Ou
Darkness

An *Elite: Dangerous* Novel

T. James

Writer and Author Press

∞

Before this novel's Kickstarter, there was a discussion. Describing it now, my writer's instinct tells me to find the conflict in the scene, the drama, to pit the two characters head-to-head in a battle of wits and will that nearly ends in failure—defeat only averted because of a clever, last-minute ruse—except the story hasn't started yet, and so I'll write this as a husband.

My wife is an exceptional woman, and it's thanks to her that you are reading this. Without her support, patience, and willingness to indulge my writing passion, *Elite: Out of the Darkness* would never have been completed.

The discussion was a short one…

'This is what a Kickstarter is'—he indicates the website to his wife and scrolls down—'and this is what I want the funding for. What do you think?'

'I think you should do it.'

∞

But that was only the start; I needed to find enough people who thought the way my wife did, and were willing to back the project. *Out of the Darkness* took flight on wings provided by the five hundred and eight stalwart souls who came forward. Their generosity still amazes me—my inadequate thank you is in the 'Community Credits' section at the end of the book.

∞

'There never can be a man so lost as one who is lost in the vast and intricate corridors of his own lonely mind, where none may reach and none may save.'

– Pebble in the Sky **by Isaac Asimov (1950).**

PROLOGUE

'As on ancient Earth, where muscle power yielded to sail, sail gave way to steam, and steam was replaced by oil, every age sees its technologies embraced as they mature; they become part of the culture, of everyday life, of humanity itself. Yet at each transition, something of the preceding age is lost even as a brave new future of possibility opens ahead.

Such a time was the early-to-mid 3270s, the last years of the old star drives. Travel between systems took days, weeks if the destination was far-flung. Becoming a pilot meant something—only a rare few could cope with the loneliness and had the resourcefulness to survive, fewer still to thrive. It was a time when to be addressed as 'Commander' made men and women feel like heroes.

But, as with all the ages of humankind before it, new discoveries and technologies brought this golden age to an end. In less than twenty-five years the latest star drives have opened new frontiers deeper in interstellar space. Now that inter-system travel takes mere seconds, humankind forges ahead, believing the riches of the universe are ripe for the picking. It is an exciting time to be alive.

Will there be new heroes? Can there be? I do not know. But I know this: if humanity is to face whatever is out there, in the darkness, we will have to find those who recall the old ways—who remember what it all meant—learn from them, and make piloting a ship mean something again.'

– Generations in the Void by Masayoshi Kishino (3300); translation by Kieron Mastersson.

1

3275

Pharos, System BD+24 543

Moira sat at her terminal flicking through the panels of glowing text hanging in the air before her. She swept her black hair away from her sapphire eyes for the umpteenth time. She had been trawling through the data on the Kishino case for over four hours and was getting nowhere—an elite pilot and his family disappeared in safe Federation space on their way to a vacation in the 39 Tauri system. No distress call, no debris, and the records were coming up empty. Like anyone with a kill list as long as his, Isao Kishino had made enemies, but their tendency to end up dead if they threatened him or his family meant any who remained alive had judiciously decided to forget their former vendettas. Isao and his trigger finger had been peacefully retired for over twenty years. *So, why now?* Moira reached for her cup of synth-coffee and eyed the cold brown sludge in the bottom dubiously. Another hit would keep her awake but not give her the godlike powers she needed to see the connections. Her intuition had curled up and gone to sleep two hours ago. *Time to quit.*

With a wave of her hand she shut down her desk terminal, its 'tasteful lighting ambience-optimised for your comfort and productivity' fading to be replaced by the Proteus Collective Security logo and plastic farewell: 'A pleasure working for you, Ms Dolan. Good night. We shall achieve even greater things tomorrow.' It was possibly the single most demoralising phrase she had ever heard. *I don't know what gets homogenised and fed to the psych-boys for breakfast, but their mouths eject the same shite as their arses. Borderline my last psych evaluation for not being a team player? Never with you bunch of fuckwits.*

She stomped towards the door, which slid nimbly into its wall recess and out of reach of her booted foot. She had *liked* the old door—it always used to stick halfway, allowing her to vent the day's frustrations on the mechanism as she kicked her way out of the office. She was sure Ferris had deliberately reported it to Tech. The man was a balletic bureaucrat, pirouetting up the corporate ladder; 'streamlining' Moira's working environment and the department were just two more effeminate prances on his way to prima-effing-ballerina. Moira was in no doubt if she did not crack the Kishino case wide open before the foreclosure window she would be the next fixture to be downsized. Private law enforcement was about contracts, deadlines, and performance percentages—justice did not pay. Crime victims were 'service users' and a revenue stream. Criminals were a way to boost your productivity rating and grab that big fat annual bonus. She missed doing it the old way, but that was a life she could not go back to. *I'll just have to learn to fit in like a good little drone.*

The lift door opened. 'Which floor, please?'

The automated chirp grated on Moira's nerves. 'Foyer.' The doors slid closed silently behind her, but the peace was short-lived.

'As per PCS Policy 11895-B to promote the wellbeing of all employees, your voice, gait, and soma-aerosol dispersal have been analysed. I am detecting high levels of stress and suppressed aggression. These are undesirable states in the work environment. For the health and wellbeing of yourself and your colleagues, would you like me to reschedule your psych evaluation for tomorrow? (I am statutorily bound to inform you that your pay will be docked in proportion to the time taken. If you choose not to accept the appointment, your health insurance premium will be increased in proportion to the assessed risk.) When would you like to schedule the appointment?'

'Go shove your appointment up your electronic arse.' Moira stared at where she thought the surveillance camera was most likely to be whilst putting her hand on the grip of her handgun. She put on her best meaningful smile. 'Not got one? Maybe I should cut you a hole.'

The lift froze, a klaxon sounded, and the lights went out. Then a 'schnik', a hiss, and the lift filled with rapidly expanding foam. Moira managed a short intake of breath before it covered her mouth and nose. She attempted to swim her way to the door as the foam congealed around her limbs. Another second and it went rigid. *Oh shite.*

'You will not be harmed. You have been restrained with PCS's patented non-irritant Immobi-Foam. It is permeable so you will be able to breathe. Please remain calm. Security officers are on their way to assist you and will arrive shortly. To help you relax, I will play a soothing melody from ancient Earth: *The Blue Danube* by Johann Strauss the Second. Your corporate account will be debited the standard one thousand credit security callout charge. Further debits to your account will be made for clean-up fees and fines for criminal charges successfully prosecuted. The Collective thanks you for your cooperation. Have a pleasant evening.'

Ferris is just going to love this.

❋

Ferris held the dataslate between thumb and forefinger as if it was covered in something nasty. Like many people, he had a cerebral implant, but when playing to an audience he did like his visual props. His other hand was poised gracefully against his smooth cheek, slim fingers affecting little spirals through his baby blond hair. Moira glared at the play of light on the immaculate fingernails as they twirled. *There's no way those aren't polished.* He had been sitting, silently regarding the slate, for the last ten minutes. His expression had not changed: his lips set in a petulant moue of disapproval and his brow creased with the frown of a vexed five-year-old. At that moment, all Moira wanted to do was pound the man's softness into a bloody pulp. *He's going to smile, I just know it.*

On cue, the lips extended sideways forming a horizontal robotic slit. The little frown smoothed. *He's probably going for authoritative and omnipotent. All I get is constipated and condescending.* The incriminating slate landed on the desk with an ominous 'clack'. *Here it comes…*

'So, Moira, the Kishino case: I trust something so straightforward won't take too long to resolve?'

What?! Moira put her tongue between her teeth and bit down, using the pain to focus on not tearing the man's head from his neck. It took effort, but she finally found her I'm-a-beat-officer-talking-to-a-dumb-superior persona learnt from years on the force. *Let the games begin.*

'I went through the file last night before I left the office, *sir*. The case is hardly straightforward.'

'You want me to accept that an operative who is facing charges of inappropriate behaviour, damage to corporate property, and wasting security officers' time, has scanned through the entire case and formulated valid conclusions after only a day?'

'There are several thousand individuals who are bereaved because of Kishino, but the man paid his debts and kept his books clean. That leaves a multitude of suspects, but none with any stand-out motive. Plus, he's been straight for twenty years. The file gives no clues as to why he and his family would be attacked or abducted now. Did I miss anything, *sir*?' *You know this case sucks like a slut, which is why you put it on my desk.*

Although his expression gave nothing away, Ferris hesitated, just for a second. Moira allowed a little warm smug feeling to grow inside her. *You know I'm good.*

'Well, I can see I chose the right person. I look forward to a definitive resolution, *on deadline*. Your completion rating is concerning me, Moira. I shouldn't have to remind you, again, that you are not working for Federal Criminal Investigations anymore. Proteus Collective Security is a commercial entity whose reputation depends on results. You are close to not meeting your quota and—after the incident in the lift yesterday—I am afraid any representation I make to the board on your behalf will have little influence on the outcome of a hearing.'

Ah, now we get to it. 'The incident in the lift? How many credits is the fine for this time? A suspension would be nice—I could do with a holiday.'

'It pleases me you feel so comfortable in our employ, but this cavalier attitude is hardly prudent—The Collective's patience is running out. *Excel* on this case, Ms Dolan, otherwise the board will not renew your contract.'

'Ferris, you know I need this job.'

'I do, but this is not just about you. Your performance reflects on The Collective, this department, and your colleagues. Ms Dolan, I've been trying, I really have, but there is nothing else I can do.'

Moira nearly hit him, nearly. *Every bum case you've thrown at me in the last twelve months should've been returned to the client. I've solved over half of them, dammit. In my old job I'd get a fucking medal.*

'I'll get it done, *sir*. Was there anything else you needed to talk to me about? I wouldn't want to impair the department's efficiency by wasting any more of your valuable time.'

'Are you giving me attitude, Dolan?'

'No, sir. But after your inspiring speech on corporate values and economics, I thought I'd better hop-to-it, sir.' Moira saw a vein pulse in his temple. She kept her expression neutral.

'Get out of my office, Dolan. It's this case or your job.'

'Sir, yes, sir.' Hiding her smile, Moira unfolded from the chair and headed for the door.

*

Moira's high spirits faded a few steps along the corridor. Policing was the only job she had ever known and being kicked out of the FCI hit her hard. Collective Investigative Officer was just another name for profiteering scumbag, but that was what she was now. *At least I try to do it right, but what does that matter? Ferris'll ensure any reference from the board is worthless trash. He's only a holofac terminal away from anywhere in human space. If I don't nail this, my employment options narrow to mealworm farmer, engine scrud cleaner, or private investigator. Holo-vidding some poor sod's lover arse-bouncing his best friend? I'll take mealworm shite or the scrud. I need to go digging, and no one's better at that than Masterisson.*

✳

While her case was pending with Internal Security, Moira was locked out of her office and contacting Masterisson on an official commlink would get one or both of them arrested. *Time to head home.*

It took ten minutes to reach ground in the lift, its neon display proudly informing her and the sweating, white-knuckled man gripping the handrail they had reached twenty-five metres per second before deceleration began. Leaving him and his vomit for Sanitary, she stepped out into the foyer and headed for the nearest Grippa-Pad. Above, a low, grey ceiling of cloud sheeted water onto the duraglass roof. Her feet hit the pad's anchor plates which turned red as they tried, and failed, to interface with her smartboots. Like every other day, she activated the adhesion manually and hit the override button on the pad console, ignoring the legal disclaimer it read out as she started to accelerate along the tube. Abusing another CIO privilege, she overrode some more safeties; the faces of the other cogs standing on their pads blurred. She wondered how many still had teeth.

✳

The security camera scan complete, she stepped inside. *Am I home?*

'Welcome, Ms Dolan, The Proteus Collective hopes you find your downtime refreshing. How can this apartment be of service?'

Even their computer won't say it's mine, she thought bitterly, *and the voice is the same as in the lift.* In a single fluid motion, Moira pulled out her blaster, flicked the safety, and swung it towards the computer console on the wall. There were no klaxons, no condescending messages, and no foam. The *Habitation Handbook* stated that residents were not under surveillance whilst in their apartments, but Moira had already found and disabled three

8

bugs in the last year. Nowhere in Collective space did she feel left alone. It was a feeling she missed.

Disconsolate, she tossed the weapon onto a table. 'Computer, change your voice—something male.'

'Is this new voice selection acceptable, Ms Dolan?'

Someone in Tech has a sick sense of humour; that sounds like Ferris. 'No, make it less camp—smoother, deeper—that host off PNF, John Graham.'

'Those rights are reserved—use will cost you seventy-five credits with another twenty-five credits for the optional personality pack. Would you like to purchase these items?'

'Yeah, whatever.'

'Would you like installation across all your interfaces?'

'Why not.'

'Initiating…'

Moira completed a quick surveillance sweep of the room and activated the scrammer before reaching for the ancient slate. Mastersson had insisted on modifying the slate's firmware so they could communicate off the Collective network. *No productivity exec with a credit-chit up his arse is listening in.* She spoke her password while it scanned her retina and fingerprints. Three green lights flashed on. Moira waited. A micro-needle pierced her skin, sealing the puncture wound with gel as it exited. Once, this slate had been top of the line; one failed security check and the concealed chemical heat bomb would melt the internals—all data rendered irretrievable. The final light went green.

'Wel—come! My name is John Graham, and I'm sure you'd like to spend a little time getting to know me, wouldn't you? I recommend previews of my next blockbusting exposé, *The Secret Lives of Spacers*, or maybe you'd like to read my biography—'

'End intro.' *Maybe the personality pack wasn't such a good idea.* 'Establish secure link to Scrudder.' Mastersson hated the name, but he had spent most of his adult life up to his neck in the stuff.

'Starting illicit comms liaison with Scrudder…'

An electronic attempt at innuendo, really? 'You there, Scrudder? I need to pick that brain of yours.'

'I'm here. This isn't a good time, Rent-A-Cop.' He sounded sharp, but his objections always faded to the tolerant resignation of an elder brother. 'What do you want?'

'It's never a good time, but this should be easy for you. I need everything on Isao Kishino, from Futen, Fujin—all the buried stuff. Here's what Collective gave me.' On screen, she waved the file towards Scrudder's icon.

'Okay, I'll just cross-reference it…'

She sat down. He would be done when he was done.

✳

'Moira, data parsing the search terms doesn't bring up anything new. Why send me a straight?'

'Come off it, Scrudder, Kishino has plenty of history.'

'The Collective file has everything in it. There's nothing new to find. Your boy's good. What's driving you, Rent-A-Cop? Were you lonely and wanted a chat? Or are you scared of doing some real police work?'

She could hear him smiling. 'Scrudder, don't—'

'Desk-bound and twenty kilos heavier, shame. Is dragging your huge rear around too much for you?'

'Discuss the shape of my arse and I'll kick yours. The boss is riding me again and if I don't get this case sorted before the deadline, I'm done. I don't have time to go door-to-door smarming everyone and patting their furry quadruped-of-choice.'

'Pretending to be nice never was your thing, was it? You'll have to do this the old fashioned way. Besides, doing a bit of legwork means you get to relive all the bits you loved about being a plod on the force.'

'Don't go there, Scrudder. I moved to Investigations to get away from domestics and having to help ancients navigate to the nearest urinal. You're telling me, with all your know-how, I've got to go back to knocking on doors?'

'Yep, 'fraid so. Now you're even lower than a plod—you're a corporate plod. Next time, don't connect just to dump on me; go find me something *interesting*. I've got to fix this toroid matrix.' The link went dead.

I think I hate him. No, I know I hate him. Moira sighed and stared at the blank screen. *So it's by the book: sniff around Kishino's social circles and where he was last seen. This could take weeks.*

2

Throwing the things she needed into a travel bag took less than five minutes; getting Ferris to approve a line of corporate credit took nearly two hours. His smiled apology about being in a meeting was shite, but if she complained he would have made her wait longer. The only reason he granted her request for off-world transport was to get her from under his feet. That, and every credit she spent solving this case was another black mark on her record.

The lift door slid open, revealing the bright lights and perfectly polished surfaces of the docking bay. This was the public face of The Collective on Pharos: professional, efficient, plastic. In front of her was a row of liveried ships, anally arranged in increasing order of size—Sidewinder to Panther Clipper—the shiny craft arrayed to ensure disembarking punters would have to pass by them and be suitably impressed. Hers would be lurking at the far end of the bay.

She waved down one of the mechs as he trundled past in his transport. 'Hey, I've got a release docket for ship PC SS645/F7. I need a ride.'

The man swept the proffered docket across the face of his terminal. A smirk crept across his face. 'It's at the far end, Ms Dolan. Sorry, but it says here you're on a special training regimen—no transportation.'

Ferris! One day I will kill him.

'The ship's called "*Flaky Jane*". Your boss must reckon you're something special; Jane's salvage and it says here we're to leave the fixing-up to you. Enjoy.' He handed her back the docket.

Before Moira could ask what the name meant, the mech gunned the transport and headed off into the distance. She was sure she could hear him laughing.

Twenty minutes later, Moira stood in a dark corner of the dock watching the shunter guide *Flaky Jane* over the pad. The number of pits left the dead hulk resembling an impacted asteroid, but the lines looked familiar. It took a moment to recall the design; she had not seen one of these dinosaurs for years. The battered hull—a compacted rectangular wedge with remnants of triangular nose—most likely used to be a Constrictor. Back in the day, the medium two-seater vessels were fast, tough, versatile, and functional. Now she had no idea what to call the amorphous mass of welded plates, jury-rigged panelling, and un-nameable lumps. *So this is how Ferris is planning to finish me off. If I die riding in this tub, the best I'll get is a dishonourable mention.*

Moira swiped her docket over the entry panel. There was the usual beep as the light flicked green, then nothing. She was just about to try again when the door slid open with a horrible grating noise. Something inside gave a whirring 'clack' and it jammed. She ducked under and picked her way carefully through a nest of exposed cables strewn across the cockpit floor. They were held down with dodgy spot welds and graftor tape. *I can't believe I'm trusting my life to this piece of shite. At least it doesn't shout 'corporate cop' like the rest.*

She shoved her duffel bag into a corner of the cockpit. *No point stowing it; looks like I'll need my tools.* The short corridor beyond was clear of debris. The cabin door slid open easily enough, but she sneezed as an outrush of fetid air disturbed some of the dust. It covered every surface, including a creased sleeping sleeve still rank with the tang of stale man-sweat. She crammed her travel bag into the storage locker above one of the tiny berths. *Just like old times.* A scuffling noise made her spin round. She took her hand off the knife at her hip. *I'll find you later. Don't chew anything vital.*

Returning to the cockpit, Moira slipped into the pilot's seat, checking the controls and harness. Both were worn smooth with use but seemed sturdy enough.

'Ship, initiate pre-flight checks.' Nothing. She scanned the console for several moments before finding the switches she needed. *It's like being a rookie again.* It had been eighteen years since she had flown anything this old, and that had been a Hawk. *Let's hope I don't have to go anywhere hostile. Even if this thing is armed with something more sophisticated than a rock thrower, I won't be able to find the right button to press.*

She checked the pre-flight indicators. A red light blinked amongst the line of green. She pulled up more details on the screen:

'Unknown life form occupying pilot seat. Initiating lethal security measures in 12 seconds... 11 seconds...'

'What the...!' Moira scrabbled at the first harness catch, her fingers sliding across the smooth ancient metal.

'8 seconds... 7 seconds...'

Finally it came loose. She grabbed for the second, trying to keep her movements steady despite her rising panic.

'5 seconds... 4 seconds...'

It popped open. The third catch was stuck.

'3 seconds... 2 seconds... 1 second...'

Moira bucked against the restraint, pushing against it with all her strength.

'Identification unknown' flashed on the display. 'Initiating termination sequence.' From underneath her came the ominous hum of a power conduit firing up.

'Oh, shite!' *My last words and that's the best I can do...?*

The lights went dark as, somewhere, something went bang.

✻

Moira lay, unmoving, in the seat. She let out the breath she was holding. Fliers told stories about these old wrecks—pressed into service on the outskirts of known space, tens of light-years from the nearest repair facility. They were patched, modded, and jury-rigged by their itinerant pilots until their original designers would barely recognise them. *Flaky Jane*'s last owner obviously took ship security very seriously—the energy surge should have cooked her; instead, there was no light and the acrid smell of burnt-out electronics. *If the ship's too old to kill me, how's it going to keep me alive?*

Fiddling with the third clasp, she eventually prised it loose and wriggled out of the harness. She was free of the seat, but trying to negotiate the cables in the complete darkness of the unfamiliar cockpit was like stepping over snakes in a crypt. At last, her hands touched the door to the corridor which emitted a resonant boom as she kicked it. *My slate's in the bag I left in the cabin, which is behind this. And just when you think the day can't get any worse, you remember no power means no comms. Oh joy, I'm sealed inside this coffin.*

She felt her way towards where the equipment locker should be. The door fell off its hinges as she released the clasp, clattering to the deck. Exploring inside, she found a battered torque wrench. *Why would there be anything useful on this barge?* She grabbed it anyway. Swinging it from side to side as she stumbled forward, it still seemed like she caught every bit of protruding metal as she groped her way across the cockpit to her duffel bag. *Iontach! A torch.* The cabin came alive in a dancing pattern of light and shadow. Grabbing her toolkit, she headed towards the primary power node. *This ship's tried to do for me once already.* Using the insulated wrench, she prised off the access panel. Fierce blue sparks played across the metal and Moira backed away from the acidic fumes that followed. *A bank of leaking chemical batteries, nice try.* She wiped her watering eyes before delving into the bag. The scuffling sounds she heard did not follow the movements of her hands over the rough material. Scanning the torch around the cockpit animated every shadow, but there was nothing obviously moving by itself. Listening hard, Moira put gloves and face mask on before peering into the gloomy recess. *The primaries are shot, but the secondary circuits look intact. If they don't short, then Flaky Jane may live again. I hope this old girl knows it's time for her to stay dead, then Ferris'll have to cough up and get me some nice shiny transportation.*

✳

Moira rerouted the power from the central grid through the secondary node and *Flaky Jane* lit up like an ancient Christmas tree.

'Damn.'

On any other ship, lights meant, 'Welcome home'. Moira was sure Jane was grinning; her lights said, 'Now you're mine.' She stowed her tools and crossed to the pilot's console and frowned at the message.

'System reboot successful. Jane welcomes you, commander. Please sit in the chair and enter your identity:'

Still 'Jane'? Great. Memory intact means it has custom system chips. A factory reset button should be mandatory on anything with a power conduit. Now what, sit and get dosed with toxic gas? The sensible thing to do was call in an experienced ship mech, but Ferris was game-playing. Every corporate credit and syndicated second would be logged to prove her incompetence. *This time I'm not putting on the harness.* She climbed into the chair and was greeted with the blissful sound of silence. The console screen cursor continued to wink at her, awaiting her input. *Another trap? This heap won't fly unless I enter something. It might as well be my real name.*

'Thank you, Commander Moira Dolan, your weight and measurements have been logged and my security system parameters amended. Please be aware: variation in your size and weight will be accommodated, but use of ship systems by non-authorised personnel will have fatal consequences. Please enter your safety override code:' The cursor was back, waiting.

Moira lifted her hands to enter the name of her first pet mookah when she stopped. *This is too easy. If I get up now, I'm probably dead. If I enter the wrong thing, I'm probably dead. If I wait too long, I'm probably dead.* She entered, 'Jane'. The prompt was still blinking. *Think. A ship called 'Jane', lovingly customised by some lonely and paranoid space hermit. No, not paranoid—I'd be dead already—possessive!* She completed the entry: 'I love you.' Moira's heart stopped, just for a second, before the screen flashed up:

'Identity verified. Running full systems check.'

But why accept my name and take my measurements? I could be the same size as the previous owner… possibly a smuggler, using different aliases? But why accommodate physical variations? Who would…? Augmentations, cosmetic surgery, and grafting—

disguises. Shite, covert ops. Jane's Special Ops hardware kitted out as a flying dumpster. I wonder what else she can do? Somehow, I don't think this is working out the way Ferris planned. This trip might be fun after all.

*

With the ship's computer online, Moira could download the ancient schematics and, more importantly, open the doors. A trip to Parts Requisition, and another comms row with Ferris about the cost, yielded some reconditioned bits and pieces she hoped would not explode when she powered them up. The repairs took twenty-three hours, by which time all her previous optimism had evaporated. The chem batteries were replaced by a portable power unit—a simple job—avoiding acid burns was the difficult part. Moira swapped out the primary power node and replaced the burnt-out circuit boards. Ferris riding her budget meant she had to leave some of the systems running off secondary power linkages. *I hope the rest of the old girl isn't as decrepit. Anything more advanced than flying in a straight line and bits will fall off.*

Finally, Jane was as pretty as Moira could get her. She needed sleep but knew the way Ferris' mind worked. Now the mandatory reports for hazardous waste and ship modifications were filed, he would wrap her in red tape and have Jane impounded for risk assessment and refitting, 'to ensure your safety'. All the shiny corporate ships on the dock would, strangely, be unavailable. *The review board isn't big on excuses. There'll be some brown-noser sitting behind my desk inside a week.* The comms light flashed blue again, an incoming message from Ferris. Moira disabled the channel but kept the connection to Pharos Flight Control.

'Vessel PC SS645/F7, your disembarkation window will be open for the next two minutes. You are cleared for take-off. Hull clamps will be released on your mark.'

'Control, this is vessel PC SS645/F7, acknowledged.'

Ingrained habit made her reach for the external camera control to check her surroundings before take-off. She stared at the orange-tinted shapes hovering above the console. *This heap has the latest holos—who'd have guessed?* Trained on the docking bay, the camera showed a transport approaching at high speed. Ferris was not wasting time. She powered up the manoeuvring thrusters. 'Release docking clamps.' There was the usual dull reverberation through the hull, but Jane bucked forward. *What's wrong with this bucket?* Moira pulled back on the stick and increased thrust to compensate. Jane reared, hurtling towards the roof of the docking bay. On the holo-vid, the transport came skidding to a halt. 'Shite!'

'Vessel PC SS645/F7, is there a problem? Do you require assistance?'

Moira eased back on the throttle and slid the stick to its level position, wondering if Jane would freefall onto the deck two hundred metres below, but she floated down, hanging in the air as if suspended on wires. *Military grade flight controls—this thing's as responsive as an atmospheric fighter.* 'Negative, Control. I sneezed. Proceeding to exit doors.'

'Very well, PC SS64—Wait, we have an incoming message from—'

'Tell my boss that I've taken on board the lessons from his pep talk yesterday. I must follow his directives and increase my efficiency and effectiveness so I can't stay around and chat. Onwards—for the department, for The Collective, and for revenue!' Moira shut the comms channel before she heard anything that meant she was disobeying a direct order and, gently, gunned the engines. Jane shot forward through the open bay doors and into the freedom of Pharos airspace. *See you, Ferris.*

She waited until she was clear of the atmosphere before her eyes scanned the unfamiliar layout of the controls. Eventually, she found the nav screen. She stared at the circle indicating the maximum jump range of the ship. *That can't be right.* It took her several seconds to find Jane's status screen. Her drive was listed as class four, with a twenty-seven light-year range. Back on the sector map, Moira checked the circle again: maximum range thirty-two light-years. She set the destination system as Fujin. Her finger hovered over the hyperspace button. *Whatever you've got under the hood is either going to get me there really fast or spread my atoms halfway across the galaxy.* Moira's finger jabbed down.

❈

The stars stretched as Moira's stomach was left behind the engines. Exotic particles released by the hull and charged by the shields formed a new ball of reality that went cascading down the spiral wormhole the hyperdrive drilled through normal space. The walls flew by, blue-shifted light surfaces flickering with wisps of matter and flashes of energy.

Slipping...

Instinctively, Moira gripped the control yoke, knowing it was futile.

Jane moved like a rotating weight on a spring, as if the tunnel walls stretched on every accentuated bend, the ship's mass too great for their insubstantial fabric to hold.

I didn't think you could tear a tunnel—

The ship rounded another curve and the seat pressure pads expanded and flowed under her, taking the extra g.

I'm not dead, but what the fuck?

She lifted an arm and watched as her pointing finger drifted, always in opposition to the direction of each curve.

She reached for her slate, anchored to the console, and set her boots for maximum grip before releasing the harness. Her boots touched the floor, and held. She pressed the button on the console that pulled up the ship status. *Good.*

Moira had been on board a boat, years ago, the deck rising and falling with each tidal swell and ebb. She moved the 'Grip' slider down on the slate and took a step, and then another. She made the drinks dispenser and flicked through the options.

A working stardreamer and a supply of synth coffee.
Strained spacetime or not, what more do you need?

Ten light-years later, Moira was staring at the pin brightness of Fujin's distant white dwarf, a wan beacon against the black. Any rookie knew to start at the missing person's last known location, but the trail was already two weeks old and a few more days would make little difference. Kishino and his family disappeared in space, the final coordinates uncertain. Any leftovers would have drifted thousands of klicks already. Besides, the Kishinos' home planet was on her way and a background check might reveal something— *maybe.* She flipped to the nav screen. *How can I enjoy this when it feels like I'm Ferris' lackey?*

3

The Fujin System

Futen loomed before her, a blue world zoned with rich greens— desert browns noticeable only by their absence. *Heavily terraformed—a nice retirement rock, hopefully with some answers.* Proteus Collective Security had purchased jurisdiction permits for most of the nearby worlds. It made things easier, but every day she stayed and every resource she used cost credits and increased the size of Ferris' smile. Clearance granted and Jane's docking computer taking her through the atmosphere with all the indicators still green, Moira relaxed—a little. Jane was an enigma. *Will she beam me direct to the surface or somersault into a suicide dive?* Something felt wrong. The telemetry showed the usual moving boxes describing the ship's trajectory. Velocity was normal, the atmospheric conditions near-optimal. *Noise, there's almost no wind noise.* Moira flicked through the menus on-screen until she found 'Stealth'. *Why am I not surprised?* The stealth selector was set to 'Auto'—a compromise between covert movement and aerodynamic efficiency she assumed, given the other options were 'None' and 'Full'. Additional settings were listed below and she was itching to hit 'Initiate', but potentially disappearing from the planetary scanners and magically appearing on the landing pad would mean too many questions. *There'll be time to play with those later.*

Moira dragged herself away from her new toy and reached for her slate. Kishino's face appeared, steadily rotating in three dimensions. With a few gestures, she navigated to his records on the local planetary network and accessed 'Known associates', shortening the list to those native to Futen. She cross-referenced again with 'Next of Kin'. *Wife and two progeny, plus paternal geriatric.* The wife's previous alias was 'Akiyama'. *A maiden name too, how quaint.* That search pulled up no results on the local grid and removing the location filter revealed her nearest relative lived over one hundred light-years away. She scrolled through Kishino's other acquaintances and cross-referenced them with the planetary census data. All were from long-established local families that arrived with the first wave of settlers, generations ago.

'Link to planetary legislative database; remove all entries with no previous convictions.' That left only eleven, and their 'criminal' activity read like a page in a minor offences handbook: driving a transport with an out-of-date permit; attempting to bypass quarantine procedures for 'Kawaii' the family's pet pewtee; urinating in public while under the influence—hardly people who would cut off your brother's toes for not paying them protection money.

The list of Kishino's associates from other star systems read like a rogues' gallery; the names scrolled by filling screen after screen. *Lovely: murder, racketeering, piracy, smuggling, extortion, assault, rape, slaving—pretty much everything you wouldn't confess to a priest.* Others were suspects for unsolved crimes. Most were labelled 'Deceased', 'Terminated', or 'Whereabouts unknown'. *A lot of deaths, to buy one retirement.* There were no recorded communications between Kishino and the motley crew since he settled here, over two decades ago. *Has he really gone straight? What's not in the records?* She pulled up the images of Kishino's immediate family. 'Missing' was written beneath all but one. She stared again at Kishino's father. The picture was blurred, which was unusual enough—*but, his features...* She shrugged.

I hate being a bitch, but sometimes it's the only way. Here's hoping I don't have to buy the old guy a new artificial bladder after I'm done.

'Vessel PC SS645/F7, you are in New Honshu airspace, please maintain the indicated holding pattern. You will receive clearance to land in an estimated eight minutes. Please have your identification, ship's manifest, and casework authorisation ready for inspection on arrival.'

One abuser of the elderly, with duffel bag, coming in to land. Maybe I should quit, and ram the job so far up Ferris' arse he'll spit it out when he coughs.

*

The one hundred and fifty click drive from the spaceport along smooth-slabbed roads winding through suburbs, fields, woods, and up into the hills to the Kishino residence was uneventful. Despite the saving, Moira refused to travel on public transport. Besides, pulling up in a commandeered local Futen-Sec wagon lent her gravitas, hopefully enough to get the old guy to cough up the information she needed without having to lean on him.

From the driveway, all she could see of the building was an old-world concave tiled roof, flaring out at its lower edges. She followed a narrow winding path of irregular white stones between two artfully sculpted hills and soon her vehicle was out of sight. *So much for it making an impression.* The house, local white-painted stone and ochre wood panelling, was deep set—just a single storey nestling into a hillside crevice lined with manicured low-lying vegetation. *Custom built, not a prefab. Retirement has been good to Kishino.*

The paving flowed around one side of the house before rounding a sharp bend. Moira was plunged into shadow; a high grey wall of closely fitted stones cut out the late afternoon sun. Set within was a circular opening framed with red wood. Steps led down into an open courtyard, the large slabs of the path crossing a sea of small stones artfully raked into swirling lines and curves. Sunlight caught the pale ridges—waves in an ocean of fire.

Very pretty.

A male figure sidled into view, his thin hands and rough baggy clothing wrapped around the handle of the rake he hunched over. *And here's the help to show me around. Time to get into character.* Men never took you seriously unless you gave them attitude. 'Hey, you, I need to speak to Isao Kishino's father.' The figure continued raking. The steady rhythm and swoosh of the moving stones was somehow intensely irritating. Moira strode through the portal and down the steps towards him, her feet crunching the gravel. 'Are you deaf? I said—' The raking continued: swish, swish, swish.

'Please, watch where you tread, gaikoku no kata.'

'I don't give a damn about your pretty little patterns, now where—ow!'

'Patterns I can re-make. There is a rock.'

The man facing her was old, his steel-grey hair tightly cropped against a head covered in skin like tanned leather. He helpfully indicated the stone that had just cut her shin. Now she was halfway across the courtyard, she could see it was one in a ring of eight. She eyed him suspiciously, but his expression showed no amusement, only concern. His eyes were a different matter.

'Did you put that damn-stupid rock there?'

'Yes, gaikoku no kata, especially for you. You are hurt. I will bring something for your leg? Please, sit.'

Leaving her gawking, he rested his rake against the fork of a small tree and walked towards the house. This was not going according to plan. *So, do I trail him like a love-struck puppy or sit on the bench like a good little girl?* Moira limped over to the seat— a single heavy beam across two sturdy uprights, the wood weathered silver with age. She could not resist giving it a kick with the heel of her boot as she sat down. The bench was as solid as the rock that cut her shin. Worn smooth with use, at least it was comfortable.

Around the courtyard, deeper shadows cavorted in the patches of shade. She knew it was the play of the breeze through the upper branches of the surrounding bushes, but in the silhouetted movements of the spindly lines there was something disturbingly familiar—her thoughts filled with remembered shadows, each one hiding another way to die. A chill ran through her, raising the soft hairs on her skin as it went. She forced her attention back to the present. *I'm in a garden. There's bushes, sun, a breeze—nothing else.* Staring down the phantasms, she fixed her eyes on the dimness until they grew accustomed to it, and the contrasting pockets of gloom between plant and rock revealed they were empty of secrets.

The throbbing in her leg began to slow with her heartbeat. There was an overshadowed pond to her left, small silver rings intermittently appearing and expanding in gentle swells to cover the entire surface. The creation of each was punctuated by a flash of orange, gold, black, or white that left a trail of bubbles in its wake. At the pond's edge was a small mushroom-house carved from stone; in the centre an island with three stones half the size of her duffel bag. It looked like something random from a child's imagination, but as she studied it, she began to perceive a pattern—an underlying order to the apparent chaotic interplay of light and darkness, texture and form. *The garden's like an evasive witness—I hate it when someone knows something I don't.* Her clumsy footprints tracked obviously across it, marring it like scars on an innocent face. *The fish here are smarter than I am.*

Her head whipped around as she caught movement from the corner of her eye. She was halfway to standing before she relaxed back onto the solidity of the bench: it was just the old man carrying a large wooden tray. On it sat a squat black kettle, two black bowls, a small wicker box, and a rough cloth that glistened ominously in the sunlight.

'What's that?' she snapped. Her voice sounded harsh in the quiet, like bones breaking.

'Tea,' the old man smiled.

Moira felt the heat rising in her cheeks. Anger or shame? She was not sure. 'No, *that*, the rag with the gunk on it.'

By way of answer, he pressed something on the lip of the tray she could not see. There was a snap and two pairs of legs dropped from the base. Moira shot to her feet, fists clenched.

'You were fast, but I believe the table was faster.' He set the tray-table on the ground and shuffled it carefully back and forth, settling the legs firmly into the loose stones. Without another word he sat, lifted the lid of the wicker box, and sprinkled what looked like dried twigs into each cup. With meticulous, efficient movements, hot water from the kettle followed, before everything was returned to its place. 'The garden speaks to everyone differently. Today it seems to be shouting.' The man gestured to the empty bench beside him.

Moira sat stiffly, feeling even more the eejit.

'Please, your leg, gaikoku no kata.'

'You are not putting that gunky shite on my leg. What does gay co-co no kata mean, anyway? If you want to insult me, you'll have to say it in Standard.'

'Not insult, "Esteemed not-like-us." Your leg.'

'No.'

'If we wait, your tea will be too strong. Your leg.'

She had grabbed others by the throat before for pushing her this hard. But those were other times, other places. Right now, she was pinned by the implacability of those hawk eyes—they pierced while the innocence disarmed.

'Leg, please.'

She lifted her foot onto the bench between them. Her trousers were soaked through with blood, but pain was something to be ignored. A knife appeared, and before she could react he had sliced the material, up past the wound on her shin. The blade disappeared back into the folds of his robe just as quickly. With another sure movement, the old man slapped the compress over the cut. It was cool against her skin and brought with it a gentle tingling sensation that gradually faded.

He indicated that she should hold it in place. 'No pain, no infection, no swelling, no bleeding. Good for "gunky shite", yes?'

'What's in it?'

'Ah, never one to trust. The names mean nothing to you: mostly *in no kenkō* and more of its friends from the garden.'

Surprisingly, the cut already felt better. 'You should sell this stuff.'

'We do. My daughter-in-law makes; my son sells—travels a long way out there.' He pointed upwards. 'He helps people now.'

She could not keep the accusation from her voice. 'But the picture—how? You're Kishino's father.'

'Yes, our family "in the business" for long time. And you?' The old man extended a hand.

He doesn't know. The realisation hit her like a wave.

'Okay.' The old man misinterpreted her hesitation and began to withdraw his hand. He seemed genuinely saddened by her lack of response.

'No, wait. Sorry. Moira, Moira Dolan.'

He took the hand she offered. His grip was surprisingly strong, muscles like cables contouring the bronzed skin of his forearm.

So much for not getting involved. I thought I would never have to do this again.

'Masayoshi. I am pleased to meet you, Dolan-san.'

'No, just Moira.'

He nodded, smiling now. 'Hai. Moira-san, you are welcome in our home, and here it is our way, yes?'

Moira watched emotions cross his face like fleeting clouds. He was obviously watching hers.

'Something is wrong, Moira-san? You are offended, unhappy? '

'Unhappy. I bring bad news.' *Now I'm even sounding like him.*

'Isao-kun! My family? Gone too long…' Masayoshi's grief animated his face—he made no attempt to shield either Moira or himself from his feelings; his distress was naked and unadorned.

Moira could feel the lock on her own heart twisting, bending, threatening to break open. *I'm not going back there, not again.* Only the force of her will hammered it back into place. She tried taking refuge in the facts. 'Mr. Kishino, your son and his family went missing while en route to 39 Tauri. Isao should have met with a business associate there, Miles Tannon; he contacted my organisation when they didn't show. Your son had deliveries due in the Minah system, correct?'

'Hai.'

'They have not been fulfilled; your family's ship never arrived. No one knows what happened; no wreckage has been found. They are probably still alive.' She felt cheap lying like this—when ships disappeared their occupants almost always did too. *Am I trying to spare his feelings, or my own?*

Masayoshi had withdrawn, his hands clasped tightly in his lap, his head bowed. Thin and folded up as he was, he looked so frail—like a small child. 'Thank you, Moira-san, for offering comfort, even though you do not believe the words you speak.' He straightened and turned towards her. He wore the tears on his face like medals, without shame. 'You say, my "son and his family", you hide them behind their descriptions. They are people, not words, Moira-san. See…' His knotted and gnarled hand went inside his robe, pulling out a small lacquered box that he placed on his palm. He offered it to her. 'Open, please.'

The box was old, but the exquisitely detailed horses that ran over it still shone brightly. In their painted lines she could see both strength and speed. She reached out, only to leave her hand hovering above the box. It was not fragile, but Masayoshi's trust and the intimacy of the moment made her pause.

'You see they are swift and strong?'

'Yes, it's… erm… very beautiful.'

'Do you see anything else?'

A trick question. She tried to remain impassive, polite, but the eyes regarding her were too knowing. She looked again. The background was yellow, the horses galloping across it—mostly in the same direction. The colours used varied with each animal, but an overall theme unified the design.

He dipped his head. 'Open, please.'

Something about the way he said it made it seem the sadness he felt was as much for her as it was his own loss. Frowning, she removed the lid. Like life in miniature, four tiny people sat close together. They laughed, sharing a meal on the grass.

Masayoshi stretched out a hand and the image expanded with his gesture. 'My son, Isao-kun; his wife, Yorimi-okusan; my grandson, Ichirou-bō; and my granddaughter, Kiyoko-chan.'

She recognised the faces from Isao Kishino's file. Seen like this, they were no longer anonymous. *The boy has his nose, the girl his cheekbones.* There were no words to say.

Pinioned like prey in headlight beams, his eyes had her. 'They may live, but you don't think so. Your job, it is to find them, yes?'

Moira swallowed the lump in her throat. 'Yes.'

'Then if they live, you will bring them home. Yorimi-okusan, she comes from a good family—not criminal.' He stared at her, waiting.

'The information I have shows she and her family are clean.'

'Hai, a good woman. My son… there is much darkness in his past. You know this, yes?'

'Yes, but—'

'You are police? You seek justice for those who are wronged?'

'I used to be… I'm a Collective Investigative Officer now and—'

'If you are not police, you would not be here. The title means nothing; it is what you do that matters. You seek justice, yes?'

'Yes—'

Masayoshi's voice carried the weight of his emotion but still resonated with the power of wind booming through an old oak. 'Good. I am his father, but I am not blind. Isao-kun has done much that is wrong. He made many enemies. But he left that life behind. I know you will not believe me when I say this, but it is true. My son became an honourable man. He has made me proud. Now something dark has claimed him. Before this, it would have been right, but no longer for him and never for my family.' Masayoshi became silent, waiting.

Moira looked down, uncomfortable with his scrutiny. *I need to get this back on track.* She tried the strange term hesitantly. 'Masayoshi-san, do you know who—?'

Masayoshi raised his hand. 'Enough. You think your questions will help you, yet we both know you hide behind them. Long ago, my son wanted to tell me everything, but I already knew enough. Now, to us and his friends here on Futen, he is only Isao-san: family, neighbour, and friend. We cannot give you what you need. Eventually he found his path, as you will find yours. Courage, Moira-san, will bring success.

'You are police—go ask others your questions. Alive or dead, Moira-san, you will find my family and bring justice to those who harmed them.'

His fervour shocked her; the certainty of his faith worried her. Moira did not know what to say. Feeling small and unworthy, she gave a non-committal nod.

Masayoshi pulled her towards him and held her close. 'Thank you, Moira-san.'

Awkwardly, she eased herself free and offered him back the box lid. His hands closed around hers. When he let go, the box sat, complete and sealed, in her hand.

'To remember why, Moira-san.'

'I—'

Masayoshi held up a reproving finger. 'You give it to Isao-kun.'

Everything inside her screamed: *Say something!* But she could not. More tightly than his arms had bound her shoulders, she found herself bound by his trust. *A promise made without words isn't a promise,* the voice inside her said. But, even to her, it sounded pathetic and unconvincing.

4

The Fujin System, In Parking Orbit Around Futen

Moira's conversation with Masayoshi-san had left her shaken, but no matter what he said, uniting the Kishino family was still just another job. *It makes Ferris look stupid, gets the board off my back for a few months, and puts credits in my account. That's it.* It was the fourth time she had repeated the thought in the last half-hour—a mantra that did not work.

After the meeting she had retreated back to Jane, wedging herself in her bunk with her knees folded up like she used to when she was a little girl. Her slate perched on her thighs, she tried, yet again, to distract herself by reviewing the case notes, but was there any point? Masayoshi-san's assertions about his son checked out—there were no discrepancies with the records. *Isao's home is a dead end.*

'Isao', why am I calling him that? The miniature scene came into her mind, two adults and two children sitting on the grass together and laughing. Moira found no joy in it. She shutdown the first wave of feeling—a practised reflex—but the guilt remained. *Dammit. Damn him!*

'Slate, place a comms call to Keagan Dolan.'

'"Slate"? I had hoped we would be on first name terms by now, please call me John. What troubles you, my mostly morose Moira?' the holo-vid host's voice lilted.

'*What* did you call me?'

'It's the way I'm made. You are my primary user. My personality programming compels me to monitor your vocal sub-harmonics, facial expression, skin conductivity, and movement. I sense you need cheering up.'

'Stop monitoring, mind your own business, and connect me to Keagan Dolan.'

'Not an option, I'm afraid. De-selecting monitoring would be incompatible with my primary personality matrix. My living self is fascinated by people, why I—'

'Just make the fucking call!' *I am so looking forward to erasing this arsehole.*

'A great idea: some social interaction will do wonders for your mood. Searching comms links… the last registered location of your brother was a residence on Aquila in the Dalfur system… …You're connected. I'm still waiting for an answer.'

'Nothing from his personal comms unit?'

'Nope. I can contact a Space Singles group, if you—'

'No! What's the local time, on Aquila?'

'Four twenty-three a.m.'

Dammit, Keagan. I know it's been a while—a long while, she corrected herself—*but you're never out this late.* Keagan always took time out to recover so he did not mess up the 'little favours' he set up for his 'friends' the night before. His life was a mess, and it took money to keep it that way.

The familiar mix of anger and exasperation was always there when Moira thought of her brother. After everything they had been through, they both needed a change of scene and a break from the other. She had thrown herself into her career. Keagan slid into anything that would get him the quick and easy credits needed for his next drinking binge. Within six months, they were regularly rowing as she sought to straighten him out and he accused her of trying to control him. After eight months, he left legality out of the things he checked for in a job description. Asking him what he was up to would mean issuing an arrest warrant or being guilty of collusion—if he told her the truth.

When they did talk, he made veiled references to his 'work' and how lucrative it was, eventually asking whether she 'wanted in'— corrupt cops made good money. Her response had not been gentle. Twelve months later, they barely spoke. When they did, their conversations followed the same pattern: short, tense and awkward, but at least they happened—the only human contact that told Moira she was not utterly alone.

Then he got caught.

To keep him out of the work camps she called in every favour she was owed and sold almost everything to raise the credits needed for the bribes. She succeeded in covering both their tracks. He had bunked with her. He promised he was going straight.

One night, she came home after a few drinks with a friend from work. Mik was a cop; he understood the lifestyle. She thought what they had might actually go somewhere. But Keagan had left his stash on the table—right in the middle of the fucking table. The always-dutiful sister, she covered for him, pretending it was hers. Mik did not want to 'party'. He had her in restraints in seconds. She should have known; Mik was nothing like her brother. It was why she liked him.

Apparently, she played her part too well. Six weeks later she was off the force. Mik had testified he saw her unknown supplier run into the night. He said he had been keeping an eye on her, that it was her first offence—she was young and feeling the pressure of her meteoric rise through the ranks, and she was still haunted by her past. Only the last part was strictly true, but she took the lifeline he offered.

'I don't want to see another good career wrecked by a stupid mistake,' he said, 'but I need something to give the prosecutors, something to convince the jury of your good intentions.' She dropped him the name of her most faithful underworld contact. It was enough to keep her out of prison and eventually get her a shite job at the blunt end of private law enforcement. Mik got another promotion and her contact twenty-to-life. It took seven years of keeping her clean nose to the grind until she had her life back on track, even if that track was taking her via the Collective.

Afterwards, she wanted nothing to do with Keagan. She told him so, even after he begged. But it could not last. He was all she had, her only family and the closest thing to a friend. And so they had reached an agreement. They never met, but on the anniversary of their parents' death they would talk.

It was not onerous, yet every year she had been the one to make the call. Every year the calls got shorter, until last year:

'Keagan, it's Moira.'

'Shhh. Sorry, Sis. There's something going down, can't talk—' There was female laughter in the background. '—Gotta go.'

He did not call back. Neither did she. This year, the day of their parents' death came and went, unmarked.

He's busy. There could be a thousand reasons he isn't taking the call... I thought I buried this, but one trip to Chez Family Kishino and I'm back to playing the paranoid possessive sister waiting by the comms unit.

The slate broke in, insistent, 'Moira? Moooiiirrraa... Your lap is lovely and warm, but I'm feeling somewhat redundant down here. What shall I do next?'

A personality algorithm feels hurt because it's being ignored. Oh, the fucking irony. 'Leave the following message on all Keagan's comms terminals: "This is your sister. It's been too long, give me a call."' *He'll call.*

Now... She felt cheap doing it, but she had to be sure. 'Slate—'

'John, please.'

'*Slate*, interface with Futen-Sec central database. Access Masayoshi Kishino's local file. Corroborate my information: especially his involvement with the "family business", appearance and medical records.'

'It's going to be like that is it? Very well, searching.'

'Family businesses: traditional landscape gardening, herbal medicines. Criminal record: clean.'

She examined every permit, quality control and export certificate. His medical file contained no record of violent injury, signs of use or addiction—nothing out of the ordinary.

You've got the file of a goddamn saint, so why the blurred image of a face that might not be yours?

But everything else checked out, including Isao Kishino's last suspected altercation over twenty years ago, with one Anatolii Barkov whose ship was destroyed in 3253 by assailants unknown.

Masayoshi's so desperate he wouldn't withhold information, and nothing's out of place except a picture. What do I say? 'I'm sorry I'm not finding your family, but I need to ask you why a camera used years ago took an unfocused image?'

'Computer, set course for Isao Kishino's last known location before he went missing.' *Nothing.* 'Jane, set course for the Manah system.' *I need voice control on this old bucket.* 'Slate, establish a link with the ship's computer. Interface voice commands with ship controls.'

'Be glad to. I'm sure Jane is friendlier than you are. Interfacing… Interface established. No! Wait! Stop! Mummy, please don't be angry. I promise I won't try your clothes on again. I—'

What? 'Slate?'

The slate was silent. On-screen, a message flashed: 'Catastrophic system failure. Reboot unsuccessful. Please contact the manufacturer for assistance.'

'Jane, what the fuck did you do to my slate?!'

She really is covert ops—I've never seen a ship with such aggressive anti-intrusion software. And just when you thought the universe couldn't work out another way of drowning you in shite. At least John Graham is now John Doe.

Damn—Ferris. He's already pissed I cut him off, and now I need to requisition a replacement slate. Jane, looks like your comms system just miraculously repaired itself. Oh joy.

5

The Wolf 1301 System; Four Months Ago

Keagan stretched, trying to ease the eternal cramp in his muscles. The nyrolon fibres of his flight suit creaked—the inbuilt decontamination enzyme-sheaths too long overworked. Dried sweat had left salts and proteins crystallised in a cocoon-like coating on his skin that cracked when he moved. His eye muscles pulled against the encrusted gunk gluing his eyelids together, but nothing happened—he hadn't been able to sleep for… how long? He pawed at the sticky mess with a stubby gloved finger. The crust came away, tearing several eyelashes with it.

'—!' He tried to swear but the curse stuck in the thickness in his throat. At least he could see, even if it was only in blurred smudges of colour. Muscles vibrated like torsion cables as he stretched out a trembling hand towards the provisions dispenser. He stabbed at the phosphorescent green blur and missed.

Fuckin' Mk I tub! How am I supposed to fly something built before my great grandma learnt to wash her arse? Ah…

Somewhere inside his sponge-filled skull, a neurone fired. He felt down the outside of his left thigh and found the bottle carefully wedged between the pads of the anti-g harness. *Come to Daddy!* He wrapped the bottle in his gloved fist and, as lovingly as a mother cradling her newborn, lifted it to his mouth. The cork had a reassuringly moist, woody smell; there was still some left. He pulled the stopper with his teeth and let it drift into his lap—the large asteroid he was parked against providing just enough gravity. The stinging smell of the liquor ploughed furrows up his nostrils and set off a neon light show in his brain. *So much better than that fermented piss from Earth.* He tipped the bottle up, and like a half-asleep babe nursing at a teat, took the tiniest drop onto his tongue.

Nothing. His breath caught, heart accelerating until he thought it would jump through his ribcage. *Mustn't panic, there's still some left.*

Keagan knew the effects: complete lucidity, a connection to self and everything around you, and no need to sleep. It would be illegal in every civilised star system if anyone knew it existed. But its unique effects on the human brain were the only reason he was still sane—alone in this wreck of a ship. The problem was, to stay sane you needed more and still more. *Will I ever be normal again?*

The liquor began to wind tendrils through his thoughts, seeking them out and pulling them into sharper, painful, focus. This was the worst part, but this time would not be any worse than the others. He had to be quick, before he lost the ability to function. He scrabbled at the cork, catching it in the bulky gloves on the fifth try. He twisted his head sideways, shoved the cork between his teeth, and screwed the bottle up onto the cork with both hands—a desperate move to protect the bottle's precious contents.

The scanner croaked a warning beep and he jammed his treasure back between the seat pads. Keagan switched on the telemetry. *Recorded for posterity—the death of another dumb-fuck trader?* There was no going home until he managed a 'worthy' kill, but shooting *anything* in this piece of shite was some kind of miracle— an argument that never swayed the boss. He throttled up and the engines coughed in response—the briefest burst of thrust. The range readout gradually decreased as a point of light spun on the scanner, the incoming ship describing a chaotic-seeming arc as his own pinwheeled end over end. From outside his craft would seem dead—ripe for plucking by any passing scavenger or opportunist.

As the other craft approached, Keagan leant forward in anticipation. If it had teeth, he could kick them in and get back to a life worth living. *Toora, loora, toora, loo-rye-fuckin' aye. A Fer-de-Lance! Somethin' worth my time.*

He spat, and watched the cockpit looping the gobbet as he pulled his ship into a crazy spiral. The liquid still hit the dial, just where he aimed it. His headache was easing, thoughts and adrenalin racing. *I love this shite.*

The other ship was closing fast. Keagan powered up the weapon systems. *Time to dance.*

*

An Aquilian Ghetto in the Dalfur System; Six Weeks Ago

This was not going to be a good day. Hunched over the table, the warm numbness filling Keagan's head was pleasant; the beginning waves of nausea were not. He had been drinking through the night and there were no more credits left to fend off the incoming hangover.

'Keagan, you pile of shit. I knew I'd find you here.'

Like balls of lead jammed into his ears, the words squeezed the brain inside his head. 'Whaddya wan', Shane?' He didn't open his eyes; even the bar's subdued lighting drove spikes through the back of his retinas.

'Officer Gerrit to you.'

Through the fug of alcohol, he was dimly aware of Shane's fingers weaving between his dreadlocks. 'Piss off. I'm restin' me head. Stop feelin' me up, you queer.' His head was yanked up and back. Keagan felt lancing hot pain as several dreads parted from his scalp. 'Fuck it! Gerroff!'

'I said, "*Officer Gerrit*".'

Shane pushed down, hard, and Keagan saw the table top coming up to meet him. His nose exploded wetly across his face; the blood turned his scream into a gurgling cry. Bucking, he tried to wriggle free, but Shane still had him by what was left of his hair. The wild swing he made at the man's stomach was batted aside like an infant's. Shane dragged him off the seat, out of the booth, and forced him to kneel. Keagan felt the hardness of a gun barrel pressed against his temple.

'Say it.'

'Say, wha'? Wha' do yer wan' me t'say?' Keagan's thoughts circled tighter as panic gripped him. He couldn't focus.

'Say it.'

'Don't kill me! I'll say anythin', anythin'.' He could barely make out his own words through the sobs, and the blood which filled his mouth.

'You're a dumb fuck. "I'm sorry Officer Gerrit." Say it.'

'I'm s-s-sorry, Officer Gerrit. Really sorry.'

'Better. Now listen, your boss called. You been getting "banjaxed" again, mouthing off to the wrong people. He wants a little chat, so get moving.'

'You know about my boss? Aw shite. I'm not shayin' anythin'; he's way more scary than you… Officer Gerrit. He'll have my legs ripped off and fed to a Keljekk.'

'You're not listening, Keagan. I work for him—a lucrative little sideline. You left a mess I had to clear up. Now get.'

6

The Fujin System, Leaving Futen Orbit; Present Day

'*Another* requisition, Dolan? I notice your ship's comms array only functions when you need something,' said Ferris.

Moira wanted to scrape his unctuous mix of gloating and sarcasm from her skin. 'Like I said, I jury-rigged it, but it's still temperamental.'

'You know I'll have tech tear it down when you get back…'

'Do what you want. You tore strips off me for my lack of efficiency, and yet I have to get your approval for every bit of equipment I need. Are you going to okay my slate replacement, or not?'

'This is getting very close to insubordination, Moira.'

I hate it when he uses my name—it feels like I've been licked— and he knows it too, bastard.

'If this continues, I'll have to make another note on your record.'

The only thing that keeps you happy is writing your little notes—fucking accountant. 'I don't think that will be necessary, *sir*, although I may need to put in my report that my superior is preventing me from executing my duties by failing to provide adequate support, resources, and equipment in the field. Oh, wait, I can't because I don't have a slate replacement. I'll just have to return and present my case to the board in person: my case failure rate has increased dramatically since I was transferred to your department, and inefficiency and delays are frequently caused by obstructive responses to field-support requests. I'm sure I can pull some interesting numbers from Collective central records.' *And so the battle lines are drawn.*

'With your history, you don't want to go down that route, Dolan. The Board knows a team player when they see one. I'll be promoted before year's end and you'll be dodging the debt collectors. Scum doesn't float, Dolan, it sinks.'

Thought of that all by yourself did you, genius? 'Well, as you're such an outstanding team player, *sir*, I assume you'll okay my replacement? You know, for the good of the team.'

'If you were a team player you would use a cerebral implant like every other operative—yet another example of your anarchistic attitude.'

'After a lifetime happily living with my decision to avoid becoming bionic; after clearly notifying The Collective of my objections in my application; after a proven track record cracking cases others can't dent—*without* an implant—I see how wrong I was. Sir, your words have inspired me; they've completely changed my viewpoint. I want the surgery, sir, tomorrow if you can arrange it. I want a special implant, sir, so that I can download your wisdom directly into my brain; maybe you could control me remotely. I—'

'Dolan!'

'Sir, I know the surgery will have to be paid for from your departmental budget because it's for work. Given the immense cost, it means our department will drop from the number one spot in the low-expenditure rankings—that would've been three years at the top. Don't you get a hefty bonus, sir, if your department stays up there that long? Such a shame, you were doing so well.'

'Dolan, I am *not* authorising—'

'Alright, sir, I understand. You can't afford to have a top quality investigator off duty at such a busy time. Very well, I guess I'll just have to cope with a slate replacement. It should be *better* though— maybe an omni-block? Otherwise it might look like you were squeezing the credits just to nail your bonus, sir—don't know what that would look like to the board.

'Now that's sorted, may I say how impressed I am with how well you retain your veneer of calm, especially working with such an ungrateful underling as myself. Sorry, sir…wait… voice link from the comms unit… playing up agai—.' She terminated the connection. *And now any delay fills your boots with shite, not mine. Three, two, one…*

The 'Requisition Approved' icon flashed on the screen. So did the incoming voice link icon. Moira's heart leapt. *Keagan?* It was Ferris. She got up from the pilot's chair, leaving the icons flashing. *Fourteen hours and three calls and he still hasn't contacted me. Probably still out chasing the next 'sure thing'. He's fine, bound to be.*

✳

System LTT 11159

Moira cracked her knuckles in anticipation. Hypersleep in the stardreamer meant her mind had mercifully been spared the worst part of hyperspace travel: the tedium. It had been a couple of months since she had been given a case off Pharos, let alone outside BD+24 543, so control-freak Ferris could keep tabs on her. Now she was free and ready to work.

She kept one eye on Jane's proximity indicator, the other on the meal that was trying to float away—some reconstituted gunk hyped as *Primal Protein*—and occasionally she flicked both to her new omni-block's screen. Going over Kishino's case notes yet again, she had not missed anything. His trail was days cold.

She pushed the memory of her handshake with Masayoshi-san from her mind. Isao Kishino was a bottom-feeding scum-sucker who, somehow, had seen the light and learnt to fly. Moira had been sceptical, but there was compelling testimony and verified evidence. *He found his way back, maybe Keagan can too. But Kishino's not living the happily-ever-after, he's been caught by his past. Keagan's been caught by his present. Three days gone and still nothing.*

She tapped the comms icon. 'Mastersson, hi.'

'Whuuuup?'

'Are you asleep?'

'I was. This is your revenge, right?'

'You've lost me.'

'Because I cut you off last time we spoke. Sorry, I was having a rough day.'

Moira felt her cheeks warming. *Oh my God, when did I become so self-conscious that a little concern makes me blush? Maybe I should work on my people skills. My best friends are a tekhead and a mute spaceship with an aggressive overcompensation disorder.*

'It's okay, you're forgiven too.'

'Mastersson, what are you on about?'

'I decided to take your silence as forgiveness. You're crabby, and I've just forgiven you too. Snap out of it, Moira—I'm the one who's just woken up. This is about Keagan, isn't it?'

'How did you know? Never mind, *what* do you know?'

'That's more like it. I have a few tricks, and people I can look up when needed… His credit balance has been showing the same peak-dip pattern for the last few years. My guess, his illegal sidelines pay well and keep him afloat until he drinks his way through the profits. Then he's forced to go on another job. There was no change until two years ago. Suddenly, he's getting paid every two to three weeks, with two periods—both around seven months—when he was paid weekly. The boom/bust pattern has gone too; his average balance started to climb and just kept on going. He made five times the money in those two years than in the previous five. But that's not the whole story—it's easier if I send you the visuals.'

'And you got all that from where, exactly?'

'I ran the numbers from the Dalfur Bank. I'm not just a pretty face.'

A graph appeared on her omni-block screen. The lines' sawtooth pattern repeated itself, then it rose rapidly, shooting off the top. 'He's never had this kind of money… What's this? His credit balance plummeted into the red—a single debit to Osmir Debt Recovery.'

'I checked; there's no record, anywhere, of a company with that name.'

'I'm not surprised—probably a legal label for some crime lord's untraceable cash repatriation fund, or similar. Keagan was always in up to his neck, but *so* much money?'

'That's why I've been expecting this chat for a while. I know you and your brother are close. What did he tell you?'

'Where did you get that idea, that Keagan and I are close?' Moira had to force the words past the tightness in her throat.

'Hey, easy. You mentioned him, and when you were kids growing up together. I just assumed—'

'Well don't. Have you heard me talk about him much in the present? No. Keagan and I speak once a year. This year I didn't bother, and I don't need you to remind me that, as a sister, I stink. It's none of your damn business.' Her fingers hurt from holding the omni-block in a death grip. There was only silence from the comms link. 'Mastersson?'

'I'm still here. You alright?'

Is the bastard trying to make me cry? 'I'm just worried about Keagan. What else do you know?'

There was a pause. 'The sharp drop—the final one—the amount is *exactly* the same as Keagan's earnings over the prior two years. Take into account his usual living expenses: transport, apartment, food—it pushed him into the red.'

'Then my brother got himself a new employer, managed to piss them off, and they took back everything they'd paid him. Any signs explaining the lack of contact?'

'There's no money coming into his account. His customised Magtrak has been repossessed and his personal messages show a final eviction notice on the apartment.'

'Personal messages?'

'Just a load of social stuff. His choice of drinking establishment changed; in the months before his cash bottomed out he went really upmarket. There's nothing overtly criminal. Even Keagan wasn't stupid enough to leave an obvious trail.'

'This is my brother we're talking about.'

'Yeah, sorry.'

'What about his contacts? Any change in the last few months?'

'Nothing. I've already run every profile; they were all clean. You know where he'd hide a gangsta list?'

'Funny. What about Keagan's criminal record? Have any of the agencies taken him?'

'Nope. At least, I don't think so. Officially he's clean, but I guess that could have been useful for someone. Do you want me to ask around?'

'Yes, and I'll do the same on the way to Aquila.'

'Moira, you can't go chasing Keagan's tail now. Let me see what I can find. Finish your current job. Most likely you won't find anything on Kishino, and digging around won't take more than a few days. The Collective will have your badge if you skip out before you're done.'

'Dammit, Masters son, Keagan is my brother! Like you said, Kishino is probably long gone or long dead.' Moira forced aside the memory of Masayoshi-san and her silent promise.

'Stop and think for a second. If The Collective takes your badge before you reach Aquila then you'll have no jurisdiction there. You're good, Moira, but visiting as a private citizen doors won't exactly open for you—keeping your badge is the only way you'll find Keagan.'

Moira grabbed the carton of *Primal Protein* and hurled it across the cockpit. It hit the bulkhead with a satisfying meat-slap before sticking there, inanimate and dead.

'What the hell was that? You still there?'

Moira quickly uncurled from the chair, nails digging into her palms. Masterson was right. 'Yeah, I'm here. Look, I gotta go. I'll chase down Kishino and keep PCS sweet. You just find something, quickly, okay?'

'Sure. Look, if you need—?'

'I'm fine. Just get me a lead, anything I can use. Oh, and thanks.'

'Any time. I'll be back in touch, soon.'

Moira hit 'Disconnect'. She ducked under a lump of free-floating protein and made for the galley to find something to clean up the mess. *Keagan's all I've got left. I should be there, not chasing after some ex-killer who disappeared playing happy families. Damn you, Ferris.* As she walked—her boots keeping her on the deck—she flipped through her contact list on the omni-block. There must be at least one favour owed she had not already cashed in.

✶

Pharos, System BD+24 543

'Theodore A. Ferris, Sub-Vice President of Investigations with Proteus Collective Security, you have come to my notice, and in case there was any confusion in your mind, that is not good.'

'No… sir. Do I call you "sir"?'

'No, Ferris, you shut up and listen, except when I ask you a question. Why are we having this conversation?'

'Sir?'

'I do not like stupid people. By the end of this conversation, you had better convince me you have something worthwhile between your ears. Again, why do you think we are having this conversation?'

'Because of Moira Dolan?'

'A child's level of insight. Instead, try showing me why I hired you.'

'Because Dolan… Because Dolan still has her badge?'

'*I* know the benefits of patience. That is a talk I intended to have in six months' time, but right now I am only hearing stupid, Ferris. I cannot believe I am about to stoop to the level of a vid-channel villain, but in your case it seems necessary. One comms call and I can make you disappear. Are we feeling more insightful now?'

'I… I… Because I gave her the Kishino case? Because she's left Collective space?'

'No. Those mistakes will only cost you a beating. You do know that what you do for me is illegal? That is why I pay you a lot of money. I asked you to keep her occupied. I asked you to keep her out of my business. Are there any lights going on?'

'K… Kishino is linked to you, to your organisation, in some way?'

'That is the only perspicacious thing you have said to me so far. So, at a time of my choosing, why am I arranging to have you beaten?'

Theodore slid his hands further around the slate to stop it clacking on the desk. 'B… Because I didn't guess there was a link between Kishino and—'

'No! *You* could not work out the link. It was because you did not think to ask if there was one.'

'I'm sorry. I—'

'Yes, yes. I know this little speech: "Please give me another chance. I can put things right, etc., etc., etc." Ms Dolan is a trained Federal Criminal Investigations operative and rather more perceptive than you are, which is precisely why I requested you not interfere with her investigation into a routine case. A tip, Ferris: if you wish to control or manipulate someone without their knowledge, then help them, become their friend. They will drop their guard and everything is much easier, and much sweeter. I reward performance; that mistake will cost you your pay.'

'But my apartment! I've already spent the money.'

'Your faith in your own abilities lacks objectivity, when you are only capable of wisdom with hindsight. We have previously discussed my liking for the three strikes method, so what was your third, and last, mistake?'

'… I… I don't know. Please! How can I put it right if I don't know? Please—'

'And by pure fluke he answers correctly, "You don't know." Part of what I pay you for is to watch my business so I do not have to. One of my more reliable employees informed me that Moira Dolan has been frantically trying to contact her brother.'

'But—'

'I was also informed that, somehow, someone has gained access to Keagan Dolan's credit account where, on my behalf, several large deposits were made. Moira Dolan now knows that her brother was involved in *something*, and when that something is my business, I have a problem. As you need everything spelt out, if I have a problem then *so do you*. Now, is the best you can offer me, "I don't know."?'

'Look, I'll do anything. I can arrange for Moira to disappear. I can—'

'No, you won't, because you can't. Your ineptitude is of a magnitude that surprises even me. Redemption is not something I believe in—you would be dead already, except you still have the potential to be useful. You do wish to be useful, I take it?'

'Yes. Yes, sir.'

'Good. Keep an eye on Ms Dolan. Do not start being nice. Do not be more obstructive. Do *nothing* without my express permission. We stick to the original plan: edge her towards dismissal. She is making it easy enough for you. I want no one to harbour unnecessary suspicions so do not arouse any. Is that clear?'

'Yes, sir. If…?'

'You have proven next to useless. The credits you were paid have already been removed from your account—the debit made to a local gambling establishment. If you are asked about your change in circumstances, you will confess and willingly sign up for therapy.

Make a mess of this, or make anyone the least bit curious about your affairs, and you will be killed.'

Theodore stared at the blank screen of his slate. He let it fall to the desk and clasped his hands together to stop them shaking. Walking stiffly, he crossed his office and checked the corridor, before continuing to the nearest washroom to dry his trousers.

System LP 413-18

Moira reached out and touched 'Call'. 'Mastersson, you there?'

'Oh, wait…' There was a loud crash. 'Shit. Ow!' Another loud crash. 'Shit, shit, shit. Ow. It's you. Erm, hi.'

'What are you doing? It sounds like I'm the last person you want to hear from.'

'No! I'm erm, ow. I'm always happy to hear from you. It's just— I wasn't expecting—'

'Fine. Call me back when you've finished with her.'

'No! Moira, it's not like that. I would never do that to you.'

'What?'

'Nothing. No, nothing. I'm fine. Everything is fine. Just ignore me. I've shorted out the main power grid and I'm on my knees praying to the gods of technology. My sacrifice is to be up to my elbows in circuit boards and insulation gel.'

'Mastersson, you are such a tekhead.'

'I'm not just a tekhead. Anyway, tekheads have feelings too.'

'… Can you call me back when you're being a bit less weird?'

'Hey, look, I'm sorry. You don't sound too happy. How can I help?' His voice slowed and softened.

Moira suppressed the urge to fiddle with a crease in her suit. 'I'm worried about Keagan. I know we talked about this, but I can't go flying off trying to locate some space-iced meat sack just to tick some boxes on my next report when he's in trouble.' The image of Masayoshi-san's trusting face stared at her from behind her eyes.

'And that "space-iced meat sack" would be Kishino? The man with the family, who are also missing by the way.'

She was taken aback by the disappointment in his voice. 'I'm not going to abandon them, or break my promise: *when* the old guy finds out they're dead, it won't change how he feels.'

'"The old guy?" You made a promise to Kishino's father to find his family and you're just going to walk away?'

If Mastersson had been in the same room, Moira would have slapped him. 'I am not walking away. I'm sending you.'

'Sending me where?'

'You asked if you can help. If keeping my promise to Kishino and his family means so much to you, then you go. Sniff around the places he was last seen. We both know there'll be nothing to find. You do the legwork, I'll fill in the paperwork. And I'll tell Masayoshi-san because I know you're not good with people. Satisfied?' She had not planned on blackmailing him into it, but if he was going to come over all morally superior, what did he expect?

'But… I haven't finished Keagan's background check. Some systems are difficult to crack. And the lab—I need to finish up here and…' His voice trailed off.

'You've not been off-world for months. The change of scene will do you good. Besides, it was you who told me there was no substitute for legwork.'

Silence.

It felt like kicking a puppy. 'Look, if it's too much… Keagan has probably fallen in with another wrong crowd. I'll dive in and pull his arse out of the trouble it's stuck in. I can sort Kishino on the way back. Not a problem.'

'It'll cost you your job. After everything he's done, you're still not going to change your mind about Keagan, are you?'

'He's all I've got left…'

'He's not all—okay, I'll do it. If you find anything new, send it to me. I'll get my stuff together and be on the next transport. I'll be in touch.' And he was gone.

Moira leant back in her seat. *What's with him? What gives him the right to lecture me like that?* She was angry with him and did not know why. Moira had spent her whole life learning to control her feelings. Now Mastersson was pushing her buttons and that made him dangerous. But she could not worry about him now; Keagan needed her, probably. Moira pulled up the luminous nav display and touched the system icons linking her to her brother's last known system: following her finger, the hyperspace lanes lit up in neon, shining heavenly paths offering redemption. *I'm just not cut out to be the angel.*

✻

The Dalfur System

Aquila was possibly the worst place in the universe to live, Moira thought as the automated taxi floated silently along the boulevard, keeping the regulation distance from the vehicle in front. The view through the taxi window was impressive. The buildings stretched high enough that their tops cut the occasional cloud scudding by, desperately seeking to escape the city along with the winds in the upper atmosphere. The hazy nebulas of water vapour above were the only natural thing about Aquilifer City, despite the greenery everywhere. Manicured carpets of plants coated the sides and top of every shining marble edifice, like the sprayed strips of face paint currently the height of fashion in parts of the Empire. *It's all so damn clean. Anywhere trying this hard to look respectable must be hiding something.* This sterile conurbation was the last place she expected Keagan to call home.

The taxi eased to a stop, drifting to hover next to the porcelain-like curb. The door slid open revealing two exact geometric squares of grass, each adorned with a spherical bush at the centre. The path separating them was so straight it could have been laser cut. *Imaginative.* The towering apartment block was white-on-white—its 'door' formed from two gleaming slabs inset into the monochrome façade. Only the perfectly perpendicular frame of leaves hinted that this was not a wall, but the entrance.

Moira turned, her attention caught by the lighter green of a flashing hologram.

'Welcome to Aquilifer City. As a visitor here, your financial credentials have not yet been verified. Please authorise payment of your fare,' read the scrolling text before her.

What kind of city has taxis that unlock their doors before you've paid? The kind of place where you can't pay in cash. Moira reluctantly waved her omni-block in the direction of the hologram.

'Payment authorised.'

With her success record, several previous employers had offered her a cerebral implant—access to worlds of data and the comms network from inside her head—but her memories of the war and mutilated bodies fused with shining metal were too vivid, too real. So were the looks of mute horror in the eyes of the broken, trapped in prisons of their own making despite their inserted happy-chips. Cybernetics was for invalids and nut-jobs.

She slid from the seat, a belt an unnecessary hindrance when every vehicle was controlled by a central computer. Grabbing her duffel bag, Moira stepped clear of her anaemic bubble and strode towards the white wall. More text rose up to greet her—the font identical to the one in the cab.

'Welcome to Celestial Living. Please stand still while you are scanned for infectious diseases and weapons.'

It shouldn't detect the hairclip.

She feigned a nonchalant interest in a couple patrolling by with their child. Each wore one of the planet's ubiquitous green accented one-pieces. These were muted two tone—a positively ostentatious declaration of the family's upper-strata social status. *How did Keagan survive here? I'd be climbing the walls after a week, and I'm the tame one.*

'Scan complete. Who do you wish to visit?'

'Keagan, Keagan Dolan.'

'Keagan Dolan's status is "Unavailable". Would you like to leave a message?'

At least I got the right place. 'I am Officer Moira Dolan, on official business from Proteus Collective Security. Here's my operating permit.' She touched the omni-block, holding it up as she spoke.

'Identity and operating permit verified. Please enter. Directions to the apartment are available on request. You will not be permitted access to other areas of the building. Enjoy your visit to Celestial Living.'

Fortunately, all the planets in Dalfur were covered by one of The Collective's standard law enforcement agreements. Ferris would have blocked her if she had had to apply for clearance. The two slab-like doors spun silently on their central axes. Moira stepped through the central corridor that formed, her footfalls echoing eerily in the mausoleum-like foyer.

She stopped and turned. 'Computer, enable download of directions, and visitor and resident movement records for the previous four months.'

Another holographic text display sprang into life. 'Directions available. Unable to comply with request to access personal data. This building's residents' privacy is rights-protected. Please apply to Central Records.'

Damn. 'Restrict information requested to specific case parameters: suspect Keagan Dolan. Download visitor list to his apartment and details of his movements, all available information fields.'

'Jurisdiction of Collective operative, Moira Dolan, verified. Information request within acceptable parameters. Information download complete.'

Moira's omni-block lit up in response to the building's computer. She accepted the data stream and a miniature rendition of the inside of the building sprang to life on the back of her wrist. It showed a light strip leading to one of the lifts. The doors were already open when she got there and the inside pulsed helpfully with a tasteful green light. *The only thing this building won't do for you is pick your nose.*

Four hundred and twenty-three floors in under two minutes and she was standing outside Keagan's apartment. Another white slab blocked her way.

'Keagan Dolan was informed of your arrival. There has been no response.'

Her heart sank. She knew she was being stupid—scraping off the last vestiges of hope clinging to the cold wall growing inside her hurt. *So, either he's out or he's lying in there—dead or incapacitated?* 'Computer, how many separate movement signatures inside his apartment?'

'This building's residents' privacy is rights-protected. Information not available.'

'Information not available' and not just restricted? No surveillance in the apartments; visits from the Law announced before it can even knock on their doors? Privacy for the privileged, but that's not me.

'Computer, open the door. Request issued under the jurisdiction of Collective operative, Moira Dolan. Purpose: questioning and possible detention of suspect, Keagan Dolan.' *Ferris will have my badge for this. On a frontier world I could break a window or force a lock without a computer tracking every move I make. Hopefully, he's too busy making someone else's life hell and any notifications will sit unread in a memory core somewhere—as if. He probably gets a message every time I sneeze. Still, too late now. Let's see how far I get before he shuts me down.*

'Jurisdiction verified—complying.'

I wonder if he has guests? Moira withdrew the decorative clip from her hair. Shielded inside was enough juice and tazer wire to take down an Altairean Monolith at twenty metres. It was a one-shot deal, but as the clip was usefully shaped as a knuckleduster she was not too worried. As the slab-door rotated, she slipped off her duffel bag and boots—the only way to move silently on these smooth, hard floors was barefoot.

Everything was quiet so she slid inside, her back to the wall. *Shite, it's like something out of Interplanetary Living.* Entering the main area of the open plan apartment, she found no one hiding behind the door waiting to attack her—*unless you count the designer. Everything's so overwhelmingly tasteful.* White marble was everywhere, except where rugs, settees, and cushions in muted greens and browns had been artfully placed. *This isn't Keagan's home, it's a showroom.* She edged further into the room, alert for any movement reflected in the highly polished walls, but only her image played across the surfaces—multiplied on wall, floor, and every furniture frame. A swift reconnoitre of the bathroom, three bedrooms, and the living areas revealed she was alone.

Moira slid the clip back into her hair and retrieved her shoes and duffel bag from the hallway. It was time to get to work. 'Computer, initiate lockdown of Keagan Dolan's apartment. Issue an audible warning at the first sign of a visitor.'

'Understood.'

She placed her bag on the edge of the large tinted dining table. Like everything else in the apartment, it seemed unused. The Electronic Surveillance Detector was secreted in one of the many inner pockets; she slid her hand into the bag and retrieved it without looking. Next came gloves, hair covering, and facemask. She flicked the ESD on and strode across to the corner adjoining the floor-to-ceiling panoramic window.

'Computer, darken the glass one hundred percent. Apartment lights to fifty percent.'

'Understood.'

Slowly, centimetre by centimetre, she began to sweep the apartment for any cameras and listening devices. After nearly an hour, the ESD had found nothing. It could penetrate a metre of rock with its active scan, even embedded passive sound conduction sensors would show up. If anyone was keeping tabs on Keagan, they either did not care what went on in his apartment or they were confident of their hold over him.

She returned the ESD to her bag and removed the battered tin with 'Lunch' scratched into the lid. The P-FAS, or Portable

Forensic Analysis Station as the tech-boys liked to call it, was her most expensive piece of equipment. Sticking it inside an old tin might seem like a stupid idea, but when her bag was stolen on Hu Delphinus it was the only item the thief had left behind.

Sampling modules were cleaned and activated, and for the next three hours she wiped, scraped, and sucked her way around the apartment. She hated working in the ULEs—*calling them that is just wrong: there's no urban grit or real living here, not in this clinical environment. Plus, finding anything I can actually use in this near-sterile box will be almost impossible. There has to be* some *clue here that'll lead me to Keagan.*

She paid special attention to the most-used sections and articles: the floors, rugs, doorways and door handles, bed covers, sofas, chairs, and cushions, the cleanser and toilet; every empty space was wanded for airborne residues. Eating and drinking utensils could still carry DNA from skin and saliva, but the open food in the cooler was too heavily seeded with bacterial colonies. Miniscule quantities of chemical salts and proteins from Keagan's sweat should have left deposits in his footwear or the groins and armpits of clothing. The insides of his pockets were emptied and material vacuumed for particle samples, micro-debris from the soles of shoes scanned. Collect enough and she could work out what he had been eating, drinking, and taking.

Dust, hair, and dried fluids were the materials she used to paint a picture of her brother's life.

Pacing, Moira waited for the P-FAS analysis; the sample sizes were so tiny that the machine could not be moved until it was complete. She checked her omni-block. *Ferris must have been notified by now. I can't have much longer.* She fiddled with the machine's display, examining its tech-spec closely. *At least the board stopped Ferris cutting every bit of the budget; this is top-of-the-line. The analysis is more accurate, but is it faster?* She checked her omni-block again. *I need to get a grip.*

The padded sofa enveloped her as she sat; there was nothing useful she could do now but think. Keagan had been living it large. The food in the cooler was pre-packed but handmade, expensive. One container was half-eaten and re-sealed: he had obviously planned to return. Nearly all his belongings were still in boxes—surprising even for Keagan after two years, even though he never 'wasted' time organising. What did arouse her curiosity was the line of tailored suits hanging in the storage closet: not Keagan's style at all. There were eight in all, six showing the subtlest signs of wear: minute abrasions on the fibres of the cloth where it had rubbed against itself. One showed a slight discolouration from spilt liquid that had overcome the material's inbuilt stain resistance; she was disappointed, but not surprised, to rediscover his propensity for drinking.

But every brand of alcohol in the generously stocked drinks cabinet was exclusive. *Before it was anything that kicked him in the head—the harder, the better.* A slate left on a side table was filled with an eclectic selection of reading material: *The Economic Realities of Inter-System Trading*; *Human Art: the Juxtaposition of the God and the Animal*; *Hedonism as a Journey of Self-Discovery*; *Military Combat Flight Techniques of the Federation, Empire, and Alliance: a Comparative Guide*; and even *Beginners and Advanced Imperial Social Etiquette*. The list went on. What Moira could not understand was that any title she opened—and there must have been over one hundred—was either finished or most of the way through. *No trashy adventures. Is he trying to win* The Natural Brain *or entertaining more intelligent prostitutes? I tried for years and he wouldn't change. Who's helping him now, and why? What the hell is going on?*

The computer's in-apartment voice sliced the silence. 'Announcement: previous lockdown command issued by Moira Dolan, overridden. Law enforcement officers have valid jurisdiction and have been granted right of entry to the apartment of Keagan Dolan.'

Shite. 'Computer, display progress of the officers, format: video.'

'Acknowledged.'

A flat rectangle of light appeared on the wall. Three heavyset men in local police uniforms and body armour were walking across the foyer towards the lifts. No notification of jurisdiction transfer from PCS to the local police force. No prior notification of their arrival from planetary officials. Uniform or no uniform, these were goons. The planet did not matter; they were the same everywhere in the galaxy.

'Computer, confirm time for the lift to reach this floor, given current usage.'

'All conveyance systems are under capacity and no delays are anticipated. The lift will reach this floor in one minute and fifty-four seconds.'

'Computer, can you stop the lift?'

'Unable to comply. Interference with an officer of the law in pursuit of their duties is a violation of civil code CC6454.'

Why am I not surprised? 'Computer, deductive reasoning: I am an officer of the law. My duty is to obtain data from this room. If the other officers enter too soon the data I am collecting will be lost and you will have obstructed me in the pursuit of my duties. The company you represent will be in violation of civil code CC6454.'

On the video feed, the lift door closed behind the goons. Moira glanced across at the P-FAS's display—three minutes until the results were processed. If it was moved too soon, everything would be lost.

'Computer, I need you to delay the lift for two minutes. I can obtain the data I need to pursue my duties, and the officers below will still reach this apartment where they can pursue theirs. This violates no civil codes. Comply.' Moira imagined she could hear the whirring of cogs and smell computer chips burning out under the strain.

'Deduction: officers have conflicting interests—gaining immediate access versus requesting a two minute delay—I will hold the lift for one minute.'

Not enough. It's so much easier arguing with a person; just put a gun to their head when you ask for a favour. Moira scanned the apartment. *There's got to be something I can use, but everything's so damn clean...*

First, she slid the biggest sofa in front of the P-FAS to hide it from sight and hopefully offer a little protection from stray gunfire. Then she strode across to the kitchen area, opened the cooler and took the half-eaten packet of food from the shelf. She threw it on the polished floor where it left a bloody smear across the tiles. *Three... two... one...* The cleaning droid came from a small, previously hidden recess in the wall, intent on re-establishing the kitchen as a shrine to cleanliness. It had travelled less than two metres before Moira withdrew her hairclip and hit the robot with four hundred kilovolts. It stopped, the little green lights of its anthropomorphically appealing face fading to nothing. She quickly hefted the smoking carcass under the hand dryer, blasting it with air to dissipate the fumes before they set off the smoke detectors. Valuable seconds were wasted smashing its head against the work surface to get to the power cell, and more searching for the utensils drawer. *Nothing but fucking chopsticks and fancy glass spoons; damn you Keagan.* A glance at the video showed the men shouting and hammering the lift doors. The computer was winning the argument, but not for long. *There has to be something!* And then she saw it, a delicate figure of nebulous colours and subtle contours formed from twisted metal wire. *From art lover to desecrator in a few short steps.* She brought the sculpture down hard on the angular table edge. *That was probably worth a few credits.* Quickly, she worked two of the free wire strands backwards and forwards until fatigue fractured the metal. Grabbing the sculpture's base, she went back to the remains of the cleaning droid.

The image on the far wall showed the lift was moving again. The men looked angry. One released the safety on his automatic. The others held theirs ready. *Damn computer—couldn't keep its mouth shut and then decides handguns are okay...*

She hit the innards of the droid repeatedly with the heavy base until the powercell broke free. The wires she bent around its exposed contacts, careful not to complete the circuit. Then she cracked open the droid's internal tank of cleaning fluid, which she spread liberally on the floor making a puddle near the apartment entrance. She eyed the video feed again. The men were stepping out of the lift, weapons raised. Moira placed the powercell and the wires at her feet, slid her hairclip over her fingers and clenched her fist, feeling the reassuring weight of it in her hand. The men were moving cautiously along the corridor in formation. *Not complete amateurs then.*

'Computer, lock on to my voice—don't accept instructions from anyone else. Video feed off. Apartment lighting down to ten percent.' She would gain vital seconds while their eyes adjusted to the gloom in the apartment.

Silently, inexorably, the door began to spin around its central axis. Moira placed her back against it and followed it round. A single man-shaped silhouette loomed in front of her. She struck, feeling the cartilage of a windpipe collapse underneath her knuckleduster. The silhouette crumpled to the floor clutching at its throat, a slick-liquid wheezing breaking the quiet as it struggled to breathe.

'Crap!'

The shout came from the other side of the door, followed by the barking report of a machine carbine discharging half a magazine into the ceiling. *That little slip will cost you.* In a single flowing motion, Moira spun and caught the powercell with her foot, sending it sliding into the puddle of cleaning fluid. The cell discharged, voltage pouring through the liquid. A man screamed. His carbine spat the remainder of its clip into the apartment, projectiles cracking the duraglass windows and shredding furniture into billowing clouds of padding. *Shite, only two down.*

Moira sprinted across the apartment and leapt over the kitchen worktop as bullets peppered the wall above. The remnants of Keagan's overripe lunch were smeared across the floor in front of her. She took a handful and rubbed it across her stomach. *Should buy me some time.* The gunfire continued for three full seconds, leaving her head ringing from the repeated sonic blows and the overhead storage unit doors full of holes. *Empty clip.* She raced around the worktop, reaching for the broken sculpture lying on the worktop on her way past—attempting to close the distance before he had time to reload. She was halfway to the looming figure in the corner when she heard the click of a mag ramming home.

She threw herself sideways and closed her eyes. 'Computer, apartment lighting to one hundred percent.' The man, blinded by the incandescent brilliance reflected from a hundred polished surfaces, fired wildly and a score of hot metal slugs flew past her. She twitched violently, doubled up face down on the rug, her clothing covered in the bloody red mess.

'Well played, Dolan.' He dropped a packet in front of her nose. It split, spraying her face with fine powder.

Writhing and clutching her stomach, Moira rolled away, onto her side. She coughed, spitting out the bitter taste.

'You're tougher than Keagan, but in the end it didn't help, did it? He was a friend of mine. Did he ever mention me? Officer Gerrit?' He waited.

Moira felt the fury rising, but kept herself still, quiet.

'Nothing to say? Your brother didn't know when to shut up. Don't suppose he's got much to say for hisself now. Wot a family. Sister comes to find drugged-up brother. Career going down the hole, she's getting desperate—here to get a piece of his action. A liddle tip-off and Officer Gerrit tracks her. She resists arrest and another Dolan goes to the morgue. Tough break.' He swung the gun.

Moira spun onto her back. Swinging the broken sculpture, she knocked the weapon aside. He was off balance and too slow. She thrust the barbs of the damaged end between his armour plating. As the metal sunk into the softness of his stomach, she twisted the base, feeling resistance stiffen then ease as the man's muscles fought, then failed, to remain whole. He dropped to his knees, vainly trying to stem the tide of blood gushing past the embedded metal and the fingers of his gauntlets. His weapon clattered to the floor.

Moira rolled away, breathing hard and trying not to throw up. Her jaw ached where she had caught it on the floor; the acrid taste of blood filled her mouth where she had bitten her tongue. She stood. The gun was useless—a custom job with a coded handgrip and inbuilt explosive. She kicked it into the puddle of cleaning fluid and was gratified when it fizzed—blue sparks dancing over its surface. *Still charge in the powercell—no need to check that body.* Moira felt nothing as she went through the motions. You did what you needed to, or you would not be the one walking away.

She regarded the man next to her, now holding out an imploring hand—the same hand that held the gun moments before. Moira turned her back and collapsed onto the couch, before wiping ineffectually at the splattered remains of the food on her clothes. *Was this the last meal Keagan ever ate? 'Don't suppose he's got much to say for hisself now.'* Gerrit's words replayed in her head. Her hands clasped in her lap, fingers knotting and unknotting in time with the pulses of blood in her ears. *Am I too late this time?*

'Please—' He barely whispered the word.

She crossed to where he lay and checked for other weapons or a comms device. *Clean. Police? Maybe. Gerrit already prepped a cover story. No need for him to lie about being an 'officer' if they wanted me dead. So, crooked, but on whose payroll? No comms units, carrying a high tech arsenal—the money wanted this done right. Shame I messed it up.*

She could still hear the shallow rasping breath of the man by the door. The noise was quieter, but the rhythm regular. *Not good. Probably trying to get to the lift.*

'I'll be back, then maybe we'll talk about getting you a medic.' She headed for the still-open door. She felt no remorse. A score was being settled.

The results of her handiwork were halfway down the corridor, gurgling as he struggled to suck enough air to crawl the next few centimetres. *Like a turtle in that armour, no exposed pressure points.* She returned to the apartment.

The holed stomach had not moved. 'Medic—' The mouth attached to it loosely shaped the sounds.

'Not done, back in a minute.' She looked over at the energy cell lying in the pool of fluid, decided it was not worth the risk, and headed to the kitchen area. She took a chopstick from the drawer and headed back to the corridor.

The turtle had managed to creep another metre or so— exhausted, weak, slow. She bent forward, raising the chopstick. Behind the goggles, eyes widened. It was easy to pin flailing arms with her knees as they waved ineffectually, *like mine did, a long time ago.* Something unintelligible gurgled through a broken throat. Moira thrust the chopstick past the neck guard and into the carotid. She stepped clear and pulled. The body writhed, a hand clutching at the hole as blood sprayed the wall and puddled on the floor. A few convulsions and it was over. She grabbed a boot and dragged the corpse back to the apartment. Although it was heavy, the soaked body armour slid easily over the smooth floor.

'Wha—what have you done?' Gerrit was still lying where Moira had left him. His skin was pallid, bluer after the bleeding expanded the slick at her feet. *Names make it harder,* she cautioned herself.

She perched on the back of the sofa. 'He couldn't talk so he was no use. So, how about we swap answers for an appointment with a medic? Who sent you?'

'I need help now. I'll answer questions after you make that call.' The tone, full of bravado; the words wavered.

Moira stood and headed towards the bedroom. She returned with one of her brother's exquisitely tailored suits. She glanced around before picking up one of the rugs from the floor.

'What are you going to do with those?' He was shivering now.

Blood loss and fear. 'You're dying. I'm cleaning up before I leave.'

The man hissed insults at her back, his breath catching every few words. As she went to leave they changed, as she knew they would, to shouted reasoning and pleas. She did not look back as she left the apartment for the corridor.

I wonder if they never take me seriously because I have a soft accent? 'Computer, close Keagan Dolan's door.' It was not that anyone would hear. Years in the field told her the noisy—and illegal—excesses of the rich meant their living spaces were usually soundproof. The apartment was at one end of its own corridor and there were doors at the other. But they were frosted and the large dark smudges of blood on every surface would be visible to anyone walking by. She hurriedly wiped up the sticky mess.

The bigger problem was legal. Her attackers had no official sanction so it was unlikely anyone would alert the authorities if they did not return, but if local law enforcement discovered the bodies she would be detained. The investigation could take weeks. *Shite I don't have time for. And a fair hearing, with three of their own dead? Corrupt cops or not, jurisprudence in cases like this is more about society's vengeance than justice. I've got to get clear, and that'll take Mastersson.* The memory of his warm tones floated through her. *It'll be good to hear a friendly voice.* She thrust the thought aside. *I've just killed people and smashed up a luxury apartment. I need to focus.*

'Computer, open the door.'

Out of habit, she tossed the rug and suit into the recycler. They would be digested and the biomass used in some unpleasant way by the city. Shoving the bodies down the chute was an ideal solution, but the opening was too small. *If I had a laser cutter and more time…* The best she could do was make the apartment look good from the outside, get Mastersson to doctor the building surveillance, and hope no one came round for a social call. Given what she had discovered that did not seem likely, but someone might want to follow up. *I won't be so lucky again.*

She went back to the man. His eyes were unfocused, his breathing shallow and ragged, the blood slick bigger than before. She had seen people die and knew how long it took. He did not have much time. 'Let's start again. You will answer my questions, and then I will call a medic. Who sent you to kill me?'

The man must have known it too. He said nothing, but raised a middle finger in the age-old salute. He held it up for three seconds before his arm muscles spasmed and his falling hand splashed in the blood, the stiffness of his glove preserving his last sign of defiance. Was it aimed at her, or the universe in general?

She quickly searched the bodies, leaving the one in the cleaning fluid. *Powercell's still live*—the smell of charred flesh, melting plastic, and burnt hair was starting to overwhelm the air conditioning. She did not really expect to find anything—it was not like the holo-vid shows, assassins did not normally keep their employer's details in a pocket—but you never knew. Her omni-block software scanned images of the weapons and armour—all custom, top-of-the-range. Precious minutes were spent throwing everything useful into her duffel bag.

Moira exhaled a rush of air when she discovered the P-FAS undamaged. Hope made her touch the controls almost reverently. There was little time, but she pulled up the results summary screen. At the top of the list of unremarkable entries, the one labelled 'Anomaly' stood out. *What the...?* She drilled down through the submenus to check for errors and isolate the source. The sample had passed the standard viability tests and verifications. *A full diagnostic and recalibration will take too long to run. Besides, I've never known one of these make a mistake.* She dived into the bag and pulled out a small reinforced container. *It's on Keagan: clothes, bedding, shoes, wash-kit.* More time was lost running around the apartment, resampling. *I just hope there's enough to use.*

She stowed the container in a pocket and the P-FAS inside the 'Lunch' box. With the box in the bag, at last she could fasten the seal. The authorities would eventually discover the bodies, and her micro-biological traces were everywhere. *But by the time they issue an arrest warrant, I should be light-years away.*

She opened a secure channel on her omni-block. 'Mastersson? Mastersson, are you there?'

No reply.

Moira suddenly felt very alone. 'Look, when you get this, contact me, okay? I need you to wipe any records of my visit to Celestial Living. If you can scrub the digital goons from the surveillance footage, great; the bodies are off-camera in Keagan's apartment. I'm going dark until I hear from you.' She fed in details of the building's location and the transaction number for the taxi. It was a round trip and the automatic vehicle would still be waiting by the kerb. *I'm coming home, Jane. I want hot food, a cold drink, and my warm bunk, and if you snore I'll poke you in the support struts.*

9

The Manah System

Mastersson's sweat-slicked palms gripped the armrests, nails digging into the padding in an effort to stop the growing scream forcing its way up his windpipe. *We're coming in too fast! I'll be smeared across the side of the station like so much Jotun landsnail slime.*

On the wall-sized viewscreen at the end of the cabin, the open maw of the cuboid coriolis station spun face-on, toughened alloy edges perfectly aligned to rip the wings from the transport and spill their bodies into the hard vacuum of space that would suck all the air from his lungs leaving a human blockcicle floating... floating endlessly in black eternal night... *NO!*

'Passengers will please remain quiet and relaxed until the Starliner Express is anchored by the station's docking clamps. To ensure passenger safety in zero-g, your seat harness will remain secured until that time. Once inside the docking bay, you will experience a slight spinning sensation—this is an alignment manoeuvre and is entirely normal. Once disembarked, be prepared for the light gravity—'Mastersson made a frantic grab for the sick bag dispenser and missed. '—move slowly and mind your head as you pass through portals or under hanging roof structures. We thank you for travelling with Starliner Travel. Enjoy your visit to Petra Orbital.'

I'm going to die... I'm going to die... His conscience gave a twinge as he heard the spattering sound of floating vomit balls impacting on surfaces and the cries of outrage from unlucky victims. But his terror-shuttered eyelids were effective barricades against the reality outside.

'Clean-up to aisle seven, we have a chucker.' The honeyed tones of the announcer had gone hard and flat.

Another voice whispered next to his ear, 'I'm sorry, *sir*, but your stress monitor has red-lined and for your own protection—and the cleanliness of the other passengers—I'm going to have to sedate you. Please do not resist.'

Masterson opened his eyes and found a uniformed, blue-eyed angel frowning down at him from on high. 'Resist? No Way. Please, please sedate away…' he managed to mumble past the chunks. There was a momentary prick, followed by an ecstatic sensation as the hypodermic slid home. *Why is flying only nice in dreams?* Blissful oblivion enveloped him in its tender embrace.

✳

Masterson's body spasmed and suddenly his world was moving. His eyes flew open in time to see a bush of thick black hair and a red bulbous lump looming up ahead. The nose smashed into his forehead, disgorging a spurt of red as it transformed into a spongy mess.

'Phnuck!' A big man staggered backwards, clutching his face.

Masterson stared at the embodiment of primal rage wearing a spray-on flight attendant's uniform—all flushed skin, popping veins, and bulging muscle. It glared back.

The muscles in his own arm rippled. A wave of pain, adrenaline coursing through his body, and Masterson's brain kicked in. *Plain room—Burly flight attendant—Stim-shot still embedded in my arm—nasty brand—Overdose—Note to self: never buy a cheap ticket—Stim?—To counteract end-of-the-flight sedative—News, three years ago, July fifteenth, on the left monitor, broken must replace—travel company sued for loss of executive's time while sedated—Thoughts too fast—Big man angry: brow furrowed, fists balling—going to hit me—Escape—Exit!—Flight attendant said low gravity.* Masterson pushed hard on the plinth sending himself pinwheeling over the man's bent head.

'Wut the—?'

Seen me—going to hit the wall. He reached down, grabbing the man's beard as he passed. *Red bulbous nose—Lavian Brandy addiction—only job he could find.* He pulled hard, overbalancing the attendant and correcting his course towards the exit. He let go of the beard. *Coming in for docking—open bay doors—hope they're not locked.* He giggled as they slid apart, despite his logical-self arguing that sailing through the air to escape an enraged flight attendant in a spray-on uniform was not funny.

He landed awkwardly, coming to a stop against the far corridor wall where he slid, gently, to the floor. Grabbing the first knee he saw, he pulled himself up. 'Sorry, madam, there will be a man with a squashed nose coming through those doors to help you in just a moment.' He capered off down the hallway to the sounds of masculine groaning and a feminine squeal as the couple collided behind him.

Plan: find a bunk—Recover from space sickness—Second plan: thinking fast, moving fast—get Moira's results fast—Then she will love me—Kishino, family, ship—dock!—Where am?—Don't know—Don't know?—Computer! Mastersson's mind tried to reach for his implant. *Instructor: 'It's like looking for something half-remembered, but when you've found it you'll never forget it's there, unless you're drunk or high on drugs.'—High on drugs?—Woo-hoo!* Mastersson giggled. *Giggling is good—people get out of my way—moving faster.* He came to a busy intersection of two walkways. He slid, trying to turn a corner, and giggled again as the people parted before him. He grabbed one, a young man, by the arm. The man tried to shake him free, but could not. *I'm stronger too—pumped—that's what the gym-gimps call it.*

'I'm pumped.'

'Let go of me you freak, or I'll call the cops.'

Cops, cops—Cops, tops, locks—Tops, locks, docks—Docks!
'Docks? Which way?'

The man waved a hand towards one branch of the intersection, as much to ward him off as to indicate a direction. 'Just follow the strips. Now let go.'

'Where are the strips and what do they do and what do they look like?'

'Computer, a nav-strip for this man to the docks.'

'Understood.'

A pulsating amber line appeared in the air.

'Oh, pretty.' Mastersson let go of the man's arm.

'Get some help or the cops will bring you in.'

The man sounded *so* grumpy. In fact, everyone in the gathering crowd looked grumpy. Mastersson smiled reassuringly and waved before skipping off, transfixed by the light.

He bounded along, stopping occasionally to shake a hand, pat a head, and perform a slow, expansive gesture in the air to indicate the oneness of the universe. He grinned at everyone, laughed too. But the more happiness he shared, the less happy everyone looked. Pondering this apparent contradiction, he stopped. He showed a few passers-by how the nav-strip played through his fingers. They passed by faster. He stopped playing and people seemed a little calmer. The man's warning bounced around his head. *Grumpy?— Suspicious! Cops, docks, locks—Cops lock—Locked—can't help Moira.*

People crossed to the far side of the corridor to get by, some pressing themselves against the wall. He attempted to remove the mirth infecting his face and managed a rictus instead. *Ha! How cunning am I? You don't see me now 'cos I'm sad, just like you. Help Moira—can't giggling—can following.* Mastersson took several sneaky steps forward. Confident his plan was working he set off, letting the strip move people out of his way because he was too stupid and poor for an implant.

*

On foot, the docks were some distance from the disembarkation lounge. He quickly lost his bearings amongst the crowds and the maze of walkways. *And yet I am not afraid. See how they part before me!* Led by the light, he continued his messianic passage through the sea of people. *I will find Kishino, for my Moira, for my love.* He stopped, transfixed, before the sign. *A revelation!*

The paint was faded and peeling with age: 'DOCKS AREA: AHEAD. Enquiries, Lost and Found Office. Touch the panel to activate a nav-strip.'

And what is lost shall be found. Mastersson reached out for the panel below labelled 'Navigate' and light flickered across it, then faded. The nav-strip he had been following faded too. *My quest cannot end here.* 'Answer my call!' He hit the old panel which sputtered into life, and a green beam lit his way. *Ah ha!*

Several minutes of barely restrained skipping followed before he arrived outside the enquiries office. A small anonymous metal door guarded the entrance. A discoloured display outside indicated it was open, but there was a five minute wait to be seen. Barely containing his delight, he stepped forward and his boot clanged against metal, scraping off several flakes of paint. *Nothing shall bar my way when I am this close.*

'Computer! Oh, Wizard of the Electrons! Open the door!'

'Unable to comply.'

'The portal, Computer, open the portal and bar me not, you disembodied fiend.'

'Unable to comply.'

It was then Mastersson noticed the handle. 'An ancient way! Forgive me, Voice-of-the-Ether, I must venture on.' He reached out and the handle swam away. Grabbing it on the third try, he managed to wrestle it into submission. Pressing his shoulder hard against the metal, the door gave, centimetre by reluctant centimetre, hinges shrieking in protest. The light of the nav-strip faded and he was left blinking at the darkness ahead.

Vague shapes loomed, ominous in the shadows. One of the shadow shapes unrolled itself.

''Ere, whaddya want?' A Cimmerian figure came shuffling towards him—an amorphous mound of degraded offcuts. Stygian recesses in the cloth hid what might be hands and a face. A nasal shield surrounded the creature, the stench pushing back any stupid enough to approach.

Mastersson coughed and took a step forwards. 'I seek Kishino. He flew, in the yonder, and was lost.'

'Yer git lost. Yer wanna know summink, go plug yerself in like alla rest.'

'Plug myself…?'

'Get jacked, metalise yer cranium, load yer nodes. Dun't stop yer bein' stoopid though, do it?'

He's from the beginning. Nostalgia warmed Mastersson. 'Oh, venerable one, it is such an honour. I am one with you now, for I also know the pain of knowledge lost.'

'Yer one o'em psychonauts, ain't cha? Chems cut yer link, did they? Git lost, unless yer won' an 'ole in one o' yer chesticles.'

Snake-fast, a yellow-taloned hand shot from a sleeve clutching a shiny black construction. In the dimness, it took Mastersson a moment to resolve the detail: a pistol stock, line, and the c-shaped bow loaded with a bolt.

It was pointed directly at him—Mastersson snapped back to reality. 'Wait, that's an Arbalist '47—fully recurved, compound-monobloc construction pistol crossbow. Where did you find it?'

The tip of the crossbow lowered a few centimetres.

'Found it 'ere, din't I. Five years an' we chucks stuff. I get ta keeps wot I wan'. Iss a perk. 'S mine; yer ain't 'avin' her.' The bow and bolt swung back up, this time aimed between Mastersson's eyes.

'No, she's yours, of course. I just never thought I would see one. She's a beauty. You silicone treat her, every couple of months?'

'Yeah, course I do. 'Ow yer know 'bout Arbalists any 'ow?'

Mastersson's head began to swim. If he went back under this hermit would stick him and drag him into a corner to decompose. He focussed on the glinting tip of the bolt; imagining it perforating his skull kept his thoughts straight, for now. He found himself

fidgeting, but the Arbalist seemed to want him to tell the truth. 'I…
um…'

'C'mon, spit i' ou'.'

'I…um, well, we used to get together in a field… and we had
these outfits and mock ancient weapons…'

Cackling, the pile of rags shook from head-to-toe. Wide-eyed,
Masterson stared at the bouncing bolt tip.

'Yer 'armless. Wot yer doin' 'ere?' The crossbow lowered, bolt
pointed at the floor.

'I'm helping a friend—'

'She's a lady, ain't she? I know 'cos yer fidgetin' ag'in.'

Masterson could not deny it, but the sweating, pumping of his
heart and darkening vision had nothing to do with embarrassment.
He gabbled through his story. 'Yes her name is Moira and her
friend Kishino went missing with his family just over two weeks
ago in midspace and I checked all the details on-grid but they don't
show anything so I thought it may help if I came and asked around
and then I got stuck full of stims by some insane hairy-butch guy
with a beard and then followed the lights here and then I met you—
so can you help?'

'My, chatty ain't cha. Midspace? Wot system? Wot ship was 'e
on? 'Ere, you lookin' funny, you awrigh'?'

'Manah. An Asp—customised.'

The talking cloth-pile grew taller and Masterson shook, all air
pushed from his lungs. He watched a bead of sweat run along his
nose and drip onto a floor that was the wrong way up. He gasped.
Darkness and dusty colours coalesced with bright staccato sound,
warring against a smell with a physical presence that lined his nose
and throat.

'Poor git's goin' under. I gots somefin' 'ere, I knows I does.'

Masterson clawed at the ground as a mountain of animated
rags filled his tunnel vision from edge to shrinking edge. The smell
crawled into his sinuses, his lungs, sliding its way ever deeper until

it seemed it was the only thing that had ever existed. He felt his stomach convulse.

'Aw, these're me bes' togs. Yer gunna pay fer tha'.'

10

''Ere drink some o'this.'

Hot liquid slid down Mastersson's throat, burning his tongue and the roof of his mouth. The world was nothing but darkness and pulsating stars and pressure as his brain tried to force its way past his eyeballs to escape into the night, to escape the smell. He did not need to ask where he was. He just wished he could be somewhere, anywhere but here. He forced himself to swallow before he choked. From what little he could taste, past the rancid odour permeating everything, it was a mix of meat and vegetables. Eaten anywhere else, it would probably have been delicious.

'None o'yer machine slime this. Fresh an' 'ome made. Nuvver perk o' the job.'

Mastersson forced open his eyes, but there was only the darkness and the oscillating colours, beating in time with the throbbing tattoo in his head and chest. A claw jabbed his midriff.

'Yer threw up on me, yer git!'

'I did?'

'Yeah, yer did.'

'Sorry—'

'Sorry dun't mean nuffin' 'ere. When yer can gerrup, clean dis.'

Something dry and crusty landed in his lap; the reek was familiar, with added eau de stale vomit. Mastersson pushed it away. 'How long have I been out?'

'Nuh, no' ou', jus' ramblin' crazy stuff. Four, mebbe five hours. Dunno. A calloused palm pressed against Mastersson's left cheek, turning his head. 'The wa'er is o'er there.'

'I… I can't see it.' The dancing lights and pain still pressed behind his eyes, blurring his vision.

'Yuh dint see th' stew, neither?'

'There's more food? Yes, please.' In spite of everything, Mastersson found he was ravenously hungry.

'Go' the munchies, ain't cha? 'Ere yer go.' A bowl was pressed to his lips and Mastersson downed the contents as fast as he could breathe. 'Eats like a funkin' fledglin'. Leastways yer ain't wastin' i'.'

The headache was easing, the pulsing colours fading to afterimages. Shadows resolved into shelves, heaped with an eclectic collection of boxes, bottles, cages, canisters, electronic circuits, and mechanical devices of all kinds. *Just like home.* The sole light was from an ancient storm lantern secreted in a corner. The pale yellow haze extended only a few metres in the close, dusty atmosphere. He lay on a pallet made from the same rags his host was wearing. *Same smell too.*

'You live here?' Mastersson tried to keep the disgust from his voice. 'Oh, thanks for the stew.'

''Sorigh'. On *Ol'n'Shabby* I's go' ever'fin' I needs. Yer gets an apar'ment an' you 'as ta go on-grid, dun't cha? I use'ta 'ave me own rock afore some git wen' ta mine i'. Done 'im wi' some hi-ex righ' down 'is scoop. Git still ruptured all me seals an' me rock use' ta creak an' groan as bits fell off. So's I go' ou' an' came 'ere, sold me 'opper an' walked aroun' untiw I foun' dis place. Tha' 'ole bloke before me says 'e wuz ready ta quit, so's I takes over. I ge's the job done an' nowun asks questions. 'Ere, yer ain't wun o' 'em inspeccers are yer?'

'"Inspeccers"'? No, I'm just a mudfoot trying to help out a friend.'

'Yeah, Moira. Yer said 'er lots when yer was thrashin' abou'. Nice is she?' Performing an alarming sashay with the bits Mastersson guessed were its hips, the lump of cloth mimed the contours of a number eight with both hands.

He shifted awkwardly. 'It's not like that. Besides, she'd tear your throat out if she saw you doing that.'

'No' an 'ome body then, is she? Dunno wo' she's gunna see in summit as scrawny as yer. S'pose yer could allez cook 'er dinner.' The rag mound cackled again.

'Look, forget her, okay? What's your name?'

'S'easier said than dun I reckon, bu' worreva yer wan'. Th' name's... name's.... Yuh 'now wo', I dun't rememmer me own name. S'pose yer can call me Ragman.' The grubby aquiline hand re-emerged from its cloth cocoon and formed a cup that caught the spittle that emerged from the hood. 'Can't shake wirrou' a name, can yer?'

Masterssons's foreboding became a suppressed shudder.

'Wotcha wai'in' for? I dunno yer, and yer dunno me, bu' I likes yer. The deal's dis: yer clean me clothes as yer chucked on 'em an' I gives yer wo' yer wanna know, a'righ'? I's even gonna chuck da stew in f'free.' Something wet rattled inside Ragman's throat as he laughed. 'We go' a deal, or no'?' He thrust his hand out further. The spittle glistened yellow in the lamplight.

Old beggar hasn't done any laundry in years. Still, I did vomit on him, and he returned the favour with food and a bed. Mastersson suppressed another shudder as the spittle began its inexorable slide towards the floor. *There's probably some honour code somewhere that says if any spit hits the ground then the deal's off.* Bracing himself, Mastersson spat into his own palm and took the old man's hand. *Next he'll probably crush my fingers.*

Ragman's grip was warm and damp, the handshake surprisingly limpid. 'Ain' gonna give a girl like yer wun o'me rock crushers, am I? Wa'er's o'er there.' The deal sealed, Ragman wandered over to an assorted pile of junk and began sifting through it, chunnering to himself all the while.

As Mastersson stood, his knees gave way. He grabbed at a shelf that came away in his hand, sending flexi-hose, wire spools, and pipes clanking across the floor.

'Oi! Wo'chit! Dat's me stuff.'

I'm fine, thanks. Never been better. Kneeling, he put everything back. *I'm going to have to crawl to the sink. I hope you appreciate this, Moira.* He levered himself up and leant on the sink side, dragging the old man's garments with him. It took both hands to force on the tap.

'An' make sure yer git some soap onnit.'

He dropped a dirty grey bar into the bowl and chased it around before getting a grip. *You get to hang out in fancy apartments. You're probably sipping cocktails with your brother right now while I'm stuck here, up to my elbows in this.*

Getting the puke out took an eternity. Mastersson nearly redecorated the room at least twice, but by turning away and breathing quickly he managed to suppress the clenching and kept the food down. With the sodden material finally draped over a shelf-end, he weaved his way back to the pallet and collapsed. *I can't believe I've wasted nearly a day. I need to get out of this smell and get my implant online.*

When the room had stopped spinning enough for Mastersson to dare to open his eyes again, he saw Ragman inspecting his handiwork.

''ll do, s'pose. Na' I'll git yer stuff.' Ragman disappeared from the corona of light. A dim white beam began dancing over the shelves.

Mastersson shuddered. *Am I going to end up like that—repulsive, senile, friendless and forsaken on my own rubbish tip?*

The seconds ran into minutes—his thoughts were his only company—in between, deafening silence. He reached for his implant and the elusive sensation of connection that would enable his mind to find the grid. *Nothing! Breathe, it's going to be okay.* It was not that he could barely stand—that would pass. His body was no more than the prime mover for his mind—coupled to the invisible cloud of information that surrounded and infused every connected human, his intellect was his strongest muscle and most effective weapon. With the stim still blocking him, he was as pathetic as a node-loader.

'Hey, Ragman. You there?' Only now did he notice how hollow his voice sounded, how quickly it trailed off in the darkness beyond the lamplight. *How big is this place?*

There was no sign of the flickering white beam. *I don't even know which way the exit is.* Ears strained for the slightest sound—anything human, anything alive. *No one knows I'm in here. Ancient crypts must have been like this. I'm going to be the first human entombed in two thousand years.* He tried standing again, but the emptiness spun around him leaving him gagging once more. Holding down the stew was all he could manage. At last, exhaustion took him.

✻

''Ere, wake up.'

Mastersson's lids flickered open, revealing the warm yellow of a sand dune by his feet. Slowly, it occurred to him that dunes did not usually smell of rotting eggs, nor did they speak.

'I foun' i'. Keeps m'word, I does.'

A surge of relief filled him. Even Ragman was company. Awkwardly, he scratched his nose.

'Yer no' lissenin' ta me, are yer?'

'You look and... erm... you look a little different.'

'S'righ', I's go' a guest—sulphur rub cleans th' skin an' keeps th' ticks off. Oh, I go' th' thing yer wanned.'

'What thing? A gold-laminated animal-friend to go with the new look? Does it bite?'

'I spen' 'ours lookin' fer tha' an' all I ge's is sarky. Well, if yer dun't wan' i', I'll put i' back.' Ragman sounded genuinely hurt.

It was the prospect of being left alone again, more than curiosity, which broke through Mastersson's haze. 'I'm still not over the stim shot. What... what did you want to show me?'

Ragman stopped walking away, but his back remained turned. 'I lives alone all dem years, an' I's th'only one tha' rememmers me Ps and Qs.'

I have a catastrophic hangover, no uplink, and I smell like he does. I need a cleanser. Instead I'm smoothing the cracks in my newfound friendship with a walking seat cover. 'Sorry. I know I've caused you a lot of trouble. Eaten your stew, thrown up on your… shirt—'

'An' 'ogged me bed.'

'—and hogged your bed. I really would like to see what you've found. Please?'

'Aw'righ'.'

Mastersson had no idea how it was possible for a bundle of cloth to relax, but this one appeared to.

'I knows i's in 'ere somewheres.' The bundle jerked convulsively, as if giving birth. 'Gorrit.'

Ragman turned and dropped a warped metal plate into Mastersson's lap. Turning the plate over, he tried to maintain a neutral expression and not think about where it had been hiding. Scorched across one surface was a trench, the metal alloy deformed where extreme heat had melted it.

'Whaddya fink?'

'It's a piece of ship's hull. This mark… is an energy weapon. Are you saying this is part of Kishino's ship?' He could not keep the scepticism from his voice.

Confident, Ragman folded his arms. 'Came in as par' of an impounded cargo, pirate's most like. Foun' 'ere—da system where Kishino's ship wen' missin'.'

'How do you know? I thought you kept yourself off grid?'

Ragman chuckled. 'I go' me inven'ry sys'em down 'ere an' I asks aroun'. Kishino 'ad a rep; 'e wuz *Elite*. An' 'e 'ad 'is fam'ly wiv 'im. 'E would've fought 'em, bu' 'e jus' disappeared; they never foun' nuffin—'cept dis.'

'Let me get this straight, the station's inventory logged a random bit of hull plate—'

'Nah. Compu'er logged dis as a par' o' a mixed alloy shipmen'. Das why no one knows abou' i'.'

'—that was picked up by a pirate a few days after his disappearance. Because it's got a burn mark on it and it's from where Kishino supposedly disappeared, you're assuming we've found part of Kishino's ship and he was taken down by pirates?'

'Yep.' The radiating smugness was now almost as strong as the smell.

All this, for a useless lump of metal. Still, Moira says never throw any 'evidence' away, and it'll hurt his feelings if I don't take it. 'Thanks, Ragman. This could be just what we're looking for. I'll make sure I tell Moira.'

'Glad ta 'elp. Now, yer fi' 'nough ta gerrout me digs? I wants me bed back.'

Mastersson stood; his legs trembled slightly, but they held.

'If yer needs t'rest, an' mebbe summit nice ta ea' an' drink, den y'can allays try "El Sircoolo d' la Veeder". Jus' ask tha' nice compu'er where i' is when yer gerrout.'

'Thanks for everything, Ragman. I'll leave you in peace, but first can you show me the way out?'

11

Mastersson turned three corners before admitting to himself he had no idea where he was, let alone how to get to 'El Sircoolo d' la Veeder'.

He stood, trying to appear nonchalant as he waited for the corridor to clear. After getting several odd looks from nearby pedestrians, he found himself alone. 'Computer—'

A little girl strode around the corner. She stopped when she saw him.

Mastersson waited, willing her to leave.

She waited, apparently to see if he was going to do anything interesting.

'Haven't you got somewhere to be?'

'No. What are you doing?'

Mastersson sighed. 'Go away.'

'No. What are you doing?'

He let his head drop to his chest before looking at the ceiling. 'Computer, display a nav-strip to El Sircoolo d' la Veeder.' A floating line appeared, blue this time.

'Hah! A *nav-strip*! My father says people who use nav-strips must be poor or stupid. Why haven't you got an implant? What's this place you're going to?'

'I have, but… it's none of your business. I'm going to an eatery that's *quiet*.'

The girl's mouth opened, about to frame some spiteful retort from the glint in her eye, when she paused, cocking her head as if listening. It often took children a few months to get out of the habit after they had their implant fitted.

'Mother says I have to come home. I sent her your picture and she says to get away from the nasty man and she says to tell you if you come near me she will call the police.' The girl, smiling gleefully, took a step towards him, then another.

Mastersson turned and, sliding one hand along the wall for balance, ran.

✶

Mastersson staggered through the outer precinct, stopping every few metres to lean against, or sit on, a convenient surface. The piece of hull plate, wrapped in mostly-clean rags, was buried in one of the deep pockets of his utility jacket, under the crook of his arm. He'd had to leave some valuable circuitry and a cooling pump with Ragman to make space. Hopefully, the bulge would not invite the unwelcome attention of some bored local cop with an overly developed sense of civic duty.

Right now, he was nursing a severe case of indigestion, muscle cramps, a splitting headache, and a simmering resentment of Moira. *Why am I doing this?* was a question he kept repeating, but he shied away from the answer, only to face another: *Exactly how far would I go for her?* That was two too many questions without an answer—*not helping my indigestion.*

He finally saw the sign: 'El Círculo de la Vida'. The smart curling letters flowed across a door daubed with a bohemian image of two open palms cradling a green and blue planet frosted with white clouds. From it, golden circles radiated out in a gaudy pattern. *Mother Earth Nostalgists—they're usually harmless.* He pushed on the handle; the wood laminate cracked under his fingers exposing the metal underneath.

The inside was tastefully lit with shimmering spheres tinted in warm yellows and burnt oranges. He bet the owners would have preferred a real fire and candles, but station safety ordinances applied to everyone. It seemed homely and inviting until his eyes adjusted. Artificial plants were everywhere. False vines climbed the wood laminated pillars and spiralled along bogus oak joists near the ceiling. Tacky plas-greenery crawled over every wall shelf and tabletop. There was no one around.

84

'Por favor, entrar, sentarse.'

Masterson spun, and the room went with him. He grabbed at the nearest pillar and more laminate came off in his hand before he steadied himself. In front of him stood what could have been Ragman's mother. *Girlfriend?* He thrust that thought aside. His eyes were assaulted by the acid green and yellow striped caftan; the psychedelic ensemble was topped off by a river of silver hair beaded and braided with all the colours of the rainbow. She even wore *glasses*.

I wanted somewhere quiet and this is dead; the décor must have frightened everyone off. 'I only speak Standard. A drink, just water and fruit?'

'Si. Gracias.' She blinked her magnified eyes beatifically at him, gesturing in the general direction of a table and chair in one corner.

She won't speak it, but at least she understands what I'm saying. He sat and began to massage his temples. The disconnect had left him tense and irritable. At least here he could nurse the stim-ache in peace. He heard footsteps and looked up, only to see the striped caftan retreating.

'Hey, the drink?' There was no response, but he did not have the strength to find somewhere else with decent service. Abandoning all pretence, he lowered his head onto his folded arms and let his mind drift. The clatter of a glass on the table top made him open one eye. Something liquid and neon glared at him from inside the glass, daring him to drink it. *Quiet, but I need quiet and sombre.* His mouth felt like it was coated with the waxy bits under Ragman's fingernails. *I hope this doesn't taste as lively as it looks.* He took a tentative sip and was surprised to find it was delicious. A few minutes passed and, with the drink finished, his head began to clear. He reached inside for the sense of his implant. *There*—like a flower opening, and coming home.

He agonised through several seconds while he came online and several more waiting to access the encrypted stream hidden under the surface flow of data on the grid. Hard to trace and harder to break, only someone better than he was could get inside. Masterson smiled. There was no one better than he was. He replayed the three deeply personal memories in his mind's eye and then recalled the four scents in the correct order. The implant recognised each neurological pattern and he was in. He paused to switch out scent number three and replace it with his memory of Ragman's—so unique it was priceless.

He skimmed his most recent history, navigating by feel as images and text flashed across his mind's eye too quickly to take in. Moira's message stood out—a glowing point of warmth amongst the cold data. Mastersson had mixed feelings about re-writing the implant's software. There was no doubt emotionally labelling all the data increased his effectiveness with the device, but the results held up an uncomfortably accurate reflection of his inner world. Content from Moira ranked highest on any scale. He tried, but could not resist. He accessed the emotionality index. Her messages were up seven points since he had left on this trip. *It's just because I'm working with her.* But he knew the ranking system did not work that way. *I need therapy; she's up to ninety-one and eighty-five is a clinical obsession.* The latest message opened with a thought and Moira's voice filled his head. He was sure he felt the index go up another point.

'Look, when you get this, contact me, okay? I need you to wipe any records of my visit to Celestial Living. If you can scrub the digital goons from the surveillance footage, great; the bodies are off-camera in Keagan's apartment. I'm going dark until I hear from you.'

The location of the building flashed as a bright point on a planetary map. There was a sub-entry labelled 'Transportation'. *Goons? Bodies? What's she got into?* Heart beating, he opened the live channel. She was not online. He desperately wanted to speak to her. Even in the quiet of the eatery muttering could be overheard, but the implant could generate an audio file from his internal monologue. Remembering the empty feeling of think-talking at nothing stopped him—there would be no reply. He left his message as text: 'Moira, I'll ghost you—no problem—but what's happening? Are you alright? Can I help? Please get in touch.' He set up an alert for any return message and buried himself in activity.

A while later and her journey on the taxi never happened. For good measure, he sent her virtual-self to a cultural museum on the other side of the city. The public transport encryption algorithm was one he had cracked a decade ago. Half an hour passed before he gained access to Celestial Living's systems. Routed via three proxies and shelled in the Presence of a maintenance droid repair firm, he was finally in. Accessing the footage from every cam that had tracked Moira through the building took another fifteen minutes. Modifying it took another hour and another five minutes saw a false maintenance check logged. Moira had never been to Celestial Living.

Someone knew she was there, and had local contacts they could call in. Someone hacked the building's security and overrode the weapon safety protocols—they'll try to remove the goons' bodies and edit the tapes the same way I did, probably in the next few hours. So, they'll see my edits and know Moira has help, which means they'll be watching for anyone with a nose in Moira's business, which also means they'll be watching for enquiries about Kishino. The question is: how good are they? But I'm just a name on a ship's manifest, and the only person I've spoken to about Kishino is Ragman. He's off grid and wants to stay that way. I'm safe, but Moira's not.

With a thought, Mastersson reopened the encrypted channel to Moira. 'If you need somewhere to crash, you know where I live. Access the data cache I told you about and it will upload a new identity to your omni-block. Don't draw attention to yourself—it's solid enough to survive a cursory customs check, but if anyone digs they'll know it's forged. The cache has a subroutine that will let me know it's been activated.

'Until then, keep communication minimal—this data is piggy-backing on a carrier signal and too much unusual activity will enable a trace—but let me know if you can't make it or need help. Hopefully, I'll see you at my place.' Mastersson terminated the recording, restraining the urge to add an emotional goodbye. Moira was not the hearts and flowers type.

12

Pharos, System BD+24 543

'Tell me why, Ferris.'

'…Why, sir?' Panicking, Theodore rubbed the back of his forearm, the one they had broken. With treatment the bones had set, but it still felt tender.

'Yes, why.'

'W—Why I tried to have Moira Dolan killed?'

'The workings of that flaccid sack between your ears are of no interest to me. Let me make things simpler for you. Which part of my instructions did you not understand?'

'Y—Your instructions?'

'You are a living example of devolution. What did I tell you to do in our previous conversation?'

Theodore's voice trailed off to barely a whisper. '…To leave Moira Dolan alone.'

'No. I told you to interact with her exactly as you normally would, nothing more. You went silent; you stopped haranguing her and failed to push her in the direction I required.'

'But—'

'Oh, do let me have the pleasure of summarising. You are self-centred and ambitious to the point of stupidity and recklessness. Twice you have disobeyed perfectly clear instructions in an attempt to curry favour with me by displaying "initiative". Twice your interventions have exposed my interests to unnecessary risk. Am I in error?'

'No, sir, but she was getting close. She found his apartment. She has access to his personal data. You said she is a good field officer; if she is able to analyse the forensics from his apartment she may—'

'And your other mistake is to assume I am stupid. Do you not think I know all this? Do you not think I am more than capable of coming up with an *effective* solution to Moira Dolan?'

'Sir, I—' Theodore's throat locked.

'She has gone to ground, Ferris, because of you. Because of you, I have to take valuable time and resources from other projects to deal with Ms Dolan. Because of you, I have to spend resources organising the disposal of your body. You were warned that I do not tolerate stupidity. You were warned not to disappoint me again. Good day, Mr Ferris. Enjoy it while you can.'

The link broke, leaving Theodore sweating in the silence that followed. He stared at his fingers, knitted protectively around his sticky palms. He could not stop the shaking. His body had a mind of its own, but he could not think what to do. He sat there, at his desk, for a full five minutes. *I'll call him back.* Theodore reached for his slate. It took him three tries to enter the decryption password correctly. He stared blankly at the blank box. Everything was gone: contact links, case notes, even his bank details. *No!*

'Computer, display personal financial account of Theodore Ferris. Retina and palm verification.' He lifted his head and hands for the security scan.

'Unable to complete. Please remain stationary—the scan is three-dimensional and authenticity protocol requires high definition.'

Theodore braced his forearms on the desktop, palms face up.

'Scan complete. Identity verified. Current credit balance: minus two hundred and forty-three thousand, four hundred and six.'

'Details… details of latest debit.' He croaked out the words.

'Latest debit occurred six minutes ago. Two hundred and fifty thousand to Osmir Holdings. Entry: Penalty for failure to fulfil contractual obligation. Status: Terminated.'

Theodore swallowed. *Everything. He took everything.* He knew Osmir Holdings would be a ghost—a virtual entity created in seconds in some vast corporate simulator and disbanded as quickly. The money in the encrypted account he had expected to disappear—he only received that when a job was done. But clearing out his personal account? He would never see that money again, and now he was effectively planet bound. He had no ship of his own; why pilot some rusting death-trap when you could be chauffeured in a luxury passenger craft?

He also had no friends—they were a luxury you could not afford on your way to the top. *I've got to get out of here.* His eyes flicked around the office, looking for anything he should take. The spartan furnishings now resembled mausoleum fixtures—more fruit of his singular dedication. Nothing that would actually help. Feeling misused, he grabbed his slate and shoved it in a pocket. *Maybe I can sell it.*

'Computer, I need a line of company credit: twenty thousand in physical currency, in this office. Now. Authorisation code: Z53P-16 alpha, Theodore Ferris.'

'Voice print and identification does not match entries in the central database. Please restate.'

What the…?

'Theodore Aloysius Ferris. Birthdate 172, 3236. Sub-Vice President of Investigations. Authorisation code: Z53P-16 alpha. Authenticate voiceprint with facial, thermal and body statistics.'

'Voiceprint and other statistics do not match any known employee of The Proteus Collective.'

This… is not possible. No one can gain access to PCS records from the outside.

'Your presence here is unauthorised. Security is on its way. Exits have been sealed. Please remain calm—your case will be dealt with fairly in accordance with Collective statutes. Please note: cancellation of employee status automatically negates your citizen's rights. You will need to secure your own legal representation. Have a nice day.'

There has to be a way out. A way out… his eyes found the words etched on the window: 'Fire exit'. For decades buildings had been relatively cheap and easy to replace. The mass lawsuit filed against a subsidiary of The Proteus Collective, when several thousand people died in the 3224 inferno, cost it billions. Now building design and fire protocol were based on one guiding principal: open up and get people out, *fast*.

Theodore kept his hand-rolled cigar collection, antique lighter, and a crate of Lavian Brandy in a recessed cabinet behind his desk. They enabled him to close deals and make money so his superiors turned a blind eye. He stroked the exquisite packaging; both boxes were handcrafted from real wood. *Goodbye, old friends, you're about to take part in the most expensive demotion in history.* If the security cameras' behavioural algorithms suspected arson, the room would fill with restraining foam. He soaked both boxes with the liquor under his desk before setting it alight. The fire suppression system would not kick in until he left the room. Every door in this section of the building would unlock. He lit a cigar in the flames and puffed, savouring a last taste of civilised living whilst the fire took hold.

Most of his stash he piled next to the growing blaze. He grabbed the last handful of cigars and stuffed them into another pocket. Gripping two bottles of brandy, he carefully pinned the burning cigar underneath them before heading out the door. Moving quickly along the corridor, the cigar set off every smoke detector in his wake. The piercing screams of alarm claxons echoed from every direction; warning lights pulsed towards the nearest exit. To a camera, he was just another executive rescuing his office contraband. Blending with the growing crowd, it would take security a while to work out what was going on, and by then he would be clear.

Theodore diverted to Johnson's office and spent a few seconds pouring alcohol on the man's bonsai collection. He inhaled deeply, cigar tobacco burning bright orange and crackling playfully. He withdrew it from his mouth and gave it a delicate flick. *My only regret is I won't be around to see the look on your face, sycophant.* The dull 'whump' noise and cavorting flames were deeply satisfying.

One more target before I join the idiots and stragglers. The cafeteria was where they ate. *A rubbish chute, how appropriate.* The lit cigar followed the flammable liquid down. More fire meant more confusion, and milling crowds meant anonymity, unlocked doors, and busy security personnel. As he joined the throng, he lifted his head and straightened. *If my data's been deleted, there's no record of my face in the security system… not so clever after all, are you, sir.*

He joined a group heading for a window evac tube. Ahead, two security guards supervised the queue ensuring no litigable injuries. Theodore took a deep breath. He wished he did not smell so much of alcohol and cigars. *Too late to turn away now, they'll only get suspicious.* The queue shortened quickly until only five people remained in front. *If they arrest me,* he *will send someone.* One after another, the men and women were helped through the window until only Theodore was left.

'Hang on, sir. Don't be in such a hurry or you'll crash into the person in front.'

'Sorry, officer.'

'Are you all right, sir? Shall I contact a medic on the ground and arrange a sedative?'

'No, I'm fine. Just nervous… just nervous of heights.'

'Been drinking, sir?'

'Just a little. Erm, had to get some courage for *that.*' He pointed at the empty hole, desperate to be gone.

'Right you are, sir. Are you sure you'll be all right?'

'Yes, completely sure, I just want to get this over with.'

'Very well. I reckon that's been long enough.'

'Thank you, officer. Enjoy your new job.' Theodore hitched his legs over the side.

'New job, sir? I like this one.'

'I doubt you'll get to keep it.' He pushed off and slid down the tube to freedom.

13

Deep Space, En Route to System LHS 1573

The attack in Keagan's apartment worried Moira—the goons had arrived so quickly and known too much. The only people keeping close tabs on her worked for The Collective. Someone on the inside had it in for her, so there was no option but to keep Jane dark: no comms and all human contact avoided, be it pirate or trader, on station or planet. Despite the ship's stealth abilities, they took detours around entire systems, skimming hyperspace fuel from the stars no one visited.

Progress was agonisingly slow. By day two, Moira gave up attempting to provoke Jane, tiring of her overly-calm replies. By day three, Moira had destroyed the *Kick-It* practice dummy, even though the zero-g sapped power from her blows. Her only respite from the increasing agitation came in deep space where she could spend short periods in the Stardreamer. You were not supposed to dream, but, on waking, scenes from her past and fears for the future melded and warped her emotions into a nameless panic. The ritual wiping of the sweat-soaked covers after each sleep was a dose of the mundane that grounded her when her mind was about to take flight.

It took over two weeks to reach system LHS 1573. The star's orange light made the small brown planet below glow golden at the edges. On a fringe world like Dustbowl, she could disappear. After several 'unofficial' days planetside, scouring the crevices of Jakon's dark quarter, she finally found Esk. The scarred ship dealer was willing to berth Jane—the deal sealed with a frozen thumb pressed to his cracked slate. The device bleeped and a skull appeared on-screen. Mastersson had set up the pseudonym several years ago and he liked to embellish—Moira had acquired the thumb for him. Out here, the tech and the locals were lo-brow.

Blunt worked, and if the melodrama kept Jane from being sold for parts and Esk's mouth shut, it was worth it.

Assuming the identity Mastersson had crafted was not as easy as he made it sound. It took visits to several tacky boutiques to find brands of DNA-active hair and skin dye that she trusted not to leave her bald and blistering. PCS paid for everything, in cold, hard, untraceable cash. Every operative took a few thousand credits 'field money' on a job. Pulling out corporate credit tokens on many planets would be the last thing you ever did.

It had taken six days, but now Moira was ready to become 'Devra Foxx', naïve galactic tourist seeking her inner self amongst the stars. Jane gave her the ability to move through space undetected, now she could move among people without trace.

Time to visit Mastersson.

*

Dustbowl, System LHS 1573

As she stepped into the back of the buggy, the slight breeze coated her skin with fine particles of sand carried from a horizon outlined by a dark haze.

'Sandstorm'll hit in about twenty minutes. You want to go on?' Her driver was local, by his thick accent.

On her omni-block, the weather-sat report estimated twice that. She killed the datastream. 'How fast can this thing go?'

'Fast enough.'

The 'road' hardly differed from the pitted, boulder-strewn land around it. Moira had thought that the outsized wheels and exaggerated suspension were for show, but as they left behind the last of the tyre tracks the buggy gave a series of sickening lurches as it careered over the landscape.

Her driver was taciturn, not even offering his name. Moira, never one for idle conversation, was thankful to be left alone, although that left her dwelling on Mastersson. She already missed the safety of remote communication.

✻

'You know what you're doing?'

Moira strained to hear the driver's shout over the wind. His raised eyebrows and tilted head conveyed more scepticism than concern. 'I'll be fine.'

He shrugged and the passenger door slid shut. The cloud of dust billowing up from behind the huge wheels of the off-roader was quickly whipped away as it disappeared into the distance. The wind was gusting now, invisible fingers tugging at the curls escaping from her hood-wrap. Sweat ran down her neck and back despite her suit's heat compensators. Mastersson's location slid across her omni-block screen as she zoomed in. *Still over three klicks to go. Fuck you and your paranoia!* His instructions were very specific. After clearing planetary immigration as Devra Foxx—a simple procedure on this chaotic frontier world—she had purchased survival gear and hired the buggy to here, the middle of nowhere. She started walking and drew a water bottle from the netting on her hip. She needed shelter and dehydration would slow her down.

Moira had arrived in the region only a few hours in advance of the storm, a big one: seasonal winds of one hundred and twenty klicks an hour barrelling across the flat landscape. Unimpeded by mountain range or breakers, they accelerated across Dustbowl's second continent, sucking up dust and stones—a billion tiny bullets. A few minutes in the open would strip the meat from her bones. The storm front was visible as a dark wall across the northwest. In the time she took to drink, it had already grown, and she was getting nowhere fast.

She headed north, running, but a few metres on her pace slowed to a steady lope. It took all her concentration to spot the even ground between the littering of rocks and potholes. *This is going to be close.* The driver had told her to wait, but storms here could last days or weeks. Hendryn's Folly was a small community

95

and its residents not shy about asking strangers awkward questions. Besides, she did not have the money; prices on this arid frontier rock were sickening.

As the air filled with choking dust, Moira activated her facemask, its dermal adhesion sealing in her ears, eyes, nose, and mouth. The unit's filters were new and the air she breathed tasted of plastics. Even with her eyes covered, her omni-block's holo-image was becoming difficult to read. *I guess implants have some advantages.* She pushed harder, bracing herself against the stiffening wind. Her breath came in ragged gasps, her body demanding more oxygen than the filters could provide. There were some fully armoured survival suits back at the colony. With self-contained air tanks and resistant to the cutting sand, they would have given her twenty-four hours before breaching. She had not bought one; the price was exorbitant. *Shiny-foil armour for gullible tourists. In a storm like this a day's protection isn't worth shite when no one can find you, and who'd be stupid enough to come looking?* According to the weather-sat, the storm centre had built a huge static charge. Communication and navigation were impossible.

The integrity of her omni-block's hologram finally failed, its photons dissipated by a thousand whirling grains of sand. *If the lead wind's that strong... Mastersson, if I die out here I'm going to haunt you forever, I swear.*

'Computer, switch to audible navigation cues.' The omni-block did not respond. *Shite. Sand-noise on the mask is overloading the mic.* Barely moving now, she tip-toed around rocks while solid walls of air hammered her from every direction. Her gloved finger stroked the screen and she was relieved to see it spring into two-dimensional life. She had to bring it within a couple of centimetres of her facemask to read it. She lost more time scrolling through the settings before she found the manual volume control. Setting it to maximum, if she concentrated she could just make out the computer's instructions coming through her inserted ear buds. *If you want tech to work, go lo.*

'Turn left, fifty degrees. Range to target: one point nine klicks.'

I'm really that far off? She began to stagger forward in a low crouch, trying to give the wind less to grab.

'Turn right, ten degrees. Range to target, one point five klicks.' She kept pushing, her lungs aching now as the filters clogged. Her throat dry, air becoming hotter, she forced her lungs—in, out, in, out. *Cooking from the inside.*

'Turn left, twenty-five degrees. Range to target, one klick.'

Blinded, groping forward metre by metre, the dust outside her mask formed an impenetrable barrier.

'Maintain course. Range to target, five hundred metres.'

Numb from the constant buffeting, she had not noticed the small areas of exposed skin until now. A sensation, like the nips of biting insects, began at the edge of her awareness. *The barrier cream, it's breaking down.* In minutes, the sand would scour its way past skin, through muscle, and into bone.

'Turn left, seventeen degrees. Range to target, two hundred and fifty metres.'

She was crawling now, using her arms to pull against the wind which threatened to tear her from the ground as it gusted. *This is no pre-frontal. The storm body's already here.*

'Turn right, thirty degrees. Range to target, one hundred metres.'

Shite, wrong again. The first stone caught her mask and bounced harmlessly away with a noise like a pistol shot. The second found a gap in her coverall. It stung. She touched the spot. Unable to see, she rubbed gloved thumb and forefinger together. The two surfaces slid easily, slimy with liquid, until the sand turned it to paste. She dug her feet into the ground and pumped with her arms, scrabbling desperately to cover the distance.

'Turn left, eleven degrees. Range to target, fifty metres.'

The stones came like horizontal hail, rattling off her mask. Another found an open patch of skin, and another. With each sting a new burning began as sand worked to enlarge the holes. Lines of blood ran across her facemask where the wind had taken the red drops and drawn a map of her future.

'Turn right, twenty-two degrees. Range to target, twenty metres.'

Muscles, pumping like pistons, started to lock. She needed more oxygen to slow the fatigue, but her hyperventilating lungs barely sucked in enough to stop her passing out.

'Turn left, s—'

She shook her wrist. She struck the omni-block with her gloved hand—the blows weak, ineffectual. *Don't die on me!*

'Atmospheric interference. Link with nav-sat lost. Unable to re-establish.'

She tried to speak: *Computer, boost signal. Compensate for interference.* Nothing escaped her throat but a wheezing rattle. Her glove spasmodically stabbed at the screen, but quivering muscles sent her hand sideways. Anger became paralysed rage. The static blocking the signal would only grow. In the grip of the storm, she was blind and stranded.

Help me.

Exposed skin screamed as it pared away; blood loss sapped her. She forced herself forward. Two metres on, her leaden muscles seized. Like a sick animal, she curled into a foetal position, but there was no shelter from the scouring sand.

No one came.

She pushed at the darkness tunnelling her vision… and knew time passed. She writhed, but she was weak, so weak. *Never weak. 'If you're weak you're dead. Fight the bastards. Fight until they bleed. Fight until they die.'* Pictures swam in front of her: shattered bodies from the past, dying again in the present: stumps, disembodied limbs, a line of intestine strung out across the ground, a skull without a top—brain-jelly seeping through the eye sockets.

She lashed out at something.

The strike was feeble, but she felt gratifying pain as her gloved knuckles connected with a surface that gave. The full force of the wind came back, sand eating at her flesh. *If you die, die free!* The smile made her cracked lips bleed.

Blows rained on her shoulder, becoming harder, more insistent. In her terror, it took her an age to recognise they had a rhythm; it took her longer to recognise it was one she knew.

'T...R... U... S...T... ... M... E'

Who?

'R... E... L... A... X'

She surged to sitting and her head collided with a hard surface. A helmet? Lights danced across her vision. She flopped back onto the ground. Flailing and fighting the dizziness, she fought to push herself upright. A wave of nausea and cramp stopped her.

Again the tapping: 'P... U... L... L... ... U... ... I... N'

Something caught her arm, stretching her shoulder joint. Her back scraped as she was dragged, stones grinding into her clothing and the holes in her skin. Stillness, then a jerk. She was free and moving again. Her head ricocheted from rock to rock. She blacked out, but pain yanked her back. *Not like this. Not taking me.* Her free limbs waved. She tried to dig her fingers and toes into the dirt, but the tugs continued, moving her metre by metre. An animal cry, keening above the noise of flying debris and the wind—her own voice. Muscles locked. Someone still had her.

Another jerk and she was sliding, repeated blows from metal bars raining on her head and back. *Beaten to death.* Every fibre wanted to fight, rend, kill. But she could not. Her body folded onto something hard and flat, chewed meat on a slab. While the world spun, every part of her body screamed, a cacophony of voices each clamouring to be heard.

Something stabbed her in the neck and she started to float. The thrumming of the sand stopped, replaced by quiet susurration, then silence. She screamed again as white light flooded her vision, hot skewers of pain piercing her skull before they too softened in the fluffy detachment. More tapping. She batted it away, her arms moving like stumps.

Then she was alone. The burning white light and the nothingness holding her still.

14

'Moira. Moira, can you hear me? The chems should be working by now!'

It took several seconds for Moira to recognise Mastersson's voice. She tried to sit up, centimetre by aching centimetre, but he pressed her back down with his free hand—the other held a syringe. Even that small effort left her exhausted, sweat-shivering and breathing hard.

'Can you deactivate your facemask? The filters are clogged.'

When she did not respond, he touched the switch behind her ear and the mask retracted into the housing around her neck. She gasped in air, even though her lungs were tender from the heat outside; the coolness brought her back. *Inside, safe!*

'I thought I'd lost you.'

Despite the brain-fog, she heard the tight edge in his voice. Her head was resting in his lap as he knelt. Medicated, she found she did not mind. He released his helmet and flung it aside. Holo-vid changed some people, but through her blurred vision he looked the way she remembered: handsome, in a homely, shaggy, pale-brown sort of way. He shifted, attempting to wriggle out from underneath her. The room spun as her head rolled from side-to-side—her chemically relaxed muscles not quick enough to respond. His gloved hands slipped on her hair and her head slid between them to land, with a bump, on the floor. The little coloured lights swimming in front of her eyes were pretty. She was vaguely surprised it did not hurt.

'Ow?'

He briefly cradled her head. 'Sorry, really sorry. You need patching up quick—you're bleeding. Right. Stay there.'

'I'm fine. Feel great. Not broken my neck, you know.' A little giggle bubbled past her lips. 'You're very gentle. You saved me, my hero.'

His eyes widened. The floundering cough that followed sounded forced. 'You're wasted from shock, blood loss, and the chems. You'll probably want to break my jaw when you return to ground zero.'

Her lips creased in a moue of consternation. 'No... I don't think so... Colder... Hold me, be warm.' She extended her arms in invitation.

Mastersson recoiled and hit a trolley behind him, sending a tangle of wires, plastic, and metal clattering to the floor.

'No time for that. You're bleeding on my floor.' He seized the trolley and hauled himself to his feet, his movements rushed and awkward. Crossing the room, he zigzagged around several piles of parts, before excavating the largest in the corner. '...in here somewhere.'

The fragile bubble of giddy happiness burst—Moira wanted to cry. She was abandoned and bleeding on the floor. The darkness was back, a pressure on the edges of her awareness. Suddenly frozen, her small body shook. 'M—Mastersson. Please, don't go.'

'Hold on, nearly got it. It's just the shock, Moira. Be right there.' He must have understood.

'Please hurry.' She needed him at her side, needed to know there was *someone.*

He finally came back carrying a silvered blanket and a tray with two cylinders on it. 'Erm, can you get yourself out of those clothes?'

Moira ignored his question and wrapped her arms around him as he knelt beside her. He held her, but stiffly, briefly, before pushing her away. 'You'll be okay. You're safe. Will you let me help?'

Resentment swirled at the rejection. Her mouth set in a stubborn line.

'Moira?' His hands began to tug at the fastenings of her top. She reacted without thought.

'Aarrgghh… ow… ow… ow… please let go of my thumb.' He held up something, blurred and red. 'Blood, yours. You've got to let me help.'

She blinked, forcing her eyes to focus. His hand dripped with it. Remembering her training, she let go. 'We used cutters.'

'I'm on it.'

She started the count, something to help her stay conscious. He was back before she reached fifteen. She wafted a sleeve at him and felt him take a hesitant hold on her wrist. '…before I pass out.'

She came to, to find him tapping her cheek. She had no idea how long it had been and felt a little uneasy.

'I'm done.' He was unsure and clumsy as he laid the blanket across her. 'It's heated. You should feel better in a bit.'

'Med canisters, used them before?' Her teeth chattered as she spoke.

'I do better with metals and an arc-welder.'

'Prop me up.'

He did, and passed her one of the canisters. She reached down to her injured side, but her hand was trembling too much, until he steadied her wrist. *Never like this with my brother.* Using both canisters, between them they managed to get enough healing gel-foam into the wounds. She closed her eyes and flopped back, spent.

'At least I can't see any more bleeding.' His voice anchored her floating consciousness. 'Is there anything else I need to do?' He tucked the blanket around her, his movements hurried. 'Let me check… contains active bio-engineered particulates capable of analysing and removing foreign bodies from tissue…'

He's reading the instructions on the back—no surprise.

'… nutri-gel with bio-active matrix which accelerates… yet works in harmony with the body's natural processes…'

The familiarity of the sounds, the rhythm of the words, drew her towards warm oblivion. This time, she let it happen.

*

Her eyes flicked open, revealing a world of ominous shadows and contorted shapes.

'Computer, lights.' A single roof panel flickered into anaemic life, its buzz an accompaniment to the almost-subliminal industrial hum emanating from every monochrome-grey surface. Moira shut her eyes against the preternatural brightness, then squinted until they adapted. *I've been touched.* The welling memory was confusing: sensations and partial awareness. She threw the silvered thermo-blanket aside. *I'm in my underwear*, but still the disconnected sense of unease persisted. *If...* There was as much threat as fear in the thought. She sat up, pain coming from a dozen places. She braced herself until the spinning eased. Another, more considered, inspection followed: four major wounds, multiple lacerations—all sealed with the pale-blue healing gel. The rest of her felt like one continuous contusion, every centimetre mottled black-purple. The underwear was hers—*doesn't he have any spare?*—the blood stains on it were wash-faded and brown, ghosts of their former selves. She sniffed an armpit—clean. Relaxing a little, she took stock. *At least a day, maybe two?* Time she could ill-afford.

The room was a juxtaposition of solid, ordered bulkheads and the scatterings of a kleptomaniac with a technology fetish. Components, tubes, wires, ducting, circuit boards and assorted fossilised casings littered the floor. The dust got thicker in the far corners. A narrow path wound between the bed, an open exit, and a door. Wobbling, she negotiated her way to the exit looking for her shoulder bag. *Shite, don't tell me it was left outside?*

In the bathroom, Mastersson had left some nearly clean coveralls draped over a trolley. She pressed the tag and the seams opened. Flailing like a stranded fish, she worked the material over her feet before hauling it up and sealing herself inside. There was a glass of water on the trolley too, half drunk. The masculine parody of domesticity was reassuring. *He's just a harmless tekhead.* The murderous rage that gripped her on waking was fading to simmering resentment. She heard the grinding of gears behind her and spun, almost losing her balance.

'Oh, er, good, you're dressed.' Mastersson stood framed in the doorway, one hand unconsciously scratching the back of his head.

Her own awkwardness made her brusque. 'Thanks, Mastersson. You're a good friend.'

'Yeah, don't I know it.'

'What?'

'Never mind. I'll, erm, leave you to it.' He turned, looking for an escape.

'Don't move.' He stopped. 'Did anything happen?' Her eyes bored into his, pinning him.

'No. Why should it? You probably removed the eyeballs of the last guy who saw you naked.'

He was hiding something, but with his fluttering panic and brightly flushed face he seemed harmless. Compulsion, rather than mistrust, made her press him. 'Mastersson?'

'Just my thumb; it still aches where you sprained it.'

New anger derailed her train of thought. 'Your thumb? What about leaving me out there? Where the fuck were you?'

He breathed out, a long breath. 'I wondered when we'd get around to that. I was working on a dynamic self-actuated comms-link re-router, DSACLRR for short. You know it's high-tech when the acronym is just as difficult to say as the name.'

She folded her arms. 'And a comms-link re-router is more important than me being left in a sandstorm? And don't tell me it stops others tracing you when you're on the grid, I know. Just answer the question.'

'A few hours before you arrived, I couldn't follow the weather… the system went down.'

'Why?'

'I was trying a little experiment with an AI module I found.'

'You eejit, Mastersson. I've seen one run amok; you're lucky to be alive.'

'Don't I know it. Stupid thing decided it could become more effective by overclocking its own circuit board. It had control of the power management and safety lockout subsystems before I could contain it—fused half my power grid. You want as much information about Keagan as I can get and if it had worked...'

'So, you were "only trying to help". Instead, I nearly get sand-shredded and, until it's fixed, you can't access *any* useful information about my brother.'

'The good news is—repairs are pretty much done.'

Moira could see the dark circles under his eyes and the thin lines on his face. 'You worked through the night?'

'The last two, when I wasn't...' He trailed off into an awkward silence.

She buried the uncomfortable feelings. 'Okay, you saw me naked and you cleaned me up. Can we get past that and move onto something relevant?'

'You're not going to poke my eyes out?' There was the faintest hint of an emboldened smile.

He was trying to find Keagan, and he did come and get me. 'Damn it, Mastersson, I want to wring your neck.'

'It'd be quicker, but maybe some food and something to drink first? You're looking a little wobbly.' His relief at surviving brightened every word.

The communal living area was kitted out in the same utilitarian décor as the bedroom. Everything was metal, struts, bare wires and conduits. Only one area was clear of junk, on a sheet of metal straddling two cargo canisters.

'Food's on the table; drink's in the flask.'

She perched on the sole chair. The place was set with a selection of light snacks and even some fruit, although she doubted it was fresh. She reached for the only mug; it had been washed but had stains you would need a sandblaster to shift. Taking the flask, she sniffed the contents. *Water, good.* She knew what alcohol could do to someone.

'I'll leave you to it. If you need anything, I'll be over there, putting things right.' He moved away, following a tortuous route between the heaped debris.

Whether he intended to be considerate, leaving her alone, or he had run off with his tail between his legs to hide in his man-corner until she calmed down, she had no idea.

He stopped before rounding the first pile. 'We'll find him.'

She forced a smile. 'Yeah, we'll find him.'

'And it'll be fun, working together.'

Fun? She stared at him.

He paused as if waiting for something more. Met only by her silence, his smile, if anything, grew broader. He shrugged and disappeared behind the junk pile.

After six years, she had Mastersson pegged. They had messaged, chatted, audio and vid linked thousands of times. *Now I've got to live with that sense of humour.* It was the side of him she was least sure of. Wasn't he just a tekhead—her go-to for info and the "grid-fu" she needed to break a case? A comforting little box, but she had the horrible feeling Mastersson was not going to fit into it as easily as she wanted. She pushed the thoughts aside. *He's just a harmless gridder.* Now was time for food, water, and more sleep. Soon, they would be on Keagan's trail and everything would be straightforward. *Yes. Definitely.*

15

Moira crawled out of bed. Her body was still a mass of dull aches, but the healing balm would keep the pain under control for several days. Adopting the civilised custom of fresh clothing every day had been another way of leaving her past behind, but there was no chance of Hotel Masterssson offering that level of service. She slipped the same coverall over the same underwear. *I know this is a bachelor pad, but there must be a cleanser here somewhere.* She hesitated, unwilling to venture outside just yet and have the strangeness of yesterday reassert itself. Their interactions were different now—closer—and she did not like things she did not understand. *It won't hurt to look around.*

Utility suits and a few, very unfashionable, travel outfits hung in the storage units. His beloved piles of junk turned out to be just that. She found no personal artefacts or effects. *No surprises there, he's always lived a virtual life. Everything he values is on the grid or in his head.*

In one corner hung an ancient video panel.

'Computer, activate this display. Leave content unchanged from last use.' An external holo-image of the planet's surface appeared, slightly unfocused. The skies were clear and the sand lay still on the ground. *He didn't see the storm—too busy working.*

'Computer, show content most frequently accessed on this display.'

She stared. She recognised them all—people she had put away with Masterssson's help—except the eight clustered together in the bottom left hand corner. 'Computer, enlarge image and information on the man in the green outfit, bottom left corner.'

His clothes were strange, archaic. He wore spray-on leggings, a tunic tucked through a broad belt that made it look like a skirt, and a pointed hat with a long feather waving jauntily from one side. He was carrying a shaped wooden branch, held bent by a taut thread, and several smaller sticks with feathers stuck to them were protruding from a pouch slung over his back. It took her a moment to remember something Mastersson had told her once: *Robin…?*

'Computer, summarise data known about Robin Hood and the others in the lower left.' She listened for several minutes, increasingly amused. *Rob Roy MacGregor, James T. Kirk, Dirty Harry, Buck Rogers, Jesse James, Mustapha Khouri, Erik Tiborann: all mavericks and heroes. How did he put it?* 'From more noble times.'

'Okay, that's enough. Computer, restore images to original configuration and deactivate.' *I knew he got his kicks on the darkside of the grid, but this…* How could he be a threat? But she was in his domain and the prospect of facing him in person still left her uneasy.

Back in the communal area, she was pleasantly surprised to find a basic breakfast complete with a flask of industrial coffee sitting on the table. She eyed the slate beside it and decided conversation could wait until she had refuelled.

Coffee drunk, Moira tentatively picked up the slate. Her fingers hovered over the screen. *Damn it, I owe him.* She was alive. He had given her a way out, a bolt hole, information. Six years of memories—and too many unpaid favours. *If he ever got caught, I would've helped…* but he never had. His help kept coming, and her debt growing. She let the slate drop back onto the table top and glared at it. *For now, we'll both have to settle for me playing the good house guest.*

She reached for the screen and an insectoid head appeared, eyes shadowed by thick dark lenses. Something glowed from somewhere underneath its chin. 'You're welding. It's breakfast time and you're welding.'

Mastersson grinned. 'Fixing things is what I do. How are you feeling?'

So, he's not finding this awkward. Give him a gadget and he's the happiest man alive. But her discomfort persisted. *I'm eating his food, wearing his clothes, under his roof.* She was sharper than she meant to be. 'Fine.'

The screen winked out.

His voice switched to her right as a door slid silently open. 'Sorry about the clothes; I don't get many female visitors. We should get you something glamorous to go with your new look.' He pointed to a junk pile behind her.

Why is he still smiling? Her distorted image copied her movements on the silvered side of one of the casings—hair: blonde; skin: dark tan; eyes: brown. Moira hated it. 'This "Devra Foxx" cover and the storm have left me looking like a one credit whore after a heavy night of S&M.'

'Oh, I don't know. It sort of—'

'My appearance is not a topic for discussion. Are we clear?'

'Crystal.' But his impish expression said otherwise.

That little box, the one she hoped he would fit in, was looking way too small. *Unless... if in doubt, confront.* 'I know me being here, in your private little playpen, is difficult for you and these boyish high spirits are your way of coping. It's fine.'

'Humour makes effective social grease, it's true, but I'm happy because we're up-and-running. And I have something that might interest you.'

'Did you find the bag, with all my equipment in?'

He was instantly serious. 'I couldn't see more than a few centimetres in front of my face. I knew you were hurt, so I pulled you in. We could go outside and look…'

She shook her head.

'What did you lose? Not the information from Keagan's apartment?'

'That bag held most of my field kit—not easy to replace. The data is fine. I always backup.' She held up her wrist, displaying the omni-block. 'Shall we get to work?' She picked up the fully laden plate and carried it across the room, happier things were moving again. When she stepped up to the door, it did not open.

'No food or drink in the lab, house rule.' Mastersson's voice carried no inflection as he spoke.

'You're serious? Every room is full of old shite. You expect me to believe your lab has a clean-room protocol?'

'The rig I built from this "old shite" is what we're going to use to find your brother. It's taken years of work to finish. No food—' He caught her glance towards the empty coffee flask. '—no drink.'

'When you broke it, you fixed it in less than three days.'

'It's my rig, and I don't want to fix it again.'

*His place, his rules—*this *is why I like to work alone.* Seething, Moira returned the plate to the table and crammed in a few mouthfuls. Empty-handed this time, she approached the door which drifted aside. *No surprise—the workroom door is the only one he fixes.* It was another huge box, its walls of welded scrap metal containing the other half of the universe's garbage. She stepped aside and let him lead her between the piles to the far corner and the white beam of a spotlight. On one of the many worktables lay an arc-solderer, a component that was almost too small to see, and a circuit board with a nest of wires that reminded her why she tied her hair back.

Mastersson sat and pulled the goggles over his eyes. 'You may want to turn away and close your eyes for a second.'

She did, but flickering blue-white light still filled her vision as he worked. 'Finished?'

'Done. What have you got for me? Is all the data from Keagan's apartment?'

'Yes: a full surface and airborne particulate inventory; chemical and DNA samples; images of the goons that attacked me; layout and décor images—the works.' Her fingers skipped across her omni-block screen as she set up a data-stream to Mastersson's network.

'Don't you wish you had an implant?' He tapped the side of his head. 'Using one becomes as natural as breathing after a few days.'

'Until one malfunctions, you have an auto-immune reaction, or it gets hacked—then you're a vegetable.'

'You're such a Luddite; these days that hardly ever happens.'

'I have no idea what a "luddite" is, but I know the difference between "hardly ever" and never. My brain's staying my own.' She felt around the coverall before remembering it was not hers. 'Did you find a small box, about so big, in my clothes?'

He looked quickly away. 'It's here… somewhere.' He stood and delved around in the mess at the back of the worktable. 'It was in your breast pocket…' He had the decency to look abashed. 'I threw everything else in the recycler. They were either bloodstained or damaged.' He passed the small reinforced sample container to her. She turned it over in her hands. It was scratched, but the seal was unbroken. She touched its screen and carefully went through the gesture sequence; getting it wrong would destroy the contents. She inspected each vial. Everything was intact.

'I kept myself off-grid since the apartment so I haven't analysed the data. It could take several days.'

'…And would I mind looking through it, setting up the results for analysis and the tools you need?'

'Yeah, something like that.' Moira managed an uncomfortable smile.

'Go on, as it's you that's asking.'

His expression took on that faraway look she was used to seeing on-screen when his attention was on his implant. In person, it was even more disquieting.

The 'File Download Request' dialogue appeared on her omni-block and she approved it without thinking.

Mastersson nodded. 'I'll dredge through this later. In the meantime, I found *that* when I went looking for Kishino.' He gestured with the solderer. 'Take a look, and tell me what you think.'

She left him to it and wandered over to another workbench. 'Any chance of some light?'

'Sure, sorry. Station three is all yours.'

Moira squinted through the brightness of the spotlight beam. She picked up the metal sheet and examined it. 'It's ship's hull plating. There's… an unusual burn mark… a gash from a high intensity beam weapon.' An uneasy feeling swept over Moira, which she buried in scepticism. 'You think this is from Kishino's ship?'

'That's what I asked, but my source was certain.'

'You have sources now, do you? I'll have to make you my deputy.'

'Ha ha. There's a multi-phase microscope. Can you make out anything?'

'Haven't you looked?'

'I use the microscope for micro-circuitry, not forensic analysis of weapon impacts. Working out how people kill other people is your department.'

She placed the metal in the microscope's sample tray. Manoeuvring the ultra-high definition camera head was quicker manually and Moira had a detailed three-dimensional image of the metal's underlying crystal structure before her in seconds. 'Computer, full topographic scan of the sample; focus on the weapon impact site.'

'Complete.'

'Computer, establish secure link to Proteus Collective Security's Forensic Analysis Database. Cross-reference with damage samples, establish origin weapon type. Extrapolate relative position and range of the firing ship. List all ship types with capability to carry origin weapon type. Scan sample's crystalline structure and cross-reference with Moira Dolan personal case notes, Kishino file. Does sample origin ship type match Kishino's currently owned ship?'

'Unable to comply. Links to external computer networks currently unavailable.'

Moira looked over towards Mastersson.

'Okay, it's just booting up.'

'Did you think I could tell what it was just by looking at it?'

'I don't know. You use your gut instinct a lot.'

'Gut instinct works best with people, Mastersson. If you got out more, you'd know that.'

'If you're asking me on another date, the answer's no—not after you ditched me and I got stuck with a smelly old guy.'

What?!

'Okay, system's up and we're on the grid. Better still, no one knows but us.'

Still flustered, she continued staring at him. Behind the tint of the protective goggles, his expression was unreadable. 'Moira, are you okay? If you're still feeling wiped out you can always go and rest.'

'I'm fine. Computer, repeat previous instruction set. Mastersson, can you take those damn things off? They make you look like a Thargoid and it's creeping me out.'

'Link to Proteus Collective Security Forensic Analysis Database established. Cross-referencing sample topography with weapon impact sub-database. Awaiting analysis. Cross-referencing sample metallic crystalline structure. The sample matches with alloys and treatments used in the manufacture of the Asp Explorer by Lakon Spaceways. Atomic stresses and trace radio-dating confirm date of manufacture to be within statistical tolerance. Is sample from ship of equivalent type and age to that owned by Isao Kishino? Ninety-five percent certainty. Is sample from Isao Kishino's ship? Unknown. The significant parameters are—'

'Computer, ignore significant parameters. Summarise results for weapon impact topography.'

'Still awaiting analysis.'

'Mastersson, are you sure you ironed out your connection glitches?' Even as she asked, an amber light flashed from within the mess of wires on his desk. 'What's that?'

'Wait. Working on it.'

'Talk to me, dammit.' He had disappeared into his implant, again.

'Your query set off a trace. They haven't isolated our footprint and the node is uncompromised. I'm going in.'

'Mastersson, Collective grid security are good. If they trace you… you can't switch that implant off whenever you want. There's rumours of induced burnouts and—'

'Moira, now is not the time to be my mother. I'm through the lockout. Now, let's see what it is they don't want us to see. Encrypted. If I can isolate the data… and we're downloading through the backdoor. Come to Papa.'

'Mastersson, this is not a game.' She was on her feet now, working out where best to hit him.

'They're looking for an external intrusion. I loaded a backdoor through your corporate profile when you started work; it's been sleeping, until now. By the time they've worked out the data's leaking from the inside and gone back years to find the insertion point, we'll be long gone.'

Hoping he was fully focused on his implant, she carefully halved the distance between them. Stunning him would be easier if he did not see it coming.

'Got it. Now if I can run an analysis on the root encryption…'

She was only a couple of strides away. She raised her hand, shaping her fingers for the strike.

'Moira, please don't. Trust me, I know what I'm about—this could help find your brother.'

How did…?

'Okay, I've got the encryption keys. Someone is locking down information they don't want found, probably the same someone who set you up at Keagan's apartment. We need this.'

She stopped, for the moment. The amber light flashed faster.

'Mastersson.'

'Yeah, I know. Damn. Let me try…'

The amber light blinked rapidly, in time with Moira's heart.

'They're getting close, aren't they? Cut the link, *now*.'

'Just a few seconds…'

The amber light's flashes ran one-into-the-next, the warning almost continuous. It went out.

'Mastersson, what the fuck does that mean?'

'It means the information was locked manually, by someone with a high security rating. The problem with using a personal profile to insert a backdoor is you can't look up.'

'Fuck that, the light's out! What does it mean? Have they traced us? Do they know you were using my profile?'

'You don't have to worry; if it turned red then we'd have a problem.'

'It was about to turn red, wasn't it?'

'Would you believe me if I said, "No"?'

She wanted to hit him, or maybe strangle him slowly with one of the many lengths of wire lying around. 'And will you take that fucking mask off! Jesus, Mastersson.'

He put the mask on the bench. 'I know I'm good, but I think "Jesus Mastersson" may be overdoing things, don't you?'

It was tempting, to blacken those twinkling eyes with her fist. 'Look, chasing Keagan is my risk to take. I should never have involved you.'

He leant back a little. 'Too late now. Besides, I think you may be interested in the results.'

'What results? I thought someone locked access.'

He grinned. 'They did, but not before we downloaded our own copy. I've got a nice little decryption algorithm or two just waiting to chew on this. Besides, denied access is the first sign this is worth looking at, right?'

'Tell me when you're done. I'm going to get a drink.'

'There's beer in the cooler. Thirsty work, grid-running; only the tough can take it.'

His jaunty tones followed her from the room. *Since when has he been this annoying?*

16

An hour and two synth-coffees later, Moira was sitting back in the workroom. 'Well?'

'I've run the decryption algorithms three times. The file is passing every integrity test.'

'And?'

Mastersson activated the holo-display with a flourish. Moira read the analysis twice:

'Impact topography of sample not consistent with any standard weapon discharge.'

She stared at the plate again. 'But it's the result of an energy weapon: the deformation, the disruption of the metal's crystal lattice, the topography. Computer, display other results: estimated range of weapon at time of discharge, estimated power output of weapon, ships capable of carrying such a weapon.'

Text appeared in the air: 'Estimated weapon power: ten thousand megawatts per square metre. Unable to estimate weapon configuration and discharge range, or compatible ship types.'

Mastersson swept his fingers through his hair. 'Isn't that high? That'd take a hit from point-blank range.'

'Yes, from a small-to-medium weapon, but there'd be deeper secondary lattice damage at the impact site.'

'So, a larger weapon fired from further away, mounted on at least a medium-sized ship.'

She shook her head. 'The beam profile is really coherent; heavy weapons tend to spread, at least a little.'

'The data I retrieved could be false—but then why would someone try to hide it? That leaves only two options: the weapon that made the burn mark was either experimental or Thargoid in origin.'

Moira suppressed a shudder. 'It's not Thargoid.'

Mastersson turned to her, eyebrows raised. 'You're not normally so quick to dismiss a possibility.'

She looked away, feigning renewed interest in the burn mark. 'Why would some high-powered corporate exec want to cover up an alien attack? No, those bastards have been ambushing humans for decades for fucked up reasons of their own. It's got to be something experimental.'

'If you're sure… The factions suppress the news feeds to avoid panic, but there's rumours in the darker corners of the grid that Thargoids operate deep in human—'

'You're not listening! There's people involved!'

'Okay, okay! So The Collective isn't above field-testing a new weapon on a major space-route, knowing it means fatalities and questions?'

'Bluntly, no. The research division's funding and resources are highly classified—people only hide the big money—they'll have the means. As for motive, since when did any corporation allow ethics to impact their profit margin?'

'I've never dealt with a corporation I could trust, but it's a massive risk, authorising the killing of an entire family travelling a busy route in Federal space.'

Her mind spinning with ideas, she got up to pace. 'What better way to prove the effectiveness of the system? And if headquarters doesn't know what's going on, maybe a rogue employee, even a rogue division? But why Kishino? Were his killers on contract? He's got enemies, but he's left enough dead, the living have left him alone for decades. So why now, after so long?'

'If a personal grudge seems unlikely, we're back to corporations where it's always about the credits.'

'People pay for superior killing power. Icing an Elite pilot would be an effective demonstration. But we're still guessing at the motive.' Moira balled her hands into fists, pressing the knuckles together in frustration.

'Then who? Do you know anyone highly placed enough to run that kind of research set-up?'

'Field CIOs like yours truly don't sit down to luxury dinners with corporate seat-warmers. It's way outside my job remit, asking that sort of question about that sort of people. I'd need to find someone I can *persuade* to be helpful, which could take months.'

'Well, what do we do now?'

'We need a more detailed analysis of the beam mark. Can you access any other databases? Faction military? Another corporation's research division?'

'No way—too many databases, with too many layers of anti-infiltration software and the latest encryption, not to mention the most aggressive countermeasures you've ever seen. Breaking that lot from outside might be possible after a few years, but security is updated all the time—when you've discovered the necessary keys, they've already changed the locks. You need someone inside or another way in.'

'Like a backdoor implanted through an employee's data files?'

'Exactly, a backdoor or… oh.'

She stepped towards him and leant over; he pressed himself back in his chair. 'Yes, "oh". When, exactly, were you going to tell me, Mastersson? You never asked.'

'I was just looking out for you—no corporation can be trusted. When you first uploaded your credentials was the ideal opportunity. If it helps, try to think of it as insurance you never knew you had. Now you get to cash in.'

'I can't deny it's been useful, but you should have asked.'

'Yeah, I should. Sorry.' His shoulder line softened and he settled back into his seat as she started moving again. His voice, higher pitched than usual, signalled an attempt to change the subject. 'Someone knew you were chasing your brother after only a few hours. I'm assuming tracking operatives is standard? Are you still carrying any company hardware, or running their software on your ship's system?'

'There's just this omni-block. There's no way Jane's running Collective software; she fried my slate when I tried to interface it.'

'Then your omni-block could be compromised.'

'You want permission to try accessing my omni-block?'

'The backdoor already gives me access to your omni-block, but you said I should ask.'

Moira could see the muscles around his mouth twitching, trying to suppress the grin that was forming. They failed. 'Mastersson, I think you're a bigger public menace than whoever's behind all this. Fine, go ahead, but if you access anything personal I'll clock you one.'

'Like… height, one metre sixty-eight; vitals of eighty-three, sixty-two, eighty-one—Ow!'

'Just—'

'Yes, ma'am. Scanning now, ma'am. Your omni-block's clear—no dodgy software, just basic corporate housekeeping. I doubt there's something hiding; I'm good at what I do. Who routinely keeps tabs on you?'

'Ferris monitors departmental communications, but—'

'Your boss? He's been hassling you. What's his angle?'

'Angle? Mastersson, you're trying too hard. Ferris is a political brown-noser, plays the system and dotes on his departmental success rating. He wants promotion desperately, which is why it makes no sense that he's been trying to derail my investigations. He allocates me cases that can't be solved and most department heads wouldn't touch. When it's all about efficiency and profit margins, my failures make him look bad.'

'But he wants you out?'

'He's hinted as much, but that doesn't make sense either. Recruiting and retraining costs credits so PCS is all about employee retention. I thought his personal hatred of me was overriding his career drive, but my gut tells me it's more than that.'

'But you're such a lovable character. What's not to like?'

Her swinging boot caught something metallic and sent it skittering loudly across the floor. 'Knock it off. What's with you?' The pacing was not helping. She could only take four steps before turning from another pile of debris. She sat back on the chair.

Mastersson's smile faded. 'Never mind. Could it be personal bias?'

'What, mine towards him?'

'Yep, you can be... You have strong opinions on people.'

'I hate Ferris' weasely little arse, sure, but his attitude towards me is getting worse. If he's involved in this or covering for someone, then his actions begin to make sense.'

'They do?'

'Keagan's financial records show he's been blowing big money for months and now he's disappeared. The low-key way of getting me out of the picture is to get me fired. As a discredited operative and private citizen, I have no reputation, resources, or authority to discover anything. Because of you, I got onto them before they were ready. Ferris knows something.'

'Your gut may have predictive powers heretofore unknown to humankind, but doesn't your job demand a little something called evidence?'

'Do I fit the mould of irrational female? Think carefully about how you answer that.'

'No...'

'*No*. Ferris is my line manager; it's his job to monitor me. I used my omni-block to pay for the transport to Keagan's apartment. That transaction was logged instantaneously in our departmental account—the one Ferris watches and the one you can't change because your backdoor is based on my clearance. I'm attacked at Keagan's shortly after I arrive—by locals. It happened fast, so they were on standby—a backup in case anyone came snooping. There were no bugs in the apartment. Ferris made a call.'

'Okay, but someone could have been watching the building. Also, the guys had weapons. Someone cracked the building's software before I did and overrode the safety protocols. They could have inserted a monitoring subroutine to report visitors months ago.'

'It's an apartment block with hundreds of residents and thousands of visitors. Spotting individuals needs heavy surveillance. I don't think anyone could watch the building—not in such an ordered society, not without arousing suspicion. Monitoring software is possible. But you're missing the human element here, Mastersson. Ferris derailing my career conflicts with his desire for promotion. People don't do that—act in a way consistently at odds with their aims—not without a reason, unless they're insane. Ferris is a git, but he's not insane. We have to go and find him.'

'We?'

She said it without thinking—just assumed he would come with her. He looked tense but had not said no.

His face lit up with a smile, but it was rueful. 'I'm flattered you asked, but do you really think with my… skill set… that I'd be any help out there, in the big bad galaxy chasing big bad Ferris and his gang?'

'Mastersson, you're a wimp.' The anger in her voice surprised her, but not as much as realising how much she had taken his help for granted.

He was angry too. 'Moira, do you want to find your brother, or not? I could come with you—part of me wants to—but we both know in a firefight or a brawl some hairy guy will have me in a neck hold with a gun to my head in no time. Access this system from my implant too often when I'm away and I'll be tracked and arrested. And so will you. You need my "arse" on this seat and the information that gets you. You may want to cross space with some machismo-moron knuckle-dragging his way behind you, but that's not me. Guys like that can't wipe their own backsides because their glutes get in the way, let alone navigate the grid. So, do you want this wimp's help, or not?'

'I just meant—'

'I know what you meant. I need a beer. I guess you'll need to get your stuff—you don't want to put off finding Keagan for too long. I'll order you a ride. The weather's calm—pick up will be about four klicks due south.'

What the fuck's eating him? She stared at his retreating back, words lost to her. Years of camaraderie shattered in just a few days together. Moira began rebuilding her walls. *This is why I'm single. It's time to find Ferris, and do what I've been wanting to do for months to the little shite.*

⊓

Mastersson stared at the tangle of wires and circuits on his desk that he had rebuilt the night before into a working tangle of wires and circuits. These days he was not a heavy drinker and the fifth bottle of beer left him feeling decidedly squiffy, but he knew what he was doing—data processing with his implant was still fast.

A few hours' anonymous trawling through seven open scientific databases for unusual molecules, locations of known compounds, products containing the samples Moira found, and organic markers left behind by their owners gave a sea of data it would take Moira several days to wade through. Optimising the search algorithms should narrow the options. As he fed the parameters into each database he sipped, and thought.

The alcohol was supposed to take the edge off his anger, but it was not working. *Idiot. Collective operative and action woman Moira Dolan was going to take one look at your tech cave and fall for you? Why would meeting in person be different, after six years of fetching every stick she threw? 'Cos you have such a magnetic personality and the body of an Imperial Marine? Hardly.*

His anger had focused on her for the first three bottles, but then alcohol and bitterness turned it inwards. He was Moira's pet, 'Scrudder'—nothing more. *Is that what I want?* He toyed with switching off the grid interface for the umpteenth time. Sweeping it from the worktop may be a satisfyingly grand gesture, but what he had built was too good to waste on some inebriated impulse. *Is it too good to waste on her?* But it was not about feelings anymore. *If I wanted to stop sniffing after Moira, I should have done that years ago—not wait until she's attacked and her brother's in who-knows-what kind of 'shite'. If I was that kind of bastard, she would probably find me irresistible. Isn't that what women want? Ask and they say a man should be sensitive and dependable, but it's always the bastards they sleep with.*

125

The results were coming in, and they were a mess of statistics that Moira would probably put together using her gut. From the three completed runs, there was something even a computer boffin like Mastersson could not miss: one organic molecule without a history: 'Unknown', 'Unidentified', 'No known analogues'. *How can that be right? My stunningly attractive intellect tells me this has to be important, but something 'unknown' is no use as evidence. Moira's no more an organic chemist or biologist than I am.* But he knew who was. The name floated up through the alcohol from the murky depths of his past. *She could help. She's probably the best— only?—help I'm going to find. Oh gods, why Helen? And now I have to call her—call the woman who used to love me to help the woman who never will. Oh, the pathos.*

Is it always going to be 'anything for Moira'? Am I really that pathetic? But he *had* refused to help when a contract obliged her to chase some poor innocent who crossed The Collective. A grim smile touched his lips. *She was so pissed.* The rant had been epic. *Moira's right though, I am a 'self-righteous shite', and right now that feels* good. *Besides, what's the alternative? Moira attacked again, Keagan dead, and another scum-sucker gets away with shafting the little people.*

Recalled to himself, he felt less like a wuss, but he still did not want to face Helen. He took another swig of beer. *I've 'found my balls' as Moira puts it, so let's get this over with before I sober up. Helen...*

Mastersson had enjoyed getting drunk. On the long nights of coding, alcohol loosened the lock on his mental toolkit. His fingers flew and walls on the grid fell before them. He made money, enough for a sub-cranial implant. Drink helped him buy it, drink stopped him using it. But alcohol was an old friend, one he was not prepared to ditch for the sake of his toy and, after months of practice, the three of them had learned to get along famously. Then he met Helen. His rapidly acquired temperance had stuck, mostly. He suppressed a small burp. *I hope she doesn't notice. Better let my mouth do the talking—thought-crossing right now would bring me a world of trouble.* A mental nudge to the implant and the connection was open.

'Gustav, is that really you?'

'Gustav'. Oh no. 'It's me.'

'Why aren't you on visual?'

Because this is already weird enough. 'I've been overusing the implant and I'm giving my neurones a rest. How are you?'

'I'm good. I can hear that slight slur in your voice and the little pauses when you stop to think. Are you back to drinking?'

Nearly ten years on and it all comes flooding back. How can you live with someone so practically perfect? 'Mostly sober—had a bad experience; now I only drink when I'm depressed.' *Why did I say that? Interacting with real humans Rule 101: never call your ex when you're on the beer.*

'I remember. Gabriel Industries was on the news for days.' Her voice had taken on a disconcerting softness—it took Mastersson a few seconds to process what she had actually said.

'How did you know about Gabriel Industries?' He tried not to sound shocked.

'When you… when you left saying you were in too deep and the headlines followed. That, and you used to hum their corporate jingle while you worked.'

'Ever the scientist, Helen. I could never keep anything from you.' *Worrying, for a grid-runner.*

'I'm just glad you got clear.' Again, that disconcerting softness. 'I was scared for you, Gustav. People who went after Gabriel Industries *died*.'

'It was too close—that's why I won't drink on a job.' *Please don't fuss. And I'm still justifying.*

'But you went back in, didn't you. The exposé of 3267, that was you wasn't it?'

How the…?! Was that pride in her voice, or something else?

'Helen, that was a long time ago. Besides, who'd be stupid enough to break back into a monitored system?'

'Gustav, I know you never truly believed you could trust me; because of what you do, you can never trust anyone. But you called me, remember? Do you think I've been waiting for a chance to entrap you, after ten years? If I'd gone to the authorities, you would be in a penal colony or long dead. Neither happened. Try and think logically, when have I ever let you down?'

Despite years of honed paranoia screaming otherwise, he knew she was right. *Moira keeps my secrets, but then I'm useful to her and she's always loved anyone who fingers the establishment, but Helen...* The memories were good ones, for the most part. She was loyal and warm. There were long conversations deep into the night. There was the time he rejigged her research equipment. The memory of her scolding still burnt his ears, but she was radiant when the scanner's increased sensitivity gave her a breakthrough after a month-long stall. Helen was caring. She was comfortable. She was someone you could settle with, if you were mature enough. *Rather than chasing fantasies.* Shocked by their direction, Mastersson's thoughts froze him like an animal in a search beam. *The beer's doing my thinking.*

'You've no answer then? Still my paranoid Gustav.'

'Sorry. I know I can trust you as much as anyone. That's why—' *Rule 102: remember the fragile female ego.* '—that's one of the reasons why I'm calling. I've got a friend who's in trouble. Her brother is missing.'

'A "friend", and you want me to help?' The tone was flatter now, the warmth cooling.

Rule 102, and it wouldn't be so bad. 'Yes, she's just a friend— of six years—and the only person in the galaxy she loves is her brother. To be honest, we think he's fallen in with some bad people. I was wondering if I could bring a bio-sample over for you to take a look at?'

Silence, then: 'You want to meet? We don't have to talk face-to-face, you could send it by courier…?'

The hanging question. Mastersson hoped by answering he was not promising more than he actually said. 'We don't have to meet, but I thought it would be nice to… to catch up, face-to-face.' *And if I let that sample out of my sight, Moira will kill me.*

'Do you really mean it? I… I would like that—' Her voice was warm again, and was it a little deeper? '—but I can't.'

Daunting as the prospect was, Mastersson actually felt disappointed; after spending time with Moira, Helen would be a relief. 'You can't? You can't help, or you can't meet up?'

'Neither, both. I can't come to you—there's another research project that I have to complete.' She sounded crestfallen. 'If you can wait… I'm guessing the sample has probably degraded and will need working up? It's likely to take a couple of weeks to run an analysis for you.' She rallied. 'I know you hate travelling, but can you come here? I can clear my other commitments by the time you arrive.'

There was no point in lying; she could always tell. 'That could bring you trouble. Moira's already been attacked. She works as a security operative and suspects someone in her organisation has something to do with her brother's disappearance.'

'She must be a good friend…'

'I'll take some of the heat off her if I can. You know the line of work I'm in, there is a risk.' This was their longest and oldest discussion. 'If they link her to me then you may get dragged in. These aren't nice people.'

'I'll help, but promise me—nothing stupid.'

'Don't worry, I've grown up enough to still be doing what I do best. I don't take stupid risks.' *Unless I have to.*

'So, what do you need from me? I don't know if my area of expertise can contribute much to police work or forensics.'

'I've got a sample that isn't recognised by any of the databases I ran it through. I've no access to a cutting-edge research facility and my one corporate pass I can't risk overusing. Breaking another system will take too long. I wouldn't ask, except I'm out of options. Does your lab have the right equipment to identify the sample?'

'Organic or inorganic?'

'Organic I think, but you're the molecular biologist.'

'Where was it found? Some context will help me refine the search parameters.'

'Her brother's apartment. Moira believes it was something on him or present in his system because of where it was found: his clothes, bedclothes, and the hygiene and food prep areas, mostly.'

'By "present in his system" you mean it could be some sort of drug?'

'Honestly, probably, but I don't know. Her brother... has a flexible definition of legal.'

'Like someone else I could mention.'

'True. Helen, this could save a life.'

'But you know that's not the only reason I'm doing this.'

Masterssson found himself blushing. 'I know, thank you. It'll be good to see you again.' He meant it too.

'Take care, Gustav.'

'And you, Helen.' He terminated the link. *And so, to save his friend's brother, the heroic Gustav bravely faces his past. Could my life get any stranger?*

18

Pharos, System BD+24 543

It had been so easy, well, easier than expected anyway. Killing Spree were specialists and had selected the area richest in large game animals to custom-build the lodge. The Faylin X790 stood propped in a corner, along with the rest of the pre-packed hunting gear. Theodore had taken just four hours to unwrap the stash of equipment, watch the holo-vid tutorial, assemble the hunting rifle, and make his first kill. It was not clean.

Theodore had watched the 'deer'—he had no idea what it actually was—limping, writhing, and finally crawling into a thicket, out of sight. He fired a few shots into the foliage, but it was over a klick away. Wincing with every step through the dirty, disorganised chaos that the oiks and philistines lovingly referred to as 'nature', he finally made it to what he thought was the right bit of forest. It took him an hour of scrabbling between branches to find the creature, its downy head resting on a root and eyes rimmed white with panic. It wriggled a little, obviously trying to get away. Theodore considered shooting it again, but decided to let it die in its own time. He already missed the convenience of civilisation and was damned if he was going to dig out more metal and bone fragments from the carcass.

Dragging the thing back took another four hours. The muscled man in the holo-vid had decried the use of a walker to pull the carcass as 'sacrilege', saying it diminished the visceral satisfaction of your first kill. As far as Theodore could tell, all the advice got him was a sprained ankle and a caking of dirt. He had even set off without charging the hunting suit's environmental compensators after hearing some bullshit about 'connecting with your inner maleness in the wild'. Apparently, that meant sweating until even the outer layers of the suit were soaked and nearly passing out from heat exhaustion and dehydration. His thing for craggy faces and sculpted arms had got him into trouble on more than one occasion. This time, when he resolved 'never again', he swore he would stick to it. *I'll contact his bosses and have 'Daxx' fired if I live through this.*

He gripped the animal by the lower jaw and skull and heaved again, arms and legs trembling with the strain of hauling it up the steps and over the threshold. By the time the carcass was in the centre of the floor, all he could do was roll over and lie next to it, panting. It took an age for his breathing to steady and the dancing spots to disappear. Only then did he realise he should have done the butchering outside. *Take a man from civilisation and he loses even his most basic faculties.*

Muscles stiff from the exertion, he staggered across to a low padded chair and dropped into it gratefully. 'Computer, play lesson seven: "How to make something edible from something dead".'

'Please clarify, do you mean play lesson seven: "Historically Authentic Butchery Techniques for Use in the Wild"?'

'Computer, as I cannot afford the luxury of communicating with anyone else, you will have to do. Do stop being so literal and just play the lesson.'

'Acknowledged.'

What followed was a collage of blood, filth, and primitive male chest beating. Theodore caught sight of the blood drying on his hands and front. He managed a shambling run to the washroom where he stood underneath the cleanser without disrobing. At last he was clean, dry, and beginning to feel human again. Retreating to his as-yet-unused hunting lodge and breaking out the gear for the free Genuine Big Game Wilderness Adventure that came with it had seemed such a good idea at the time. Now all he wanted was his apartment and the sanity of modern living. *Except I don't own an apartment anymore.* Not yet ready to face his future, he seized on hunger to provide a much needed distraction. That still left the process of preparing the food. *I am not doing it Daxx's way.*

He strode through to the main living space and faced down the animal's accusing stare. Late evening sunlight poured in through the open door, turning the blood on the floor a burnished orange. *The colour of my couch at home.* Before he was swept away by another bout of melancholy, he decided to ferret around in the supply cabinet for something more advanced than a twelve centimetre knife with a sawtooth blade. He found what he was looking for in the medpac—one of the few untouched trappings of civilisation that Killing Spree had not desecrated in their drive for an 'authentic' experience.

Using the laser scalpel, the meat separated easily from skin and bone. There was a perverse pleasure in imagining Daxx's response to the sin he was now committing. The lodge was so spartan that the only cooking facility provided was a fire pit. At least there were some genuine reconstituted plant matter logs '…to tide the budding huntmaster over until lesson eight: *"The Wilderness Will Provide: Ancient Techniques of Fire Making."'* He was supposed to be rubbing sticks together, or something, but the logs lit in seconds when subjected to the intense heat of the scalpel beam.

Despite the primitive set up, Theodore started enjoying himself as the smell of skewered meat chunks filled the room. Initially certain he would be dead by the end of the day, he had outsmarted his unknown boss. He could use a weapon now and there would soon be food to eat. For the moment he was alive, if not comfortable, and that was something.

'Alert. Movement sensor number thirty-six activated in sector seven. Live holo-vid footage is available. Do you wish to view it?' The computer spoke without inflexion.

'It's probably just something else furry to shoot.' Despite the bravado, his throat tightened and his heart beat in his chest. 'Computer, display the footage.' The sky was darkening now, muting everything grey in the twilight. 'Computer, colour enhance moving objects.'

'Acknowledged.' The image broke into a confusing kaleidoscope of variegated shapes as the late evening breeze stirred every branch, leaf, and blade of grass.

Theodore could not contain his temper. 'Don't be so literal! Remove colour enhancement. Isolate the trigger for movement sensor thirty-six and enhance.'

'Unable to comply. Movement trigger has now left sensor range. Movement sensor number thirty-five is now reporting activity.'

'Computer, how far is movement sensor number thirty-five?'

'Approximately one klick from this location.'

Theodore was sweating, despite the cool of the evening, but he had to know. 'Computer, display movement trigger for sensor thirty-five. Enhance and track.' The image zoomed in. It took a long, hard stare for Theodore to make out the shimmering pattern against the monochrome background. Even on high magnification it was only a distortion in the air, passing from tree to tree. 'It' was moving with care and purpose, and did not want to be seen.

How could he have found me so soon? Theodore forced his aching legs to carry him across to the rifle. *You think I'm just your errand boy, but I've already learnt some new tricks.* He sealed the heavy door's locking mechanism and carried the gun to the open window. He connected the energy cell of his hunting suit to the charger and switched on the reactive camouflage. *Two can play at being invisible, and I know you're coming.*

19

Crouched deep in a heavily leaved stand of trees, Moira watched the small walker propel itself silently over the tangled roots. The deft movements of her fingers on the omni-block guided it into the dense undergrowth, its vid-stream beamed to her wrist bobbing and blurring with the motion.

Ferris had boasted about buying the hunting lodge and the parties of superiors he planned to entertain in a summer-long campaign of arse-licking his way to the next promotion. *With his credit line cut and the survival instincts of a candy-bug entering a kids' crèche, where else would he go?*

The light was fading fast, the wrist display dimming with it. Bringing her omni-block to her face, she was just able to determine the relative position of the hunting lodge. Her stealth suit status displayed as 'Operational'. She began following the walker southeast, the range indicator showing just over a klick to the target, to Ferris.

The EM scanner spiked—a game-tracking sensor triggered by the robot, now a hundred metres in front. Moira flicked on the walker's holo-projector. *That should get his attention.* She ducked at the sound of a shot, a high velocity round shredding leaves and snapping branches. Her eyes darted about, but there was nothing to see except trees, all intact. *Eejit rookie!* She dropped the gain setting for the walker's mic, allowing herself a grim smile as her heart steadied. *If I'm jumpy, Ferris'll be crapping himself— shooting at ghosts that don't stay dead.*

Before moving forward, she signalled the walker and the holo-emitter powered down. Negotiating the heavy cover and guiding the walker made for slow progress; Ferris was a beginner, even though his hardware was designed to help civilians put large holes in moving furry things. As if providing a demonstration, she heard two more rounds passing through the vegetation, both wide of their potential targets.

The lodge was nearer when the second EM pulse fired. Moira imagined Ferris's voice as she switched the holo-image back on. *'Oh, mummy, why aren't they dying? Did I hit one? How many of them are there?' Three… two… one…* another shot. *As long as he's focusing on the hologram, I won't take the hits.*

She added little variations to the game as she closed, but her amusement at Ferris' ineptitude dulled every hundred metres, concern replacing it. *If I can work out where Ferris is, we'll have company soon.*

Moira dived forward as a heavy branch overhead cracked and swung towards her. Her earphones pumped out a confusing cacophony of noise, sounds ricocheting from every direction and she pressed herself into the dirt. Leaves fell, swirling like snowflakes as flying splinters split the air around her.

The firing stopped. The rustling did too as everything airborne finally reached the ground. Nothing moved. There was no sound.

On the back of her wrist, red text flashed a warning: 'System failure—please retrieve mobile unit'. *Bastard got lucky!*

She got up, moving quickly in a low crouch. Replacing a rifle magazine took seconds and even a moron like Ferris could isolate her movement if there was nothing else to look for. *So far, he's doing everything he can to earn the title 'amateur'—he'll forget the periphery.* She swung wide.

Moira hit dirt when the lodge appeared through the black-purple bushes, the faux-rustic roof and walls making it look like something from a historical database. Ferris' gun barrel balanced on a tripod on the window sill, the stock appearing to rest in mid-air instead of against his shoulder. It pointed straight ahead. *Keep using those brains, Ferris; it'll make this a lot easier.*

Moving only below the elbows, she armed a self-propelled grenade before easing it over the launcher's gas chamber. She felt it click onto the housing. *Shite.* The barrel of Ferris' gun was moving, the scope exploring the extremes of his field of vision. Her only protection, her suit and the surrounding foliage.

She inverted the launcher; its feet sank into the soft earth and anchored. A stream of targeting data scrolled by as she zoomed her goggles in on the open window. The rifle barrel was swinging towards her. Touching the aim icon, she waited. Figures for air pressure, trajectory, range, projectile velocity and weight, wind force and direction slid across the display. The gun's muzzle was visible, as was the huge lens of the scope.

'Trajectory locked.'

Ferris pointed the rifle directly at her. She threw herself to one side. A tree trunk as thick as her thigh exploded into splinters behind her. The mass of wood hung suspended for an instant before gravity brought it down. *Fuck, atomiser rounds.* She rolled and kept rolling as the tree fell. Leaves rained down and branches shattered as exploding shells filled the space she had occupied moments before.

The cracking of wood sounded from every direction as she struggled to get clear—she was not fast enough. Branches became bars that caged. She froze—movement or sound would kill her. All she could see was greenery. Experimentally, she moved each limb a fraction of a centimetre. *Nothing broken.* The only sounds were the rustles of drifting leaves and creaking wood settling into place. Amateurs usually kept shooting. *Atomiser Rounds—fewer in a magazine, or is he waiting for me?* Very, very slowly she eased her left arm across her before feeling for the display with her other hand and touching the screen. Suppressed, the 'phut' of the compressed gas release was barely audible.

'Launch successful.'

The grenade detonated with a dull 'whump'.

She let her head slump back onto the earth, resting there for a moment. The neurotoxin released would act in seconds. *Now, if I can just reach my chain-knife.* It made quick work of the surrounding wood; she was free. *He shouldn't be walking around for hours, but no point being stupid.* Rolling off her equipment pack, she dug around inside. She found a flybot and sent it zipping towards the window. An interior scan of the lodge with the micro-cam showed the rifle lying on the floor next to a distortion in the air. *Good.* She set off for the window.

Inside, a quick spray of Metal-Mist and an electric discharge from the accompanying powercell revealed Ferris curled up like a newborn. Moira reset the motion sensors and strode up to him, stim-shot in-hand. He was sweating, dilated pupils rolling in his head.

'Hello, Ferris. Not pleased to see me?'

To start with, all he could manage were moans.

'Swallowed something? Too much brown-nosing?'

'Moina. Tho thorry. I didn't know id wasss 'ou.'

'It must be the chems talking. If I heard properly through your horrible diction, it sounded like you were actually apologising.'

'Moina. Moira. Thanks for coming for me. Help me up and we can get going.'

'You seem to be in a hurry. What's the rush?'

'… Someone has a hit out on me and if you can find me so can they.'

'A hit. Who could you have offended, with your charming personality? You haven't worked it out?'

'I… we… every minute we stay here is dangerous. You could have been followed.'

'True, or you could've been. That's why I need answers *fast* and I'm not the patient type. *Who* could have had me followed, Ferris? Was it the same person who had me attacked on Aquila?'

'I… I don't know what you're talking about.'

'You're not a good enough liar to play this game. Not, "You were attacked? Where? When? Who by?". Those are questions a concerned boss would ask. "I don't know what you're talking about." means you're guilty. Who ordered the attack, Ferris?'

'Moira, I promise you, I don't know anything. What did they look like, the men who attacked you?'

'I think you've given me enough excuses.' Moira kicked him in the stomach. She waited until he could breathe again. 'How did you know they were *men* Ferris? No one's keeping tabs on me except PCS, except *you*.'

'Are you crazy? Why would I—?'

She kicked him again and stepped aside as he threw his guts across the lodge floor.

'Time's short and you're still stalling. This boot has a reinforced toe cap. How's your stomach, Ferris? Who are you scared of? Who's more scary than me right now?'

He coughed, shaking his head.

She stamped down on his kneecap and felt the tearing of muscles and tendons as it gave way. 'Does this help you focus on your priorities?' She flicked her foot out, pushing the fingers cradling the shattered knee into the wound.

He cried out, subsiding into whimpers as tears streamed down his face.

'You can make this stop. Something happened to my brother— the only family I have—I want to know what. If you don't know, you know someone who does.' She caught three of his fingers under her boot and pressed down.

He screamed.

'I'm your only way out. Talk to me and you can get out of here before your friends show up.' She eased the pressure but did not raise her foot.

Through sobs, the words poured out. 'I don't know his name. He contacted me, said he could arrange promotions and money. There was lots and lots of money.'

'I need a name, specifics. If he can arrange promotions then he's either high up in Proteus or knows someone who is. Which department? When he contacted you where did the link come from?'

'I tried a trace. Dead-end. Within five minutes, ten thousand credits disappeared from my account. He threatened to kill me if I tried it again or told anyone. You don't want to get more involved,

Moira. Get me out of here and I'll pay you well. You can leave, go wherever you want, start a new life.'

'Too late, but loyalty isn't a word you'll ever understand. I want my brother. I want my old life back. Tell me *everything* you know. Don't lie. Don't miss anything out.' *I was certain he would fold. He's still shielding someone, someone who has him absolutely terrified.* She checked her omni-block. *I've been here too long already.* She regarded Ferris again, pondering how to get the leverage she needed.

'I'm done here.' Moira grabbed the medpac and started rearranging the equipment in her backpack. 'Computer, where's the communications array?'

'This facility is not equipped with that item.'

Saying nothing, she looked meaningfully at Ferris and held his gaze. His face was one of the hunted. Casually, she picked up every piece of his equipment and tossed them, one by one, out the window. She kept it up until he took the bait.

'What are you doing?'

She did not answer. Every few seconds there was another thump as an item landed in the dirt outside.

'I said what are you doing?' The pitch of his voice was rising, hysteria gripping the edges.

After a slight pause, while she opened the next equipment bag, the rhythmical sound of the impacts continued.

'You've got to get me out of here. He'll be coming for me, for you too.'

Still she ignored him.

When she had spread the contents of all six equipment packs on the ground outside, she took a small box from her own. 'Do you know what this is? It's an incendiary charge. Everything will burn. The lodge has a fire suppression system, but I'm disabling it. The back door will be open; you'll be able to crawl outside. You may even make the treeline, but you won't be able to hide your trail. The smoke will be visible klicks away. I'm sure whoever you are scared of is monitoring my Proteus account. I'm going to tell him where to find you. I try not to kill helpless people, but I bet your friend isn't that principled. You can die here, or tell me what I want to know.'

She was stepping over the threshold when he called after her. 'He… he told me to keep you away from Keagan, so I set you up with all those dead-end cases and Kishino. That made him angry. I didn't know he'd made Kishino disappear as well.'

'You said, "disappear"; you mean Keagan's alive?'

Ferris' reply was lost as the security warning filled the room: 'Proximity alert. Motion detector twenty-two, range seven hundred and fifty metres.'

'Shite. Give me audio and video.' The wall display sprang into life. In the darkness, there was nothing to see.

'He's here, we've got to—'

'Shut it, Ferris.'

There. The whirring sound was rapidly quietening. 'Your friend's sent at least one buzzer, and that means troops in the trees and coming this way. Spill it. Now.'

'That's all I know. He wanted you kept out of the picture, quiet. I don't know why he wanted Keagan or Kishino. He never told me anything—never gave anything away. Whatever he's doing, it's been going on for years. He's powerful, well-connected. He accessed my accounts and deleted everything. *Please*, we've got to leave.'

She stared at him, marking the shaking, the sheen of sweat, and the smell of urine and shite.

'I believe you.'

'Oh, thank you.'

'I believe my brother could be dead because of you. I believe you're too stupid to live. Didn't you think your boss would find out about this place? That, or you've allowed yourself to be used as bait and only now realise you're utterly expendable. Whatever, it doesn't matter. Moira Dolan, stupid security grunt—that's what you think? I've been here twelve hours already—enough time to circumnavigate your sensor perimeter and leave a few surprises of my own; they'll kill a few. When the survivors find you, he'll know you betrayed him.

'Computer, access the last three minutes of surveillance footage. Play back in a repeating loop.' She lunged and struck Ferris in the throat, crushing his voice box. Two twists and a blow dislocated his shoulders and remaining knee.

'Can't talk, can't move—you can't disable the video playback. We security grunts call it "evidence". Goodbye, Ferris.'

The first shots burst through the wall, up near the ceiling. *Long-range speculative fire. Looks like Ferris' friend wants to know who hacked Keagan's account and apartment building.* She activated her stealth suit and hit 'Execute' on her omni-block. Lying amongst the pile of equipment she had thrown through the window and spread in an arc in front of the lodge, the canisters of EM reactive gas exploded, blocking the line-of-sight of every gun scope she knew of. The slight breeze was carrying the smoke west. She selected the eastern compass point on her display and hit 'Detonate'. The explosions were too far away for the noise to carry to the lodge, but anyone nearby not caught in a blast would move that way to see what was going on.

After slipping on her backpack, she jumped through the open window. Hidden inside the smoke cloud, she walked away, feeling her way between the trees.

After they had fixed his throat, Ferris would be kept alive as long as he kept talking. But it would not be long before he had nothing useful left to say.

20

Adab, the 51 Arietis System

Mastersson sat, feeling uncomfortable despite the shape-memory alloy of the chair conforming to the contours of his rear. Head heavy, he balanced it on interlaced fingers and elbows spread on the table top, his arms forming a perfect weight-bearing triangle. Everything in Helen's apartment was about geometry and straight lines—the furniture and architecture a testament to clean and straightforward living. It made his skin itch.

Life was so easy for Helen: top honours at graduation, ever more prestigious job offers as she was headhunted by a series of research laboratories and corporations followed by her inevitable meteoric rise through the ranks. He knew she was too good for him and he never understood what she thought he could offer in return.

The cliff-top patio was constructed from a transparent material that left him with the disconcerting feeling of floating in mid-air. *Helen's future: always clear, always bright.* The sun was one-third risen, its golden light creating a monochrome patchwork of black and bronze over the buildings set in the parkland around the lake below. Mastersson replayed the thought; a mantra to persuade himself that what he was about to do was not completely shitty. Helen's clear and bright future should not include him. He knew, deep down, he was unnecessary clutter. He also knew she would not see it that way.

'There hasn't been anyone else since you left.'

The memory of her words the night before burned him in the growing daylight.

He had laughed. 'What, no one?'

She had looked hurt. He had tried to find words as disbelief turned to apprehension. Her green eyes had him. It was always worse when they were so close. And she never, ever looked away. He remembered coughing, his cheeks burning with the embarrassment that followed his desire. The best he came up with was,

'I'll get another drink. What would you like?'

His disbelief had nothing to do with thinking her a liar. Honest was all she knew how to be. It made her fascinating, intoxicating, and the most frightening woman he had ever met. He was incredulous someone had not taken his place in the intervening years.

'Gustav, turn around.'

The unbidden memories played behind his eyes and his grip tightened on his glass. Trying to focus on what he was about to do was impossible when he only wanted to look at her again. But could he face what would come after, and especially what would come after that?

Her hand had fluttered to his shoulder. He could not bring himself to shrug it off. Relief and disappointment had warred within him as he turned—she was still clothed. The wrap-around dress would have come free so easily—just a touch to her shoulder, as she touched his.

Angry that he had fallen so easily, he had attacked, trying to push some distance between them. 'The dress? What did you think was going to happen tonight?'

'You know why I wore this dress.' She stepped back a little, but her eyes never left his.

'Us—it wasn't working before. What makes you think it would be different now?'

'I don't. I think we could have what we had before.' With each word she moved closer, her voice softening. Now her eyes were the only things he could see.

'Before, I walked out on you.'

Her hips and breasts were warm and soft against him. 'I haven't changed, Gustav. I think we should find out if you have.'

The heat, the melding together—shocked at the intensity, he snapped back to the present. His physical response under the table jabbed him with guilt. *And now I have to face the after, after that.*

The sun was higher now, only deepening the shadows. Mastersson reached for his glass and sipped the tart green liquid— the juice of some local plant. Even with the sun rising, the air had yet to warm. The cold soaked through his clothing, gripping him like his fatalistic certainty. He could not leave without facing her, not again. *That much of me has changed.* Helen would still give him any information she had—there would be no game-playing. It only made him feel worse.

'Good morning. Lovely, isn't it?' She chose the chair across from him.

He was surprised, and a little disappointed. 'The sunrise? It's a little—I don't know—*bright*, don't you think?'

'You get used to it and learn to appreciate the subtleties in the light and shade.'

He glanced over and found her looking directly at him. She wore a plain white robe that left only her feet and hands exposed as she sat with her arms wrapped around her knees, curled up against her chest. She was still.

He wondered at these times whether she was touching something deeper than he ever could. 'Are you talking about us, or the sunrise?'

'You know the answer is both.'

'And you guessed what I'm thinking.'

'…That last night happened too quickly, and shouldn't have happened at all; that you are working out what to say to me—how to tell me that you're leaving, but can we still be friends and work together.' There was no hint of a question in anything she said.

'I hope the answer is "yes" to both of those?'

'You know you don't need to ask, but I do have a question for you...'

A wave of dread swept over him. *Why do I keep leaving? Why before? Why now? How can I—?*

'One day, maybe, you will find answers to whatever you're thinking about and be happy to tell me, but it's none of those.' Her smile was rueful. 'You're not still here just to make sure I analyse the sample—you know when I offer to help I don't go back on my word. But you didn't run, and so something in you is different. You've grown, Gustav.'

Uncomfortable, he could not resist the urge to interrupt her train of thought. 'It doesn't feel like it. I never knew what you saw in me.'

'You are the bit of chaos my life lacks—a breath of fresh air; I value your creativity. Whatever you think of yourself, I know you have a good heart. Men who are interesting and caring aren't easy to find. What we shared last night—everything that is right about us is still there. Tell me what you need and I'll get my analysis to you as soon as I can. In the meantime, is it too farfetched to imagine— as you can change—that maybe, one day, you could change enough to decide to stay?'

Helen smiled—calm, small, sad—before uncoiling in one smooth motion and heading back inside, pausing for a moment to stroke his hair as she passed.

Masterson turned his head to watch her go. He remembered the rhythmical sway of her hips as she walked—it was still as entrancing as ever. She disappeared inside and he turned back to look out across the valley, as if the beauty of the panorama could provide a release from the paralysis of his mind. His feelings for Moira could not be denied and, despite the fact there was nothing between them, being with Helen felt like he had betrayed her somehow. But being with Helen last night had reignited something—something at least alive and real, if he wanted it to be. Whatever it was, his feelings for Moira were tainting the soil in which it was trying to grow. *I came here looking for answers and found, what? Only more questions. I sound like a cheap philosophy pamphlet.*

Despite his cynicism, the questions were real enough. *It isn't simply a choice of who, or even between holding out for the impossible or holding onto the inevitable. Who do I want to be, and am I even ready to make that choice?*

21

Dustbowl, System LHS 1573

Moira felt skanky. Days on board ship had left her too aware of her body despite her regular wash routine. The enclosed cubicle and chemical biocides she schlepped onto her skin left her feeling like the inside of a disinfected animal transport. Now she stood on an empty desert plain, sweating from every pore. Fine flecks of sand stuck and made mud with the moisture. *Disinfected and in a desert, yet somehow still damp and dirty.*

She turned slowly around, sure she had followed his instructions correctly this second time. There was nothing to see but rocks, sand, and clear blue sky.

Mastersson was nowhere around. Neither was her lost duffel bag. *Of course the storm took it, but when you're having a shite day, a little luck wouldn't go amiss. I just hope I don't need the equipment; I can't exactly call Ferris for replacements, now he's dead. At least the data uploaded.*

She spent several minutes scuffing at random patches of sand and rolling over the biggest rocks, expecting to see a door or some cunningly hidden control panel. Finally, she gave up. The fact Mastersson had hidden his—home? den? lair?—so well annoyed her. Everything about him annoyed her. It was petty, but she needed a win. She was back on his home ground, owing him her life and an apology. Men never made Moira feel small, but Mastersson had without trying—the fact he had not meant to just made her angrier. *I can't even find the damn door without him.*

They had barely spoken over the past few days. He had muttered something about keeping their data overhead low to avoid detection, which was fine, but they both knew they were avoiding each other. *Maybe this time will be better.* Bringing her duffel

148

bag—her home away from home—to Mastersson's last time felt like she was moving in; *obviously not a good idea. I've got a light rucksack and I'm a guest visiting a friend. This is not going to be complicated.*

'Mastersson? You there?'

'Depends who's asking.'

Oh no. 'I'm outside.'

'Fine. Fine. Just leave the delivery in the usual place, ok.'

'Mastersson, you shite, quit dicking around and open the door.'

'Moira? Moira! Shit, coming.'

'You've got someone in there with you?'

'… … … I'm flattered you think I might have.'

That was a long pause.

A gritty scraping and rivulets of sand slipping through a widening crack alerted her to the stairs. They descended to a stone door that ground slowly open, adding to the cacophony. *I was so close.*

'It's amazing you've kept this place hidden for so long, given the noise that makes.' She nodded back at the opening as she stepped into his junk-filled parlour.

'The secret's not to go out much. It's safer in here.'

And we take refuge in banter, suits me. 'I like what you've done with the place since I left. Charming.'

'But I haven't—oh, right.'

I shouldn't... 'Mastersson, are you alright? This is okay, right?'

'Yeah, it's fine. Do you want a drink or a shower?' There was no eye contact; he was already heading to the kitchen.

'Look, I'm sorry. Now stop acting like a dick.'

'Sorry for what? …Oh *that*. We both know I'm good with computers. The tech guy, that's me.'

Moira stared at his back as he busied himself pouring some green sludge into two glasses. She did not know what to say. They had fallen out plenty of times in the years they had known each other, but there was a wall there now. Usually, Moira hit 'Disconnect' and next time they talked everything was fine. This physical proximity was stifling. 'Where should I drop my stuff?'

He turned, his expression still unreadable. 'You're in my—the same room as before.' He paused, then extended a hand, offering her a glass.

'I'm not touching that, it looks like manifold coolant.'

'Suit yourself. I think I may be getting a taste for it.'

✻

He can't be too pissed off with me if he's loaning me his bed. Moira finally began to relax as the water soaked her hair and cascaded down her back. Her head was clearer too. She reached through the spray and touched her omni-block.

'Computer, interface with local network.'

'Voiceprint and total lack of respect for security protocols identifies Moira Dolan. Link established.' *Sense of humour's still intact.*

'Computer, cross-reference all records for Keagan Dolan and Isao Kishino. Report all common associates; locations they both visited within six months of each other; similarities in background, social status, financial circumstances, and known criminal activities; known personal preferences and habits; common memberships or alliances with any corporation, political or private group.'

'Warning: the data is incomplete. Results for such broad search parameters are likely to be inconclusive. Do you wish to proceed?'

Sometimes, one thing is all you need. 'Yes, computer, proceed.' She let the familiar facts wash over her—allowing her free-floating mind to rearrange them into new patterns. *Context is everything.* They had no associates or locations in common. From their backgrounds, the only commonalities were periods of poverty. Isao came from a stable family; she and her brother only had each other.

Isao's father's image—a gentle, wizened man content in his garden; the passionate plea for closure—swam into view. On board *Flaky Jane*, the memory caught her in the quiet times, only to be rigorously dismissed. *My parents would have been around his age.* Masayoshi had forged a bond—she tried, and failed again, to permanently file it under 'inconsequential'. She had to find Keagan first. Yet now Isao's and Keagan's lives were linked. *I need to—*

'Computer, repeat last ten seconds.'

'Both have exceptionally high combat rankings, as recorded by the Pilot's Federation.'

'Computer, specify.'

'Isao Kishino was finally ranked as "Elite" based on combat performance—'

'Computer, no details. Specify latest ranks and years achieved.'

'Isao Kishino achieved an elite combat ranking in 3248. Keagan Dolan achieved a deadly combat ranking in 3275.' Moira stopped wiping the cleanser over her legs. *Keagan took years to crawl to dangerous, and suddenly he's deadly?*

'Computer, verify current combat ranking of Keagan Dolan.'

'Accessing Pilot's Federation database. Current ranking of Keagan Dolan: Deadly.'

It did not make sense. Her brother was a good pilot, but by necessity, never choice; he was happiest scrabbling around back alley planets scavenging his next sure-fire deal. *There has to be a connection… surely not?* 'Computer, cross-reference the known locations of Keagan and Isao over the previous two years. How many times have they coincided?'

'There has been one incidence within twenty light-years.'

Shite. It was not likely Kishino had been teaching Keagan, but tenuous links were the only ones left. Until recently, the idea that Keagan could achieve Deadly status in less than a year was laughable.

'Computer, from the data, what could explain Keagan's jump in pilot rank?'

'Keagan had a teacher other than Isao Kishino; he had access to a ship faster than known models; he has an extremely high aptitude for piloting skills and was able to rapidly assimilate teaching from a passive source or personal experience; Kishino and Keagan had methods of deceiving multiple security systems across human space as to their actual whereabouts and activity.'

None of those sound likely. 'Computer, access records for specific events that increased Keagan's combat ranking. Specify number of kills, ships destroyed per encounter, locations and video footage from Pilot's Federation records.'

'This system does not have access to that data. Pilot's Federation security systems equivalent to, or exceed, military grade.'

'Computer, specify Keagan Dolan's known whereabouts for the last three years.' Moira listened as the computer read out the locations. There were no surprises, only his new home planet, Aquila, and several of his old haunts where he had established contacts. *But he's not visited his old stomping grounds in over two years.*

'Computer, confirm: the records of Keagan Dolan's ship arrivals and departures to and from Aquila during the last two years have no recorded destination?'

'Confirmed.'

So where were you going? 'Computer, display the cargo manifest for each of Keagan Dolan's trips in the last three years.' Moira moved her face from under the stream of water and wiped her eyes. *The first year's classic Keagan: a few cargo canisters of cheap legitimate junk as his alibi for what he's really carrying, but since moving to Aquila?* She could not quite believe what she was seeing. The station docking itineraries showed his hold was stuffed with tens of thousands of credits worth of computers, luxury items, platinum, gold, and gemstones—the same items every trip, outward and inward bound. *Except for the small assortment of extra canisters he brought back. Keagan, this isn't like you.*

And two trips with no cargo at all?

She had to be sure. 'Computer, confirm the following statements: in the last two years, on every trip except two, Keagan Dolan's ship carried an unchanged consignment of expensive cargo; when he returned his ship carried extra canisters with varying content.'

'Those statements are true for ninety-two percent of the data.'

'Computer, specify reasons for the eight percent anomaly.'

'Records indicate that some canisters were destroyed in transit.'

Here we go. 'Computer, over the last two years, has Keagan Dolan's ship been repaired? Access original Aquila Station records. Cross-reference with the dates the cargo canisters were destroyed.'

'Displaying available records.'

'Computer, where are the other records?'

'These are all the available station records. Cargo canisters were destroyed on two trips.'

Moira waved her hand in front of the wall panel. The flow shut off immediately. She shed the water from her eyes and hair, sweeping it back down her neck and over her shoulders. In quick succession she touched each hovering data record, glancing through the details before moving to the next. *Nearly all repairs indicate damage from weapons fire.*

'Computer, graph severity of ship damage recorded for each repair on a timeline.' The image faded out and back. *Minor damage, several occasions, but both trips with severe damage were followed by another that lasted over six months! Got your tail kicked, so decided to take a long holiday, Keagan?*

'Computer, display all available details of the two longest trips.'

No destination given. No cargo. A different ship each time, never used again—both medium sized and kitted with a fuel scoop—so long distance travel? What the fuck were you up to? You fly for a month, take some minor damage then get your arse kicked before running off in a borrowed ship with your tail between your legs. Then you come back, get back in your old ship, stay longer but repeat the pattern. Then, after returning the second time, you take barely any damage...

Valuable cargo, added to with each local trip: bounty hunter bait for pirates with ship scanners. Lure them in, show them the error of their ways, and the extra scooped cargo's sold to help the cash flow. But...

'Computer, who owned the two borrowed ships Keagan used for the seven month trips?'

'Both ships registered to Shane Gerrit, resident of Aquila in the Dalfur system, at the times specified.'

A cop's wage buys two spacecraft in eighteen months, and then he loans them to a complete stranger with a criminal record for a months-long trip to nowhere. Yeah, right.

'Computer, display list of previous owners of both spacecraft.'

On-screen, two words: 'Osmir Holdings.'

A name I've heard before. 'Computer, display ownership transfer documents and details of Osmir Holdings.'

What a surprise; both ships 'bought' from and 'sold' back just before and after each trip, to Osmir, a company that, apparently, never existed. Shite—you need powerful friends to launder money and move property on that scale.

'Computer, display Aquila Station security recordings on ship ownership transfer dates, limit search to sequences including Shane Gerrit and anyone ident-tagged to Osmir Holdings.'

'Unable to comply, files corrupt.'

'And station docking records? Same search parameters.'

'Unable to comply, files corrupt.'

A ghosting Mastersson would be proud of; they have a payroller on the station. Doesn't help me a metre—it'd take months to set up a cover and sting operation, if they haven't already swapped out my target for another sleeper.

Moira tightened her fist and hit the wall. *Fucking dead end. There's got to be something.*

'Computer, display a timeline of all these events.'

She touched the screen, again, and again. *So why did his ship take so much damage in the first month? And why such severe damage on the local trips just before each long voyage to nowhere? Then, only minor scratches in the last few months before he disappears—ship still docked and his last recorded location surface-side on Aquila? He either started picking weaker targets or his combat skills improved at an incredible rate.*

And what about the long trips? No weapons damage to either borrowed ship, but repair records show both needed major maintenance on their return. He's spending a long time in space, going somewhere off-grid—either it's way out or he's complicating his route to throw possible pursuit.

'Computer, how many days between departure from, and return to, Aquila Station for Keagan Dolan's two longest trips?'

'Two hundred and fifteen days and two hundred and eight days.'

Assume a common destination; take the shortest route, and halve the time for a one-way trip. 'Computer, assuming constant hyperspace and system travel, stopping only to scoop fuel, what is the maximum distance Keagan Dolan's ship could have travelled from Aquila in one hundred and four days?'

'Please specify journey parameters: systems visited.'

'Computer, remove all limiting parameters except those already mentioned. Exclude only systems with no available hyperspace fuel source. Include systems where illegal trade activity is suspected.'

'Working. Depending on direction and route taken, the maximum achievable range from Aquila varies between one hundred and five and one hundred and thirty light-years. Would you like the results displayed?'

'Yes.' Figures and text morphed into an expanding disc of clustered stars. The four major spiral arms of the Milky Way froze in place, centimetres from Moira's nose. A small red blob winked in one of them. 'Computer, overlay three-dimensional representations of human space—explored systems in yellow and colonised systems in blue.' Two more coloured blobs appeared, interlocking with the red.

'Computer, make display interactive—standard hand gestures.'

'Acknowledged.'

She reached out and zoomed in on the highlighted areas, blinking as suns and planets flew at her face only to disappear as the sheer scale of the virtual distances left them far behind. The computer could manipulate the image for her, but Moira needed to feel what she was seeing. Keagan's maximum travel distance occupied an irregular volume, the shape flowing with the distribution of the star systems. It extended beyond the edge of colonised space.

'Computer, disregard all colonised systems with governmental organisation ranked higher than feudal.' Two thirds of the inner stars disappeared, leaving over three hundred lawless human worlds in the colonised band. There were still hundreds of explored but unoccupied systems, and thousands as yet unexplored.

'Computer, redisplay and highlight colonised systems where Keagan Dolan has known contacts within indicated regions.' In the hologram, nothing changed. 'Computer, access all available records on Keagan Dolan, check for known associates and the star systems in which they have operated. Redisplay and highlight systems.'

She waited, but nothing changed. 'Computer, extend search one level: include all associates of Keagan's associates. Redisplay and highlight.'

'Working.'

She waited several seconds.

'Search complete. Result positive.' A single light flashed.

'Computer, that positive result is Keagan's home planet, Aquila?'

'Confirmed.'

So, a friend of a friend on home sweet home. 'Computer, display data summary of individuals within the positive result set.

Moira glanced at the rotating face then stared. She had shoved a sculpture into his gut and left him to bleed out on her brother's apartment floor. *Ferris' goon.* 'Computer, detail Shane Gerrit's career path, 3265 to present.'

'Shane Gerrit. Local law enforcement officer. Whereabouts currently unknown. One count of demotion for taking a bribe in 3273.'

She listened as the computer described his reinstatement and rapid rise to the rank of Warrant Officer. *All in the last two years, no doubt 'helped' by the same person who's been 'helping' Keagan and Ferris.*

'Computer, highlight systems occupied by Shane Gerrit's other known or suspected criminal associates.'

'Shane Gerrit has no criminal associates, known or suspected.'

'Then who bribed him?'

'Information unavailable, file corrupt.'

And the pieces fall into place. 'Computer, transfer all data from this session to my omni-block.'

'Acknowledged. Transfer complete.'

Her awkwardness with Mastersson forgotten, she only just remembered to grab a robe on her way out.

'Stop what you're doing, I've got something.'

22

Mastersson had tried hard to listen when Moira came in, but attempting to keep the live electronics on the workbench stable with a syringe of liquid nitrogen was demanding most of his attention. This needed a steady hand, and avoiding the impulse to shake his head was proving difficult. 'I'm not convinced.'

Three drips, ten C down. That should do it. He looked up. Moira stood—hands on hips, lips drawn into a tight line—giving him one of her most formidable glares; it seemed much more intense in person. 'Look, at the time Keagan was around, Gerrit had no active criminal associates, no local network, no back up. It's the way these people operate, Mastersson—it's all about connections. Gerrit wasn't a hardened crim. My bet, he was kept on retainer by Ferris on behalf of his unknown boss then put to work keeping an eye on Keagan. The minder system is common: one key individual, someone they have leverage over, controls local operations. His two friends, the men with him in Keagan's apartment, show as clean. Three officers paid very well to do a little baby-sitting on the side; easy money. Either that or another incentive, maybe blackmail. Everyone has a button.'

'Yes, but—'

'Ferris, or his boss, recruited Keagan and had him working as a bounty hunter—although I've no idea why—from Aquila. The strange thing is, Keagan didn't get all his repairs there when he got shot up—bounty hunting isn't illegal, so why travel over one hundred light-years to get fixed up? He went elsewhere for a reason—instructions? Keagan's then left to effectively operate alone. Gerrit's just the minder, his friends, local grunts —I've met the type hundreds of times—they wouldn't be given access to privileged information. Keagan would have no way of locating a hidden repair facility unless Ferris or his boss gave him one. Ferris' boss has a secret facility within this'— she gestured at the hologram—'area of space, most likely hidden in one of the lawless or un-colonised systems.'

Good. Mastersson reached over and powered down the board before swivelling in his chair. Moira's arms were crossed, fingers tapping on her elbow. He braced himself. 'Why recruit Keagan as a bounty hunter? I thought you said he preferred living under a rock and rubbing up against the other invertebrates.'

'He's my brother. *I* get to call him whatever I want.'

'Okay, sorry, but ballsy space jock hardly fits his MO, does it?'

'"His MO"? You've been studying the lingo since we last met?'

Mastersson found himself grinning. With the quest for her brother oiling the works, their tension was easing, old patterns guiding them through the awkwardness like well-used rails. 'You know I've always wanted a life like yours: full of action and romance, suave space captains wining and dining me on board their bridges before exploring the possibilities of zero-g—'

'Enough, Mastersson!'

She's actually blushing. Moira Dolan was so rarely vulnerable. *Her brother's losing her sleep.* He suppressed the urge to point out how much her new colour suited her.

'I don't know what's with Keagan. He changed after the war. I got used to the person he's become—even though I don't like it. But now? His part in this makes no sense.'

'And Ferris didn't know anything?'

'Nothing, other than whoever he was working for also arranged Kishino's disappearance.'

'"Was"? Oh.'

'Don't look at me that way. I didn't kill Ferris; I just roughed him up a bit… and left him for his boss to find.'

'That won't end well. But we aren't any closer to this boss— let's call him Mister X—'

'Let's not, and it could be a woman—if she's disguising her identity. Ferris has never actually seen him, or her.'

'If I accept you as a paragon of femininity, it could absolutely be a woman, but why would Mistress X want her own space corps made up from crims and ex-crims?' The circuit he had been working on began to buzz. *Damn, forgot to—*. Masterson grabbed it with the forceps and sank it into the crucible of liquid nitrogen where it sizzled and spat white gas. When it quietened, he put it back on the workbench, bleeping gently.

'Okay, if you insist on a name, it's going to be Ferris' Boss, FB, got it? As to why, money.'

He had seen that gleam in her eyes before; she thought she was onto something.

Her voice was full of confidence. 'Computer, from Aquila Station records, total the cost of repairing Keagan Dolan's ship over the past two years. Include replacement of damaged cargo from his original inventory. Use this figure to estimate the total cost of damage and cargo losses over that period, assuming repair costs remain constant regardless of location.'

'Total costs due to repair and cargo losses estimated at twenty-six thousand four hundred and thirty-six credits.'

'Computer, based on records of commodity prices in the Dalfur system when Keagan Dolan is recorded as selling goods there during the last two years, calculate his total income from those sales.'

'Total sales: forty-four thousand seven hundred and fifty-eight credits.'

Masterson interrupted, 'So he's making some profit, and the bounty payments would boost that, but, presumably, he has to give a kickback to FB.'

'Agreed. That's not much to show for two years work and the risks are way higher than any he's been willing to face before. It was never about the money; he's always wanted an easy life and he's not going to find one on that income.'

'Maybe Keagan's been recruited to become a good guy? He gets to earn a little cash on the side.'

She looked at him, one eyebrow raised. 'Keagan as righteous space crusader? You want to try again? You were doing so well.'

'They kidnapped the Kishino family and tried to kill you, so not working for the good guys.'

'I know my brother. If you give him a cargo hold full of valuables he would sell them in a day and drink the profits in a week. No, someone has him tightly leashed. I just don't know how.'

'Or why.'

'My bet would be some territory war between rival gangs of pirates or smugglers—buy-in expert pilots and eliminate the opposition. Bounty hunting is a cover, a way of legitimising a series of executions. With no competition, they could establish a monopoly on local goods or enjoy bleeding the main trade routes. The investment would be paid back in a few years and new rivals would go elsewhere.'

'Sounds feasible, and if it's true your brother could still be alive—he's useful to them as a pilot.'

Moira's face lit up. 'Thanks, Mastersson. And maybe Kishino's alive too. We just have to work out where they're being held and get them out.'

He was pleased to see Moira infused with renewed hope—but her voice was edged—was it only a veneer over brittle desperation? *Her brother is everything to her, the only one that stops her feeling utterly alone. Lose him and who does she have left? Me?*

Memories of his night with Helen played like a violin bow over his heartstrings and tugged on his conscience. He felt smaller, and angry thinking about Moira made him feel that way. *Do our choices define us, or does who we are define our choices? How much control do we have?*

'Cheer up, Mastersson. I know there are a lot of star systems to hide in, but we've still got your friend's molecular analysis. Combine that with the other results from Keagan's apartment and we should be able to figure this out. Everything will be fine. Trust me.'

I trust you know where you're going; it's only me that doesn't.
'Wait a second, you've been analysing data all night and still haven't finished with what you found in Keagan's apartment? Moira, how did you reach these conclusions?'

'Routine protocol: explore the wider possibilities and cut them back stage by stage until you can't go any further.'

Oh shit. 'Using meta-search, on the grid? Which systems were you logged into?'

'In Standard, Mastersson.'

'Asking a computer to process queries with thousands of possible results and modify them based on additional factors you give it—that's what you've done?'

'Of course.'

'Please tell me you weren't logged onto The Collective's security database?'

'Why's that a problem? It's custom designed to deal with the broad datasets and open-ended queries that are a normal part of casework. Besides, you said you had multiple layers of protection between your system and the external grid. You would have told me not to use my account or disabled it if it wasn't safe, right?'

Despite his implant, Mastersson could not stop himself shouting, 'Computer, shut down all access to the grid. Start with every active connection and then close all passive backdoors. Do it *now*!'

'We can't go off-line now, not when we're so close!' Moira gripped the edge of the workbench, her knuckles turning white with the pressure. 'I need to cross-reference more information to finish. I need that access.'

Mastersson tried to keep the anger from his voice. 'It *was* safe for small-scale data exchange, but the complexity of a meta-search query isn't dictated by the length, or even the number, of questions you ask. It's the number of possible permutations in the result-set generated. Asking open-ended questions eats petaflops of computer power that *always* draws the attention of some nosy systems admin. Couple that with the fact you're AWOL from The Collective but are still using their resources and I think that maybe, just *maybe*, some alarms are going off somewhere.'

'Can't you do your tekhead stuff and get us out of—' She saw his expression. '—Can't you weave some of your tech magic and block a trace, or remove records of the search queries?'

'Your account doesn't have sufficient clearance and, like I said already, infiltrating that amount of security without a backdoor can take weeks or months. I suppose I could try and engineer a false trail across the grid for them to follow. How long ago did you start asking Collective computer central open ended questions?'

'I don't know exactly—I couldn't sleep—about four hours.'

'Then we're stuffed. Going back online means they'll only track us faster. As it is, they're probably on their way already. We have to leave.' Mastersson caught the glowing in the corner of his eye. The circuit board was red now. He gripped it in the forceps and threw it across the room. It landed with a pop, and pellets zinged from behind the piled salvage that intercepted the hot metal. He winced at the unnecessary damage to his now-abortive plans. *Doesn't matter now.*

'But I asked a few simple questions. It may have strained the brain of the computer at the other end, but the answer sent was very simple, just a localised galactic map.'

'Note to self: never allow children to play with technology unsupervised. If an approved user asks a computer an open-ended or multi-branching question with no security qualifiers, then the computer will load *everything* of relevance to that query from *every* connected system. My records are safe, but all the case information on your omni-block has already been copied onto the corporate database. They know exactly what we know about the case, and that we're getting closer. Given they've already tried to kill you and hackers like me are corporate enemy number one, I think they will try very hard to ensure we don't leave this planet alive.'

'You should have—'

'Time for recriminations later; that flashing red light—passive external monitors just detected a data trace. The Collective has subsidiaries—depots—throughout this sector, doesn't it?'

'I think so.'

'Then they could be here any minute. Get what you need, and only what you need. I've got a detonation to rig.'

'Detonation?! What detonation?'

23

Moira raced into Masterssson's bedroom. It took her seconds to retrieve her belongings from the floor, but longer to throw on some clothes before stuffing the rest into her rucksack. She slung it around her shoulders and returned to the common room. Masterssson was not there. 'Where—?'

'Down here.' His muffled voice surfaced from somewhere underneath yet another pile of boxes and wires. 'You done?'

'I didn't bring much.'

'Now don't flip out and go all women's lib on me but—'

'What's women's lib? You had your nose in too many historical holo-vids again?'

'It's from when men were selfish and women resentful. But you know you're the equal of any man?'

'Of course.'

'Good, glad you think so. I'm really busy here, so could you go and pack me some clothes and any useful equipment you see lying around? My tunics and underwear are in the boxes under the bed and there's survival gear piled in the closet. Thanks.'

'Do I look like a domestic droid to you? Get your own stuff.'

'Setting these explosives is tricky so, in the interests of speed, it will not diminish your value as either a woman or a human being one iota to keep things moving by helping out, will it?'

'Masterssson, one day I'll—'

'Don't waste your anger on me. As some great spiritual teacher somewhere once said: channel it and you will do great things.'

One day, I really will kill him. She turned and re-entered the bedroom and ventured under the bed. *If there's anything alive in his underwear, I'm going to make him eat it.*

The time she spent ransacking his room was worth it. For a civilian, he kept an impressive selection of useful equipment. She took a step towards the door but was thrown backward onto the bed as the room shook and reverberated. Everything spun around her. Her head felt like it would burst; for a while, all she could do was lie still. She gripped Mastersson's bag and dragged it behind her as she crawled back into the common room.

'Sonics!' Her lips shaped the word, but she could not hear it. She touched her ears with her free hand—there was blood on her fingers. *Shite.* Pressing the hostile environment control on her collar instantaneously covered her ears, eyes, nose, and mouth. *Reduces my vision some, but I shouldn't get stunned again.*

Still too dizzy to stand, she knelt and looked around the room for Mastersson. The persistent humming in her ears masked all other sounds. Through the lessening blur, she saw the collapsed pile of equipment but no Mastersson. Leaving his bag, she scrambled across the room on all fours. She was pushing past a heavy metal box when another pressure wave shook everything, sending her sliding across the floor on her face. With her sensory organs protected the disorientation lasted only seconds, but her body ached like she had been run over by a juggernaut. *Much closer—they're analysing the seismic waves.* The intense pulsed sounds devastated subterranean structures, concussion disabling those inside. Scraping herself off the floor, she scanned the bunker walls; they were still intact, with no obvious signs of fracturing. There was no time to wonder why; she had to dig Mastersson out.

She tore at wires and hauled aside boxes hoping—dreading?— to see a hand, foot, or face. After bracing her feet, she was yanking on a particularly stubborn thumb-thick cable when lights appeared above her left wrist.

'What are you doing?' The text floated in the air, looking at her. She spun her head. He was standing not five metres away, a quizzical expression on his face. Anger rose with her relief.

'Mastersson, you fucking shite! Where were you?' The silent-sounds tore at her throat as she threw them at him.

Amusement creasing his face, he mimed looking at her omni-block display while his mouth opened and closed like a fish. She read his hovering text. 'I'm deaf too. Didn't hear a thing you said. Have you finished playing with that cable?'

He just loves showing off—like I don't already know how useful direct implant comms would be right now. But… uurghh! She let the heavy cable fall to the ground.

He nodded towards the back wall. 'This way.'

Moira spoke into her omni-block mic, which beamed the electronically coded sounds direct to his implant bypassing his ears: 'Where were you?'

'Had to find this.' He waved a T-shaped component under her nose. 'I've been meaning to tidy up and catalogue everything for years, but there's always been something more interesting to do. Here.'

She took hold of the scratched component and stared at it. 'A ship's core regenator. What are you up to?'

'Oh, not much.' Each word dripped smugness. He reached out and pressed his palm to a blank area of wall. A black line appeared, reaching from floor to ceiling.

As it widened, Moira saw an ancient reactor in the chamber beyond. 'Your bunker's a ship! Don't tell me you're planning on flying us out? They'll shoot us down before we clear the atmosphere.'

'No, this old bird's buried too deep, and she's missing a few essentials—she'd break up before take-off.'

'So your genius plan is to blow it.'

'There's too much data here—stuff I've been collecting for years. If it got into the wrong hands—'

'You mean the authorities.'

'Them too. Let's just say more than a few lives, planetary governments, and system economies would be ruined. I can't leave until I've taken off the safeties and set up a power feedback loop.' He started for the reactor.

'But this is your life's work. What's a hacker without his data? They're only chucking sonics, and even an old ship can withstand that.'

He sagged. 'Do you really think they will stop at sonics?'

'Probably not.'

'I've unlocked the corridor behind you, to the left.' A hole in the wall was opening, one she had not seen before. 'There's a way out. I'll meet you in a few minutes.'

'If you're about to give me an "If I don't make it" speech, you're wasting your breath. I know my way around old ships. I can help.'

He looked at her.

She stared back.

'Okay. The console's over there. Just follow the on-screen prompts. I'll need that back.'

She tossed him the regenator and watched him dismantle the safety panel that allowed access to the bowels of the reactor.

The console controls were intuitive and they quickly fell into an efficient working rhythm, instruction and action passing smoothly between them.

'Nothing on the reboot, just the same three error messages. You haven't tested this have you?'

'Assessing my new home's self-destruct mechanism when I moved in wasn't the highest thing on my priority list. No.'

'I've got some—'

The entire room bucked as another sonic charge detonated. Moira flew backwards and hit the wall, breath exploding from her lungs. She slid to the floor. Every centimetre of her body felt like it was bruised or bleeding. She tried to breathe, but could not take in air. For a time, all was gasping, pain, and spinning colours.

Great, they know where we are. How long before they figure the sonics aren't doing it? Her vision focused and she sought Mastersson. He was pulling himself back up using an exposed strut. He paused for a moment before offering her a shaky thumbs-up and vanishing down his hole. Was she imagining the faint clanking of him back at work? On jelly legs, she leant back over the console. The first of the three error messages disappeared, replaced by '1st stage initiation: Reactor priming circuits online.'

'Just the fail-safes.' His message appeared, floating over the back of her wrist.

Between shallow breaths, she started to disable them while he staggered around the reactor's bulk looking for the manual overrides. She paused, waiting for him to catch up. *We make a good team, he and I.* She looked over to where he worked—the cramped conditions meant there was nothing she could do to help. His curly tawny-brown hair covered the visor around his eyes. She knew they were hazel.

Accessing secured systems was illegal throughout human space. Mastersson liked to use the old term: grid-runner. He would lose everything when the bunker went up—all his equipment, all his accumulated knowledge, gone. Her mistake had taken his livelihood and his life—no insurance covered gear that would land you in a penal colony, or dead. She doubted his implant—designed for networking, not local storage—could carry even a tiny fraction of the knowledge he had amassed over the years. *And he would rather lose everything than see it in the wrong hands. He's more than a petty crook.* Guilt hit her harder than any sonic charge. *I have to make this right, but how?*

Reappearing from down below, he ruffled the dust from his hair and then looked up and beamed—dishevelled yet triumphant. Time stopped, as if she were caught and held by something indefinable.

His brow furrowed. 'You okay?'

She shook herself. 'I'm fine. Ready for the last step?'

He did not reply. Instead, his eyes took on the faraway look she hated—he had gone inside. When he came back, his face was set hard. 'Sensors have picked up vibrations on the outer hull—they're cutting their way in. We have to hurry.'

She turned to the console and started the next sequence, powering up some of the peripheral circuits.

'Heads up.'

A readout appeared on her wrist: 'Estimated hull breach in 2 minutes... 1 minute 59 seconds...' They exchanged a glance then focused; working in unison, they moved through the rest of the sequence.

'1 minute 43 seconds... 1 minute 42 seconds...' Everything on Moira's panel went green and she turned, but Mastersson was still fiddling with something on the far side of the chamber. 'You not done yet?'

His face was grave. She checked the screen of her omni-block, half-guessing his words before she read them. 'This will only take a little while. There's nothing else you can do.'

'I'm not going.'

'It's delicate work. They'll come in shooting. If they get here before I'm finished, this has all been for nothing. When the reactor powers up, there's no way to stop it. I can trigger it remotely with my implant and we can get out of here. If you want to speed things up, go ahead and open the vehicle bay for me.'

Moira folded her arms. 'I can hold them off; give you the time you need.'

'It's too risky. The computer's reporting hull breaches in two locations. They'll be coming from different directions and you can't keep them all off my back. I'll catch up.'

She glowered at him, feet locked to the floor. 'There's another way.'

'No, there isn't. We know what they're capable of—they mustn't get hold of what's stored here. Please don't fight me, not now. You can rescue Keagan and Kishino—I don't have your ability to hurt people.'

The remark stung, but she knew how he meant it. She knew what it meant to her. 'This is my fault. I need to put this right.'

'They want me alive—they're not bombarding us with high-ex—there's a chance. There's no chance for Keagan or Kishino unless you go.'

If she stayed, maybe she could help. If she stayed, maybe her brother would die, maybe Masayoshi would never see his family. Maybe they were already dead. Deciding was tearing her apart.

He stood, resolute, looking directly at her. His expression was expectant, and confident.

She was not the person he thought her to be—she had always known that—she was harder, and darker. But looking at him now—looking at her—she wanted, for once, not to let him down. Their eyes locked for a second and years of shared experience passed between them.

Maybe, if...

Yeah, right.

She nodded, turned, and ran.

24

In seconds, she was leaping between the heaped junk in the common room, heading for a door that was already sliding open. There would be no tears. *'If you cry, you can't shoot straight. You wanna be dead too, girly?'* The imperatives of her training guided her feet as she took refuge in movement, focusing on escape.

The empty rectangular tube of the corridor opened before her and she plunged along it—leaving Mastersson behind made her feel like shite being flushed down a pipe. She slid to a stop, coming up just short of a second metal door. She heard the first closing behind her, followed by the resounding thud of a reinforced locking mechanism. It was too late to go back now, even though she wanted to.

There was an old fashioned keypad on the wall and a note on her omni-block: 'Happy Birthday. You've just won a set of wheels. With love, Mastersson. xxx'

Angrily, she punched her birthdate into the keypad. *No tears. At least he's still alive.* The second set of doors creaked as they juddered back, exposing the space beyond. 'Thanks, I think. What *is* that?'

'Your ride.'

'It's supposed to be yours.'

'I never thought I'd be entertaining; you're my first guest and there's only one seat. They're close—gotta go. Play nicely and don't scratch it. I'll see you later.'

She stood, staring at the omni-block for longer than she should, but there was nothing else. *You've lost people before—this isn't any different.* The words were empty.

Walking into the dimly lit space, the bulkhead doors closed behind her. Facing her from the shadows, a dark cavernous mouth and an array of tubes. She walked around the vehicle and met a wall of wheels, three of them, each a head taller than she was. As she came closer, her boots disturbed a layer of dust that clouded around her feet. The same dust covered the machine, as thick as her finger.

She climbed the stepladder; with each step her boots dimly sounded out a deadened 'thunk' rather than ringing on clean metal. She coughed as she reached the top. A transparent bubble containing a harness chair perched atop spidery metal strut-work. The lights overhead flickered, briefly went out, before coming on more brightly. Bolted to the back was a large tank and… *Oh, shite.* The mess of tubes and a metre-wide flared nozzle of an ancient rocket engine were also covered in dust. *Why do I get the feeling this has* never *been driven?* A thin sheet of metal was hammered around the rocket housing—apparently as a safety barrier between the high temperature exhaust and the fuel tank. *No, not reassuring.* Keagan's boyish voice played through her mind: *'Sarge says always check your equipment. If it don't work when the other guy's does, you're dead.'* Nearly all Sarge's expressions had ended in 'you're dead'. A quick examination of the fuel tank confirmed her fears. The dust on the side had long-dried tracks in it—either fractures or the seals were shot. She hit it with her knuckle. A hollow sound echoed from inside. *Typical Mastersson: build it but don't test it.* The sound of cutters broke her train of thought. Mastersson's killers—*no, captors*—were already in the passage. She wondered how long the bulkhead doors would last.

Balancing on the top rung of the ladder, she scanned the dark recesses of the makeshift garage. There were several cargo containers piled in the far corner. A fluid slide and she crouched on the floor before springing up and sprinting across the open space, sneezing as she went. She glanced over her shoulder. A line of glowing molten metal oozed down one of the doors from a black gash that flashed white with heat from a cutter. It would not be long before the hole was large enough to push a gun barrel or a grenade through.

She scraped the dust off three sides of the nearest container before she found the display. *Just mechanical parts.* Rubbing another two canisters revealed only out-of-date generative protoplasm and industrial cleaner. *Like that was ever going to happen.*

The cutter was halfway around its circle. Not long and they would have a clear line of fire. She clambered over the front row of containers and saw the sign on the wall: 'Fuel Line'. She grabbed the hose and hit the release with her foot. It was heavy but flowed easily from the wall as she hauled it behind her, until it stopped. Her feet slid in the dust and she dropped into a crawl to gain the purchase needed. Shouts came from behind the doors although she could not make out the words over the noise of the cutter; it was three quarters around the circle. She pulled harder, but the cumbersome line pulled back. *I need more time.* Bracing the line with one hand, she felt inside her holster for her handgun. *Shite. Probably shaken loose by a sonic.* She hoped Mastersson had found it and was putting it to good use. *But that doesn't help me.*

She spun around and sat, digging in her heels and jerking the line again and again. On the sixth tug something in the mechanism finally gave, sending her toppling backward. She rolled with the movement, bracing against the pull to stand, before shuffling past the rear of the vehicle towards the doors.

Moira pointed the nozzle at the gash and the flaming cutter. More shouts. Her finger squeezed the trigger. She kept the burst short—an arc of inflammable liquid connecting her to the ignition source threatened to incinerate the whole vehicle bay. The cutter's light disappeared.

Damn.

The fuel hit the door, still glowing molten orange, and hissed as it vaporised on contact. She shielded her eyes as the flammable mist reached its flashpoint and exploded. She was gratified to hear more than one scream. *Now they'll think twice about trying to get through*—her sense of triumph vanished—*and instead set enough charges to bring the whole place down before I can get clear.*

She turned back to the wheeled—*what the hell do you call* that? Leaning against the line proved useless as its coils tried to snake in the opposite direction. When she was a child she had wanted to be more like Keagan and the other boys in the squad—she was quicker but envied their strength. She had learnt to stay alive by becoming faster, smarter, tougher, harder. Locking the line in the crook of one arm, she pulled up the omni-block interface for her smartboots—not standard issue, these could grip almost anything.

'Computer, reverse boots' vacuum function, fifty percent power, and activate nano-adhesive.' The blown dust billowed around her, her feet gripping the floor securely for the first time. Muscles straining, she wrestled the recalcitrant line into submission and several steps later had it straightened out and connected to the intake valve on the side of the six-wheeler. She hit 'Pump' and looked over her shoulder. She did not spot the snooper right away, its slim head protruding a few centimetres from the gash. *How long's that been there?* It withdrew and the cutter started again, sounding louder than before through the humming in her ears. Less than a ninety degree arc of metal remained before they were through. And there was nothing she could do to stop them.

It was probably futile, but she raised her omni-block to her mouth anyway. 'Mastersson?'

The display remained empty.

It's just a dampener field—no signal. But she knew, in combat situations, chaos reigned: safeties were off, trigger fingers twitched, bullets and energy beams strayed. *What if he fights back? What if he doesn't cooperate and...? What if the reactor blows before...? He's not dead. I know he's not dead.*

All she could do was wait.

25

The cutter had nearly completed the circle. The usual catcalls of hunters cornering prey were absent. Someone had done her the courtesy of sending professionals. The half-filled fuel tank was leaking again, despite Moira's efforts at patching with generative protoplasm—it really was out-of-date. New dark tracks cut the dust on the tank-side where volatile liquid had sprung afresh. She disengaged the fuel line and dropped the end in a puddle of protoplasm, which was tacky enough to hold it as it spewed flammable liquid in front of the doors. She sprinted to the six-wheeler and threw herself up the ladder, snapping back the manual access clip of the driving bubble. The flimsy clack of it resealing was not reassuring. *At least the harness looks like it will hold.* The straps tightened automatically when she shoved the fastening home. She blinked when the heads up display sprang into life—she had not expected Mastersson to bother, then realised how much in character it was: put a computer inside a homebrew death trap.

'Computer, open outer doors.' She could just hear her own words.

Text flashed across the HUD: 'Voice recognition identifies Moira Dolan. Welcome to the Mastersson Sand Cruiser—a wheelie great ride. Data-file download available, do you wish to proceed?'

Grief. 'Yes, proceed.' *Sent after I left, but that doesn't mean he's still alive. No time to read it now.*

The 'Complete' icon flashed above her omni-block. She looked up; the doors were only a metre apart and moving slowly, struggling to shift years of piled sand.

'Computer, rear view on HUD.'

'Acknowledged.'

The cutter's white light was gone. A still-glowing metal plug slid outwards, before falling and rolling across the floor. The exit was still too narrow to allow the sand cruiser through.

'Computer, initiate engine ignition, minimal thrust, brakes on full.' There was a sputtering from somewhere. 'Computer, reinitialise engine ignition. Repeat previous instruction set.'

More sputtering. Dull thuds echoed as shots ricocheted from one of the tyres. Designed to hit rocks at rocket speeds, bullets would be no problem. The jury-rigged fuel tank was a different matter—they no longer seemed interested in taking her alive. Dry, her throat croaked he words. 'Computer, repeat previous instructions.'

Still nothing, except the empty 'chuck-chuck-chuck' of some valve behind her left ear. More bullets—the sharp rapport of projectiles on metal. *Shite, sparks.* 'Computer, increase power to ignition circuitry two hundred percent and then open propellant flow valve.'

'Warning: these actions—'

'Dammit, Computer! Override safety protocols and carry out instructions. Now!'

As projectiles whined around her, she waited—tense and nervous. About to ask the computer for a temperature readout, she heard sparking behind her. Vibrations thrummed through her seat as the old fuel pump started up. Another tense few seconds passed. *At least the outer doors are open.*

The force of the ignition eased her back into her seat, filling the bay behind with smoke and flame. She clenched her teeth as the pressure increased, hurling the vehicle outside like a child's toy. On the HUD, fire spewed into the opening behind her only to curl back, greedy fingers reaching for the fuel tank.

They were snuffed out by the pressure wave from the bunker's exploding fuel store. It kicked her in the back as it hit, sweeping the rear wheels up the side of a banking dune. Gripping and fighting, she twisted the controls. The six-wheeler began to tip, threatening to roll. She gripped harder, driving the front wheels into sand but still the vehicle overbalanced. She flipped the throttle to minimum as she spoke,

'Computer, initiate parallel driving.'

'Please clarify: do you mean crab mode?'

'Yes, crab mode!' All six wheels realigned and she accelerated, righting the sand cruiser as it rose up the dune. She crested the top with wheels airborne, but the suspension caught her gently and she powered ahead, the rear view showing only rapidly receding sand. *But the troops, probably mercs, must have transport.*

The HUD flashed a warning: 'Bunker generator detonation imminent: please ensure you have reached the minimum safe distance.'

'Computer, what safe distance?'

'Approximately two klicks.' There was no point asking for a countdown. She would either make it, or not.

'Computer, standard driving mode.' She caught and controlled the skid as the wheels realigned and opened the throttle. *Okay, Mastersson, let's see if this is more than a toy.*

The sand cruiser soared over the crest of another dune, gliding for several seconds before the wheels hit dirt. She pointed it straight ahead, locking her arms as the acceleration compressed her insides. *Shite, this thing can move.* The ground blurred and still she accelerated, out across the open plain stretching level to the horizon. Mastersson had done a superb job with the ride. Despite the wheels skipping over rocks the size of her head, she felt only a steady buffeting inside the bubble. *It's like flying an atmospheric fighter.*

'Bunker detonated.'

Seconds later, the earth bucked. The six-wheeler left the ground. Stones kicked up by the passing subterranean pressure wave tore into the fuselage. Two hit the bubble, leaving star fractures. *Please don't let that be his grave.* She did not know who she petitioned, or care.

She eased back on the throttle as she watched the ground come up to meet her. The wheels hit hard, the suspension struts grinding the dirt as they tried, and failed, to compensate. She heard the snapping of metal and a central wheel began to shake. The vibrations resonated through every part of the frame and the once stable horizon became a blur of vertical movement. A crack. One of the stars had a tail, snapping its way across her visual field. Another split extended from the other impact site, growing with every vibration. She eased the throttle back, the cruiser almost coasting, before checking her rear-view. *If the detonation left a hole that big, surely it took out any support vehicles?* There was no way to know.

She had traveled another half-klick before she saw the buzzer floating off to her left, matching her pace. The sleek craft pivoted on its axis, bringing its primary weapons array to bear. *Shite.* Moira gunned the throttle and the six-wheeler shot forward as a line of detonations crossed the ground behind her. *They must have weapons lock—warning shots.* The loose wheel finally broke free, careening over the ground and bouncing into the distance. The vibrations changed frequency and intensified, ramming her teeth together like an ore crusher's. Sounding like a machine pistol going off, the cracks in the screen leapt the remaining distance. They joined, opened, and wind rushed in, tearing the top off the bubble. Moira threw the cruiser into a sideways skid, hoping the large wheels would shield her from debris as she came spinning to a stop in a cloud of dust.

A helmeted face appeared on the HUD. 'Stand down. Exit your vehicle immediately. Lie face down on the ground. Try anything and I will not hesitate to kill you.' The face blinked out.

Not big on conversation. She gave a thumbs-up before wriggling, as if struggling with the harness. She scrabbled around the cab and under the seat. Mastersson had left her a blaster, some rations, and a first aid kit. *I can't conceal the blaster's power source at close range, and throwing food at them isn't going to work.* She pressed the release button on the straps and bent forward to cover her movements. The first aid kit was beaten up but opened at her touch. *The contents better be good.* She found the canister she wanted and gripped each end before twisting, letting the liquids inside run together as the internal seal broke. A quick, vigorous shake and its status light turned green. She sat up straight. Despite her eye coverings, it was difficult to see through the dust. *There!* The buzzer hovered a few metres away, its internal rotors whipping up a miniature sandstorm. Its weapons array pointed unerringly at where she sat. The blaster was still tempting but would not scratch the buzzer's armour.

Moira clipped the canister to her belt and screamed as she hauled herself clear of the shattered cockpit and onto the ladder. Her right leg dangled uselessly, and she cried out as she hopped down each rung on her left. She hit the dirt hard, her body folding, arms protecting her leg. She lay there moaning, and waiting.

The buzzer alighted on the sand, its engine slowing slightly to a dull thrum. She could make out two helmeted figures inside. A door swung upward like a bird's wing and the passenger stepped out, pausing to maintain his balance against the buffeting winds generated by the rotors. The buzzer's weapons remained trained on her. The figure, a man by his build, walked towards her in a wide arc, unholstering his sidearm as he closed the distance. Moira remained still, other than to draw an occasional gasping breath.

The man pointed his gun at her. 'What's wrong with your leg?'

She replied through gritted teeth. 'Broken. I've got a canister—pneumo-cast—I need to use it before I can walk.'

His jaw set and eyes hidden behind reflective lenses, she could not read his expression. Eventually, he nodded. 'Throw the canister here.'

She kept her expression neutral as she worked it free of her belt and rolled it across the ground. He took three steps and picked it up, his gun barrel never wavering from her face. After a brief inspection, he threw the canister onto the ground. 'Don't take too long.'

She allowed her leg to drag behind until she reached it, crying out as she stretched the last few centimetres. Her fingers closed around the tube and she tried to bend and reach her leg. She lay back in the dirt, breathing hard. 'I can't. Please, help.'

He paused, as if weighing the threat she presented. He lowered his gun as he stepped forward. *Apparently a short woman with a broken leg doesn't scare him—at least not enough.* As he bent towards her, she knocked the gun from his hand.

He snarled, 'I'll break your other leg, bitch.'

'Who said it was broken?' She wound her leg back before propelling her booted foot under his solar plexus. He staggered back, collapsing to his knees, winded. Moira rolled. An instant later the buzzer's weapons array blitzed the ground where she had been. She guesstimated the distance and kept rolling. The buzzer fired again, the rounds hitting dirt and then pounding into the body of the kneeling passenger, his armoured torso shielding her from the shells. *And now the pilot goes into shock.* The thumping ended as the pilot stopped firing. In one easy movement she came to her knees, took up the canister of pneumo-cast, and hurled it into the air intake of the buzzer's rotor. She saw the pilot smile as she heard the rotor chewing easily through the canister casing. Cat-like, she smiled back. *The gel should start to set about... now.* Like a wounded animal, the buzzer screamed, the shrieking of metal tearing against metal. It bucked wildly, nose pitching forwards into the dirt. Moira got to her feet and started to run. She gained little speed on the uneven ground so she threw herself down, trusting to dumb luck. She turned her head in time to see pieces of razor sharp rotor blade exiting from all sides of the craft. One came through the cockpit, spraying bits of the pilot into the air on the way out. A hiss of white gas plumed and the red-orange flames inside were instantly snuffed out. With the sound of metal rasping against stone, the buzzer rolled over and lay there, dead. *At least the fire suppression system is working.*

✳

The sand cruiser's bubble was cramped and uncomfortable, stuffed with the equipment Moira had salvaged from the buzzer. With a wheel missing, the suspension shot, and a shattered cabin, it took several hours to make the distant landing site—Jane's stealth systems were good, but not perfect. *Not that it makes any difference now; they got Mastersson because of me.* She locked the thought down and filed the last few hours with the other memories that threatened her ability to keep going, to survive; still her vision blurred. Angry, she wiped her eyes on the back of her glove. *Damn you, Mastersson.* Part of her wanted to bury herself like Keagan had—after their parents were killed, after the war. He found his solace in myriad criminal and chemical distractions. She would not settle for such a neutered existence, so she decided to change things. By looking forward, she never had to look back. Mastersson was a wound in her side. Dead, she could forget him. But he had skills and information—he was useful. *If one buzzer managed to get clear there might have been another.* Hope stopped her cauterising the hole. Most people needed hope's light to live, but some things you do not want to see. It was easier, to shut them in dark places where they would not grow—the long-dormant ghosts she was still not ready to face. *It's a job. Get it done and Mastersson, Keagan, and the Kishino family come out alive.*

There was nothing to see at the landing site, just more flat sand and rocks, but that was the point. She slid down the ladder and spoke the code into her omni-block. The vibrations came up through her feet, building until her knees shook. The air around her began to pulse, a deep thrumming she could feel in her ribcage. Ripples passed across the surface of the sand in front of her, dislodging even the bigger stones. Finally, the upper surface of *Flaky Jane* was visible, sand falling in rivulets down her sides, and still she kept rising. The sonic micro-emitters in her hull powered down. *That's a neat trick—Mastersson would've...* would *like it.* Moira ferried her gear between the cruiser and Jane's cargo hold, stowing the most useful items in her small cabin. In a few minutes, she was ready to go.

'Welcome back, Moira.'

'Jane, seal the door. Engage active atmospheric camouflage and scan-disruption, and match our heat profile to the environment. That's a mouthful. Jane, from now on label those instructions "Atmospheric Cam Protocol".' The chair straps enfolded her as she sat. 'Jane, manual control for take-off.'

'Acknowledged.'

Moira eased off Dustbowl's surface. She was desperate to leave, but had to keep their airspeed low so Jane's camouflage systems were not overwhelmed. They could easily fool a casual observer, but if subjected to an active scan they would only buy her time. She hoped there were no other flight-capable vehicles nearby. *How many people do you need to take on a short-arsed girl and a tekhead?*

Atmospheric conditions were calm and the flying easy, so she took the time to define several more camouflage protocols. *But I can't hide forever, so where next?*

'Jane, display latest file downloaded to my omni-block.' *Let's see what Mastersson has to say for himself.* She told herself she felt nothing. It almost worked.

'Acknowledged.'

She had expected some pre-prepared, 'If you are watching this then my enemies have me and you must go free…' speech. Instead, there were just a few lines of text. *His last thoughts before I left the bunker, sent from his implant.*

'Helen knows what to do with the sample. Now they've found us they may try to find her. I suggest you move Helen and the sample to the following location. Feel free to be persuasive if she's stubborn, but don't damage her, please? Good luck, Moira. I… …take care.'

Jane read out, '-23, -30, -54.' the coordinates for the 51 Arietis system.

Moira sat, rigid and lips pursed. 'Jane, search onboard records only of—' She had to think briefly to remember his first name; it had been so long since she had used it. '—Gustav Mastersson. Cross-reference with "Helen" and display her profile.'

'Helen Mastersson, former wife of Gustav Mastersson, was born Helen Dewart on the fifteenth…'

Moira did not hear the rest.

26

Adab, the 51 Arietis System

Late evening was Helen's favourite time—a stillness after work was over—but now the dying embers of the day brought no consolation.

The deep indigo of the sky faded to an empty blackness pierced by crystal points of light. The air was crisp, clear, and still. Sitting out on the balcony normally lulled her mind, cleansing away the concerns of the past few hours. But not tonight. Focusing her attention inward, she tried again to find the antidote to her worry. She had called three times in the last two hours, and every time her implant reported that Gustav was unreachable.

Delaying contact had seemed like a good idea. It was not like him to be back in touch straight away, and any attempt to press him about their future would only push them apart. But Moira's brother changed things. *'We think he's fallen in with some bad people.'* Gustav's life was entangling with hers again and now she was unravelling. She could no longer bear not knowing. *What are my options?* The only way she could deal with this was to break it down and analyse it, but this was not happening in the controlled conditions of a lab.

Another sip of the sharp tasting juice brought with it the hope of some clarity. Querying her implant with new combinations and rephrasings of Moira, Keagan, possible locations and connections, she waited. Her answers were the same as before: *Not enough data to determine identity.* Just the same old loop.

She swilled the juice around the base of the glass, collecting the bits that remained, tipped it back and swallowed. Above, the distant blanketing of stars swathed a cold emptiness. She turned away and retreated inside towards her workroom, now her refuge.

Hippoc Bioceuticals had willingly paid for the installation, despite the expense, and Helen paid them back with longer hours. The muted magenta and cream décor of the entrance matched the rest of her home so she could forget it when not feeling inspired to test her latest theory.

She was retina and DNA scanned as she moved inside. Decontamination in the airlock followed as did being sprayed with an organic shield membrane after her mask was in place. The lab computer was kept secure on a local network isolated from the grid—the only access in person via the terminal. She checked Gustav's sample in the store area. A thought initiated the research status summary: *Sample work-up successful. Analysis complete.*

'Finally!' *Computer, display a 3D model of the molecule.* Moira's guess appeared correct: the discovery of the sample on Keagan's bedding and clothing meant he had been taking it. *Pinpoint likely places of origin and extrapolate effect of sample ingestion upon human physiology.*

Working...

She waited, but her answer was flashing lights and a message on visual, aural, and mental channels:

'Alert! Unauthorised access to main area. Please stay calm. You are safe behind the security door. Law Enforcement has been notified and will be with you in approximately five minutes.'

They've found me, already! Gustav wasn't being paranoid. Computer, display a video feed of the intruders.

A single figure was moving like a dancer across the room, pirouetting between pieces of cover with practiced grace. *She's slight, and she looks like she hasn't washed for a while. Not exactly what I was expecting. Computer, open the locks on the outer decontamination chamber door.*

Helen watched the figure make a circuit of her home. She moved quickly from room to room, passing places where valuables or confidential documents might be stored. *She's looking for someone, not something.* The intruder, dressed in a black one-piece with her dark hair tied back in a loose ponytail, approached the outer lab door; it looked like every other. *That's it, just a little further.*

The antechamber inside was a little minimalist but styled like the rest of Helen's home. The intruder stepped cautiously across the threshold.

Computer, close and lock the outer door. Initiate gaseous flush stage of the decontamination cycle, then suspend until I give further instructions. In seconds, the small woman had her handgun out and released a barrage at the security doors. Helen winced, closing her eyes to the bright flashes and digging her nails harder into her palms with each blast.

Quiet. Helen unscrewed her eyes. Surveillance showed the small woman turning her gun on the control panel. The impacts were muted as the projectiles shattered the casing of the unit and disappeared inside. Helen leant in to the image. The woman was kneeling, attempting to make connections between the components behind the shattered panel. When this had no effect, she lashed out, destroying the remnants of the circuit board. Helen swallowed—the blow was powerful and precise. Did she feel it through the wall? *Assassins come in all shapes and sizes.* The woman stood, hunting for another way out as her chest moved in and out like a piston. *It won't be long until she passes out.* Realising she was trapped, the woman began pointing at her mouth as her lips moved.

Computer, play audio from decontamination chamber. The woman dropped to all fours. On the threshold of hearing, between empty rasping breaths, Helen thought she could make out some words:

'…mast…er…son… … … sent…'

Mastersson sent? Computer, get some air into that chamber and open the door!

Caution. Last action aborted due to ongoing security situation.

Helen was relieved to see the figure seemed to be breathing again. *Computer, remove alert status. Notify security everything is normal and their assistance is no longer required, and open the inner lab door.*

Unable to comply. Standard security protocol mandates all reports of a security breach must be investigated. Staff safety protocol prevents execution of your last instruction.

They'll find her. Computer, opening the outer lab door will not compromise my safety. Activate intercom. 'Sorry about cutting off your air. It's Moira, isn't it?'

The woman gasped in lungfuls of air before speaking. 'Why do people ask questions like that? Whether I say "yes" or "no", I could be anyone.'

'True, but Gustav told me I could recognise you by your accent. Law Enforcement are on their way. I'll instruct the computer to open a secure storage area in the hallway, through the back. You should be safe in there until I can get rid of them. Look, I'm sorry abou—'

'Fine.' And without another word she left, weaving an unsteady course towards her hiding place.

*

It took Helen several minutes to dismiss the security team and open the storage area.

Moira slid from the narrow space. 'About bloody time.' She scanned Helen from head to foot—dismissing her in an instant—before surging to her feet.

Helen stepped back and lowered her proffered hand. 'There was no other choice. I'm sorry it took so long to get rid of them. They've set the computer system running a full diagnostic, but we only have a little time. Is Gustav all right?'

'If we need to get out of here sharpish, then we don't have time for questions.'

'Leave? Are they—the ones who took your brother—are they coming here?'

Moira squared her shoulders and took a deep breath. 'Yes, probably. They are quite capable of killing anyone linked to Mastersson. The danger to you is real. Mastersson… He wants me to keep you safe. I'll tell you the rest when we're out of here. Take this.' Moira handed Helen a fist sized package. 'It's a re-breather. You'll be able to breathe normally in and out of water. Put it on now because it won't be as easy later.'

'I don't understand. Why do I need this?'

Moira took another deep breath. 'Shite, I just love working with civilians. Our ride off this rock is at the bottom of the lake. There's a rappelling line hanging over the side of your balcony. The people after us have powerful corporate connections, and The Collective has links with Hippoc Bioceuticals. There could be sleeper agents here. They've already tried to kill me twice. Now, stop being dumb; I need your head in the game.'

Helen bit back what she really wanted to say. *She turns up out of nowhere, expects me to drop my life at her say-so, and treats me like a child while she does it. I can't think why Gustav would count this woman as a friend.* She took the re-breather. 'How does this work?'

'Put your nose into the depression and press the button.'

Helen started as the mechanism instantly reshaped itself and flowed around the back of her head, covering her eyes, nose, mouth, and ears. Claustrophobic, she reached up, her instinct to tear the mask from her face.

Moira gripped her wrists. 'Look at me. Relax. The air doesn't flow as easily as in a suit. Inhale, exhale, slowly and deeply.'

Helen wanted to break free, but the woman's grip was too strong. She forced herself to draw in air—it tasted artificial and metallic—but the mask was comfortable and breathing easy enough with a steady rhythm.

Moira released her, leaving alternating pink and white stripes on her skin. 'Collect anything you need, and if you find anything useful that could help Keagan and Mastersson, I suggest you grab it and destroy any records you leave behind. Do it quickly.'

Helen flushed, hating her sudden feeling of incompetence. 'There's some results in the lab and a few personal effects. I won't be long.' She felt Moira's eyes burning into her back as she left. *What did I ever do to her? Is she always this hostile?*

She dashed into the lab, her mental commands deactivating the lock protocol, bypassing the door controls Moira destroyed. She threw the sample into a transport flask and paused to regard the intricate holographic molecule still spinning in the air. *What are you, to cause so much trouble?*

Helen looked around—years of work and research, her career. Gustav had told her about the viral subroutine he hid on her system. A single command and everything she had ever researched at Hippoc would disappear from the local data-core. Her company had copies of her summaries and results, of course, but all her notes and unpublished theories—everything that was *her*—would be gone. *I can't, I just can't. Computer, override isolation protections and establish an external link via my implant. Download a copy of all data relating to research sample MAST01 to my implant memory. Encrypt and send a copy of the entire database to Kimberley Landred with the following message: 'Kimberley, I've had to go away for a while. Please keep this safe. I'll explain everything when I get back. Thank you.'* She followed with a single thought that set the virus eating away her life. She fervently hoped it was one she could come back to.

She turned at the sound of footsteps.

'What *are* you doing?' Moira demanded. 'We have to go.'

'I just have to grab some clothes—I don't want to end up looking… like you.' She was cross, flustered, and the words were out before she could stop them. Helen watched Moira's hands ball into fists, but her expression carried more disdain than anger.

'Get your soft corporate arse onto the balcony and down that line or, so help me, I'll throw you off.'

The women's eyes locked, but time was running out. Helen shouldered her way past Moira who offered no resistance, simply flowing around her.

'At least you have some fight in you. Hold onto that, you're going to need it.'

Helen felt the woman's palm pressing into the small of her back, hustling her along. She shrugged her off and sped up until she was on the balcony. Without stopping, she reached for the mechanism hanging from the top of the line. Moira stood back and watched as she fumbled with it. Wordlessly, Helen thrust it at her. Three deft movements, a couple of clicks, and a tug and Helen was pulled forward a pace.

'Right, you're done. This'—Moira indicated a lever—'lowers you faster the harder you press. I'm going to follow and discourage anyone that wants to look over the railing. If you feel my boot soles on the top of your head, you're going too slowly.' Moira took her gun from its holster and gestured to the edge. 'Remember, no implant communication or we'll be found. Over you go.'

Determined not to give Moira any more ammunition, Helen quickly climbed over the rail.

'Good. Brace your feet—a little wider—and push off. Squeeze the lever as you do. Don't look—'

Helen froze. The lake, one hundred metres below, rushed up to meet her, before vertigo dropped it back taking her stomach with it.

'Helen! Eyes straight ahead. Look at the rock face, nothing else. Now push off... and press the lever. Good. Again. Again. Don't stop and think. Just do it. Again.'

With each push and release Helen felt the world swing round her as the rock face blurred, slowed, and blurred again as her feet left, stopped, and came back towards it.

She heard Moira's voice, shouting from overhead. 'Okay, the line to your left may whip. Don't worry, it's just me coming down.'

Curiosity told her to look, but fear glued her eyes to the cliff side. She was sweating now. The grip of her hands on the line and the lever felt slick and uncertain. The other line flicked her shoulder. She glanced over and her limbs went leaden. The wall of purple-grey stone stretched out, disappearing into the gloom of a night only dimly lit by stars. Beneath her was an empty void. She tried to work out how far down the cliff she was, but now her face was against the rock her perceptions seemed distorted—from her balcony all she could remember was the huge sense of space;

reaching the bottom seemed impossible. She hung, helpless, like a fish on a line.

Some boots, then Moira, came into view. She reached across and rested a hand on Helen's shoulder. 'All you have to do is begin to sway, in and out, slowly. Just push with your legs, then relax.'

Her voice was softer than before, and Helen felt the rushing in her head slow, the dizziness retreating a little. 'You can do it, gently—keep your feet on the rock until you've got the rhythm. That's it. Now look straight at the rock. Keep the rhythm going.'

'You must think I'm pathetic.'

'I froze my first time.'

'You did? How long have you been doing this?'

'Since I was eight. Don't take your eyes off the rock. Now you've found the rhythm, push off—that's it. Now push off and press the lever a little. And you're moving.'

Helen felt herself drop, but she was in control and, with her confidence growing, she allowed each fall to get a little longer. In a few minutes they reached the bottom, an irregular strip of rocks piled at the base of the cliff holding back the water a couple of metres away.

Her eyes adjusted to the gloom—above the dark wall loomed over her. She looked away as another wave of dizziness threatened. 'Coming down was hard enough. How did you get up there? You can't have climbed.'

'I've been climbing since I was nine, free-climbing since I was ten. Now, hush your mouth a second.' Moira's words were blunt, but Helen heard no insult in the tone. 'It's really easy to get disorientated under water.' She unclipped both ropes before attaching another—retrieved from her belt—linking their harnesses. 'We can't use lights in case we're seen. Just follow where I lead. Can you swim?'

'I'm not completely useless outside a lab, you know.'

'Just checking.' Moira turned and disappeared into the water, the line trailing after her. *Does this woman ever apologise?*

Determined not to embarrass herself again, Helen followed before Moira pulled her in.

27

Helen thought she was a strong swimmer, but soon the line was taut, tugging at her harness as Moira forged ahead. Although the lake was clear—kept that way for the workers and their families by the company's massive filtration works on the far side—it was pitch black near the muddy bottom, too far from the dim starlight above. The re-breather was advanced, easily interfacing with her implant. Switching to infra-red did nothing to increase visibility, except enabling her to spot a few previously hidden fish.

The line had gone slack. *What happened?* Helen gripped it and tried hauling herself through the still water, only speeding up as the line tightened. Ahead, a shimmering glow. Closing in, an undulating shadow resolved into Moira, who held her position with the easy strokes of an accomplished swimmer—the light of an omni-block transcribing graceful arcs with each movement. *Is that how she's navigating? It's so primitive.*

Moira was moving towards her now, extending her free arm. Helen paddled backwards, but Moira was too quick—her hand catching the side of Helen's mask. 'Don't be stupid; we have to touch to talk—sonic transmission, conducts by contact. Why did you tow me back, are you hurt? Is your re-breather not working?'

Something inside Helen wanted to crawl into a deep hole and hide. 'The line went slack. I thought you were in trouble…'

'I'm not a tekhead with an implant. I don't swim as fast when I have to get my bearings on this.' She waved the omni-block under Helen's nose, a little too close for comfort.

'But why—?'

'We don't have time, and it's none of your damn business. Can we go?' Without waiting for an answer Moira pulled away, breaking their connection, before disappearing into the gloom.

Charming. Helen trailed after, feeling too much like a pet on a leash.

✻

By the dim light of the omni-block, Helen watched Moira apparently tracing a symbol onto a rock. Spaceships were designed to tolerate high mechanical stresses and, being airtight against the vacuum of space, there was no logical reason why being deeply submerged would be a problem. However, she had never heard of a ship that looked and felt like an underwater boulder.

Moira stopped and touched Helen's facemask. 'We'll have to wait until the airlock fills with water—shouldn't take long.' An indicator on her omni-block went green. 'After you.'

Helen swam into the dimly lit hole; it was cramped with both of them inside. The door slid shut and she felt the faintest of vibrations transmitted through the water. Above, a pocket of air grew rapidly as pumps evacuated the liquid. As soon as her face was clear, she retracted her re-breather, glad to be free of the constraint. The air smelt of ship. She tried to forget about all the unpleasant things she knew about onboard recycling. *I can't blame Gustav for hating space travel. It's not pleasant, even if I don't get space-sick.*

'Welcome home, Moira and guest.'

'Thanks, Jane; that will be two for dinner.' Moira shrugged. 'The previous owner was a paranoid-eccentric. The first time I tried to fly her, Jane nearly killed me. If I'd replied differently, she would have incinerated you. Don't touch anything.'

Helen smiled—it faded as she realised Moira was completely serious. 'Is there anything else I should know?'

Moira started to strip off her gear and stow it in a locker. She nodded at another in the corner. 'Don't go anywhere or do anything without my say-so. Don't look at me like that. Jane's a potential death-trap and I'm nowhere near finished working out her configuration; she looks like a heap, but she's full of cutting edge covert-ops equipment. I've been around ships for years, but never seen anything like this.'

Helen let her facial muscles relax. *Maybe this can be turned around after all.* 'Covert-ops. They use bio-agents—poisons, neurotoxins, and the like. Does this ship have a biosciences terminal?'

'Who knows? I find new things every time I go looking. How far did you get with your work up of the sample?'

'Far enough that, with the right equipment, I should be able to find some answers. Gustav will be so pleased when we tell him—I know contacting him now isn't safe, but I can't wait to see him.'

Moira's lips thinned. 'Yeah, well first we need to get you kitted up.' She reached into another locker and pulled out a folded flight suit. 'It will automatically—'

'—adjust to fit. I know. This isn't my first time.' Helen took the suit. 'Can I change somewhere down there?' She indicated a door. 'Or will I be disintegrated on entering?'

'You can use my… the cabin. Don't open anything… and don't take too long. We can't go anywhere until you're togged and in a flight chair.'

Helen quickly suited up. Moira's look of surprised approval was gratifying. She was still conscious of Moira's gaze as she slid into the co-pilot's seat and felt the padding and her flight suit morph into a single unit, cinched by the harnesses. She only half-listened as Moira took Jane through a series of standard pre-flight checks, although she wondered how many ships' checklists included 'stealth protocols' and an 'impeller system'.

Her eyes wandered around the cockpit. The ship really did look the part: panels were scuffed and worn smooth with decades of use. Two large fuselage patches were flaking with age and looked incapable of holding out the cold vacuum of space. *Unless they're cosmetic. I* hope *they are cosmetic.* Several internal panels were missing, exposing the guts of the ship. Arterial cables and conduits threaded across the floor, walls, and ceiling; in places they were tied to struts or glued directly to bulkheads.

Moira must have caught her expression. 'Jane's been through a lot.'

She's proud of this… mess. 'How did it get you here?'

'She's a lot tougher, and smarter, than she looks.'

'And old. I'm no engineer, but the latest scientific equipment won't interface with outdated models. A few years ago, I tried to retrieve information from an ancient database using a new terminal—the information was erased and the terminal died. Isn't there a risk using these jury-rigged systems?'

'Normally, yes, but whoever put Jane together was some kind of insane genius. She's riddled with interfaces and crossover boxes I've never seen before.'

'So if we hit even a simple problem, you can't fix it.'

'Depends what it is, but maybe not. Look, either get off now or stop complaining—Jane's the only way to get to Mastersson—it's your choice.'

'I want to see Gustav.'

'Good, so do I. Jane, ahead six knots. Take us to the surface, engage atmospheric stealth protocol, then retrace our entry trajectory back to deep space. Monitor the integrity of our stealth profile, and maintain the maximum velocity that won't degrade performance.'

'Understood.'

There was no sensation of movement; the lake was still and the ship tilted at a barely perceptible angle. After several minutes of awkward silence, the colours on the viewscreen changed from matt black to ultramarine as the first glimmers of weak starlight began to penetrate the depths.

This woman is impossible. Helen tried to resist the urge to tap her fingers. *It's going to be a long trip. I need to do something.* She tried, but the ship's computer refused to interface with her implant.

'Moira, your guest has attempted to gain unauthorised access to my systems. Should I terminate or incapacitate?'

'Jane, neither! Her intentions aren't hostile.' Moira shot Helen a look. 'I thought I told you not to try anything. You're lucky I downgraded Jane's automatic threat responses.'

'You could have turned them off!'

'Actually, no I can't—"off" isn't an option. When I said to check with me first, I wasn't on some petty power trip.'

'Okay, sorry!'

Helen bore Moira's accusing gaze for several seconds before she relented. The prospect of a silent war lasting days in the cramped confines of the ship seemed to soften her a little.

'Jane, allow Helen Mastersson access to your non-critical systems.'

'Is that wise?'

'What? Jane, please just follow the instruction.'

'Acknowledged.'

'Does it have a personality chip?'

'I doubt it; her computer core is one of the original parts and was built before personality chips became fashionable. There are times I wonder, though.'

Helen felt her implant report the status change. *Computer, give me the specifications of any onboard scientific terminals.*

Her only reply, total silence.

'Is the computer's interface working? I'm not getting anything.'

'She won't take mental commands—her original owner may have used a hard-coded implant. It took days for me to work out the verbal interface. She likes you to call her "Jane".'

'Would she like me to say "please", too?'

'Not sure, but if you're too sarky she may irradiate you while you sleep.'

Shaking her head slightly, Helen tried again. 'Jane, please give me the specifications of any onboard scientific terminals.'

'I am equipped with a Mobi-Lab-Tek prototype, mark thirteen. There have been several modifications made since installation. Do you require details?'

The viewscreen suddenly cleared and filled with stars, the remnants of the water swept away as the ship reoriented and began to accelerate, pressing Helen gently back into her seat. Other than the change in engine noise and acceleration, the transition to flight had been barely noticeable.

'No, Jane, thank you. That's impressive. My company—now probably my ex-company—is only just trialling the mark fourteen. How did you find this ship?'

'Dumped on my local dock-side. My ex-boss thought he was fobbing me off with some junk, or he knew about the security protocols and wanted to kill me.'

'That's not a joke either, is it? Did he have something to do with Keagan's disappearance?'

'Everything and nothing. He was a pawn, but I still have no idea in whose game.' Her every line was taut, like a hunting bird mid-dive.

Helen felt the cold rage emanating from Moira's small frame and remembered the first time she had seen her—as a potential assassin. Pride forced the fear down and she rallied. '"Was?" Did you kill him?'

'I thought about it, but I figured Ferris' boss would want that pleasure so I left him incapacitated, for collection.'

Shocked, Helen floundered for a response. *What do you say to someone like Moira?* She considered asking about her brother, but thought better of it. 'Gustav is lucky to have a friend like you. When things get difficult, like now I mean.'

Moira's response did not come straight away, and when it did her voice was soft, her words stilted. 'No, he's not. I got him into this... and I couldn't get him out.'

'What do you mean? I thought we were going to see Gustav.'

'I was at Masterton's. I made a mistake and they tracked us there—sent in two squads. I couldn't... there was nothing I could do. He told me to go—he refused to leave before he'd destroyed everything.'

The flight was still smooth, but Helen's stomach turned over. 'Is he alive?'

'I don't know. I hope so. He has information and skills they could put to use.'

'I can't believe you just let them take him.' The other possibility was too much for Helen to process.

'You weren't there!'

'No, *you* were. Was this your brilliant plan, to come knocking on my door and ask if Gustav just happened to leave his kidnappers' forwarding address?'

Moira gloves creaked as she tightened her grip on the flight stick. 'That sample Mastersson brought you, I was hoping that huge science brain of yours would find something useful.' Her words, edged with anger and fear, were spoken through clenched teeth.

The helplessness mirrored Helen's own. They were playing longshots. She took refuge in what she knew. 'Jane, please upload file "Mast01" from my implant to your science terminal and display the analysis.'

'Acknowledged.'

Helen regarded the contortions of the complex molecular chain and the statistics listed below. She was aware of Moira eyeing her hungrily but ignored the insistent pressure, letting her mind clear and focus on what mattered. 'This is highly unusual.' She gestured and the hologram flowed towards her. 'See here, here, and here... It's a protein with multiple active sites. The conformation... Jane, extrapolate the most likely protein structure assuming it was bathed in human synaptic and cerebrospinal fluids, lymph, and blood. Colour code the areas of altered structure. List physiologically active molecules native to humans that the protein is likely to interact or bond with.'

A few seconds later, the display shifted again. Four shapes now hung in the air, each with multiple sites flashing in different locations. Below each shape were listed several hormones, many neurotransmitters, and a host of other organic compounds. 'This is like no other protein I've seen.'

Moira broke in. 'Communication is, hypothetically, the passing of understandable information from one person to another. If the expert would condescend to explain to the layperson, in non-scientific terms, maybe actual communication could take place?'

'Sorry. This molecule should not exist. It changes its shape, and the effects it has on the human body, depending on where in the body it's located. The effects of consumption would be profound—it's both psycho- and physiologically active. For something like this to evolve—it would need to share an ecosystem with humans for millions of years, but there's no way this is from Earth. It's been engineered, artificially assembled in a lab. Given its wide-ranging effects, I would guess it would be highly addictive. Rapid withdrawal could cause multiple organ shutdowns and be fatal.'

'So it would make a very effective street drug. Someone could be controlled by it?'

'Yes, by threatening to withdraw supply, but, given the high cost of manufacture and the specialist equipment needed, I doubt that's its main use, just an advantageous side effect—from the perspective of a supplier.'

'That explains why Keagan suddenly started acting like an automaton before he disappeared... Wait, the books in his apartment—he was never intellectual. And his newfound combat abilities—his kill ranking shot up in a few months. Could this protein augment someone's intelligence, perception, coordination, reaction times? Could it help them learn new skills, fast?'

'Quite possibly. It acts both physically and mentally, so yes.'

'But why? Whoever took Keagan also took Kishino—an Elite. Why submit the best to an expensive drug regimen to increase their abilities? They must have deep pockets or wealthy backers: one of the bigger corporations or faction militaries. If we're dealing at that level, then something like this could tip the power balance across known space. If the Imperials use it on their pilots, the Feds and Independents have to buy it to maintain the status quo—a chemical cold war. The only winner is the manufacturer, who could charge what they liked.'

'So that's why they came after you and Gustav, but how did your brother get involved?'

'I still don't know. He was a low-life, a nobody. He had no distinguishing features except an unerring ability to make the wrong choices.'

Moira's frank assessment surprised Helen. 'Maybe he was part of a different test group.'

'I don't follow.'

'Standard scientific protocol is to have different groups of several test subjects—some exposed to whatever is being tested, some not—a control group. Maybe they wanted to see if a failure like Keagan—sorry.'

'Carry on.'

'Maybe they were testing to see what effects the drug could have on someone's life? It could be sold to billions of people who want promotion, who want to succeed. It may not have a military application at all.'

'Granted, but how do you explain Kishino? He was taken by the same people that took Keagan. He was already an elite pilot. He's happily retired with a family, his enemies dead or running scared. There's no motivation. He's already got everything he needs. Why jeopardise that for a highly addictive, untested, drug?'

'It does seem strange. What about Keagan? If he's a test subject, someone would have to watch him. Were they?'

'Definitely. They've been trying to keep me away from him for months. His lifestyle changed completely. The evidence was easy to spot. '

'I can't get away from how much this sounds like a social experiment.'

'No, it's not. Mastersson found a section of hull plate, probably from Kishino's ship. There was a mark on it, from an energy weapon that matched none of the standard designs in the databases.'

'You said, "Probably." You don't sound sure.'

'I work with "probables" all the time. You're a scientist: you test samples again and again until you've eliminated all the possibilities. Sometimes, by rote is the only way to do police work, but cases take years to solve. Real breakthroughs come with intuition and experience, by being able to see what's not there, being able to read people. You can't get those from a test tube.'

'A good scientist needs intuition, formulating hypotheses—'

'From a rigid matrix of known facts. That's why technology is so often ahead of science: the creatives, the visionaries, they see the potential and make it happen. Science explains what they've already discovered and put to work. In police work, when coincidences start clustering you're on the right track. The plate *could* be from another ship with the same configuration as Kishino's—but discovered in the same system and around the same time that he disappeared, and with an inexplicable weapon burn across it? Everything in me says *not*. Keagan, Kishino, an experimental weapon, and a drug that makes pilots more lethal, all linked to the same group of people. Something big is happening and we're just scratching the surface.'

Physically Moira could be daunting, but intellectually Helen was not so easily cowed. 'Well, that shows you don't know everything. I did not have a "rigid matrix of known facts" in front of me when I analysed this protein—I used my expertise and intuition, just as you do. I'll concede your point about it having a military application, but I still think they are conducting a sociological experiment. To me, it seems like there are two cohorts of people: the sample, those… with a lot of potential for the drug to unlock like Keagan; and a positive control, those who have already excelled through natural ability like Kishino. It's the best way to confirm the efficacy of the drug and demonstrate it to potential buyers. There may be military applications, but the methodology is social.'

Helen waited for Moira to try and shoot her argument down. Instead, she was silent for a time before replying, 'Okay, that makes sense. We can't go on-grid without risking detection, so can you think of any research facilities or anyone who has conducted this type of research, legally or not?'

'Drugs research, with kidnapping and murder? No one I know in the scientific community would ever willingly engage in a venture like this.'

'Setting aside your professional ethics for a second, what about rumours, gossip? Every community has its intrigues and secrets, its pariahs, even the scientific one. Could someone you know have been bought or forced? Any of your peers suddenly behaving differently or changing their lifestyle?'

Never before had Helen questioned her own morality. She knew Moira was right: people gossiped at conferences and nodded knowingly to each other across the tables at institute dinners, but she had always kept away from such intrigues. It was one reason her career had progressed so quickly. Now, her lack of insider knowledge could cost Gustav his life.

Moira, who had been watching her, rammed her head back into her seat padding. 'Let me guess, you're a good girl who always kept her nose clean. Mastersson was your illicit thrill—even though you knew what he was doing was illegal, you never notified the authorities. Being his accomplice was exciting, but because you nudged, nagged, and encouraged him to go straight you could convince yourself you weren't doing anything wrong—in fact, you were the angel in his life. How very convenient. How very hypocritical. Convince me you're not whiter-than-white and I can at least respect you for being honest with yourself.'

'How dare you! My relationship with Gustav is none of your business. And I *have* heard things, I *do* know things. There was the Johns scandal, but he was an inorganic chemist…' It hit Helen; she had been played. She did not know what made her angrier: that she was gullible or that Moira had read her so easily.

They both stared straight ahead.

It was a while before Moira broke the wall of silence. 'That was a low blow. Sorry. It's a cop trick, a reflex. I use it on suspects and my leads all the time. You've schooled yourself so carefully to be professional it's impairing your ability to think. That, and all close-knit communities are self-protective: there's always an understanding—even if it's unconscious—to keep outsiders, outside. *Everyone* knows something. I need—Mastersson needs—

whatever you know. If you keep your community's secrets, we won't find him.'

It was all too much: weeks of worrying, the break-in, being uprooted, Masterson gone, their lack of progress, and now the accusations. Helen's righteous anger warred with her shame. She wanted to scream, 'This is all your fault!', to slap Moira, to make her hurt. Only Moira's apology and her need to find Masterson kept the dialogue open. 'Apology accepted but don't do that again. Sometimes you can just ask, and give someone time to think. It's obvious you disliked me from the moment we met. I'm not a cop, so I don't play mind games as well as you do, and so I've no idea what it is about me you don't like. How we feel about each other doesn't matter: we both want to find Gustav—' Helen glanced across at Moira and was surprised to catch her looking down, almost shyly. '—I'll do my best to remember something you can use, but I think better when I'm not under attack.'

When Moira spoke, her voice was quiet. 'Alright. Let me know when you have something.'

All Helen could find was a weak, 'I will.'

'Can you tell anything about the origin of the protein from its structure?'

'It bears a superficial resemblance to a couple of protein groups, but that won't help us isolate its origin. And there is… something… but I can't pin it down right now.' In front of her, white wisps of cloud reached out to caress the viewscreen before being left behind, empty-handed, as Jane flew on into the void of space. Helen pulled her fingers through her hair, feeling suddenly exhausted. 'Do I need to be here, as there's no emergency?'

'No, you—'

'I've been in zero-g before. There are two seats, so I assume there are two bunks. Is yours the top or bottom?'

'Bottom.'

Helen released her harness and orientated herself expertly towards the exit. 'Fine. Wake me if something important happens.

She pushed off the control panel and glided through the opening door, glad to be away.

28

Deep Space

Moira slipped from the sleeve on her bunk and glided gracefully from cabin to cockpit. Years in space meant she found moving while weightless easier than an aquatic found swimming. *What's hard is trying to get to sleep with someone constantly snuffling. It must've been two hours before I blacked out. Why did Mastersson marry her?*

'Jane, status report.'

'All systems operating within normal parameters. Current location: deep space in 51 Arietis, approximately two hundred thousand klicks from Adab. No objects within scanner range.'

Good, no one will trace a jump from way out here. But a jump to where? Moira could not rid herself of her seething resentment of Helen. She had risked detection and arrest, gambling on Mastersson's ex-wife and her scientific expertise. Mastersson had trusted her, but so far all Moira had seen was someone so locked into rigid group-think she was incapable of imagining anything outside her tiny box. *Take her away from her lab and what's left?* She pushed herself over to the dispenser.

'Jane, synth-coffee, medium-hot.'

'Enjoy.'

'Erm, thanks.' She took the sealed container, pushed and spun mid-flight before catching the pilot's chair arm with her free hand. Pivoting, her momentum carried her smoothly into the seat. It felt good to be alone again on her ship, to have room to think. *She has to know something useful, but how to get at it? She's too intelligent for the usual cop tricks. How can I derail her enough so she actually starts using that huge brain? Everything depends on her.* The thought was not reassuring.

Moira heard the characteristic pad…pause…pad…pause of someone navigating quickly in zero-g—pushing on the walls and pulling on handgrips, gliding across the intervening spaces. *I thought she'd be a boot-shuffler. I need a few more pleasant surprises.* 'Breakfast's in the dispenser. Help yourself.'

'Thanks. How did you sleep?'

Great, superficial pleasantries to fill a perfectly good silence. 'Fine,' Moira lied, 'You? You seemed pretty restless last night.'

'Not a wink.'

It was obvious from her jaunty tone Helen was itching to tell her something. 'Remembered a useful fact or two since our last conversation?'

Helen floated gracefully over to the co-pilot's chair, carrying her breakfast in one hand.

Cereal-cake and a carton of fruit juice. Why am I not surprised? Moira braced herself for a dose of smug.

'I used my expertise and intuition to work out who's behind this.'

'You got that from a protein?' Moira made no effort to keep the scepticism from her voice.

'It's all there, if you know what to look for… and you're not pushed too hard.'

She's angling for another apology or a pat on the head. I can't wait to give her back to Masterson—cute, helpless, and high maintenance. Moira waited, keeping a lid on her still-simmering resentment.

'We are taciturn this morning, aren't we? You should try eating naturally, it'll improve your bad temper. Synth-coffee will do that to you.'

Payback for last night? Maybe she's got a spine. 'It's all from a dispenser; none of it's natural.'

'What defines it is what it's made from.'

'Which is presumably a deliberately obscure reference to our protein. So give me the names, or are you waiting for a drumroll?'

'We both know you don't believe I've found anything significant. You're a cop—'

'Ex-cop, and now ex-investigative officer. Your point?'

'My point is you think like a cop, and you won't believe a word unless I lead you step-by-step through the evidence. What do you know about molecular biology?'

'About as much as you know about stripping down a Lensmann P43GRL.'

'I'll try to keep it basic. After I got up, I spent most of last night having a closer look at the protein. It *really* should not exist. In the centre is a theoretically impossible structure, a Giurgea Pivot. It's what gives the protein its unique ability to change conformation—'

'Conformation?'

'Sorry, the shape a protein chain makes when it folds. This protein radically changes its conformation—its shape—when dissolved in different bodily fluids. It's this ability that enables it to profoundly affect so many systems in the human body. Without the Giurgea Pivot, this wouldn't be possible. The problem is that the Pivot is an entirely theoretical structure. There have been several attempts to synthesise it over the last fifty years or so, but none even came close. It's just not feasible with current human technology. In fact, some of the most eminent researchers in the field hypothesise it will never be synthesised.'

'Except now it has been. Am I to assume from this you think Giurgea is our guy?'

Helen smiled. 'No, Giurgea died seven hundred years ago. The man who's most recently been working on the synthesis is someone I studied under. Jane, please call up the profile of Carl Linnaeus from the onboard database.'

'If Jane has his profile stored locally he must have a rep.' As Moira spoke, the data began to scroll in front of her.

Helen summarised, 'He's Imperial by birth. His father and mother were unremarkable, other than being nostalgists. They ran a business, which failed. The family were sold into slavery. He went through the standard genetic screening: his owners saw his potential and sold him on, with his parents' blessing by all accounts—his sale cleared the family debt and left them with a tidy profit. Since then he's been pathologically self-reliant—excelling at everything he turned his mind to until he developed a fascination for biosciences. He hasn't looked back since.

'I've not seen Carl for years, but we have corresponded in a professional capacity. He's a genius, a visionary whose work is years ahead of his contemporaries. It's not immodest to say my peers consider me one of the foremost researchers in my field, but there are several of his theories I struggle to completely understand. Some of those who failed attempted to discredit his work, but at every turn Carl has publically humiliated his opponents or undermined them in some way. He's in Jane's database and infamous in the scientific community not only for his brilliance, but... there have been rumours—that's what you want isn't it, gossip?'

'What I want are facts, but I'll take gossip if that's all we've got.'

'When I knew Carl, he was always driven, always passionate, and that could make him seem ruthless sometimes. They've tried to link him to several books and papers published over the years under different names—horrible things he would never be willing to write.'

'Are you just going to stand there defending him or tell me what "they" say he's done?'

'Carl's outspoken when it comes to politics, but these texts expound a belief in engineered social evolution and the unreached potential of humankind. Their manifesto includes the use of selective genocide to improve the genetic health of humankind; the sterilisation of anyone with an IQ less than one hundred and thirty; and the withdrawal of all social support and welfare to allow competition and natural selection to weed out "those too weak to survive without help".'

'And here was I thinking scientists were too unimaginative to be immoral.'

'Very funny. He's less immoral than amoral—a misguided idealist.'

Moira was silent for a while before she spoke. 'So, he's realised a theoretical concept. That's barely a means—someone else could have synthesised the Pivot before he did. Even if I assume the gossip is correct, that doesn't establish motive. Have you got anything more conclusive?'

Helen looked at the floor before speaking. Her words sounded forced. 'There were other rumours, years ago, that he had applied for research licences that weren't granted. After, he disappeared for a couple of years. Others were quick to assume the worst: that he was supposed to have reached agreement with the leader of an unnamed feudal world, who offered the planet's populace for experimentation. Deaths were mentioned.'

'But you don't believe it.'

'Nothing was ever proven.'

Moira raised a sardonic eyebrow. 'We both know proof and innocence are different things. Besides, if you believe he's innocent, why bring up his name? Is he capable of a project like this and hiring killers to work for him?'

'It's hearsay that he's… less than kind to underlings and those who get in his way. He was… he never seemed like that to me. He's only having people kidnapped that we know of; he could be working with or for someone who ordered the killing.'

'Only having people kidnapped'? *There's something else behind this, something she's not willing to face. Something for later.* 'But you can't think who this other person might be?'

'No names come to mind. Actually, I wasn't thinking of another person. If you look under "Career Progression", Carl's name is listed as a consultant for the bio-research division of Argent Aerodynamics Amalgamated Inc., the company I worked for sixteen years ago.'

'What was Carl working on, back then?'

'It's classified, of course, but it had to do with the Thargoids.'

Moira's teeth dug into her tongue, her blood a pulsing rush in her ears. She stared, watching as Helen scrolled past the data. Relief flooded her, and she jumped at a way out. 'It's a big leap from human experimentation to Thargoid involvement. We need more than blind guesses.'

'It's not a blind guess. Carl consulted for Argent Incorporated as a specialist in exo-biological research and exploration. He made me sign a non-disclosure agreement before he told me, well bragged: he was one of the original members of the Alliance delegation that met with the Thargoids back in 3253. According to him, he was pivotal in the negotiations, and in minimising the diplomatic impact of the INRA's attempt to sabotage the meeting.'

The exit was closing, and Moira felt her throat constricting with it. Only the cold beads of sweat ran freely. She wiped her forehead, thankful Helen was still staring at the hologram. 'It's the first I've heard of it—hardly the testimony of a reliable witness. Besides, the fact that he's an expert on aliens doesn't establish their involvement. It's barely circumstantial evidence.'

Helen frowned slightly, but her voice was steady, overlaid with the annoying patience of someone used to lecturing others. 'There's clues in the protein structure of the Giurgea Pivot. Carl hypothesised that the Pivot could only be synthesised at temperatures well below freezing—conditions favoured by the Thargoids. And there's no human technology I know of that can synthesise something so complex. This evidence is circumstantial, but there is some that isn't: the particular combination of stereoisomers and beta and delta amino acids in the Pivot's protein chains; they are characteristic of Thargoid biospheres. The protein complex you found in your brother's apartment is xeno-terrestrial.'

Moira felt herself locking down—the numb ice of panic freezing her thoughts and clenching her guts in a solid grip. She forced out the words. 'In Standard?'

'Proteins are made of smaller building blocks—amino acids. Each carbon-based biological system will tend to have characteristic combinations of amino acids, which are differentiated by their structure and three-dimensional shape. I'd need to do further tests to be certain, but these chains are made up of some amino acids occurring on worlds terraformed by Thargoids; your brother's sample is an artificial grafting of molecules from alien and human biospheres.'

This can't be happening, not again. 'But—'

'Hear me out. Last night you spoke about clusters of evidence. Jane, pull up an image of the hull plate from Mastersson's file. What if the burn mark wasn't caused by a human weapon, but one of Thargoid origin?'

It looks just like—Moira tried to block the memory, tried to force it back down, but there it was: the black smeared burn-line, spread like a gash across the metallic wall… the patterns the blood made on the ice and metal… the way her spine folded back on itself, wrapping around—she could not face the rest.

Her words rushed out, an uncontrolled torrent of panic. 'Jane, emergency—release pilot's harness!' Moira threw her synth-coffee across the cockpit. The carton passed harmlessly through the hologram before spattering across the external screen: a dark liquid sheet resolving into quivering globules floating in the air before the starlit panorama.

'Moira, what's wrong?'

'Get away, hide, stay safe.' Keagan's boyish voice filled her mind and took control of every muscle. She grabbed the back of the chair and pulled, flying wide of the exit in her haste to get away. She heard a muffled woman's voice. Was it concern? It didn't matter. Her hand found the door jamb and she pulled herself through before the door was even half open. She ricocheted along the corridor, one spasmodic movement after the next battering her body until she was inside the cabin.

The words barely hissed between her clenched teeth and passed her knotted fists as she curled into the far corner of her bunk: 'Jane, emergency lockdown. No one gets in… No one gets in.'

29

Helen sat in the semi-darkness, looking at 'Lockout Active' flashing in front of her. Jane had not made any overtly aggressive moves since Moira triggered it, but who knew what the ship was capable of? She had not dared leave the co-pilot's chair, and Moira was not responding to her attempts at communication.

Moira had been in hiding for an hour and a half. Not that Helen wanted to face her in her current mental state. The woman was terrifying: an unpredictable storm of pent-up aggression. Fear chased her thoughts in yet another circle. *Does she have an episodic mental illness? Unlikely if Mastersson has been her friend for all these years, but then he does have a soft heart. Is she his latest cause? Maybe it's an infection, something tropical? Where was Mastersson's bunker? That's not likely though—he's so careful, and wouldn't choose a planet with indigenous biohazards—but which planets has she visited in the last few months?* The prospect of being stranded, alone, with a trained killer who had complete control of the ship and was losing her mind was not a pleasant one.

Helen sat for several more minutes, re-evaluating the conversation and weighing her options. *It has to be the Thargoids—there's nothing frightening about a protein—post-traumatic stress?* The possibility was more appealing than the alternatives. *If that's right, do I wait it out, or talk her round?*

Without access to Jane's systems, there was nothing she could do. Could a delay put Mastersson in more danger? Or, worse, would Moira hurt herself if left alone for too long? She'd heard of it happening. There seemed little choice. *Hopefully, Jane won't try to incinerate me.*

She reached across for the harness release and, holding her breath, pulled. After a few seconds, she breathed out. *Okay...* Slowly, she disentangled herself. A gentle push and she was gliding towards the exit. The door did not open. Having Moira shouting back did not appeal, but she had to try. 'Moira? Are you okay? It's Helen…'

Has she locked comms, or is she too far-gone to respond? She scanned the bulkhead around the exit; her eyes found a small panel labelled 'Manual'. Would Jane interpret an attempt to open it as tampering and respond in-kind? She gripped the wrist of her trembling hand as she reached for the catch. The cover popped open easily. There was a lever inside. *I've come this far…*

The door slid aside, exposing an empty corridor. She sagged against the jamb until her breathing slowed. *Hopefully, the access Moira granted will open the cabin.* She pushed off down the corridor and saw the 'Do not disturb' sign lit over the entrance. Although she was not attacked for using the access lever, the light remained stubbornly on. She tried shouting, but there was no response. It was then she noticed the button under a small grill. *An ancient intercom?* Tensing, she pushed it.

'Moira? It's Helen.' Again, there was no response. 'There's only me here. Can you unlock the door and we can talk about it?' The silence continued. *Is it working, or am I talking to a wall? What can I say that might get through?*

'If you're too scared to help find Keagan and Mastersson, then it's up to me. There must be a way I can get Jane to respond… Perhaps there's something behind one of the panels I can use to bypass the lockdown…' In case Moira was watching her on holo-vid, Helen pushed herself around and back along the corridor.

She was just passing through the cockpit door when the shout came from behind, 'You stupid shite, don't touch anything!' The door closing severed further communication.

Helen controlled her bounce from the back of the co-pilot's chair and caught the handle next to the drinks dispenser. She chose a synth-coffee from the list of favourites. There was a thump from the other side of the barrier. *She's going to be really cross…*

Adopting what she hoped was a non-threatening pose and a pleasant smile, Helen turned to face the oncoming storm. 'Synth-coffee?'

Moira shot through the narrow gap with the wrath of an avenging angel. Helen dodged artfully as Moira made a grab for her, overshot, and continued straight on towards the viewscreen. Helen's mouth opened, but before she could say anything Moira kicked out with her legs and turned mid-flight. Her boots struck the heavy polymer with an ominous thud.

Helen held up the coffee carton like a shield. 'I thought you could do with this.' It was all she could do to squeak the words under Moira's feral glare.

They stayed there, in frozen tableau, for several seconds.

Moira shook her head, her jaw set in a hard line. Her body seemed to stiffen, like something inside was turning in on itself, becoming small and brittle.

Are those tears?!

Moira looked away and pushed off the bulkhead towards the exit. As she floated by, Helen let go of the handle and caught at her ankle. The response was immediate: the other foot shot out like a snake, catching Helen's wrist and sending her spinning, out-of-control, across the open space. She was only dimly aware of her own screaming, all thought wiped away by shock and pain. Curling protectively around her injury, she drifted, barely noticing her back hit the far wall—lances of red agony shot along her forearm, piercing her hand.

'Oh, shite. Why did you have to go and do that?'

Moira's indignation fired Helen's reply. 'You broke my wrist!'

The response was brusque and business-like. 'I doubt it. You barely had a grip on me. It's probably just a sprain. Let me see.'

Helen pulled her wrist more tightly against her body, gasping as another wave of pain overtook her. When she looked up, Moira was within arm's reach.

Helen could not stop herself recoiling as Moira reached out. 'Don't!'

'Fine.' Moira pushed off again, heading for the opposite wall. 'There's a medpac in here.' She tugged open a panel. 'Good luck putting it on yourself. And, by the way, it's never a good idea to make a grab for someone who's been combat trained. Reflex is faster than thought.'

'Obviously.' She caught the medpac that Moira tossed. A surge of anger came with it. 'How much longer are you intending to rationalise hurting those around you, Moira? You need to talk to someone. You need to let someone in.'

The remarks bit home; like sentries told to stand at ease, the hard lines on Moira's face softened and she was suddenly vulnerable. Her eyes glistened, briefly, before her expression reset. 'It's none of your business.'

'No, not normally, but Gustav and your brother are missing, so is Kishino and his family. As far as I know, we are the only two people looking for them. We have to trust one another; we have to help each other or *this*'—she gestured at the cramped confines of the ship—'isn't going to work.'

'I work alone, always have. You're a civilian—' Helen could feel the distaste in the word. '—and you'll get us both killed. I should find somewhere safe to drop you off.'

'And then you'll do what? Go where? You don't know the first thing about bio-sciences which, at the moment, is all we have to go on. And even if you do figure it out, you don't know anything about Thargoids.'

Moira rocked back, as if she'd been slapped.

'So, it really is—'

Moira lunged and caught Helen by her flight suit, knotting the thick material into a ball just under her throat. She pulled them together until Helen could feel Moira's breath as it slid across her cheek and caressed her ear. 'What do *you* know? A little bit of *theory*? If you went up against the Thargoids, they'd kill you. I won't watch another—. You've no idea what they're capable of. You're a weak, spoilt little princess who thinks she knows how the universe works because she's been watching it from the top of her tower. You're useless, spineless, and you wouldn't last five minutes out there by yourself. This trip is over for you.' She pushed Helen, sending her spinning away.

Despite favouring her injured wrist, Helen managed to right herself. 'Moira, you're the one who is barely fit to go on. Look at you: you're sweating, you've got the shakes and with any mention of "Thargoid", you lose it. You need help to get past this or your brother, Mastersson, and the Kishinos are gone forever.'

'Why don't you just say dead?'

'All right, dead.' Getting through to Moira was like soothing a skittish animal. Helen watched as the coffee carton floated by, undamaged. Gentling her voice, she tried again. 'Why don't we retrieve that, and you tell me what happened?'

'I don't see what good talking will do.' Moira's reply was sullen.

'As you've never opened up to anyone, how would you know?'

'Is this what Mastersson sees in you, this softness, all this *empathy*?'

Helen's nose wrinkled. She couldn't work out what was behind the question. 'Empathy isn't a dirty word, and Mastersson knows I love him.'

'Yeah, I bet he does. So, what does "Doctor Helen" want to know?'

'All of it, if we're going to work together. Let's go through to the cabin.'

30

The nano-stik mattress held Helen down in the zero-g as she perched on the end of Moira's bunk, waiting. Moira huddled in the back corner. It was fascinating and alarming, seeing her like this: wide eyes staring at nothing, arms locked around her knees, hands toying with a small yellow lacquered box covered in animal figures that had appeared from inside her flight suit. Her shoulders rose and fell in a rapid rhythm, her breathing shallow as if struggling to find enough air to speak.

Helen waited several minutes before asking, 'Is that keepsake from Keagan?'

'No, Masayoshi-san, Kishino's father. He wanted me to give it back to his son.' Moira turned the box over again, never taking her eyes from it. 'Our life... as kids we travelled hard, we fought. Keagan sometimes made me things from rags or scraps; nothing lasted, or it was lost.' She tucked the box back into her suit.

'What happened, Moira?'

It was a while before she spoke. When she did, her voice was a whisper, flat and cold. Helen leant closer to catch the words.

'They appeared in-system with no warning. The first we heard surface-side was a comm from an asteroid mining colony they attacked as they passed the outer rim—one of the miners got off a short burst of garbled speech before the signal went dead.

'I was eight, and I remember bombarding my parents with questions. We were a Survivalist family, and Dad believed in never withholding the truth so he told us what was going on as it happened. At first it was exciting—there were *Thargoids* in our system. Keagan and I, we wanted to see one—after the victory and our security force had captured some. I wanted one as a pet. I remember Da's smile as he said, "No, M., you can't even clean up after your mookah."

'They beamed everything over the comms, live as it happened. All us kids hated the rock-jocks. When we heard the last of the miners die and their comms went dead, I remember thinking, "Serves them right—too dumb to squish a few bugs." And then the bugs were coming for us.

'The call went out, to rally the ships and for those without one to take cover in the colony's bunker. I remember the shame—the other kids had parents who were flyers, but mine were both farmers—I wanted parents who would be heroes, not ones that were going to hide like scared cattle. I kicked and fought Ma as she dragged me over the frozen ground and down the icy steps into the underground shelter. I wanted to go and fight and preserve our family honour. I could already fly an agro-skimmer. How hard could it be to pilot a ship and go up against some stupid bugs? I only quit when Da gave me a clip with his free hand. I hadn't noticed his other resting on the sidearm at his hip. I couldn't think why he needed it. He obviously knew nothing about fighting, and our flyers were in the air. I could see the coloured traces they left behind as they flew away. Of course they would win. I'd have to face the smug teasing from the other kids at school tomorrow. I looked at Keagan; he was pushing his fingers hard into his palms, thinking exactly the same thing I was. He gave me a wink though. We'd fight the other kids together and give as good as we got—we always did.

'We sealed ourselves in. There were—what?—about thirty families and a few kids who had both parents on board the ships. The grown-ups were scared, and it was that as much as anything that silenced us kids. Some of the others started to cry, but Keagan was holding my hand and when he nodded I knew everything would be okay. Voices streamed unedited from the ships—we were all gripped, hanging on the words that determined our future—I can still hear them:

'"We have them. Oh, gods, so many!"

'"Morley, Davies, where are you going? Come back! Cowards!"

"'Hold it together. Perez, take your team in from the left.'"

"'Perez has gone. This is Lenton. Should I take her team?'"

"'Gyo here. What about us? You want us on the right or down the centre?'"

"'Hold on, not all at once. Yes, Lenton, take Perez's team—'"

"'Lenton's an asshole; he'll get us all killed. Let me—'"

"'Joyce, this isn't the time. Lenton, you're in charge. Gyo, take your team left.'"

"'I thought Perez's team was going left?'"

"'Fuck this, Kendal. Everyone, this is Abati—follow me, we're going in…'"

'Over the comm, everyone started shouting at once. I was a kid, but even I knew they were dead. Me and Keagan, we were a team. The rock-jocks and the flyers didn't leave us alone in the beginning, but we taught them to—by working together. You won as a team, or you lost. Seconds later, the angry shouting changed. The flyers were screaming and pleading, and dying. It only lasted a minute, maybe two.

'The silence on the comms channel meant there was nothing between us and the bugs. The colony defence batteries weren't finished. Da had been cursing the council every night for months for prioritising work on the harvesters, just to make a profit. Ma said he shouldn't live as though he was always scared of something. I'd called him a coward. He hit me when I did. Now I know he was right.

'With the last of our ships gone and no ground defences, the bugs sat in orbit and bombarded the colony. We could hear the muted thump of the explosions and feel the kick of each detonation through the walls and floor. Inside, children and adults alike cursed, wept, and screamed again. I didn't. Neither did Keagan. We gripped hands while our eyes locked. Several people threw up or shat themselves. The stink was disgusting. Da held onto Ma as she wrapped an arm around us. We could feel them both shaking. Everyone flinched when another blast went off, until the sound of each explosion ran one-into-the-next, like fist-size hail on a windscreen.

'I've no idea how long the bombardment lasted. It seemed like hours, but was probably only minutes. The bunker was the only structure to survive. It was worse when the noise stopped. A few panicking airheads were wondering if they had gone, but Keagan and I knew they were coming. Some of the airheads raised their voices, asking to be let out to search for some loved one who hadn't made it inside in time—as if anything could have survived *that*. One stupid woman even wanted to go and find her pet. In the end, enough council members shouted them down and, when the people with weapons sided with them, common sense prevailed and everyone decided to stay inside. It was Keagan, not my da, who told people the bugs would stand less chance of finding us if we stayed quiet. After that, they managed to keep it down to muted sobs and whispers.

'Hours passed. We couldn't see or hear anything from outside— all the external sensors were dead. Comms were out too; the bombardment destroyed any chance of calling for help. A couple of fights broke out as people blamed each other for not sending a distress call when we could. The peace officer 'cuffed a couple of the hotheads. Everyone else subsided into silent despair. No one was coming. No one knew the Thargoids were here.

'Ma had her arm around Da as he wept. When Keagan retrieved Da's pistol from the floor, neither of them noticed, but I did. I remember the look he gave me—not fear, just shame and anger. We both knew it was fight or die. "'It's just like school, but the bullies are bigger. When they cut their way in, stay close. Got it?"

'I nodded. I knew he would get me out of there.

'We started to run out of air before they found us. The scrubbers must have taken a hit and finally packed up. The heat started to build and everyone was sweating and panting, people lying around like dying fish. When Old Mr Jackson passed out, it was decided we must open the doors. Anyone with a weapon was called out and jostled into a semicircle in front of the entrance. After a discussion that seemed to take an age, the council asked for a volunteer to go outside. I saw Keagan move the arm that wasn't around my shoulder. My heart dropped into my stomach at the thought he might leave me alone. He must've seen the panic in my eyes as I squeezed his arm. He nodded and smiled. At that moment I could've burst with pride—if not for me, he would have been the first to volunteer—*my* brother. There was an awkward pause before Lissa stepped forward. I liked Lissa: Keagan followed her around like a kit and I followed him, but she was always kind to both of us. I could feel Keagan's arm trembling under my hand. He was staring after her, tears in the corners of his eyes as he bit his bottom lip. I still wonder what he wanted to say to her. He would've gone after her if not for me.

'Her friends and family looked tense, afraid, or openly wept. Far more were visibly relieved they weren't going. I cursed and hated them: Earth-grubbers and cowards, every one. That day, I swore that I would never let myself get like that: just meat for the slaughter.

'We never knew what brought the Thargoids. The bombardment must've destroyed any tracks we'd left on the ground and the bunker entrance was well hidden. Maybe they picked up on the vibrations as the huge doors rolled backwards. Maybe they could see the plume of hot air that escaped into the frigid atmosphere as the seals were broken. Lissa stepped cautiously through the gap, crouching low as she worked her way up the steps and out of sight. Moments later, we heard the 'crack, crack' of her pistol discharging and then the rhythmical drumming of their limbs on the hard ground as they came.

'Someone had their wits about them, and the sounds outside were drowned out by the grinding of the door gears as they were thrown into reverse. But it was too late—they were never going to close in time. I didn't see what happened next because Keagan grabbed my arm and yanked me forward through the milling crowd. I wanted to pull away, to run in the opposite direction, but he seemed so sure and I trusted him more than anyone. So, as those around us fled from the light that flooded in through the too-wide gap, we ran towards it. I wanted to stop, to see what they looked like, but Keagan pulled me forward faster and harder. I glimpsed a bulbous silhouette, taller than a man, pause in the doorway. Then Keagan jinked sideways and dragged me behind a storage canister to one side of the doors. He bundled me tightly in his arms as we crouched there, barely out of sight. I tried to fidget free—to see what was happening—but he bent his mouth to my ear and hissed,

'"Still and silent. You and me, together."

'He drew my face further into his chest, his hands gripping tightly. He wasn't going to let me look, but I could hear the discharge of weapons and more shouting. If the Thargoids made any noise, I couldn't hear it. Keagan was sweating, body locked rigid except where his lungs worked like an agri-pump. Suddenly, I felt him exhale, the muscles throughout his body going slack. I turned my head. A crustacean-like body, mottled brown and yellow, lay in the middle of the floor nestled in a tangle of inert plated limbs. Blue-green liquid spilled from several holes in the upper dome of its ridged and plated carapace. The liquid steamed misty-white vapour as it spread. Bits of the people I knew were scattered around it: arms and legs piled with disembowelled torsos, friends' and neighbours' faces torn apart or stuffed into the back of their skulls.

'It was Keagan's voice that drew me back. Someone was screaming, just another noise in the maelstrom until Keagan whispered her name,

'"Ma."

'He must have become aware of me then because his hand found my mouth and muted me before my cry could escape. The thing held Ma in two arms, her feet dangling a metre off the floor. It looked like it wanted to hug her. As if drawing her into a protective embrace, the flat flanges on its 'forearms' aligned like shields down her back. But red streams flowed down her body as its claws—fingers?—pierced her shoulders.

'Da was there too, standing close by, someone's discarded handgun shaking in his inexpert grip.

'I can remember that picture now; it haunted my childhood nightmares. All the anger and shame I felt towards them. The hatred of who they were and what they made me. While everyone else ran and cowered at the back, my parents, farmers, came for me and Keagan.

'It's too late, I can never tell them I'm sorry.

'Da pulled the trigger. He'd never trained and the first one went wide, but he kept trying, pumping out the shots. Where I was frozen inside, I felt the warm surge of triumph as bullet after bullet struck home. He kept firing, even after the clip was empty. Then it turned its repulsive dome towards him. I remember the wave of disbelief: the hatred and the anger; it should be dead. Da shot it—and when you shoot something it dies, everyone knows that. But apparently you can't kill a Thargoid with a low calibre weapon, even at close range. The slugs ricocheted off—didn't even mark it. And it looked at him, straight at him, as it reared on its back six legs, arms lifting Ma higher like some kind of offering, or trophy.

'The two front legs unfolded and reached up until the claws touched Ma, under each breast, before moving to meet in the middle. Blood flowed as the claws pushed into her skin and under her ribs. It was still looking at Da as it took a hold of something inside her and pulled. Her ribs cracked open like a gekhan nut. He ran forward then—my da, the farmer—and attacked it with his fists. One of its legs shot out like a lance, skewering him under the chin and lifting him into the air until he hung there, level with Ma. It flicked him away then, and he slid and rolled across the floor until he was stopped by another body.

'When I looked back it was reaching inside her, inside Ma. It looked like it was playing with her, until it took out her heart; I could see it still quivering. Then the alien lowered my ma's heart to its jaws and spat something. There was a violent fizzing, a hissing as plumes of white vapour erupted. The heart quivered, then stilled as it inflated, before bursting with the dull 'whump' of a soft tyre deflating. All the alien held was so much minced meat.

'I'd forgotten Keagan. He must have held his breath because he gasped, a ragged intake of air. Then we were moving. I didn't want to go. I didn't want to leave them there, like that. But Keagan's fingers bit into my arm and he half-dragged, half-carried me through the doors just before they closed behind us.

'After that, everything was a blur of running and hiding—Keagan hissing at me to do what I was told, telling me we must work together to stay alive. He promised he would always be there for me. He said he was Ma and Da now, and we had to survive. Through the numbness, I heard him. I listened. I believed. He's the only reason I'm still alive.'

31

They sat together, in silence, for some time. Helen watched Moira through a blur of tears—she hardly moved, just stared inside at another world in another time. *Curled up like this, she looks like a frightened little girl, but no wonder, given what she's been through.*

'Why are *you* crying?' Moira asked, scraping her own eyes dry.

Helen dabbed the tears with her sleeve before replying. 'What you said… it explains a lot: why you're so angry, so difficult to get close to. It doesn't make sense, but many who witness violence feel guilt, as if they were to blame—which of course they're not. Is that why—?'

'I didn't tell you this so we could spend hours analysing and empathising. But to answer your question: no, I don't feel guilty. I was eight; I didn't even have a gun. Those fucking aliens killed my parents. Is that what you wanted to hear, *doc*?'

'I want to understand. I'm sorry if you feel I pushed you into this, but when you're being… spiky, now I don't have to take it personally.'

The lines of Moira's frown shifted, more puzzled than defensive. 'Knowing this stuff helps you toughen up? How does that work?'

'No, not toughen up. It helps me understand. For someone who has to know about people to do her job, you have some huge blind spots.'

'Now I'm really sure telling you this was a bad idea. When I made you nervous, you didn't criticise. I prefer the way it was before.'

'Oh, you're joking.'

'Partly.'

'I wasn't criticising. I'm just honest, if a little too direct sometimes.'

'Let me guess, that was something else Mastersson liked about you.' There was no sweet, in the bitterness.

Helen looked away. *Where did that come from?*

Moira must have relented because her voice softened a little. 'I don't *do* this girl-to-girl sharing stuff. If seeing me break down helps you and means we find Keagan, Mastersson, and Kishino, then fine. Let's move on now, shall we?'

That was breaking down? I've never known anyone so desperate to keep it together. She hesitated before asking Moira the question. 'Can you remember anything else, anything more about the Thargoids?'

'You're asking if we can find a lead from a twenty-year-old memory?'

'You're probably too close to see, but I thought, together, we could find more "clusters of evidence". We know Carl's connected with the Thargoids in the past, and this project—whatever it is— has likely been running for years. Our evidence suggests Thargoid involvement. I'm guessing what happened to you as a child was on a planet on the borders of human space, in the area that we looked at on Jane's display earlier?'

Moira paused. 'Fafner, in the Jotun system, but over time the border would have moved outwards as new territories were colonised...'

'But Carl could have met with the Thargoids around then, couldn't he, during their incursions? How else would they have begun collaborating? I can't imagine aliens welcoming someone landing outside their front door unannounced. Afterwards, he most likely arranged liaisons on the edge of human space, or just beyond.'

Moira sat up straight. 'I suppose it's possible, but everything that happened after the bunker is a blur.'

'There's nothing else specific, nothing that stands out?'

'No… wait.' Moira's voice tuned out like a weak comms signal, going quiet and flat. 'The only other thing… Lissa's broken body. Keagan stopped running when we saw it. It looked like she'd been thrown, the way her spine folded back on itself and wrapped around—I think it was the landing gear of one of their ships. I remember the patterns her blood made on the ice. There was a burn mark across her and the metal she rested against—a black smear that spread like a gash. And just above… there were some markings. Then we caught movement in the ruins of the colony so ran and hid, and ran again.'

'The markings, did you recognise them? Could you draw them?'

'No, but—' Moira reached out and activated her omni-block. She traced several curves in the air with a finger. The eight-pointed star had crudely drawn back-sweeping arms. She added several approximations of swirls in the centre. 'The first and largest symbol. The rest were too complex to remember—probably writing.'

Helen stared at the shape. 'I know what that is—the pattern inside, it's fractal? There's a smaller circle in the centre?'

'Yes… I think so.'

'Carl uses it on correspondence—the logo of a subsidiary of The Proteus Collective, Natura Mutabilis Incorporated. He's carved out quite a niche for himself there. He often boasted about his 'obscene' budget and tried to use it to entice me to come and work for him. His hints that I would be free to pursue *any* line of research, without worrying about oversight committees or ethical audits, were hardly subtle.

'But working for him was never going to happen. He can't help but gloat, in private, how he 'owns' NMI and everyone that works for him. He negotiated almost total autonomy from The Collective and seems to be accountable to no one as long as he keeps innovating and bringing in the money. That he chose to so overtly use a Thargoid symbol as the company logo isn't surprising; Carl's brilliant and utterly egotistical. He demonstrates his prowess by playing little games. For the brighter-than-average, he dangles bits of bait only to trap them in a power-play when they bite, all for the pleasure of seeing others humiliated.'

'He does this a lot? Has anyone ever beaten him?'

'Carl game-plays any chance he gets. I don't know of anyone who's gone up against him and won.'

'That's what he tried with me—using Ferris to sideline my career so I couldn't help Keagan. What about you?'

'Me? I was smart enough not to play.'

'Well, we don't have a choice. If NMI operates outside colonised space, they would have to register any land claims—standard procedure. We should be able to narrow down the locations he could be operating from by checking where NMI's been in the last few years. That's going to need grid access.'

'I know Carl's cronies could find us—if I understand what Gustav told me—but how else can we find the information?'

Moira tapped her cheek with a finger. '…unless… Jane, can you access the grid covertly, so the data and link can't be traced?'

'I possess basic data encryption and trace prevention abilities. Avoiding a trace depends on local network conditions, the amount of data, and the length of time the comms-link is maintained. Do you wish me to establish an external comms-link to the network?'

Moira looked at Helen, who leant forward slightly, nodding. 'Please…'

'I don't suppose Linnaeus ever piloted his own ship?'

'Never.'

'Thought not, and I need an official PCS permit to access NMI vessel flight records. But even if I'm still on PCS's roster, Linnaeus will be monitoring my account…' Moira shook her head. 'Jane, task sequence, execute with the following security parameters: maximum data stream rate, save to local storage only. Use all available protocols to protect the data and our location. If you detect a trace, or as soon as the task is complete, sever the connection.'

'Security parameters understood.'

'Jane, task sequence follows: Download information on the systems NMI has explored and/or registered claims in over the past fifteen years. Restrict search to specific sources: the central Pilot's Federation database and publicly available information. Cross-reference with our previous data inquiries and include only systems occurring within those areas of space.'

'Acknowledged, working.'

'At least this way, Jane only has to compile a list from publicly available files; that shouldn't set off any data mines. Without Mastersson—Jane, can you hack into secure systems?'

'I am most definitely not equipped with suitable AI subroutines. Recommended action: find a human with relevant expertise. Caution: these activities are illegal in most systems.'

'Erm, yes, thanks, Jane. Mastersson, where are you when we need you?'

Moira's voice had taken on a wistful quality that surprised Helen, but her chain of thought was broken by Jane.

'Search complete, no trace evident. Would you like me to display the results?'

'Yes,' Helen and Moira answered together. Only Helen said 'please'. Her heart beat faster as points of light sprang into the air before them. *The light from one of those suns is shining on Gustav.*

Both sat, staring at the motes of hope before them. Helen lurched in shock as Moira punched the wall. 'This is what happens when I get all girly—I don't think straight. Linnaeus isn't going to choose somewhere this obvious. He'd pick a dark system—a brown dwarf or similar—something difficult to find.'

Helen jumped in. 'Jane, please display only dark systems.' Thousands of stars winked out.

'That's still too many and doesn't show us what we need. If Linnaeus wants to hide, even he won't have registered where on an official database.'

'We have to try something.'

Moira's voice was resigned. 'Okay, Jane, show us the system details.'

✻

Over twelve hours passed as both women pored over the data, sifting the information using every keyword they could think of and factual commonality they could find.

Moira pushed free of her chair. Her boots hit the floor and stuck. She began to pace, the movements oddly disjointed in zero-g. 'This is shite. Look, Helen, none of these systems stand out. Linnaeus could be in any one'—her wave dismissed the hologram—'or hiding in plain sight in one of the many we "eliminated" before. He could have a disguised facility elsewhere in human occupied space. And how much fucking unexplored space is there? Maybe he goes on camping trips with the bastards every few months. The information we've got isn't detailed enough, and what we need may not be here at all.'

'We can't give up. Is it too much of a risk to request research papers published by Carl and NMI with subjects relating spatially to these areas? It could give us some clue.'

'Really? Linnaeus is going to put a map showing his secret base in the middle of an appendix?'

'Do you always get this caustic when things don't go your way?'

'Are you always this blindly optimistic? It's like watching an insect head-butting a window. Maybe if you turned that blonde science brain of yours to the problem we might get somewhere.'

'I'm trying, but you seem to think you know everything.'

'So what do you know that I don't?'

'I know Carl. He may have left some cryptic references to this project in his papers if he was bored and wanted to go fishing for more players for his games.'

'That query will download an unspecified amount of data and put us at risk. Do you really think he'd be that stupid?'

231

'Carl is never stupid but always craves stimulation, and we've nothing else to go on.'

'Really? The way you talk about "Carl" is very familiar.'

'I don't know what you're getting at.' Helen forced herself to keep eye contact.

'I think you do. If you have a history with someone I might have to kill, I should know. Our last girly sharing time was *so* enjoyable, we should do it again. Your turn.'

'I thought you were going to drop this aggressive cop front?'

'I thought you'd be honest.'

Helen looked away.

'You want me to say, "please"?'

'There's no point in trying, and I know I won't get a "sorry" either. Carl… Carl always likes to have the best. I've almost as many patents and research citations to my name, if you take my age into account. I'm one of the few people who grasps his theories— although not easily.'

'Details. Specifics.'

'We first met when I was twenty, a student at the Ekhi Biosciences Institute. I don't know what the faculty thought he was going to teach us; they presumably paid his exorbitant lecturing fees for the prestige. One semester, he gave a series on his Pivot theory. He was showing off—the content was way above student level and, back then, had no practical application. Where everyone else endured the talks to meet their attendance quota, I thought I could see something—a beauty and underlying simplicity—despite the obtuse presentation.'

'You make it sound positively gripping.'

And suddenly Helen understood—the unlikely friendship between them had been bugging her from the beginning—Moira saw Gustav as her sounding board and sparring partner.

'What are you smiling about?'

'Nothing. I like to know the people I'm working with. Did you want to hear the rest?'

'If we can skip more of the joy of science.'

'Carl was impressed with the questions I asked, and he invited me to dinner.'

'And your cleavage had nothing to do with it?'

'No. I don't know. Carl is a little more complex than that. He's a celebrity, in his field. Being rich, influential, and not bad looking draws attention. I expected him to be a user; even back then I wasn't completely naive. But, as I got to know him, I found he didn't respond to overtures from men or women. He's too private, selective, and likes to be in control.'

'But he asked you to dinner. Let's skip the dessert. Did you have sex?'

'No!'

'What about later, when he fell in love with your mind?'

'After a few months, he asked me to come and work with him, when I graduated.'

'So that's a "yes" then. Don't be shy; you know my secret.'

'I don't see why it's so important.'

'For someone who's so interested in other people, *you* seem to have some huge blind spots. I've been working in law enforcement for years. Believe me when I say—and because it's you, I'll use a nice word—coupling makes a difference. People act like they have shite for brains.'

That was enough. Helen grasped for something, anything to hit back with. 'Did you like it when you slept with Gustav?' She realised how stupid she sounded as soon as she asked the question.

But Moira looked like she'd been slapped. Her voice was taut, awkward. 'Mastersson and I never slept together. Being his ex-wife, I suppose it's natural you'd want to know.'

Helen's relief deepened, solidified—the thought of the Gustav she knew being attracted to someone like… No. She caught Moira staring at her, expectant. 'I'm sorry, I should never have pried. Your friendship with Gustav is none of my business.'

'Can we drop Gust—Mastersson and get back on-topic? Having sex changes things. *If* we ever find Linnaeus, and *if* he doesn't kill us first, and *if* we are in a situation where my arse is on the line and you have to make a snap decision, I need to know you aren't going to freeze or do something mental. I normally work alone, and never with civilians—this is why. Bottom line: if your head's messed up because of Linnaeus then I could get killed because you fucked up. Did you have sex with him? Do you still have feelings for him? And, on the spur of the moment, will you choose Linnaeus over me? If the answer is "yes" to any of those, we have a problem.'

'Yes, we were sleeping together but it didn't last, and I don't think I would choose Carl over you. I mean, everyone's depending on us.'

'That you used the word "think" bothers me. You need time to double-check your priorities.'

'But—'

'You know Linnaeus well, so download those scientific papers and see if you can find anything useful. If they're advanced, I can't help, and right now I'm tired and I need to crash. Are you staying to sleep or leaving to do some research?' Moira's voice was hard.

Without a word, Helen peeled her flight suit loose from the bunk and pushed herself towards the exit.

32

The mood on board ship was claustrophobic and stagnant. After the argument, Moira had barely slept. Worse, they were stuck. *If I don't keep busy,* someone's going to get strangled. She had chosen parts cleaning, useful as an excuse to be alone and it left her mind free while her hands worked.

Linnaeus: location unknown, money and resources, well-connected, in league with aliens. She sucked at the knuckle she caught on an edge. *Me: no squealer network, face-shifters, four-block equipment stockpile, tekhead department, permits, or backup. No ideas. What I do have: a quirky old ship and a civilian scientist in denial about her evil overlord fetish.*

Worse still, she had seen first-hand the way Linnaeus operated. *Capable of subtlety, forward planning, and he isn't leaving loose ends. If the bastard is as arrogant as Helen thinks he is, then where's the flashing sign declaring 'Future Ruler of the Universe lives here'? This project must be too important for him to take his usual chances. Humanity's most accomplished xeno-biologist and biochemist teamed up with Thargoids…*

'Shite!'

The ultrasonic cleanser glided away. Moira made a grab, but the folded cloth in her hand sent it spiralling. It hit the ceiling and slid along until it came to rest in the far corner of the cabin. Two small globules of blood followed. Moira wrapped the cloth around her knuckle before looking around for something to readjust. She pulled the magnetised calibrator off the wall and got back to work.

They're experimenting on us.

Squeezing, an effusion of red blossomed through the cloth. She forced her grip round the metal calibrator to relax. She stared at the once-white material, now coloured with her blood. *Helen would give this a name: anger, fear? Paralysis*; cold and numb was all she felt.

But she could still think. *This is my job: to sniff out and wipe up the galaxy's shite so that privileged people like Helen Mastersson can keep their shoes clean.*

Moira found a feeling and clutched at it—she hated the woman. Right now, why did not matter. What did was that she was camped out between Moira and her supply of comfortingly synthetic coffee. *You know where you are with synth.*

Moira and Helen had succeeded in 'avoiding' each other for most of the day—physically, a difficult thing to do given the confines of the ship. When circumstances forced them into close proximity, belligerence and determination kept the walls in place. They ate separately.

Helen had buried herself in the research papers while Moira, at a loose end, probed Jane's recesses to inventory the available equipment. Some surprising discoveries roused her curiosity about Jane's previous owner—now growing into a welcome diversion and a source of nagging doubt.

'Jane, display the profile of your previous owner.'

'Unable to comply.'

Computers, helpful as always. 'Jane, specify the reasons you are unable to comply.'

'Unable to comply.'

This is beyond unhelpful. 'Jane, remove all encryption, access blocks, and security protocols surrounding all data and requests for access about your previous owners and all related topics.'

'Will not comply.'

'Will not comply'? Not 'unable'? What the fuck?

'I'm done.'

Moira spun.

Helen stood behind her, every line of her face and body tense. 'What are you doing? Looks like a bomb's gone off in here. What's in all the piles?'

'Equipment. I've been looking for anything useful. It's not going to help now though, is it? You didn't find anything.'

'Nothing. Absolutely nothing. I was so sure. Carl always left clues. When I read his papers, I would keep an eye out for the subtle hints; he enjoyed it when I found things his colleagues missed. There were ciphers, microdots, word plays, and more, but there are no references to this project—explicit or tangential. Maybe he's increased the complexity or subtlety and I can't keep up.'

Helen looked so exhausted and broken that Moira actually felt sorry for her. They wanted the same things after all. 'I doubt that great science brain of yours is failing; I think Linnaeus changed his game. Normally, you intellectual types need something keeping you busy and your minds turning over. Mastersson likes to battle with security systems and you throw yourself into your research. Bored, Linnaeus is a puppeteer. But now he has something more interesting to do—running an illegal operation right under the noses of his corporate paymasters. This project is so important he's defending his investment—ruining lives, not for intellectual stimulation, but because people get too close. He doesn't want this discovered.'

Helen shook her head vigorously, wrapping her arms around her sides. 'We've got to get Gustav out of there, Moira, but I don't know what else to do.' She shifted sideways and came to rest on a storage crate.

'Don't! That's delicate.'

'Sorry. What about his headquarters? He must have something on file at NMI.' Sudden hope made her face glow.

Moira took no pleasure in slapping her down. 'You're not thinking. Surely someone like Linnaeus would never rely on an external data store?'

The light faded. 'You're right; he's too arrogant to trust anything or anyone else. He only ever used his implant and his memory never let him down. He won't have told anyone about the project, at least no one he doesn't completely control—and he's very good at that.'

'That's my assessment.' Moira regarded Helen as they shared their despair. She could guess why Mastersson had found her attractive. It was not just the physical, there was something inherently feminine about her—soft—*everything I'm not*. Right now, she carried that vulnerable air about her, a silent plea written large in every line of her posture. *Men always like the girly crap.* The helplessness and despair she could cope with—they mirrored her own—it was the pathetic dependence that made Moira want to hit her.

'If you weren't so wet I could use you.'

'What?! You're resorting to insults again? At least I'm not afraid to show what I'm really feeling. I don't have to hide behind a wall of repression, and then fire barbs at anyone nearby to release my pent-up emotions.'

Their eyes locked.

Push her, and she pushes back. But the hair, and the manicured nails, and the perfect complexion, and those doe eyes. 'It wouldn't work. You're too soft.'

'I thought we agreed to drop the game-playing and try a little openness.'

'I wish this was a game. What are you made of, Helen? Take away the intellect, the cultured manners, the sparkly-dust feminine charm, and what's left?' Moira backhanded Helen across her cheek. When she pulled her hand back, there was blood on her knuckles. 'I *know* what I'm made of. Keagan and I fought for years to stay alive. We fought *back*. When he went down, I kicked the man pinning him to death to make sure my brother was okay. Keagan killed a man with his fist, broke the leg of a woman with a crowbar, before bashing in another man's skull. She was watching while they tried to rape me. I was eleven. Keagan may be stupid, and thoughtless, and self-destructive, but whatever else he is, he's a survivor, like me. He's the only family I've got. If we find where Linnaeus is keeping him but balls things up, he'll end up dead. Mastersson will end up dead. Kishino—his entire family—dead. If we leave things alone, then they may be imprisoned, but at least they're still alive. I don't *know* you. Fuck, *you* don't know you. You've never been pushed near the edge, let alone over it. You're soft, untrained, untested—a massive risk. What's making me so fucking angry is I could do this—I could get them out—but there's no way I can get *in*. You, you could get in, maybe, but you'd dissolve like shite in a downpour. I'm not betting Keagan's life on you. I need a soldier, not a scientist. Just stay out of my fucking way.'

Moira stood and shouldered past the girl. She took three steps towards the door before Helen caught up and yanked her head back by her hair. The response was automatic, reflexes honed over the years switching on her muscle memory. Moira twisted, leaving the hank of her hair in Helen's grip. One sharp blow below the solar plexus and Helen fell backwards, gasping for air.

'That's why I can't use you.' A curt dismissal meant to end to their 'conversation'.

But Helen had not finished. Moira was so sure she was down she was not looking when Helen's boot caught her knee. It was a lucky blow. Moira felt the cartilage give as her kneecap slid sideways across the bone. She went down and Helen, wheezing like a broken ventilator, was on top of her in a moment.

Moira got her hands up before the blows rained down. There was little power behind them, but the flurry of fists and pain in her knee left her momentarily stunned. The storm could not last. Moira looked through her fingers. Helen was purple. Still winded, all her energy was going into trying to breathe—except for the raised fist she was about to let fly. Moira caught the wrist as Helen swung for her. Her reflexes told her to twist, just so, and the bones in the forearm would be a mess of splinters. Managing to override the impulse, she rolled Helen aside. Ignoring the pain in her leg, she pulled herself along the floor a short way using the handholds on the wall for purchase before turning around.

Helen was trying to squeeze out words with no air to make the sounds. Eventually, she managed a whisper. 'Selfish coward.'

'What, for not chancing the life of my brother against your ability as a commando?'

Helen forced several more breaths into her lungs. 'Selfish because this isn't about Keagan, it's about you being afraid to be alone. Your brother is living as an animal, locked up until the drug destroys his mind and breaks his body. And there's Masterssson. If you know him, you know he values his freedom and independence over anything else. Kishino—'

'Alright, I get it.'

'Really? I don't think so.'

'Talk all you want. I've been lied to too many times by too many people—'

'So you're going to let them rot because this is really about how little-girl Moira hasn't grown up enough to trust.'

'I wasn't finished. Your words aren't worth shite. But, just now, you showed me you would fight, not fold. Finally, I've seen some spirit, although you still hit like a coddled princess.'

'I broke your kneecap.'

'A lucky shot. You wouldn't have a hope against anyone with training who was prepared, but then maybe they will see what I saw. Maybe we can use the way you look.'

'Bleeding, with my hair everywhere?'

'For fuck-shite, will you stop *worrying*! Nobody here fucking cares. You look harmless. You look pathetic. You look weak. We can use that. I reckoned you for a pampered doll, but you proved me wrong. Maybe you can prove Carl wrong.'

'What do you mean?'

'Part of you is still hanging on like you've got a crush. If you're acting that way, it's probably because he ditched you. My bet is you'll become interesting again when you start to exceed his expectations. I don't trust you, not yet, but there's enough about you to give me some hope.'

'Your plan—whatever it is—you're willing to give it a try?' And suddenly, Helen was alive and animated.

Moira groaned inwardly. 'We'll see. We have time to beat you into shape. You know I'm a bitch. If this is going to work, then that's pretty much the only side of me you're going to see from now on. Think you can handle it?'

'I think I can handle you. What's the "it" we're talking about?'

'The freedom fighters that picked me and Keagan up after the Thargoids left, they didn't allow hangers-on. You joined, learnt, and fought as one of them or you were shot and dumped. I'm going to train you the way they trained me.'

33

Deep Space, System LTT 10787

I hope this isn't going to be a long tearful goodbye. Moira's manner was brusque. 'Are you ready?'

Helen grimaced as she pushed the words past her broken lip. 'It still feels like I've got so much to learn.' A little blood trickled down her chin as the split reopened.

You do, I hope this is enough. 'That's not what I meant.'

'I know. I wanted to say "thank you" for—'

'It's okay. Look, about the beating…'

'I said I was okay with it. This has to look real. You did what you needed to.'

'I wasn't apologising. I was going to say, you took it well.'

'Apologise? Never!' Another drip escaped when Helen smiled. She winced.

Still so soft—but Moira wasn't about to quash Helen's vulnerability when she would need it as a shield.

'With you as my instructor it was inevitable my pain threshold would go up.'

Moira felt she knew Helen now, and tried to find the words she needed to hear. 'You worked hard. You've learnt a few tricks and you've toughened up. I wouldn't risk Keagan or Masterssson if I didn't think you could do this. Good luck. Now, are you ready?'

Tension in every line of her face, Helen nodded.

When it looked like she would say something else, Moira shook her head. 'I'll see you later. Act weak and think strong, and we'll bring them home.'

*

Helen reached between her knees and yanked on the release handle for the co-pilot's escape pod. She fought the claustrophobia as the mask unfurled across her face and the harness tightened, locking her securely into the seat's pressure gel. Metal sprang from above and below, isolating her from everything outside. Then something shoved hard from underneath and her eyes unfocused, leaving only a dark tunnel where the universe should be.

She blinked, waiting for the blurred double-image before her to sharpen. The viewscreen ahead showed stars rolling with the spiralling motion of the pod. And there was Jane, already resealing herself against the emptiness as her escape-bay door slid back into place. *Goodbye, Moira. Don't get caught.*

'There is no need for alarm; you are safe inside a fully equipped Vega Line Corporation escape capsule. This is an advanced piece of technology designed for your comfort and to ensure your safety. The stars outside are moving because the capsule is automatically orientating itself towards the nearest space station. No action on your part is needed; this craft is programmed for self-navigation. If the view of the stars is causing distress, please give an appropriate instruction to the onboard computer. You may also adjust the environmental controls within safe limits.

'However, due to space restrictions, we regret to inform you that supplies of available liquid and solid nutriment are limited. To ensure you arrive at your destination in optimum physical and mental health, an induced sleep will be necessary during transit. There is no need for alarm; the procedure is painless and perfectly safe. You will be woken at your destination and attended to by expert medical personnel. We apologise for any inconvenience. Please note: the costs of your medication, transport, and consumables will be covered by any standard galactic insurance policy.

'Before sleep, do you have any further instructions or queries about our service you wish answered?'

Helen scratched her left ear where Moira had injected the sub-dermal nano-transceiver. Eardrums did not itch, but knowing the irritation was psychosomatic did not seem to help. Linked to her implant, she could activate it with a thought. All she got now was static; she was already out of range. But despite the lack of contact, she did not feel alone.

'Computer, no, I'm ready. You can induce sleep now.'

All she felt was a slight pressure on her upper arm. Her doubts and the memories of her last trip to Carl's headquarters whirled around each other before beginning to slow. As she drifted into unconsciousness, she thought of Gustav and Moira... but lost the sense of it as the darkness took her.

*

'Escape Capsule 1 of 2. Vessel of Origin: PC SS645/F7.

'Status: Clear of asteroid field. In motion.

'Current System: LTT 10787.

'Destination System: Toci.

'Intra-System Destination: Harvest Dock Station.

'Occupant identity: confirmed from emergency implant file as Helen Masttersson.

'Next of Kin: recorded as Gustav Masttersson. Status: notification sent.

'Occupant Status: Stable—Monitoring reveals dermal contusions and lacerations. No deep-tissue damage identified.

'Prognosis: Occupant should reach destination safely without immediate intervention.

'Estimated flight time remaining: 87 hours, 4 minutes, 59 seconds.'

Harvest Dock space station comms computer received tens of thousands of messages every day. The inserted monitoring subroutine intercepted them all, checking their contents against its list of pre-defined keywords. This message was different.

###COMMUNICATION>SCANNED###

###KEYWORD-FLAG>POSITIVE###
###COMMS-SUBR>ACTIVATED###

###MESSAGE>RELAYED###

✽

Deep Space, En Route to the Toci System

Moira stretched, flexing herself as much as she could within the confines of the harness to work out the kinks. She had been awake for twenty-three hours straight, tailing the escape capsule at a safe distance. Long stakeouts or tails were not easy, but experience had taught her to focus like few others. Unfortunately, watching a distant, flickering blob on the scanner did not occupy enough brain power to stop the rest of her mind wandering.

Jane's stealth systems were the most advanced she had ever seen; there weren't many other ships outside faction special-ops that could pull this off. And yet the doubts remained. She had no access to Jane's computer firmware. All such requests were greeted with variations of, 'Unable to comply'. What dormant instructions and subroutines lay hidden inside, Moira had no idea.

She had pried into Jane's guts numerous times over the past few weeks, but much of the engineering that held them together remained beyond her. Somehow, a previous owner had managed to jury-rig ancient and modern into an aesthetically displeasing but functional whole. *If she was human, Jane would be a cyborg-schizophrenic without a warranty or character reference. And I live inside her. Joy.*

More than once, Moira had pondered the strange coincidences that had led to her acquiring Jane. *Or did Jane acquire me? She came to me via Ferris, Linnaeus's lapdog. If there's a backdoor into a subsystem, it would only take a single comms-link instruction—from anywhere, at any time. Linnaeus could detect, shut down, or destroy us on a whim. Is he out there, waiting and gloating? But when this all started, surely I wasn't that much of a threat? He only wanted to run me out of my job, or is that what he wants me to think? I fucking hate clever criminals.*

Maybe Jane is part of a set-up, but not of Linnaeus' making. If the Feds, Imps, Indies, or any one of a dozen major corporations, had an inkling what he's working on, they would intervene. But why would they choose me?

I hate surveillance—maybe another synth-coffee will take me to my happy place.

She was reaching for the harness clip when the proximity alarm went off. *Shite, what the hell is* that *doing there?* Another blob was on the scanner, moving rapidly towards Helen's escape capsule. Moira risked diverting more power to the engines and Jane accelerated.

The ship—massive, sleek—was already on top of the escape capsule when they came into view. *Running dark too; there's no other way they could have got this close. But why become visible now? Unless… shite!*

'Jane, optical zoom on the ship, maximum magnification.' *Imperial Cutter, brand-new, customised, no identifying marks. I bet even a full active scan wouldn't tell me much—it's probably screened to the top of its Imperial skirts. I can't get to Helen in time, and that will easily have us outgunned.*

Moira took the yoke, expertly manoeuvring to maintain range and bring Jane around in the wake of the new ship. She could only watch as Helen's escape capsule was swallowed by the massive scoop on the front. *At least they've taken her alive, but who are they and what the hell do they want?*

'Jane, report: status of all stealth, propulsion, and scanning subsystems?'

'All systems operating within acceptable parameters.'

'Jane, run every optimisation routine you have. If that thing knows we're following, you're space junk.'

This was not part of the plan. Remember your training, Blondie, and don't fall apart on me now.

34

?

... ... Floating. ... ... Where? ... ... No... lying on... something? Soft. Comfy. Heavy? Why am I heavy? Can't open... want to open... see...

'Ow!' She could not restrain her cry as she finally managed to lift her leaden eyelids and was hit by glaring brightness. She told her hand to cover her eyes, but it flew sideways and hung, useless, in empty space.

'Doctor, the corpse is waking up.' The overly-loud male voice made her teeth ache.

'Milton, we'll have words later about your bedside manner. You can go.'

She cringed. Even sotto voce, the soft feminine words were icicles sliding through her ears. A rhythmical series of bumps followed, each more subdued than the last. She wanted to rest in the quiet.

'It's all right; you've just been brought out of hypersleep. It normally takes a little while before you feel orientated.' The voice, barely above a whisper now, was much easier to listen to.

She tried to form words but heard a stream of unintelligible babbling. It took her a moment to work out the noises were hers.

'Don't worry; your speech will come back soon. Helen, isn't it? Can you understand me?'

Helen gave a slow nod and someone else moved her head while the world spun around.

'Do you mind if I call you Helen?'

She rolled her head a little, side to side on the pillow. It felt easier, but something was still not right. She gabbled again; her tongue felt like rubber.

'What you need to know is that you're safe.'

'Nuh. Nuh ri'.'

'You really are a talker, aren't you? Give it a few more minutes—'

'Nut rit.' Fear gripped her.

'"Not right?" What isn't right?'

'Sleeep—nut rit.' She tried to sit up, only managing to get her head a few centimetres off the pillow before she flopped back, the room spinning. In her near vision, the only features distinguishable from the blur of her surroundings were a dark smudge over a larger white one. 'Toa sic.'

'I'm sorry, I don't understand.'

Helen forced herself to concentrate, shaping each syllable with exaggerated care. 'Tooo ssick forr trip.' An edge of panic had her now. *Wrong… Why…? Where…?*

'I shouldn't be the one breaking this to you. He'll have my head.'

'Telll mme!' Helen tried, again, to rise; the doctor caught her before she slid to the floor.

'Your pod was picked up by a ship that brought you here. It was a long journey. You're experiencing the results of extended hypersleep.'

'Wwhere amm I?'

'I can't tell you that.'

'Soo nnot safe.'

'I can't give you any more information. I'll be in trouble already.'

Helen heard an almost-silent swishing. *Door opening?* She tried to look towards the sound, but her view was blocked by the doctor.

'Milton, what are you doing here? I didn't send for you.'

'Move aside; time for the patient's meds. Orders.'

'How dare you go behind my back; she can barely talk, let alone stand.'

'That's why I've got this; it'd get a blart moving.'

'You're not giving her that. She's under my care.'

'She's alive; I'd say your job's done. He's not willing to wait. If you have a problem, take it up with him.'

Helen's vision was a little sharper now, and she saw a smaller female figure shouldered aside by a large male, dressed as an orderly. She could not make out his features, but he was holding a tube shaped object in his hand.

'No, I donn wann'—'

He took her arm, none too gently. She was too weak to resist.

'I'm having no part in this.' She saw the doctor heading for the exit.

'Wai—donn goo!'

'We don't need her. This won't hurt a bit.'

She tried to pull away, but it was useless. He placed the tube against her forearm. She recognised the warmth of a dermatiser discharge.

'Whaat, haave you given me?'

'A fast acting stimulant. It'll kick you in the head like a heavy-g hangover eventually but, for now, you're prepped and ready to go see the boss. He almost seems excited.' His jeering tone negated the surface politeness.

'Who's your "boss"? And where am I? Some pirate base? A terrorist cell?' *If I'm here, then where is Moira? If I've been brought so far, how will she find me?* She let the fear show on her face, just like they had discussed. *Let's see if Moira's tricks will help.*

'See, you're thinking more clearly already. He said he wanted to answer all your questions himself. Small tip: you might want to keep your tongue civil. C'mon, get your legs working.'

She slid gingerly from the bed and caught herself on Milton's thick arm. It would do no harm for him to think her weaker than she was. 'Thank you.'

Milton gave her a surprised look, as if unused to courtesy. 'This way.'

He evidently did not want to keep his boss waiting. The stimulant quickened her mind, but she did not have to fake the trembling in her legs as she was half-dragged along, her vision swimming. The corridors they went down were an endless flow of bends; even in the 'straight' sections the walls, floor, and ceilings twisted as if desperate to break off into their own tunnels. It was like being inside an intestine, one intersected by junctions and octagonally framed doors which folded, fan-like, before disappearing into the floor as they approached. *Not something you see every day.* The smooth walls were tawny-brown, covered in unfamiliar sworls her blurred vision could not resolve. The industrial light panels and crude ducting that ran along every ceiling—although functional—looked like bolted-on afterthoughts.

'There's gravity, then? Are we planetside?' Helen tried to make it sound like idle conversation, but Milton's leer made him look like a grinning stone. Either she had been too obvious or he did not like the company of women, at least not on an intellectual level.

'We're here.' The big man stopped. These doors were larger than the others, the octagon quartered by bars that received the folding fan leaves before sliding into themselves and disappearing below. Other than a breezy susurration, they made no sound.

Milton prised her fingers loose from his forearm. 'I think you can manage. Have fun.' He pushed her over the threshold.

She spun her head as she was propelled forwards and caught Milton's jaunty wave before the door assembly rose, spreading across the opening and sealing her inside. She was alone. Fifty metres away, there was an open exit. A computer console stood sentry, overlooking an otherwise empty room. Lists of data, diagrams, and video feeds hung invitingly in the air above it. Her attention wandered to the opposite wall: its entirety was covered with a hazy pastel shade of blue—the colour combination with the ever-present tan-brown spiralling on every other surface managing to be both bland and tasteless at the same time. *What is this?* Something bothered her, beyond the strangeness of her surroundings and the precariousness of her situation. There was a familiarity here she could not identify. She stood, studying her surroundings as she waited. As her eyes adjusted, she tried to make out other shapes in the dark corners. The octagonal theme continued, the edges of the floor, walls, and ceiling were bevelled surfaces at roughly forty-five degrees to the vertical, but the joins were organic—no line was parallel or perpendicular to another. The effect was of being in an underground burrow, one carved by machines.

Still she waited, her implant counting the minutes as they passed. The ice blue haze on the right wall shifted and pulsed. *No—flew.* For a moment, vertigo took hold. *They're clouds. A projection or a window?* She looked away and steadied herself. *This place is designed to disorientate. It's a test...* She knew why it seemed familiar. *Carl!* He designed every office and meeting room to throw visitors off-balance. *He's watching me, gauging my response. Will I go to the exit and look for a way out, or to the console for information?* Helen lowered herself to the floor and sat there, legs crossed. It did not take long.

'Helen, I'm impressed.' Carl's speech, as always, was clipped yet languid—layered with disapproval and seamless self-assurance regardless of what he actually said. She turned; he was standing a few strides away, a panel closing behind him. She kept her expression neutral and his dark beetling brows drew together in a slight frown of disappointment that creased his, usually, smooth face—despite the passing years, he had not aged.

'Hello, Carl. Most people would have opened with, "Nice to see you," or, "How are you?", not by abandoning a guest in their playroom.' *'Act weak, think strong.'? If I can't charm Milton then it's not going to work on Carl.*

Carl's brooding eyebrows arched; his slightly hooked nose wrinkling as if he smelt something unpleasant. Helen crossed her arms to hide her shaking hands. *When was the last time that someone spoke to him like that? Is this the man I remember? If I can't act, how far can I push things being real? I'm alone here. What use is the plan with Moira light-years away?*

Shifting as quickly as the clouds outside, Carl's expression changed—a mask of artificial civility. 'I'm sorry, old habits and all that. Welcome to my current home.'

And dramatic pause as he waits for the applause. She stood.

Carl did not offer his hand.

Nothing changes. She let anger give her voice an edge. 'It's… distinctive, but in the circumstances I'm finding it difficult to register much admiration for the architecture. I was on my way to a safe space station when I was picked up, without my consent, by an unknown ship. When I'm finally roused from hypersleep, I wake up here. Where am I, and what's going on?'

'I see you've already spoken with the doctor. What exactly did she say to you?'

I know you were watching the medbay. Back to playing… truth or dare? 'I pressed her for answers and she told me about a ship— nothing I didn't already know. Coming out of hypersleep never felt like that before.' She watched for it and caught the gimlet-glint in his eyes. There was nothing she could do or say to change the outcome for the doctor. 'Carl, where am I, and why did you have me brought here?'

'You are in my office, obviously. Perhaps you had best tell me your story. There is somewhere we can relax through there'—Carl gestured to the exit at the far end of the room—'and take a drink. What would you like?'

He'll tell me nothing until he's satisfied. What does he suspect? 'All right. I'll have chaddon juice.' Helen strolled slowly across the space, Carl waiting until she passed him before herding her towards the exit.

'Don't give them what they want unless you have to and, if you do, make them wait. If they're agitated enough, they may let something slip.' Moira's voice played through Helen's head.

'Milton told me the stimulant would be effective for a little while. Are you feeling tired?'

'I'm starting to, but I can talk if I'm sitting down.' She resisted the temptation to look at the console as they passed. Anything Carl left on display would have been chosen to unsettle her, to make her confused and unsure. Where Carl was concerned, there were no accidents.

The corridor was short and they soon reached another door which fanned open before them and closed just as quickly behind. Carl's implant must have signalled the environmental controls because the smaller room was on the colder side of fresh. Her wakefulness was intended, but she welcomed it.

The décor was neutral to the point of boring, the soft furnishing, deep carpets, and green plants arranged in deliberate disorder—a forced homeliness. *Disorientate your subject first and they will drop their guard in familiar-feeling surroundings. Then a drink, probably laced with something to loosen the tongue, and a casual chat to follow.* Which box had Carl placed her in: a nothing to be squeezed for what she knew then discarded, or someone he valued? She hoped for the latter. *'It's all about leverage.' One of Moira's, and brutally pragmatic as always.*

'Please, take a seat,' he said, gesturing to a soft curving chair that was halfway to a bed. He crossed to a drinks dispenser and returned with her juice. She took it from him and he sat across from her, perching on the edge of a footstool. His hands were clasped, elbows on knees. Having known him for years, Helen could read the expectation in his posture, and the suspicion clouding his forced-neutral expression.

She sat. In the awkward silence, Helen decided that real emotion was still her most effective weapon. *I'll have to play with the facts as I go.* 'We're together again after not meeting for —what?—five years? And nothing has changed; you're obtuse and still make things stupidly difficult. Why did you have me picked up?'

'What were you doing in an escape capsule in the Toci system?'

'I knew your headquarters were there, so I set that as my destination. I needed your help.'

'I'm listening.'

'Do you know Moira Dolan?'

'Why don't you tell me how you know Moira Dolan.'

'She took me, by force, from Adab. She's… psychotic, delusional. She told me this crazy story: that you had kidnapped her brother, Keagan, and Gustav Masterson too. She said her boss was working for you and you'd tried to have her killed.' Helen wondered if there was the faintest change in his expression. 'She said she used to work as an investigator and she had linked Gustav to me, and me to you. I had a chance to get away and I took it.'

'How convenient. So Moira Dolan brought you near my headquarters. To what end? Surely you can see this all seems…'

'Suspicious? You think I'm working with Moira?'

'A possibility, of course—you would agree because of Gustav. Just answer the question, *please*.'

'She wanted me to infiltrate your offices, so I could find out where you were.'

'Ah, the bruising.' His tone was dismissive. 'Your story is that Moira Dolan attempted to force you.'

Fear and anger warred within her. 'I don't know Keagan and I didn't think you would actually kidnap anyone—yet here I am. Do you have Gustav?'

He pretended not to hear the question. 'Was Ms Dolan's plan to drop you off on some remote part of the planet with a distress beacon? Or maybe she was going to put you on a transit ship and you'd shuttle down and walk in through my front door? Or, maybe arriving in an escape capsule would be the most convincing?'

'Her idea, not mine.' Helen's semblance of control was weakening. Each question prised another finger loose from the hope she desperately gripped. She felt sure he could see the rapid pulse beating in her neck. She steadied herself. *It doesn't matter how we got here, or that he's worked it out, all that matters is what he thinks my motives are.* 'She said the escape pod would be most believable: you'd be suspicious of a planet drop because you would want to know how I arrived, and you would expect more from her; the transit ship would make me look like an accomplice and so she settled on this.'

'Honesty. Refreshing. Were the bruises also her idea?'

'Yes.'

'And you agreed to them?'

'My only option seemed to be to go along with her. When I was safely away—'

'You were going to tell me everything and then turn to me, your new protector, to shield you from this "psychotic, delusional" woman. How is that little scheme working out for you?'

'You're mocking me. I thought, because of our past… We didn't part on bad terms… I've answered your questions, put up with your insulting manner. I don't deserve this. You had me kidnapped, or has that "little scheme" conveniently slipped your mind? I hardly think I'm the criminal here.'

'I would be careful about the words you choose.' His tone was cold, the threat real.

Helen matched his stare. *How far is too far? I would never have pushed him like this when I was younger*. But there was something about his manner, some reserve, control as well as threat. *He wants something.*

He leaned back, a slight upturn at the corners of his mouth. When he spoke, he sounded almost reasonable. 'There are not many people I permit to take that tone with me, but for you I will make an exception, this once. After everything, you must be feeling disoriented as well as tired and, as you say, we have a history. The how and why of your arrival is interesting, intellectually, but not relevant to your immediate future. Whether you believe Moira Dolan or not, the choices you make *here* are the important ones. You must have questions—ask away.'

So now we play at being friends? 'Moira let me contact Gustav to prove her point, and he wasn't reachable. Your actions are… a little out of character. What's going on, Carl? Do you have Gustav?'

The 'smile' did not change, nor his eyes break contact, as he tilted his head. 'Do you still love Gustav?'

'I'm sorry, how is that related to our discussion, especially as it's none of your business?'

Again the look of disapproval, quickly glossed over. 'Helen, my dear, ever the scientist. You presume to theorise about me, but you are reliant on old data. Let me dispel a few of your illusions. You are far outside human space, human law. No one knows where you are. This'—his expansive gesture indicating the structure they were inside seemed incongruous in the cramped room—'has been built to my exacting specification. What happens here happens because I wish it. You are here because I wish it.'

Another push? 'So, what is this if not one huge ego trip? You wanted to play petty despot and rule your little kingdom in the middle of nowhere?'

His expression hardened. 'That you think so little of me, knowing everything I've accomplished, demeans you, not me.'

'Surprisingly, this isn't about you, Carl. I'm angry. What's demeaning is being hauled halfway across the galaxy and receiving evasions and power-plays instead of meaningful answers. Are you going to do me the courtesy of a single straight reply, or gloat before you have me thrown out of an airlock?'

'Forgive me. I forget that you aren't the little college girl I knew. You're a woman and a scientist—'

'I'm glad you noticed.'

'What I was attempting to convey, before our misunderstanding, was that you would be a valuable addition to my project. I think you will wish to consider it, when I've shown you what I'm working on. Walk with me.'

A door opened behind him. He made his way towards it, weaving through the furniture. Seething inwardly, Helen followed.

35

Helen followed Carl through a series of identical doors and corridors. Any signs and viewports had been concealed—she was only going to see what he wanted—but she was beginning to get some idea of the scale of the place. Her implant told her she had been walking for over ten minutes, each step adding to the map it was building. Although, without external reference points, it was not going to help find her location—either the grid was being blocked or his assertion they were far outside colonised space was correct. *Is this part of his game? He wants me feeling alone and helpless. Did the ship that picked me up even leave the sector?* Helen brightened at the thought. Maybe Moira had followed after all, and even now she was only hours from being rescued. Still unsure of the sub-dermal transceiver, she decided using it could wait until she was alone. They approached another door, just like all the rest.

'This place—the room, corridor, and door designs—they're not Federal, Imperial, or Allied. From what I remember, this isn't your style either. I thought you said everything was built to your "exacting specification".'

'*Specification*, not appearance. It's a question of function and priorities.' Carl stopped walking and gave her a pointed look, one she still remembered from their endless discussions about her 'wanting to look like a doll'. There was a pause, presumably for some additional security checks, and the door opened. She had expected a laboratory packed full of equipment, busy minions in crisp white coats sitting at terminals and hunched over imagers. That, or a display case containing Carl's latest creation. Instead, lying on a bunk on the far side of a small room, she saw Gustav.

She ran to the barrier. 'Is he hurt, injured?'

'Simply incarcerated.'

Beyond the transparent screen separating them, the room was bare of everything but a computer panel and personal facilities—obviously a cell.

'Gustav, wake up!'

Shocked at her lapse, she recalled Moira's words. *'Carl is a control freak; let him think he can manipulate you—showing your vulnerabilities may make him overconfident, careless.'* Carl knew her; it served no purpose to adopt a pretence. 'What's he doing in there? Get him out.'

'He is in there because he meddled in something that was not his business, and because he is uniquely skilled.'

'You mean you would've had him killed if he wasn't useful. Carl, what happened to you?'

His eyes narrowed. 'Do you want to talk to him, or not?'

'Yes, please, I'd like to talk to him.'

'Very well. Take a little time.'

They would be watched, every word recorded. But even though they were prisoners, it was wonderful to find him alive, to be able to talk to him again. *Now...* Her implant remotely activated the transceiver. It picked up vibrations conducted through the bones in her inner ear—everything Helen heard and said, Moira would hear. ... *if only she's not too far away.*

To avoid detection, the transmissions were focused data bursts, low power with a limited range—broadcasts had to be kept short for the same reason. In the time they had, Helen fervently hoped to hear the sharp yet familiar voice that meant rescue, and hope. Whether or not Gustav could tell them anything, at least Moira would know he was alive and well. Questions about Keagan would only multiply Carl's suspicions.

As Carl walked away, Helen tapped on the clear surface. Gustav did not stir. *I thought he wasn't hurt!* She rapped harder and then hammered. At last, Gustav propped himself up on one elbow, wiping his eyes with a palm. She let out a breath. *Get a grip. He always could sleep like a rock, anywhere he came to rest.*

He looked around, dazed, before catching sight of her. He bounded out of the bed and made straight for the barrier, pressing his hands against it. She mirrored the gesture with her own, his response warming her.

'I'm really glad to see you.' His face fell. 'But not here.'

'I'm just glad you're okay. Did he hurt you?'

'His goons were a little heavy-handed when they took me, and he has ways of getting you to do what he wants. Where's Moira?'

'I don't know.' *How can I tell him there's a plan?* 'I thought she'd gone crazy, claiming you and her brother had been kidnapped. When I left her, she was set on freeing Keagan.'

'Then she's alive, at least.' Some of the tension left him, but not all. 'Did she say… mention anything?'

She tried to squeeze just enough inflection into her voice, willing him to get the reassurance without giving anything away. 'She seemed very determined, and she's resourceful.'

He seemed suddenly downcast. 'She didn't mention me at all?'

This isn't working. 'She told me you were friends, but she planned to use me to get to Carl—you too if necessary. After she had finished beating on me for answers I couldn't give, she became desperate; she said you were expendable.'

'What? She wouldn't…'

No, don't!

But then he got it. She saw his features settle, his body relax. He kept the tension in his voice though. 'I thought she was a friend. I've been helping her for years. I knew she was shit-crazy about Keagan—some kind of emotional dependence thing—but I never thought she would sell me out, or beat on you? Was it bad?'

Please, don't overdo it! 'I'd rather not talk about it.'

'Right, I understand.'

'But you're okay?'

'Fine, apart from being locked up as Carl's pet tekhead.'

She did not want their connection broken, but Carl would end their conversation when he felt there was nothing else to learn. 'What's he got you working on?' She knew she had pushed it too far as soon as the words came out.

Gustav did too. 'I'm working on a little something for him, to help.'

Helen terminated the transducer broadcast an instant before she heard Carl's voice behind her.

'Ah, renewing old acquaintances is so pleasant, but Helen has been in extended hypersleep and it is only the stimulants we gave her that are holding her up. She needs rest. Gustav, I think you should be getting back to work after your little nap.'

It was time to stand her ground, at least a little. 'Carl, I want to visit Gustav again, tomorrow?'

'There is much for us to discuss, after you are rested. Shall we?' He indicated the door.

Although outright defiance seemed unwise, she wanted to make her position clear. 'Goodbye, Gustav. I *will* be back tomorrow.'

'I hope so.'

When they went to press their hands against each other the barrier blocked their touch, but Helen felt the contact.

The silence was infused with Carl's impatience; there was nothing to be gained by pushing him further. With a final smile to Gustav, she acquiesced and walked through the door, Carl steering her from behind.

✳

Carl had said little on the escorted march to Helen's quarters. When they parted, his manner was curt. That had surprised her and, recalling her conversation with Gustav, she could find little that would have annoyed Carl or given too much away. *It must be a good sign: he left disappointed.*

From what Gustav said, he had embraced the role of conscientious objector, but this time he had been cautious and compliant—there was none of his usual humour. *Carl's using me as leverage.* Tomorrow's conversation with Carl would be about her motivator: she cared for Gustav. *I wonder what dance Carl will have me do, when he starts pulling my strings.*

Her quarters were larger than the lounge room she had been in yesterday. The walls, ceiling, and floor were set up in the same general octagonal configuration as every other room: floor space lost to curves at every junction. But no two were exactly the same. The colouration could be thought bland: beiges and browns, with hints of faint sand-yellow and muted reds, but, looking closer, the detail was disconcerting. Every surface was subtly different: myriad small shapes inset into a pearlescent resin-like material. *Shells in clear amber here; the undersides of mushrooms, thin-sectioned there; different, again, everywhere else.* They formed complex patterns, natural, symmetrical arrangements that ran—one spiral to a circle to another—into a larger indefinable asymmetry; there was no beginning or end, only flow.

She was distracted and tired; the intricacies seemed to move, turning languidly in on themselves. *Like they're waiting for something to happen.* She blinked and the motion stilled. *At least the furnishings are plain*—the only concession to her aching eyes.

She tried the door to the corridor but was not surprised when it failed to open. The room was more comfortable than Gustav's cell, but it was a cell nonetheless. She suspected the better Carl's prisoners behaved, the better their accommodation.

She crossed to the display on the wall, positioned for easy viewing from the bed and the small chair next to it. *Not exactly Mithrian levels of comfort.* She slumped into the chair, trying hard to fight the despair that sat cold and heavy in the pit of her stomach. Since ending the last transmission to Moira there had been no reply, no sign anyone was listening. Scenarios played in her head: Moira losing track of the ship; Moira taken, Carl enjoying knowing she was locked in the room next door; Jane destroyed, Moira dead, Carl saving the revelation until she defied him—the termination of hope completing her subjugation.

Moira's voice came to her, but only as a memory: *'Standard practice for breaking a prisoner: leave them to focus on the unknown and their own fears will do the work. Always stay positive. Always stay focused on your goal. It's the only way to win.'*

That's all very well for you to say, with all your training and the disposition of a hellcat. If you're not coming, or dead, where do I find my positive? If there's no rescue, what's my goal?

Her memories of Moira answered, *'Contingency. There is always a contingency.'*

Helen gave up trying to think of one after several useless minutes. She toyed with the idea of trying the transceiver again. The interface with her implant only offered a virtual on-off switch; to communicate she had to speak. Alone in a room seemed like the ideal opportunity, but she was in no doubt Carl was watching. If she started talking to herself, he would take even that slim hope. *Maybe, maybe she'll come.* They were just words.

So I'm left with nothing, unless I can figure this out. Where would Moira start? I need information, but how does Carl make contact with the outside?

'Computer, list available forms of entertainment.'

'The onboard library of visual and auditory entertainment is extensive. Detailing the index would take approximately twenty-seven standard galactic years. For maximum utility, please make requests specific.'

'Very well. Computer, detail availability of current news sources.'

'Those services are unavailable.'

'Computer, display the latest published research paper in the field of xenobiology.'

The paper—by one of her colleagues, Zolan Ross—was dated two months before her abduction. *There were at least two more papers whose publication was imminent. If Carl's ships download the latest updates as they pass through human space, then none have been here since mine arrived. That, or he knew I would try this and he'll only grant me more access if I agree to whatever he proposes tomorrow.* She did not bother to re-read the familiar manuscript; it was flawed in several places.

Body, mind, and options exhausted, Helen decided to surrender to sleep. Pointedly, she lifted the covers on the bed and undressed underneath. She had one new goal, however trivial it seemed, and tomorrow there would be words.

36

Helen's eyes blinked open, slowly adjusting to the diffuse red-orange ambience emanating from walls, floor and ceiling. The room's furniture was barely visible—dark contours against the dim background. She rolled over and white light from the ceiling panels flooded the room. Shielding her eyes and grabbing the sheet, she wrapped it around herself and stood, disorientated and ill-prepared to face the day.

Breakfast was a lavish affair. All Helen's favourite foods from fifteen years ago had been set out on the table in the corner of the room. A stylish but ostentatious outfit was draped across the comfortable chair. Evidently, Carl still favoured the pretensions of Imperial styling. Trying to sweeten her up, he had only succeeded in creeping her out. Someone had been in the room while she slept. She dived under the covers to dress. Out of sight, and rustling her clothes to cover any sound, she risked a whispered conversation.

'Moira, are you there? I hope you can hear this. Gustav is alive and well. I haven't been able to find out about Keagan or Kishino, yet. I think I will be safe in the short term.' Lying still, all that came back was silence. 'Please contact me when you can.'

She made herself eat. *'In a hostage situation, take food and water whenever you can get it.'* Moira's advice seemed sensible, but Helen had to force breakfast past the dryness in her throat. She still had no backup plan. Moira, the expert, was supposed to listen in and advise. *How can I do this on my own?*

As she tidied the leftovers into the recycler, the door to the corridor opened behind her. No one waited outside. She looked across the threshold; the lighting panels fixed to the ceiling flashed, a crass intrusion into an already bleak-looking day. Their makeshift design obscured the intricate fractal whorls patterning the ceiling. The forms morphed subtly as they continued down the walls and across the floor, only to disappear as the stark white light from the closest panels dimmed and those further away lit, proclaiming a baleful invitation.

Before leaving, she eased on a pair of couture slippers. The rumours persisting in the scientific community were true: Carl still liked his women aesthetically pleasing as well as competent. *As long as they don't try to express any individuality.*

The pulsing panels guided her through a series of doors that opened as she reached them and closed behind her. She did not bother trying doors that were not indicated. Knowing her implant was compiling a map, Carl limited her access to new information. She was a rat in a maze of his making.

Following the tortuous route, Helen confronted a closed door fifteen minutes later. Unlike the rest, it stood, inanimate, making Carl's point for several seconds before opening. Walking into the chamber from the confining corridor, she could not help but turnabout, her eyes drawn upwards into the immense space; eight decks high judging by the rows of viewing ports lining the giant octagon's five back walls. The remaining three sides were totally transparent. Her breath caught as she stared at the sweeping star-scape suspended in the black above the horizon-arc of an azure gas giant, its opaque clouds a shining aureole that framed the scene from below. Upon them, the station cast a massive hazy shadow—an organic confusion of tendrillar arcs and gibbous forms that shifted with every movement of the vapours below. *We must be in the outer atmosphere; I've never seen a station orbit this low.* High above hung a segment of moon: vague hints of a terrestrial blue and green surface escaping through a monotonous blanket of white cloud.

'Magnificent, isn't it?'

She had not noticed Carl approaching. 'Being so close to the planet lends drama, but the moon's surface is too obscured to see much of interest. It doesn't compare favourably with Amar's Marbled Mountains or Sippar's Crystal Sphere.'

Carl frowned, and she realised he was studying her to see if she was being deliberately obtuse.

'I was not referring to the scenery. One solar system is much like another. I meant *this*.' His arms swept around, indicating the ceramic-sheened walls encircling them. Such boyish pride was almost comical in someone as accomplished as Carl Linnaeus, but bruising it would have repercussions.

She killed the smile-that-might-have-been before it reached her lips. With it went any sense of charity. *He'll make no concessions unless his memories of me are tinted with a little fondness—too little for me to hide behind.* 'Kidnapping is rather an extreme way of getting an audience, don't you think?' *Not the most diplomatic opening.* She tried to minimise any damage with a diversion. 'Zolan's paper was thought-provoking. I thought he made some interesting points.'

'What? His hypotheses on ammonia-soluble protein folding behaviour in sub-zero temperatures are ludicrous!'

'How did you know that was the paper I pulled up last night? Zolan's had a long career and has published on a wide range of subjects.' He could lie, but they would both know it.

Carl inclined his head. 'Touché. I can understand that waking up far from home and being assessed—'

'Assessed? I've never stayed somewhere before where "guests" are subject to surveillance while they undress and wash.'

'A necessary precaution, I assure you.'

His reply was so smooth she thought she would slide on it. *He'll find out I've changed.* 'Why? I was picked up in an escape pod. I didn't dock here selling dangerously outdated military supplies.'

'You were coming to see me. That speaks of *intent*.'

'I was forced. How does that justify spying on me? You're not being logical.' The accusation was an old trump card. It usually worked.

A feigned stillness failed to cover his awkwardness, or keep the anger from his face.

'I want your word that you will stop any spying in my quarters. No matter what my intent, I'm no threat to you here. You wanted a discussion, but we can't move forward unless we can establish at least a little mutual trust.' It was a risky gambit, but necessary if he was to see her as a more equal partner. *I need the leverage; I just wish I knew how to use it.*

'Very well.'

'Your word, Carl.'

'You have my word.'

She knew he would keep it; he would not demean himself like one of the 'devolved masses' who were 'vacuous and fickle'.

With that small victory gained, it was time to smooth his ruffled ego. *As Moira once said: 'It's not about capitulation or submission. Appeasing a "dominant" male's fragile ego gives you room to outmanoeuvre.'*

'Thank you.' She made a show of re-examining the room before gesturing at the looming shadow on the clouds outside. 'From the little I've seen, the scope is impressive. But why the unusual design ethic—the external shape; internally, the open duct work and lighting. Your tastes have changed.'

'*My* taste? Surely you—of all people—must recognise the superstructure?'

Of course I can, but you'd be resentful if I denied you the big reveal. 'I remember the pictures you took, during the human-Thargoid talks. Why emulate them?'

'Why indeed? The fittings and equipment are the very best our race has to offer.' His tone was disparaging. 'However, this station is a commission, built at my request.'

She tried hiding her burning curiosity behind a mask of disbelief. 'They built it? Why? If you're collaborating with them, what are you hoping to achieve?'

'We'll talk more about that later. First, I need to know that we will be able to work together.'

'It would help if you told me what you want.'

'In time. Take a seat.' He led her over to a padded bench set a few metres back from the transparent wall. Sitting, she gripped an edge hard as vertigo threatened to take her. Under her feet clouds roiled, and the ceiling was lit by stars.

She swallowed. 'A personal theatre?'

'More.'

Carl made an eloquent movement as if conducting. Two points of light appeared and converged on the centre of the giant panorama, each leaving diminishing propulsion trails behind. As Helen wondered how she was supposed to see any detail, the image split in two and zoomed in. She flinched and leant back as two small ships, resembling bats with twin lance-like talons, surged towards each other. It reminded her of the primitive jousting matches on Earth that Gustav spoke so enthusiastically about. This was just another archaic testosterone-filled chest beating session re-enacted with bigger, more dangerous toys.

She looked sideways at Carl. *This has to be a joke, or one of his tests?*

His face was rapt, an earnest and hungry expression framing eyes fixated on the two craft.

Stiffly, she stood. 'This is disgusting. I won't watch people murder each other for "entertainment".'

He did not even look at her. 'Sit down.' His voice carried the hard notes of command and finality.

She looked around the space they occupied. The closed doors suggested the chance of escape but quashed it. They were alone. There was no doubt they would stay that way. *I can't afford to have Carl as my enemy.* She swallowed her morals and sat down.

One of the pilots performed a spiralling manoeuvre that flowed into a loop. Across the emptiness between them, an incandescent line of fire flashed against a sheet of blue, briefly obscuring the rear of the second ship. From the edge of her seat, Helen willed the shield to hold.

'Watching this, it's impossible to live entirely in your mind. You feel it—don't you?—the visceral thrill of watching the superior eliminate the inferior.' The cadence of Carl's words carried his jubilation, despite them being little louder than a whisper.

Helen stared resolutely ahead, not wanting to catch his expression. 'I see a pointless waste of a life.'

The second ship broke away, releasing a missile as it decelerated and turned sharply. Altering course, the ship came between its projectile and enemy, a flurry of energy bolts impacting its shield. The missile, unharmed, arced around, closing on the first ship, the second manoeuvring to block the line-of-sight.

Appalled yet fascinated, Helen followed the balletic movements.

The first ship launched a missile of its own, but they were now too close together and it overshot the second ship as it arced away leaving a clear path in its wake—the first missile struck home, engulfing the craft in a wreath of yellow flame.

She jumped from her seat, an accusing finger pointed at the destruction outside. Her horror mounted as she heard the voice of the station computer.

'Field test eight thousand and sixty-seven complete. Result: clear victory. Pilot 'A' kills: five hundred and eighty-two; pilot 'B' kills: three hundred and sixty-four.'

She glared at Carl.

'Intoxicating, isn't it?' Carl waited, as if expecting her lavish praise or fawning question.

Helen wanted to wipe out that condescending smile by breaking his nose. *This must be how Moira feels most of the time.* Fighting to keep her voice steady, she managed, 'Death is always compelling. Toying with it, perfecting it—repellent is the only word I can find.'

'It was always one of your shortcomings: to be defined, and so limited, by petty morality. You need not worry. Suitable test subjects are difficult to locate and expensive to replace—the ships are equipped with custom safety equipment and their computers governed by strict protocols. There is little danger of death or even major injury, both are inefficiencies I cannot afford.'

Relieved, she watched the 'destroyed' ship fly from the arena, trailing the victor. 'So, what's all this for? What part of your "masterwork" are you trying to show me?'

His smile grew wider. 'I've perfected the Pivot.'

'The pivot?'

'The Giurgea Pivot.'

She kept her expression neutral. 'You're jumping from space combat to fictional biochemistry. That protein structure can't be made. In your lectures… you stated it was hypothetical—an interesting mind-model.' She hoped he could not see her pulse pounding in her throat.

'No longer fictional or hypothetical. I synthesised the precursors eleven years ago. And now I am perfecting it. I want you to be part of that work.'

For a moment, all she could do was stare at him. The chance to be involved in something so monumental, a single leap so great its achievement would push forward the boundaries of practical and theoretical biochemistry by decades—it was her lifelong dream. And Carl held it in his hands.

He took her silence and cooling excitement for disbelief. 'I can forgive your scepticism, given the short time you have had to assimilate the facts, but I am disappointed that you, of all people, would think me a liar.'

What will he believe? 'This is big, Carl, even for you. Show me. I need to see the research, or at least a three-dimensional model where the underlying mathematics can be verified.' She put eagerness, even a plea, in her voice. It was not hard.

He inclined his head and she turned. The planet, moon, and star-scape disappeared, clinical white replacing the transparency of the outer walls. Twenty metres tall, the Pivot hovered before her, the atoms and molecules moving smoothly as their bonds stretched to accommodate the transitions from one impossible conformation to the next. It was exactly as she remembered seeing it on Jane's display. She allowed her jaw to slacken, her mouth hanging open until she realised this may be too much and closed it.

'The mathematical model.' A table, figures, and symbols appeared to one side. 'Would you like me to interface it with your implant?'

She almost said 'yes', almost. Implants were supposed to be secure, inaccessible from the outside, but given Carl's formidable technical resources… 'No, this is fine; my thoughts are still disordered from hypersleep. I need to spend some time with this; do you have a terminal I could use?'

He smiled paternally. 'I'll have one brought. Notify me when you are ready to talk again.'

As he walked away, she told herself what she was about to do was necessary to avoid arousing his suspicions. She *could* have resisted the compulsion to know more; the twinge of guilt was because she did not want to.

37

Helen had stayed in the chamber past lunchtime, through the afternoon and evening, eventually grinding to a halt in the early hours of the following morning. She did not stop working when the service droid brought her food. Even when the doors opened so she could deal with her bodily needs, escape did not enter her thoughts. Her mind was soaked with new understanding: impossibilities made real by sub-atomic nuances; intricacies buried within a simple beauty. Being on the threshold of comprehending the workings of the Pivot was a frenzy of discovery and a heady joy she could not explain to a non-scientist.

As she finally crawled, naked, beneath the sheets, she remembered the times when she had tried to share her enthusiasm for her work with Gustav. He would smile, nod, and ask intelligent questions. He did not even look bored as he listened to her long explanations. But she could never convey the wonder of the biological systems she studied—he was all algorithms and machines. And this, this was the most incredible discovery of all. She longed to tell him everything: the possibilities, the *meaning* it had for her. *But he isn't here.* He was in a cell, a prisoner, just as she was. Shame washed through her, souring her mood. *I'm supposed to be finding a way out, but this opportunity—it won't come again.* She lay, staring at the ceiling, her heart and mind at war.

At last, weariness dragged her into a fitful sleep.

*

When Helen woke, her eyes gummy and sore. She tried the transceiver again.

'Moira, are you in range?' She hissed her query three times, pausing for several minutes between each as she waited for the hoped-for answer. *My only contingency may be to work for Carl.* A stab of self-loathing followed—it was not an appalling prospect.

She dressed and breakfasted, feeling more comfortable in her quarters after Carl's guarantee of privacy and discovering her morning 'gifts' were brought in by a droid. He wanted her to feel indebted, but she resented the captivity more. She hardened her resolve. He would not buy her with finery, or the glamour of working on the Pivot.

She was reassured to see that her door did not open until she touched it, and surprised to hear the voice of the station computer:

'Please turn right as you exit, then proceed to the next junction.'

Carl's feeling more amenable this morning. She followed the step-by-step instructions that took her along familiar routes. When her implant reported she had reached the junction she wanted, she stopped and spoke into the empty air.

'Carl, I know you're listening. Although I'm intrigued to see what you have planned for me this morning, I would really like to see Gustav before we start.' *And find out how much freedom working with you would leave me.*

There was a pause. 'Very well.' His voice was flat. The door on her left opened. 'I know you can find your way.'

Disapproving or disappointed?

The walk seemed to go more quickly. *Probably because I'm directing my own steps.* She found Gustav hunched over his terminal, typing furiously on virtual keys. Their glow seeped under his armpit and elbow, but she could not make out the symbols he entered.

Carl's disembodied voice broke across her thoughts. 'Don't be long.'

She had anticipated his impatience and that the visit would be cut short, but the tone was antagonistic. It sounded like a warning. *I've done nothing to provoke him, so it must be aimed at Gustav.*

✳

Gustav stretched, trying to ease the lines of fire that played across his shoulders. *There are so many easier ways of coding than this.*

'Don't be long.'

His heart leapt in his chest, as it did every time he heard Carl's hard tone. But there followed a welcome voice—soft, warm, and feminine.

'Good morning, Gustav.'

'Morning, Helen. Mine just got brighter, how's yours?' She was so close, just on the other side of the barrier. He stood and pressed his palm against the cool surface, his last human contact an eternity ago.

She returned the gesture. 'It could be worse. The accommodation is comfortable, if a little restricted, but the catering and room service are good.'

He knew he would pay for it later, but he could not resist. 'Someone has a nasty taste in clothes, though. If dressing in outlandish outfits is a chore to be borne by the privileged, you should try rebelling, like me. I get my own little box and a simply-tailored utility outfit. You'd look good in one of these.' He expected her to smile, like she used to when he teased her.

Her voice was tight. 'I'm sure we all have our own ways of coping. I'm doing what I can to get by.'

This can't go wrong, not now. 'I know. It takes some getting used to...' He searched for the right words. 'Do you remember when we first met—on Argovia—you spent months negotiating with a local warlord for research access while I was there, working on contract?'

She looked directly at him, her eyes intense but her voice gentle. 'I remember.'

'We'll be fine. You'll be fine. You always were stronger than you knew, and still are.'

She smiled, her face radiating warmth and a little too much relief. He flicked his eyes up and back to hers. Tears glistened on her lashes. She gave an almost imperceptible nod as she quickly wiped them away.

Good. Mastersson felt the tightness in his own muscles loosen.

'That's long enough. You can see each other later,' Carl's voice intruded.

The familiar knotting was back in a moment. *If we both do as we're told.*

The external door opened, reinforcing the instruction.

'You take care, and remember—be good.' He felt his heart lift as she smiled.

'I'll see you soon, Gustav.' She turned by the door to wave before she left and he smiled as he lifted a hand.

As the door shut behind her, he balled his hand into a fist and let it fall back by his side. 'Okay, Carl, you can punish me for a trivial quip about your clothes sense, or I can get back to work. What's it to be?'

'Given your slow progress, you had better get to work.'

He turned to the terminal. *Oh, I will.*

✲

With every new corridor Helen walked, her implant map expanded but, caught inside Carl's information bubble, she still had no overall sense of the base. This was the first time a door had opened onto a decline. The descent began gradually enough but grew steeper as she rounded the first spiral turn of the corridor. There were no handrails or steps; the risk of starting a slide she would be unable to stop was very real. She sent an instruction from her implant to activate her footwear and was relieved when the soft shoes responded, their increased grip enabling her to make better progress.

As she reached the second bend, she had to turn and side-step to keep her balance. Carl's grandiose sense of the dramatic played out in his choice of locations—not reassuring. *This place is definitely not built for humans. I wonder if he will introduce me to one of them?*

She decided it was worth the risk, and her transceiver went live. But, with each downward rotation, the static in her ear increased until there was nothing but a wall of white noise. *Interference? Does Carl want to meet here because he knows about the transceiver?* Her pulse racing, she switched it off.

She sidled down four more revolutions before reaching a door set perpendicular to the slope of the floor. It was easier to touch the base with her shoe than with her hand. It opened as easily as the others, but as the fan blades disappeared she was hit by a frigid wall of air. The cold pinched her skin; biting the back of her throat, it tightened her airways. Dressed as she was, temperatures like this would become dangerous in minutes. The hairs on her arms were already standing up inside her dress. *Another test: risk pressing on or turn back.*

She knew the solution had to be in there. As she slid forward, the slope eased, flowing smoothly into the level floor of the room. The sibilant hiss of moving air sounded behind her as the door closed. Being left alone was no surprise. For Carl, it was a dominance thing.

At least waiting isn't going to kill me. In the corner, hanging over crude renditions of human torsos, were several baggy environment suits. She took hold of the nearest, but even her numbing fingers could not stand to touch the frosty material for long, the pain was too intense. She sent an interface command from her implant to the suit, instructing it to warm. *It's like his life isn't complete unless he's pushing someone.* She had heard of Weltschmerz Syndrome—but the morbid risk-taking did not usually start until the sufferer was over one hundred and twenty. Carl was barely in his eighties. *Maybe his mind runs through life's pleasures faster than the rest of us.*

She waited a few seconds before touching the inner lining of the suit. It was cold, but the dusting of ice crystals had disappeared. Shivering, she wrapped the sleeves of her fashionable-but-useless dress around her hands and pulled the suit from the mannequin. Her leaden fingers struggled to maintain a grip through the gauzy material, but she managed to wrestle herself into the thing. It sealed, automatically adjusting elastic nano-fibres to fit her form. She relaxed as the hood and faceplate eased themselves around her head. *Just like standard biohazard protection.*

'Welcome.' Carl's tone sounded reverential—a holy man welcoming an acolyte into the inner sanctum.

She turned to see him wearing an outfit identical to her own. There was no point challenging him about his latest amusement. He rarely gave a justification, and never an apology. 'You seem expectant. Do you often meet them here?'

'Not often, but we meet here. Few others have been accorded the honour of their presence. One day you may be, on my recommendation.'

Helen breathed out heavily, her mask fogging. *'One day.' All this, for nothing. But what's the alternative to playing along?* 'You seem to admire the Thargoids, but every factions' newscasts carried the same stories about the negotiations: there's little common ground between our species.'

'Newscasts are little fictions to soothe an easily frightened populace. They are not ready for the truth—humanity has yet to recognise its new gods.'

Helen stared at him. 'Even for you, that's a little grandiose, isn't it? I never thought to see you in the subordinate role of alien evangelist.'

He frowned. '*I* have no gods, but—galling as it is—humans need theirs to remind them they do not dwell on Mount Olympus' summit. And, this time, Prometheus will not be chained. I don't work for them; our arrangement is reciprocal. I synthesise the Pivot with their technology and they benefit from my discovery. That they acknowledge me as an equal is the crowning glory of my career.'

'What, above discovering the Pivot, above all your contributions to science? You've spent your life pushing back its boundaries.'

'Huh. Decades of work and the Pivot is the only thing I achieved of any worth. Without it, I would be a mere simulacrum, duplicating things they achieved long ago.'

Helen had seen Carl passionate before, but this bordered on mania. 'Their technology may be superior, but that hardly makes them gods.' The words stuck in her throat, but she had to acknowledge the truth. 'You're human and your research has surpassed theirs. You are proof that humanity won't always lag behind.'

'Blind optimism you cannot help, Helen, floating inside humanity's little delusion-balloon as you are. Your isolation engenders that dangerous combination of naiveté and arrogance that colours all human thinking, and will lead to the extinction of our species.'

The utter certainty with which he spoke chilled her. She hoped he was insane because the alternatives were too terrible to contemplate. 'Carl, you told me humanity has existed alongside the Thargoids for four hundred years. We held them back in the Thargoid Wars. They attack ships and occasionally outlying colonies, but more people are killed each year by pirates.'

'Your citation of this circumstantial evidence shows as much understanding of their military capability as an insect perched on an Imperial Admiral's lapel.'

She tried to keep the impatience from her voice. 'Carl, you've been working with them for—'

'Years.'

'For years, exactly. So how can you expect me—'

It was as if he had not heard her. 'The Thargoid "Wars"? A skirmish. No one has ever met a "Thargoid"—a term used by the ignorant, coined when mankind—monkeys in spacesuits—found a bit of wreckage with symbols on they could not read. Humanity survives a few brief encounters with the Oresrians and thinks it can stand against the whole race.'

'Oresrians?'

'Some 'authorities' speculate they were centuries ahead of humans… they have been in space for *millennia*. Once, the great age and inertia of their culture was to be our salvation. Mankind is fickle, brains jumping from one thing to the next, forever tinkering, so, for a few decades, we begin to catch up while they stagnate. But they are intelligent, Helen, oh so very intelligent. An aeon of ingrained tradition cannot atrophy minds such as theirs indefinitely. Why do you think this place exists? The Oresrians have been watching, learning. Each day they discover more, they become stronger.

'In a technological age, the evolution of a species cannot be measured by the glacial speed its biology alters, but by how much and how fast it can learn. The fulcrum of power tips when a species acts on their new knowledge. Earth history is replete with examples of technologically advanced cultures destroying or assimilating primitive ones. Played out on a galactic scale, can you see another future for our species?'

She stared in horror, wilful disbelief warring with a deeper certainty he was telling the truth. 'You're helping them! You want me to help… All so you can have the aliens you idolise dote on you like a favourite pet. Were you planning to watch from the sidelines when they destroy us?!'

He struck her then—not his usual backhand, but with a clenched fist. He was not a large man, but the blow sent her reeling. Her helmet struck ground, head whiplashing inside. Blood fountained, filling her mouth. She coughed and spat out a tooth which clattered as it bounced into the faceplate. She stared at it dumbly, too shocked to react. Her old self urged her to stay down and gave her permission to lie there, sobbing. Instead, she forced herself to her feet, wobbled, and steadied. She was gratified to see him rubbing his knuckles through the back of the thin glove.

'You took that better than expected. An effective demonstration, I think—while we can all grow, real change and progress require *impetus*.

'I am not a traitor to my species—I am humanity's saviour. While the Oresrians watch us, I watch them. They are beautiful in their purity, their efficiency. What humans label as brutal, they call purposeful. They epitomise our concept of survival of the fittest. There is no tolerance of weakness or sentimentality. What is necessary, is *done*. When pressed on several fronts by the Klaxians, a second "Thargoid" group, the Oresrians deemed it necessary to shift the balance of power in their war; so when I offered the Pivot and a ready supply of elite human pilots—'

She tried not to cringe as she spoke, fearing another blow for the interruption, but she had to understand. 'As interesting as alien politics are, you've lost me. How do their plans fit with yours?'

His smile was beatific. 'Surely you've discerned the Pivot's potential for augmenting human cognition?'

'The Pivot would be neurologically active, and in several areas of the brain at once. Adapted, it has the potential to cure several chronic mental conditions. It could benefit millions of people.' And then she remembered Keagan; she had thought little of Moira's brother over the past few days, but Moira said he had changed: uncharacteristic appetites for learning and bettering himself, and his newfound lethality in a pilot's seat. 'Keagan Dolan, you took him as one of your experimental subjects. Was he piloting one of the ships I saw yesterday?'

Carl inclined his head, the teacher acknowledging a slow pupil. 'Yes, the one that lost. He is consistently underperforming—not something I shall allow to continue for much longer.'

Helen's heart ached for Moira, but there was nothing she could do or say that would help. 'But how do the Oresrians benefit?'

'Another question? Disappointing, but very well… The Oresrian changes represent a great awakening of their species. The necessities of survival mean they are eager to learn, and I—a human—am teaching them! They are the perfect pupils. They observe and retain everything. By comparison, most human intellects are little better than the average gastropod's. Each of us has to learn independently: verbally or via direct observation and experience—a clumsy and inefficient process. Oresrians can pass their experiences directly to others of their species. What I show the Oresrians here, every Oresrian will know when they return home.'

'This is crazy. How does making Oresrian pilots more dangerous make you the saviour of humanity?'

'Stupid girl. Oresrians will not work alongside ordinary humans. Only I have the Pivot to offer, something so valuable they would agree to truck with one of our species. Augmented by the Pivot, our spontaneity, creativity, and adaptability means that my enhanced pilots invent new manoeuvres and tactics. The Pivot makes their erratic monkey-minds valuable. The Oresrians here learn from my little demonstrations. When they pass that knowledge to their kin, they will have the combat edge they need to eliminate the Klaxian threat. With that threat removed, the Oresrians will not be pushed towards human space. By giving the Oresrians the ability to defend themselves, I buy humanity the time it needs.'

It took Helen a moment to digest what he was saying. 'But our very best pilots will be no match for theirs. What if you're wrong? What if they come for us after their war with the Klaxians is over?'

'Humanity could not stop the Oresrians if they move against us. Choosing to bestow my gift on either party would not change that outcome. The Klaxians already push into Oresrian space, seeking to expand. Who will stop them, if not the Oresrians? Let them weaken each other before they turn on the Homo sapiens.

'Their intra-racial fighting buys humanity time. Afterwards? Culturally they still move slowly by our standards. Our species needs that delay. We are at a fulcrum point in history. After the Oresrians leave, I will develop more effective versions of the Pivot. I will sell each new iteration to the highest bidder. There will be a biochemical arms race between every major human power. They will bid, or their pilots will be left behind—effectively useless.'

'So you end up our species' richest dealer.'

Carl shook his head. 'No vision, which is why humanity needs someone like me. Money has nothing to do with it, other than as a measure of economic power which, in turn, is a crude but effective measure of the evolutionary fitness of a society. A society that cannot compete economically will lose the ability to defend itself. It will be consumed by a stronger, more worthy, society. For too long mankind has languished in a pseudo-peace. Each year we pour billions into looking after the sick, coddling the inadequate. Each year, billions of pathetic lives incapable of looking after themselves mate and reproduce—making more pathetic lives. Each year, humanity's gene pool is diluted—our species weakens. Now the Oresrians are learning to learn, they will evolve and move on to greater things while humanity masturbates in its own genetic filth—devolving with every generation back into the primeval soup from which we came.

'The moralists and do-gooders deny humanity the potential of genetic engineering. By what right do they decide our fate, when they are blinded by their own self-righteousness? By releasing an improved Pivot to humanity every few years, I will stretch every economy. Resources will be diverted from pampering the inferior. Societies and individuals will strive against their peers, and humanity will once more be exposed to the perfecting evolutionary forces from which it has so long sought to escape. Within a few generations, augmented by my Pivot technology and honed by natural selection, humanity will emerge fitter and more able to survive than it has ever been. *Then*, we will be great, *then* we will deserve our place in the universe. And then, if the Oresrians will not give it to us, we will be strong enough to *take* it.

'That is what only I can give humanity: its ultimate perfection and best chance of survival.'

Too shocked to absorb the full implications and knowing she must hide her real feelings, Helen stalled. 'So I'm to be part of the development team for the Pivot?'

'You make it sound so mundane, but yes; I am offering an unparalleled opportunity to engage in research at the cutting edge, to work alongside a superior species, and engage in an endeavour that will secure humankind a future.'

'How many others have you recruited? Is Gustav part of your great work?' She managed to hide the sarcasm.

'As for biologists, you are on a shortlist of one. Mastersson is currently working on other projects, but, if he shows himself to be more willing, his talents could be used to hasten humanity's perfection.'

'You mean for espionage and eliminating those who get in your way?'

'I have nothing to fear from direct opposition, but Mastersson's skills could purge the weak at a faster rate.'

It was getting harder to hide her anger. 'You sound supremely confident. Every human power will ally against you when they discover what you're doing.'

'By the time they work out I am not offering exclusivity, it will be too late, there will already be a power imbalance. Those ahead will be loath to lose their advantage, and those left behind will not dare open water for fear of being swallowed by bigger fish. Humanity is fundamentally selfish—the concerted effort needed to discover my location or impede my progress requires levels of cooperation those in power do not have the ability to achieve.'

Desperate to find a flaw, she flung the question at him. 'Every human faction, nearly every corporation, has a covert strike team; one will get to you.'

'You think so? The Oresrians are not short-sighted. I am a proven asset, one too valuable to risk—they will protect me in case they need me again. If they require a greater return on their investment, then I will think of something. Due to their high regard, they have already acceded to my request for a deterrent.'

Her heart sank. 'A deterrent?'

'When humanity becomes curious, the Oresrians will launch a pre-emptive strike on ten outlying systems. Too late, ships will come and swarm ineffectually over the dead, before they flee. Humanity's leaders are terrified: they give credence to superstition when the unknown should be acknowledged, and uncovered. All they know: the Oresrians have technologies they cannot match. Humanity will soil itself at the thought of crossing a territorial boundary marked by that much devastation.'

She turned her back on him, hiding her knotted fists under crossed arms. *I can't lose control. And I can't reason with him— he's become a monster.* She forced her breathing to steady. *Humanity won't be that easily cowed, but we have to stop this. Gustav must have something, he must! And where's Moira?*

'Is something troubling you?'

Helen buried her feelings. 'I've… never been made an offer like this before. I do have an issue with the degree of personal choice available.'

'We are both adults. After everything I've told you, I can hardly let you leave, can I?'

'And Gustav? Will my decision have any bearing on him?'

'We live in an interconnected universe. Both you and he have the opportunity to benefit from the situation.'

Or not, she thought bitterly. 'I need time.'

'Assimilating a new worldview and re-evaluating your place in the universe takes an emotional mind a while—I understand that—but things progress and I need those around me to be as focused as I am.'

'I'll give you my answer as soon as I can.'

'Yes, you will. Until then, I have things I must attend to. If you have further questions, we can schedule another meeting.' He nodded to her, a dismissal.

She nodded back, turned, and walked from the room. The door opened before she reached it. When it closed behind her, she initiated the environment suit's release sequence. Unable to wait, she scrabbled to remove it, scraping it off her like something dead and repellent. She leant against the corridor wall, breathing hard. Away from Carl—with each intake of clean air—she felt less constricted. He would be watching, but she could not make herself care. There was so much to process, but first she needed to retreat to her room and wash.

38

Deep Space, the Peregrina System

Moira settled deeper into the seat as she reset Jane's flight program and felt, rather than heard, the reverberation of multiple stealth-plates realigning on Jane's outer hull before the system shut down. Through her visor, she watched the console displays wink out. Starved of power, Jane was going to sleep.

Inside the survival suit, Moira was cut off from the ship and the essentials she offered. Survival was possible for weeks with the re-breather and four tons of liquid oxygen in the hold. The suit would stop her freezing for at least a week before its power cells gave out. But the suit's newly-replenished survival rations would last, at most, four days. Masterson had described internment inside an ancient-Earth sarcophagus to her once; she could not think of a better analogy.

Brainstorming had yielded no alternatives. None of the standard avoidance methods would work—their heat signature would be too intense and there was nothing to hide behind. This way left them not just vulnerable, but helpless. She ejected the doubts, yet again. It was necessary.

Jane's trajectory was pre-set. Moira hated giving away control, but from three hundred thousand klicks out, a fraction of a degree off and they would miss by tens of thousands of klicks, or slam straight into the planet. Like throwing a stone, the only opportunity to alter their track was at the start. Everything else was unpowered freefall down Eurynomus' gravity well before momentum carried them clear of the gas giant. *Hopefully.*

Jane took over the ship's manoeuvring thrusters before powering up her main engines; this far out, the exhaust heat was undetectable. Despite the g-protection from the pilot's seat, Moira still felt the kick in her back as Jane shot forwards. Her fingers dug into the armrests as she held on—a primal instinct she never quite managed to override. She gritted her teeth against the pressure and could do nothing more until Jane reached her target velocity.

Finally, weightlessness—the only sign the engines had shut down. Jane would be a block of ice long before they arrived. *Now, we wait.* As Moira reached for sleep, a familiar thought surfaced: *I hope this time is different.*

✳

She awoke groggy and unsettled. Reaching up with a glove, she scraped the ice from her facemask. The environment suit kept out the worst of the cold, but Moira still shivered. *Being awake makes no difference—with every display powered down, I'm still blind.* She released the harness and pushed herself over to the viewport. Lifting the scraper from her belt, she set to work on the crystals that filmed the duraglass. Over the hours, the cold had transformed her breath into a thin frost that covered every surface. It was irrational: the human urge to see where you were and watch the scenery go by. If she saw death approaching through the viewport, it would be too late; Jane was down too deep to come back in time to fight or flee.

She could just see Peregrina's star setting behind the gas giant, the last of its corona disappearing below Eurynomus' blue horizon. Staying in the planet's shadow increased their chances of staying alive. Thinking of Jane as a person was sentimental, but, out here alone, she was Moira's only company.

The gas giant grew, parallax accelerating the rate, until the viewscreen contained nothing else. Her omni-block flashed a simple acknowledgement: 'Recording.' Jane's passive scanners were juiced with the little power they needed, the results retained in memory to be analysed later—anything to keep her energy signature below discovery threshold. Passive scanners were incapable of resolving detail, but all Moira needed were the flight patterns of the Thargoid drones.

After so many passes by the patrol perimeter, Moira was angry.

During the first fly-bys: cold, icy panic; the whirr as the suit struggled to compensate for the sweat; uncontrolled shaking; commands to Jane that had to be shouted past the blockage of a dead tongue locking her throat—barked between pumping intakes of air—blood when she had bitten it. In scanner range: an unknown number of Thargoid drone-ships—only Jane's ability to re-align and distort her outer hull plates and alter the coating of inorganic chromatophores standing between them and discovery. Her resemblance to a rogue asteroid was far from perfect.

But there is only so much fear the mind can take before going numb.

Jane described more tangential tracks—how many, Moira did not know, insensate in her enveloping blanket of nothing. Each time her vision narrowed, tunnelling past the point where she could act, think, or care.

Hours later she would come back, small, pathetic, and hating herself.

It did not last. Moira's temper had warmed, simmered, and heated to boiling. Then, her parents; now, the Thargoids were between her and everyone that mattered. Childish fantasies of revenge—Jane flying untouched through an ineffectual hail of alien weapons' fire—had come with the fatigue as she stared at the passing planet-scape through the port. But the results from every pass were the same: there were too many ships, their flight paths forming a tightly coordinated web with holes too small to squeeze through. The frustration became worse than the fear.

As she had waited—and recalled Jane's systems to life time after time when they reached a safe distance, only to turn, wait, and try again—her anger hardened to stubborn resignation. So she pushed, repeating until total burnout threatened, endangering them all.

At last she gave in and attempted some of the—'silly' she had called them at the time—mental exercises Helen had shown her. During the first couple of passes, they made no difference. Her frustration and exhaustion left her barely functional in a maelstrom of disordered thoughts. But, out of desperation, she persisted. At least now she could sleep for most of each run—except when she neared the planet; except when she came close to the people she cared about.

Moira was unused to melancholy. She had faced the worst the galaxy could throw at her and come through fighting—at least with some of her family intact. Keagan was a dick, but she would kick the arse of anyone else who said so, even as she agreed with them. *It's been so long since he's been there for me, but he's the only person in my life; then Masterssson came along.* Out here emotions loomed large, and these disturbed her. Helen's mind-gymnastics helped, even though she suspected the techniques were not designed as a distraction. Thinking about Helen left her feeling ambivalent, and that surprised her. The woman was everything Moira was not and a lot she despised. She expected the memories of her time with the scientist to yield a cold indifference or an intense dislike, nothing mixed or positive; it made no sense. *Unless, somehow, shared experience has made us 'friends'?* She prodded and poked the concept around her mind before putting it down, unsure where to file it.

A glint in the viewport caught her eye. She rubbed the duraglass. It was not light playing off an ice crystal. The last rays of the sun caught the moon behind them, the reflected beams illuminating *something* whose path paralleled theirs.

Shite.

There was nothing she could do. Powering Jane would be like activating a distress beacon. *And their ships are fast, probably faster than us. We'd be swarmed in minutes.* She remembered to breathe out and a sheen of mist clouded her visor. In the moment it took to clear, the point of light disappeared.

Did you turn tail?

Cold sweat ran down the back of her neck. Moira counted five seconds passing, ten, fifteen… and it was back, rebounding light playing off it from another angle. *I'm not taking this.* She pushed off the wall, grabbing both armrests of the pilot's chair as she spun into it. *If I go down, I go down fighting. I'm coming for you, bastard!*

'Jane…' Her mouth was dry. Unable to finish the command, she scrabbled with the harness clips. Her frantic hands wrapped around the control yoke, the creases of her gloves digging hard lines into her palms with the pressure she exerted. She flipped the safety caps from the trigger and missile launch controls. Her finger and thumb pressed both at once.

Both switches responded with their usual reassuring click, telling her they were there if she needed them, but were inert without power.

'Fucking shite bastard shite! Jane!'

She wanted to hurt one, wanted more than anything to blow one apart. But she would die before she got the chance, and then Keagan would die, and Mastersson would die, Helen, Kishino and his family too.

She tried to find her centre. She could not. But as she started to breathe, the rhythm found her. It was enough. She released the yoke and placed her hands on the armrests.

The seconds crawled by. A minute passed, two. All the while Jane gently accelerated, the planet's gravity working to slingshot her clear and back into the darkness, and safety.

Moira drummed her fingers on the chair. *Helen probably saved my life.* The thought vexed her. She did not know what to do with gratitude, but irritation made her feel like herself. *Time for a synth-coffee and to analyse the footage. Maybe this time I'll find a weakness.* But Moira was long past optimism; all she had left was the law of averages.

39

In the middle of nowhere, Jane floated, at peace. *Safe.* Moira sat, staring at the three-dimensional image. An hour was enough. The gas giant hung in space, the zoomed image fading out at the top and bottom. *There has to be something there, a base, a ship. Even dumb-fuck aliens don't set up a defence perimeter if there's nothing to protect.* She threw the third empty synth-coffee carton. The net of yellow ship trajectories shifted and changed, but remained tightly wrapped around the prize. From over twenty passes, only two scans showed gaps big enough to pass through undetected and for one, the probability of success was less than fifty-fifty. Her brain was flatlining.

'Jane, hide or steer? Why can't you do both?'

'Please rephrase your query. I do not understand the current parameters.'

'Never mind, Jane. How are you at thinking in tangents, because straight through isn't going to work.'

'Tangential, from the root word tangent: in immediate physical contact, touching. The most commonly understood definition in geometry: it is used to describe a line or plane touching a curve or surface at a single point. Please specify how this relates to my cognitive functions.'

'Jane, you're a genius—terrible at conversation, but a genius.'

'Thank you. My systems have been designed to achieve maximum user satisfaction. Do you wish me to perform a maintenance check on my communication matrix?'

'Thank you'? Don't flake out on me now. 'Jane, no check is necessary. Now please shut up so I can think.'

'Acknowledged. Verbal communication will now cease until resumption is requested.'

Moira glared at the screen. *Sometimes I swear this box of bolts has a sense of humour.*

'Jane, change the virtual viewpoint: take us five thousand klicks from the surface of the gas giant's atmosphere. Display the drone ship patrol perimeter, and show where it intersects with the gas giant's atmosphere. Increase brightness of the ships' trajectory trails. Now, maintaining relative distance, follow the extrapolated intersection line around its perimeter. No, too fast. Good, maintain that pace. Now, superimpose recorded images of weather patterns.'

Minutes later, and the virtual circumnavigation of the patrol perimeter was complete. *This is still stupid, but it has to be better than suicide.*

'Jane, turn us around. We're going sightseeing. I hope your rust-proofing is still in warranty.'

✳

Moira set her jaw in a grim line. *This time.* The receding moon, Undine, filled the gap scraped in the ice on the rear viewport. The timing of their arrival had been exact; the body of the moon shielded them from any outlying Thargoid scouts as they approached the planet from the darkside.

She turned up the low-light gain on her visor, resolving Undine's features into hazy-grey shapes. Today the poles were clear, rendered as light monochrome domes cupping the upper and lower parts of the globe. Darker blotches were interspersed with lines of intermittent white that traversed the equator. *Mountains shielding patchy forest; probably a nice place for something to live. But why here? What's so special about this system, this planet, this moon?*

The thick wispy spiral of a tropical storm crossed the darker grey of the equatorial ocean, hiding it from sight. Over the years, Moira had heard men waxing lyrical about the supposed womanliness of stellar bodies. Was this moon feeling shy—modestly covering her midriff with cloud? *Eejits.*

This was as close as Moira got to becoming sentimentally anthropomorphic about a ball of rock: reason told her the storm below was the one she wanted to enter. *Only three hundred klicks across, perfect weather for a holiday compared to where we're going.* A graceful turn and a push and she floated back along the corridor towards the cockpit. *Time to face the monster.*

She knew looking out of the front viewport—again—was a bad idea. Dwelling on what she was about to do would not make it seem any saner. Tens of thousands of klicks away and it was clearly visible. No one could find a romantic metaphor for the vortex that broiled across the surface of the gas giant. Jane had measured the storm-spiral at over four thousand klicks across. The wind speed around the central eye was gusting at over five hundred and fifty klicks per hour, the white flares of lightning strikes averaging six to ten per minute. *This mother has more than a mild case of indigestion, and we have to get through without getting turned to shite.*

✳

Moira ran Jane dark, cold, and silent for the descent—every system dead, except Jane's central core that limped along on an aging emergency powercell.

It had taken three days to get this far. Compared to most interstellar objects, they were hardly moving; the problem was most interstellar objects moved at tens of thousands of klicks an hour. To reduce the chances of detection during deceleration, the engine burn-time had to be short. Whether *Flaky Jane*'s ancient retro-boosters were up to the job, Moira could not be sure. She tried not to think about what they would look like after plummeting through the upper atmosphere only to be crushed by the near-limitless pressure below. But the gas giant loomed ahead. *Jane'll be squeezed to something smaller than your average cargo canister.* Neither staring nor brooding would make a difference. *It's time.*

She glided easily across the cabin, spinning as she travelled. She landed bottom-first in the pilot's chair and swept the straps across in one smooth motion. The click of a harness was reassuring and business-like. *Now we're getting somewhere.*

'Jane, on my mark, activate pre-programmed entry protocol. And de-ice the viewports—I want to see what I'm doing.'

'Acknowledged.'

A few seconds and the tumultuous weather front could be clearly seen. The epicentre of the swirling mass of cloud glided towards the far horizon spinning anticlockwise, trailing whips of wind as it went. Moira watched the altimeter readout.

'Jane... now!'

The thrum shook Moira's bones as Jane's engines piled on the deceleration. She gripped the flight yoke and eased it back, lifting Jane's nose towards the tail of the storm. They were coming in too fast.

'Jane, more reverse thrust.'

'Thrusters are operating at maximum safe capacity.'

'Then exceed it! Now, Jane.'

If they hit the outer atmosphere too fast with no shields, Jane's hull would crumple like foil. The engine thrum turned into a whine as an arrhythmic vibration gripped the ship, setting Moira's teeth on edge. The collision with the outer atmosphere hammered Moira deep into her seat. Despite its protection, her insides jellified as Jane bounced off gas rendered as hard as diasteel by their speed.

Moira pushed the yoke forward, hard, forcing Jane's nose down. Her muscles strained as she fought to prevent Jane from skipping like a stone on a pond. Jane rebounded once... twice... and Moira was pushed backwards as the storm caught them from behind, carrying them in its swirling wings.

Catching the storm's trailing edge effectively knocked hundreds of klicks per hour off their speed, but now the winds sheared across the ship's hull. Moira threw her weight against the yoke as Jane slewed sideways. *If she flips...* The whine of the engines crescendoed to an inorganic scream—a grating pressure that felt like it would tear Moira's skull apart.

She shouted, 'Jane, hull polarisation, now,' but the roaring swallowed her voice.

Jane's cameras analysed Moira's lip movements and flashed a visual confirmation on the screen: 'Polarisation active.'

I hope this works.

Moira's muscles burned, the shearing winds and turbulence draining her strength minute by relentless minute. She had seen computers attempting to handle chaotic situations; instinct was the only thing she trusted. But she was tired, so very tired.

An erratic vibration was pounding through her seat. *Not good.* She risked a glance at the display, their speed relative to the storm was coming down, but was still outside safe limits. The lancing pain from the whine of the thrusters was becoming intolerable. It was a risk, but Moira had to take it.

'Jane, reduce thrust to within safety limits.'

Immediately Jane began to buck, slicking through the air like wet boots on ice. Then she was turning, and turning.

Wait…

Moira twitched the controls and Jane flipped sideways-on to the sheering winds. She checked the velocity display again.

Finally.

Jane moved with the storm. Gusts kicked her from all directions, but Moira found she could compensate if she did not fight against them. *I'm sure Helen would have something suitably sage to say.*

Sailing with the winds, there was a savage freedom in being part of the maelstrom. She took Jane down into the storm, away from the watching scanners of the Thargoid ships. The lightning was there to meet her.

'Jane, status of hull polarisation.'

'Functioning.'

'Functioning' is not the same as optimal. We've no shields, and if the residual charge on Jane's hull doesn't exactly match that of the surrounding air, the lightning's going to short Jane's circuit breakers—the ones keeping us airborne. This is a dumb plan, except it's working.

Riding the gusts and currents by feel, she felt her tired muscles relax. For the first time in a long time, she smiled. The storm was moving swiftly, its path paralleling the equator. The disabled shields, wind-beaten clouds, the ferocious electrical discharges, and the fact that Jane was travelling with the spiralling vortex would mask them from Thargoid scanners.

In a few hours the storm will pass underneath the defensive perimeter of waiting ships. Edge to the limits of the storm when we are far enough away, let the wind sling shot us out and we go dark again—right behind enemy lines, hopefully with a clear run to whatever's in the centre.

Now that just leaves finding everyone, freeing them, and escaping. Easy as kicking a snarb in the tentacles.

But it was not a plan; it was a list of things to do. If you had a real plan, you had answers for the *how* part.

40

'… Wake up, Mastersson.'

The dream had been beautiful. Moira—or was it Helen?—and the gently rolling hills of a lush green planet. He remembered the gentle caress of warm sunlight on skin—

'Mastersson. Wake up!' That intrusive voice again. Hard. Masculine.

Oh, crap. Carl. 'Whaddya want?' Mastersson prised his head from the flat top of the computer terminal. His arm muscles were tight and stiff as he attempted to gain the leverage he needed to reach vertical. More muscles cramped as he worked on balancing his head on top of his neck. 'I'm awake.'

'Barely.' Carl radiated coldness, Mastersson's lack of consciousness apparently a personal affront. 'You're not ill. You sleep hunched over your terminal and you eat hidden under the covers of your bed. Did Helen divorce you because her attempts to drag you kicking and screaming towards civilised behaviour failed?'

The jibe surprised Mastersson. 'She's been here a week, and I don't see her rubbing off on you. Still hoping your pliable protein will make you King Thing of the universe?'

'Trivialising betrays a small mind, Mastersson. Yours obviously requires more education.'

The spasms shook Mastersson off his chair and left him writhing and groaning on the floor. When he could move again, he wiped the drool from his chin. 'I thought that was going to stop when Helen arrived.'

'Did your attitude? Your flippancy is a shallow pretence. You care for her and feigning otherwise offers her no protection. The ruse is transparent, pathetic, especially after your displays of affection.'

'What's pathetic is you spying on our displays of affection.'

Mastersson's eyes rolled back in their sockets as more power surged through him, bringing renewed spasms in its wake. When the pain stopped, he gulped down several lungfuls of air.

'This is necessary, Mastersson, because your manners fail to improve. Be glad Helen is more valuable to me than you are. My little motivator is always available if you remain intractable, or she does not prove her worth. Now, given your reputation and the number of hours you spend at this terminal, why is your progress so poor?'

'You ask, after injecting me with a choker?'

Carl raised an eyebrow. 'As if I would let *you* loose with a neuro-implant! Without it, I have one less thing to worry about. You've had time and a terminal, so where are the results?'

'The ice-breaking software on your system is so basic it's unusable. It's like starting from scratch. I need my equipment: interfaces, servers, relays, decrypters—the works. If you're the genius you're cracked up to be, maybe you should have thought of that before you sent in your goons with their concussion grenades and automatic weapons.'

'Excuses. Every piece of technology here has been sourced from the most reputable companies in their respective fields.'

'There's your problem. You went to *reputable* companies, not custom. It took me years to write the code I need. The safeguards reputable companies build into their equipment prevent it being vulnerable, but also prevent it from attacking anything else. You have no isolation buffer, no disconnect software, let alone a retracer or rerouter. What you've got here won't get me inside a medpac with a cracked lid. Worse, if I went live with this, it would be traced and neutralised in seconds. This system can't protect itself from external intrusion. How were you planning on defending yourself? I can try to strengthen your security, although what I can do with *this*'—he made a derisive gesture towards the terminal—'I don't know.'

'You will focus your efforts where I tell you, nowhere else. If we were in human space, you would have a valid point, but, out here, my security is taken care of.'

'You mean the Thargoids.'

'If no one can get close and we are not on the grid, I am in no danger.'

Yeah, right. 'Your faith in them is… admirable. I'm sure we're in good claws, tentacles, whatever.' Mastersson braced himself as Carl's anger distorted his features, but the expected shock never came.

'Get to work, Mastersson. Give me a reason to keep you alive.' Carl turned on his heel and strode to the door.

That man needs to relax—but I'm not going to let that happen.

✳

It was idiotic, taking food to his bunk like this, but, as Mastersson had every night since Helen got here, he settled onto it, crossed his legs, and pulled the covers over his head. *I'm five again.*

As Carl became more and more displeased, the food had gone from delicious spreads that charmed the taste buds to pilots' emergency rations. Nutritionally, the stuff was excellent, guaranteed to keep a minion working at optimal efficiency. From a gourmet point of view, it tasted like Gippsworld pig.

As crazy plans go, this one has to be right up there with asking Hengist Duval to make me Emperor. But without my gear…

He ate three quarters of the dark brown paste, trying not to think of the animals in the concentrated residue. Eating fresh-cooked meat that had once walked around on its own was a rare delicacy, but this reconstituted mush diminished the nobility of the sacrifice.

The remnants he smeared across his palm, carefully shaping each letter. Cupping his fingers to shield his hand and give the daubings a chance to dry, he wriggled clear of the sheet and stood, placing the carton on the terminal before he returned to the bunk. He closed his eyes and settled himself, moving carefully but as naturally as possible. *I need to sleep, but this will come off on the covers. It's going to be a long night.*

✳

Mastersson forced himself to lie still—any change in routine would arouse Carl's suspicions. Each minute seemed to last an hour. Eventually, his implant told him it was time.

He heard the droid enter bringing breakfast, another cold carton of sludge. With two armed guards accompanying it, there was no way out through the briefly open cell door. It left, the grunts returning to their barracks in the next block. Carl had taken great pleasure in pointing out that, at a run, they were seconds away. As every door could be locked remotely by Carl or Steen, the thug in charge of security, escape had seemed impossible—until Helen arrived. *I don't want to put you at risk, but I can't see another way.* As far as he could tell from their brief meetings, Helen had seemed willing enough to try something. *I hope she can keep it together because when this starts there's no going back.*

He did not change; his habit of staying in the same clothes for several days was a petty form of rebellion—an opposition to Carl's tailored business-like lines. He strode across to the terminal, concentrating on not swaying from fatigue. *Let's make this look good.* He sat and started work on his assigned task. He had something after an hour—an alibi in case he was interrupted. The next two hours were spent double- and triple-checking his own code. *One shot is all we're going to get.*

Helen was due in half-an-hour. For the look of it, he switched back to Carl's project.

Even behind the barrier, he felt her entry like a breath of fresh air. He stole a surreptitious glance—seeing her filled him with warmth and courage.

Like every other time, he continued to work—this time pretending not to notice her arrival. Like every other time, he turned and smiled when she tapped on the glass—this time tension meant it was a little forced. He approached, trying to read her expression. She brushed her hair back, something she often did when she was nervous. *She can't know today's the day—.* He stopped the irrational thought. Second-guessing things would tie him in knots. He paused and smiled reassuringly before reaching up to the barrier and placing a palm upon it. With the barrier separating them, routine in the smallest things replaced their lost intimacy. Helen stopped, her right hand falling to her side as she realised he was only reaching out to her with one. Years before, when they had been together, he loved the fact that her face was always so open—her emotions passing across it like clouds scudding across a sky.

Her face radiated concern.

He tried to intensify his smile without it turning into a grimace. 'It's really good to see you.'

'You too?'

'I'm good. You seem tense.'

'Carl spoke to me yesterday. He wants me to stay and work for him.'

'On the Pivot; I thought he would ask. He's already shown me how our futures are linked.' He moved against the screen, pressing his closed left hand to it. Helen was between him and the camera. 'I would like to show you… how much I care, but sometimes I need your help to do that.'

The hoped-for response came in a few wordless seconds: the slightest crease of a frown, the softening of her face, the sparking of hope in her eyes, and the tightening of her jaw as her resolve hardened.

He opened his left hand, placing the palm flat against the barrier.

'I wish you could hold me.' She leant forward, bowing her head and pressing it against where his chest would be. Her blonde hair cascaded over her shoulders—no one could see his palm but her. Nervous, he worried there was not enough light getting through for her to read it. They stayed there, just for a moment.

She straightened. This time there was nothing timid about the way she swept her hair clear of her eyes—they locked with his.

I swear I can see the cogs going round. He closed his hand and let it fall to his side. 'What else has been happening, with Carl and everything?'

'I… I suppose if he's already told you about the Giurgea Pivot then it's okay to talk about it. He has this master plan. He wants to become the saviour of humanity. He's working with the Oresrians—'

'The who? I thought it was the Thargoids.'

'I'll tell you more later. I'm tired of the game-playing. If we've got to stay then all this secrecy makes no sense. I don't see how he can object if we talk openly.'

She's much better at this than I thought. 'So, tell me everything, about the Pivot, about Carl, and the Oresrians.'

There was a hint of a smile. *She's beginning to enjoy the game. Not too much, I hope*—but the smile disappeared.

Helen's expression was characteristically her: earnest, intense. 'I'm glad I'm here with you. It will be difficult, but at least we'll be together.'

'Talking will make it better; you bring a little bit of freedom.'

Another smile. 'Carl told me about two groups of Thargoids: the Oresrians and the Klaxians…'

And so they talked. She told Mastersson about the aliens, how Carl saw himself, about his work, and his plans for the Pivot. Through it all, Mastersson willed his tired mind to process everything. More than once he wished she could spell out some of the terms she used.

An hour later, Carl told Helen it was time to leave.

Now we've finished talking about you. Narcissism apparently goes with megalomania.

He returned her wave as she left, watching her step lightly from the room. He turned and walked to the privacy of the waste cubicle—one of the few 'privileges' he had not lost yet—and pushed his hand into the cleanser. He watched the letters scrawled onto his palm—'P A S W R D'—wash away. *Let's hope our overconfident Overlord has left me a loophole.*

✳

Mastersson forced himself to keep working through the rest of the day. He needed sleep before he tried the potential passwords— if he got into the system peoples' lives would depend on him quickly grasping its intricacies—there would be no going back and no time to rest. He gave up the charade in the evening. *I've pushed*

302

all day which should keep Carl sweet, and trusting me after Helen's extended visit this morning. Still dressed in the same clothes, he crawled onto his bunk. He was asleep in seconds.

❖

They were back in Carl's office. It took all Helen's control not to betray her feelings—the tides of fear and hope that threatened to sweep her thoughts away like so much flotsam.

'Helen, I hope we have an accord?'

'We do. I know you could hear us talking. Mastersson is very special to me. If you do right by both of us, I think you will be happy with my contribution.'

'I had hoped for a little more enthusiasm. You are, after all, playing your part in the single greatest human scientific discovery since the development of the interstellar drive, not to mention the rebirth of the human species.'

'I won't lie to you Carl. The work is fascinating, but your choice of application—you know I can't condone that.'

'So, this is all for the love of one man.'

'Not exactly. I don't want to live in the universe you are creating. Here, at least, we will be protected from the pandemonium you're about to unleash.'

'Self-preservation, extended to those one loves—a most logical instinct. If I am pleased with you, you will not find your time here unpleasant. Now, shall we go and tour the laboratories?'

41

The Thargoid defensive perimeter was far behind and passive scans had been clear for the last twelve hours. Powering up the main cockpit console raised Jane's heat signature another notch, but Moira needed up-to-date information. On a galactic scale, the distance from the patrol perimeter to its centre was minute. But using gas-jets to fight the tailwinds of the storm meant they had clawed their way klick by klick. The propellant-based manoeuvring thrusters were ancient, but Jane was much less likely to show up on an infrared heat scan.

Even with the storm passing, the clouds provide plenty of cover. They were nearly opaque, and still filled with high levels of electromagnetic charge. Linnaeus and the Thargoids seemed confident the perimeter would be enough; no ships patrolled nearby. *They set the net too wide.*

Jane's proximity alarm went off. Moira eased back on the power and began decelerating. The insistent beeping continued. Jane's passive scanners could reveal little detail at this range, but with something that big it did not matter. *Finally!*

After so long, her eagerness for action and the hope of seeing those she cared about filled Moira with a heady euphoria. 'Jane, maintain current rate of deceleration.'

'Acknowledged.'

'Jane, we really ought to broaden your range of responses. Show a little personality.'

'Acknowledged. Please specify parameters of personality as they apply to a ship's computer.'

Moira's sneaking suspicion grew—Jane did have a personality and it had a very dry sense of humour. 'Later.' She was out of the harness and across to the viewport in seconds, scraping the frost off the glass.

Wreathed in cloud, a structure hung over the gas giant's pole, its shape hidden at this distance. As Jane closed, multiple pinpricks of light played through the clouds, their pattern irregular. *Reflections from the sun.* She stayed by the viewport watching, transfixed by the end of her long journey growing closer, but the haze and play of reflections still made it impossible to make out any detail.

At last, she began to see individual outlines floating amidst the vapours. Indistinct at first, they resolved into a series of protuberant biconvex chambers, the outermost edges with the most defined arc, the innermost anchored to a central core of irregular spiralling stem-like tubes. The long axes of the two or three chambers she could see lay in a plane parallel to the curvature of the planet. Cold realisation hit like a slap to the face. The forms were undeniably alien. *Like maggots in tree fungus; Linnaeus has Thargoids building his little project.*

Jane drew closer. The 'fungus' nodules were joined with a series of tubes, most sitting in the same horizontal plane, but others formed spirals that disappeared down into Eurynomus' atmosphere. *It's like a burrow. If Thargoids are like insects, they'll be hiding at the bottom. How do I turn it into a grave?* Hatred, dark and seething, swept aside all other thoughts—there was so much to overcome before she could be reunited with everyone. Squinting, she could not make out any more 'fungi' deeper in the dense mists—the hypnotic swirling motion created half-seen illusions of shapes which disappeared when she blinked. *It must have a weak point.*

The tangle of tubes and bulbous shapes floated quiescent as the clouds broiled around it. Moira watched, but the structure remained inert, waiting. She turned and hauled herself—handholds and boot-steps—back into the pilot's chair, fighting against the deceleration pulling her to the nose of the ship. Secured, she took the controls and rechecked the instruments and the little she could see through the viewscreen. *Still nothing. Maybe the hardest part will be leaving.* Jane was fifty metres away and getting closer. *It's a risk, but…*

'Jane, initialise external cameras, and give me a live feed on the holo-display.'

'Acknowledged.'

'Jane, zoom in, maximum magnification. Flip through all available wavelength filters, and let's see if we can find a way in.'

'Acknowledged.'

As Jane descended deeper, the cloud thickened—planes, curves and edges fading to silhouettes before they too disappeared. And then, a break. *Holy shite.* The—*polished stone, plastic?*—walls of the station were less than ten metres away. At least three spiral tubes dropped from above, linking to more bean-shaped structures spread horizontally around the central mass of vertical stems. *Like the head of a flower.*

Carefully, she eased off on Jane's thrusters, allowing gravity to draw them down. As they travelled the length of the central stem, more of the fungal shapes loomed beneath. These were irregularly arranged compared to the ones above, and Moira twitched Jane's laterals so they zig-zagged between them. The convoluted tubes of the central stem were also becoming more unruly, some spreading out like disordered roots anchoring the base amidst the clouds.

She eased Jane through a narrow gap between two tendrils. Passing only a metre from the surface of the station, she could see it was patterned—recursive, organic forms swirled over it, the occasional ray of sunlight playing across the smoothness like a lacquered shell. *Huh. Pretty. It'll look better when I've put a few cracks in it.*

And still they went down. *How big is this thing?*

It was the orderliness of the eight-hemisphere spread that initially caught her attention. Moira had no idea what wavelength Jane's imager was using, but faux-shadows slid from the upper edges and extended around their long vertical axes into the gloom below. If they were like the smaller bean shaped chambers above, then each could easily extend a klick beneath them.

If those are living quarters, there could be thousands—Moira froze; her childhood memory of that *thing* taking her parents apart paralysed her. The insistent beeping of Jane's proximity alarm brought her back. She backed the throttle, a red hot pounding behind her eyes insistent she depress the trigger—fear embracing bloodlust, together threatening to quench the embers of who she was in a tidal desire for vengeance. She flipped the safeties, her eyes hungrily scanning the surface for the weakest spot. *Smaller tubes, spheres? Pipes—machinery! These aren't living quarters.* From the revelation, the seeds of a plan grew—something for her sanity to hold onto.

She flipped the safeties back over the triggers and increased power to the thrusters. Jane began her glide back up. *It's about time a Dolan had the last word.*

*

Moira took Jane in slowly, before flipping her so her undercarriage reached for unseen stars beyond the atmosphere. Jane slid easily between the spiralling tubes until she hovered under one of the horizontal fungus structures. Modified landing gear adhered softly to the smooth surface before solidifying the bond.

Out of sight—and into harm's way. Moira hung from the harness, already red-faced from the blood pooling in her head. Her exit from the pilot's chair was far from graceful. She gripped hands, palm to palm, and hit the release button with her thumb knuckle. She fell like a dead weight until her arms caught against the harness loop. Ignoring the ache in her shoulders, she dropped feet first onto the cockpit ceiling.

'Jane, maintain minimal power and full active stealth.'

'Acknowledged.'

Playing with the controls on her omni-block, she ensured its silence and activated her smart boots. She walked across to the airlock and straddled the top of the door before scrabbling over and into the airlock.

'Jane, report: survivability of external atmosphere.'

'High Pressure, low temperatures: exposure is fatal within minutes. Mean wind speed: approximately six metres per second;

beware of gusting. Gases: non-breathable: hydrogen, helium, ices of ammonia and water. Outcome: hypoxia, unconsciousness, hypothermia, and death.'

'Thanks, if a bit morbid.' Moira pulled a survival suit from its cubbyhole, slipping into it with an ease born of experience.

'Jane, standard airlock evacuation. Deploy the landing ladder.' The cabin door closed. A few seconds passed as the gas pressures equalised. Moira pulled the lever and opened the outer hatch. She could feel the tug of the wind as she stepped out, hauling herself up the wrong way 'down' the ladder. Her smartboots adhered easily to the rungs. Reaching the end, the underside of the structure hung, just out of reach, above her head. *Getting off is going to require some gymnastics. At least it doesn't matter what this thing is made of; these boots will stick to anything.*

Head down and gripping the ladder, she crab-crawled her legs over Jane's underside. She was moving and then sliding as a gust caught her, momentum wrenching at her fingers trying to tear her loose. Instinct took control and she swung her legs out and away with the motion, her arms pushing off with every bit of strength she possessed. She could feel the planet tugging at her, pulling her back. *I'm not going to make it. Think!* She hit several suit buttons in sequence and started pulse-breathing as the cavity inside her suit inflated, threatening to fold her ribs in on themselves.

As her helmet folded away, Moira forced the breath from her lungs, purging them along with the suit. Air rushed past her face, sending her hair cascading out in a black halo. The push was just enough. Her feet connected, her boots clinging to the surface of the station.

Freezing gases scourged her skin before the suit resealed against the elements. The pain in her ribs eased as the internal atmosphere normalised. She allowed the purifier to replace the foul air before restoring circulation and risking a breath. *Nothing broken, crushed or burst—just a damn headache. I need to get the right way up.*

'Let's see if there's anyone around to let me in.' She touched her omni-block, activating the transceiver, and whispered, 'Helen, this is Moira. I'm outside.'

42

Sitting hunched over his terminal, Mastersson drew a hand over his chin, the predictable rasping of stubble a counterpoint to his cycling thoughts. *What am I missing? I've been through everything she gave me—every permutation of spelling I can think of. So it must be something personal…*

He entered: 'Helen'.

Again, the same response: 'Access denied.'

Who else does he care for? It could be someone he hates…

Neither 'Gustav' nor 'Mastersson' achieved anything.

Then, something he believes in.

'Evolution.'

'Access denied.'

'Natural selection.'

'Access denied.'

'Survival of the fittest.'

'Access denied.'

Mastersson bent forward, pressing his forehead against the flat, cool surface of the terminal while trying to rub some life into his brain by agitating the roots of his hair with his knuckles. *What else did she tell me? If I've forgotten something… Carl won't fall for this twice.*

'Human perfection.'

'Access denied.'

'Oresrian supremacy.'

'Access denied.'

He wanted to pound the terminal, but Carl could be watching. *My guesses are getting wilder. Think! This is Carl. What is it about Carl? What makes him tick? No… Surely not?*

'Saviour of mankind.'

'Access denied.'

Damn.

'Saviour of humanity.'

Mastersson's self-coded text box disappeared. An octagonal star, Carl's company logo, flashed full-screen.

Shite, I'm in. It took an immense effort of will not to jump from his seat and run around the room. *Yes! Carl's a control freak, and now I'm inside I can play with* everything.

Helen said she did not like the self-satisfied smile he got when doing something morally dubious. He did not hide it now. *Carl can wonder what I'm smirking about while I unpick his little empire, one subsystem at a time.*

✻

Helen did not want to be impressed, but the facilities were state-of-the-art. *I could do the best work I've ever done. And I'd be here with Gustav—kept here.* She tried to square her feelings with recent events; it was not all negative. But the claustrophobia would not lift. Neither would the feeling of being used or the outrage she felt at what she was being asked to do.

'Where would you like to work? Any one of these rooms can be fitted out to your specification.' Pride dripped from Carl's every syllable.

Gustav, you've got to find us a way out of here. He would catch an outright lie, so she tried to think of something diplomatic to say. 'I would be interested in seeing some of the Oresrian technology involved in the synthesis process.'

'I am the only one allowed down there. Maybe, in time… I thought we could spend the next session examining the Pivot's structure in more detail, now you have acquainted yourself with the basics. My work area is this way.' He moved off, confident she would follow.

Mute and obedient. She trailed after him. Halfway across the room, the main lights went out. She froze, crying out involuntarily.

'What?!' Carl sputtered, indignation rendering him incapable of anything more articulate.

All she could see was black, and the glowing shapes of the now-dead light panels dancing yellow echoes across her vision. She turned, trying to orientate towards the exit. *Gustav, is this you?* Groping her way forward, she stumbled, knocking something delicate, and probably expensive, onto the floor. Angered, Carl was unpredictable; this was not a good place to be. She felt sideways along a bench, sending what sounded like a chair clattering to the floor in her haste. Following the noise, she turned and found she could make out the silhouette—a black angular shape against the dim red-orange glow emanating from every alien made surface. She had moved quickly, but Carl knew the layout of the room. A sinewy grip caught her wrist and she felt something hard and metallic press against her neck.

'What is going on? Tell me. You are not irreplaceable.'

I can guess, but Gustav will let you know in his own time. As if he had read her thoughts, the main lights came back on, blinding her again. She toyed with the idea of fighting back, trying to get away, but Carl pushed the cold metal harder against her skin. She did not know what she had expected to happen, but it was not nothing. *Please, Gustav.*

Carl held her for another uncomfortable minute before pushing her away. The small pistol glinted as it disappeared inside his lab coat. He was still frowning.

'Carl, why overreact?' Her voice broke, but after being held at gunpoint, it would not be suspicious. 'What happened?'

'The system is reporting an unknown glitch in the power sub-system.'

'I thought Oresrian technology would be more reliable.'

He was distant, offhand. She guessed his implant was quizzing the station computer. 'It is, but I've been forced to live with humanity's best for the infrastructure. Attempting to integrate their technology with ours would take years of research that I can ill afford. Some… compromises were made.'

'Blackouts have happened before?'

'Not for several months.' The look on his face said whoever was responsible would not live to see tomorrow.

Not because their incompetence may put lives in danger, but because they hurt his pride.

While Carl was distracted, she took her chance and approached the lab door. It refused to open. *Carl still has control.* She sat, deflated and hopeless, on a nearby chair. Her back to Carl, she could not bring herself to look at the man she would spend the rest of her life working for.

✳

'Dammit, dammit, dammit!' Mastersson slapped his palms down flat on the terminal-top. *Carl's mentally interfaced with the system—I've got a manual terminal and ten sausage fingers. He's quick and already familiar with it; how long before he figures out I'm inside? That last try nearly cost Helen her life. And why is a bio-boffin like him carrying a handgun?*

He rubbed the back of his neck as he unconsciously did several times a day when coding. He did not know where the choker had been injected. *I'm blind, deaf, and stupid with my implant disabled.* His hands balled into fists as he fought back waves of anger and impotent jealousy. *Carl has everything I need*—But giving up? He steadied himself and his breathing—*and it's time I took it back.*

He stared at the infographic of the system. His fingers stroked the screen, scrolling, panning, and zooming the image, the movements fluid from his recent weeks of practice. *This is what I do—how isn't important.* He found he was starting to believe it. He paused, fixating the pattern of lines and colours in his mind. Then he moved it again, and paused, and again, and paused. He pulled the live video feed of Helen and Carl to the centre. Timing was critical.

Gustav Mastersson drummed his fingers lightly on the terminal-edge, like an ancient concert pianist warming up for a virtuoso performance. *This is just like the good ol' days: a screen, a brain, and a set of pinkies. If I can't get through, I'll go around.*

✳

'Helen, this is Moira. I'm outside.'

It was so unexpected, Helen's head whipped around to stare at Carl, wondering if he heard it too.

He returned her gaze, frowning. 'Is there anything wrong?'

No, suddenly things have started to go right. Helen activated her transceiver. 'No, Carl… I was wondering if you could set me up on the terminal over there. There's one of the sub-units I want to look at in more detail.'

'Very well.' He gestured, shooing her away.

She weaved her way across the room until she reached the screen, which lit—waiting for something to happen. Sitting, she pulled up a series of complex electrostatic orientation diagrams. Glancing over her shoulder, she saw Carl perched, motionless, focusing inward on whatever data he was processing.

Helen turned back to the screen, her fingers manipulating the information automatically. Increasing the gain on the transceiver, she carefully shaped each almost-soundless word. 'Moira! It's so good to hear from you. You've been gone for so long…?'

'Yeah, yeah. I'm glad you're still alive too. Now, I need to talk to Helen the soldier—the one I trained, remember her?—not Helen the scientist. I'm on the outside of the station—'

'You're on the outside? But how—?'

'Helen.'

'Sorry.'

'As Carl's nearby, I'll keep to questions needing single word answers.'

'Don't. It won't look natural. I'm looking at something on a science terminal. Carl will assume any muttering is me thinking aloud—something I stopped doing years ago, but he doesn't know that.'

'If you're sure, but don't push it if you want me to stay alive long enough to fly you out of here.'

'It's okay, for now. Mastersson is alive and well—'

'Máithreacha na bhFlaitheas!'

'I'm sorry, what?' *An expletive, or a prayer?*

'Never mind. What about Keagan?'

'He was piloting a ship for Carl a few days ago, but…'

'Give it to me straight.' Despite the bluntness, Helen could hear the longing in Moira's voice.

'Carl's unhappy with Keagan's performance. I don't know what he's intending to do to him.'

'Okay, and Kishino?' Moira's tone was brittle.

'I haven't been able to find out anything—asking would make Carl suspicious.'

'Fine. You did right, not pushing it. Now I need you to stay calm and answer a difficult question without squealing. Can you do that?'

'Yes. He's still engrossed.' *I thought I'd earned at least a little respect.*

'I want Carl dead. Will you get in my way?'

Shock—at first—but it faded. *What's she going to do out here, arrest him?* Moira's doubt stung, and that lingered. 'You still don't trust me?'

'You haven't blown it, yet. Standard practice: if there's a rookie with you, test them before things get dangerous. And?'

It sounded plausible but felt personal. She knew Moira wanted an honest answer, but still she hesitated, working out what she really felt. 'You said you always worked alone.'

There were a few seconds of static. 'Not when I was part of the rebel cell Keagan and I fought with after the Thargoid attack. Enough with the touchy-feely, answer the question.'

The real question was: could she, would she, pull the trigger? *Why's Moira asking me? She's the one with the training. It's not my responsibility. She can do it. She knows I'm green. She knows I feel...* Helen remembered the bruising on Mastersson's face and hands, his carefree expression gone now he was confined. The anger, the resentment of Carl's arrogance and assumption of ownership, not just of her, but of everyone who worked for him, simmered inside her. *And he's willing to wipe out ten systems and sacrifice billions of lives for his vision of human perfection.*

Yet the Pivot's possibilities still tugged at her—its beauty, its potential for saving lives and furthering human understanding. *If Carl dies, the knowledge of how it's made dies with him. Jane's database only contains a diagram, a theoretical model. Moira's sample was minute and will have degraded... Can I condone such a loss to humanity?*

But Carl stood in the way. *There's not an altruistic bone in his body. How would he put it? 'If you are too pathetic to discover the secrets of the Pivot for yourselves, you do not deserve it.' He won't change.* Helen sat straighter on her chair. 'If you don't do it, I will. For you, it's personal, but it's not just about the people we care about anymore. You don't know what he's planning—evil is the only word for it.'

Helen summarised while Moira listened in silence. 'I can't think of an alternative—we have to find a way to destroy them.'

More static.

'Moira?'

'Can't be done. There's a flotilla of Thar—what did you call them?'

'Oresrians.'

'Whatever. Hundreds of drone-ships surround the base. Even with every Elite pilot free and iron under their arses, just punching through the perimeter could be impossible. Taking on so many is suicide. We go in, get our people, kill Carl. Let the fucking bugs fight it out. Threat eliminated.'

'And when humanity loses the only edge we have, our better pilots, what then?'

'Since when have you been a strategist? The bugs have interstellar communication too. They'll already know what we do.'

'No. Carl didn't go into detail, but although Oresrians learn by direct observation and experience and pass their knowledge directly mind-to-mind, they need to be close enough to do it. If we destroy them here, nothing passes on.'

'Can't be done. There's too many.'

'The Oresrians were the "Thargoids" that killed your parents.'

Yet more static.

'They've agreed to wipe out ten star systems, as some sort of deterrent. Insane or not, it doesn't matter. They'll repeat the massacre your parents died in—this time on many human worlds.'

Still more static.

'Moira, this isn't just about you and Keagan anymore. Surely you can see that?'

'I see it. I was just trying to work out what I can do about it.'

Helen struggled to force the words past the dryness in her mouth. 'With a fleet out there, don't we only have one option? We have to detonate the base, create the biggest explosion we can—maybe overload the generators—and hope their ships are caught in the blast.'

'Helen, I'm impressed. That's very commando of you. I think I trained you too well.'

'I don't understand your levity. We're going to die stopping Carl.'

'Before jumping to that conclusion, let's define the term "expendable", shall we? In battle, every member of the smaller force is more valuable. I didn't come all this way to sentence Mastersson or Keagan to death, or even you for that matter, although it's tempting.'

I think she's losing it. How am I going to do this by myself? 'Moira, you're not making sense.' She could not keep the fear from her voice. Her gut clenched again when she heard Carl's voice.

'I notice you still mutter. Could you keep it to sub-audible levels?'

Helen swallowed before glancing over. 'Sorry. Have you found the source of the problem?'

'No, not yet, and I will not if you keep wittering.' He turned from her, eyes unfocusing once more.

Helen felt wet tears pooling. *Gustav failed, and now Moira…*

'Charming isn't he.'

Checking over her shoulder first, she wiped her eyes. 'I don't know how to deal with you like this, Moira. Can't you keep a level head?'

'Stop worrying, you're an icer—your logic gets you through. You find out your type when you get into the action. I'd say we're there, given you're in the same room as Dr Doomsday. Sometimes I ice, but when the odds get longer I become a rusher, riding the adrenaline. Lots of vets do. Adding a hint of crazy keeps you sharp. Happier, now I've psych-analysed everything?'

'No.'

'You should be, I may have come up with half-a-plan that deals with the Thargoids and gets us out alive—and don't correct me, the shites have been Thargoids to me for years and don't deserve my respect. Next: your ideas? You've been on the inside. How do we get to the cells?'

Helen's heart sank. *I've got nothing.*

And something caught her eye. Small letters flashed in the bottom corner of the display: 'Heard about the biologist with no research project? She had to cell herself to pay the bills. Touch here for more.'

What…? Mastersson!

The text-box opened up, words scrolling quickly past:

'Hi, Helen. Things are tricky. Carl's running diagnostics to isolate his problem. He doesn't know it's me, yet. I got into the surveillance and environmental systems, but there was nothing I could do earlier. Sorry. I'm working on it. Say "hi" to Moira from me. I set up a variable audio filter and upped the gain: I caught most of what she said and only deafened myself when I was late switching when you and Carl were talking.' *He can never skip the tech part.* 'Can you relay this?'

'Helen, you've gone quiet. What's wrong?'

Moira actually sounds concerned. 'Mastersson just sent me a message. He says, "Hi".'

'Tell him to stop goofing around and get his mind on the job. What subsystems does he have access to? What can he do?'

More words appeared on the screen. 'The station schematic shows all the human facilities are on the uppermost level. I can't direct her to the cell block until I know her relative position. It's going to take me some time to gain access to the security subsystem and lock things down here. Oh, tell Moira that I love her too.'

Helen repeated the words, although she was not sure her awkwardness conveyed his playful mood. There was a really long pause. 'Moira, what do you think?'

'Mastersson can hear me, can't he?'

'Yes.' Helen had an odd, caught-in-the-middle feeling.

'Mastersson, you're a soft shite. Just get a grip on that system. We've risked a lot as it is, communicating for this long. I'll be busy for a few hours. Later.' And she was gone.

Signal static tickled the inside of Helen's ear. 'Wait—' Her eyes fixated on Mastersson's text-box, her only link to a friendly human being. Words appeared quickly:

'Don't worry, Moira knows what she's doing. This needs my full attention. Hang in there. I'll be back.' The text-box winked out.

Yes, but what am I supposed to do? Stay calm and distract the resident homicidal maniac? As she thought it, she knew she had her answer. *Okay, Carl, let's talk about our past and a future I pray will never happen.*

43

Moira touched her omni-block with her suit finger and cut the transceiver link. She felt split in two: her mind settled on her plan while her emotions jumped and skipped like the giddy girls you saw in holo-vision adverts. *Mastersson and Keagan are alive! Mastersson said he loved me; he must be joking. And Keagan's probably hurt.* The upward surge spiralled and hit dirt. *There's work to do.*

She turned back towards Jane; placing one booted foot before lifting the other was the only thing preventing her plummeting down the planet's gravity well. Clouds flitted by, carried by a wind, unconstrained. It would be easy to let go, to float away. Many times growing up, it had all seemed too much…

Suspended upside down, blood pounded in her head—the reality of the pain grounded her. At least she had a freedom of sorts after so long cooped up inside Jane. But what use was freedom without absolution? All the times Keagan had been there, giving her the courage to continue—older brother and surrogate parent. She recognised the feeling: a little sister's blind adoration. She spent her life, first protected and then driven by it—but Keagan never wanted her help. Later, when he had, she had stepped in like their mother, bailing him out of trouble of his own making. They shared their childhood, but where she grasped at normal life, Keagan set himself against it all. *Anaesthetisation from everything by using anything. How much is he the victim here?* Her feelings were more ambivalent than she expected. *If the urgency isn't just for Keagan…* but what she felt for Mastersson she had no name for, and unknown emotion scared her.

She touched the omni-block again and Jane's silhouette appeared a few metres to her left, the ship's contours mirrored as a distorted outline on the station's underside. The station *they* built.

Her fear found another focus: the memories of an eight-year-old girl.

This, I know—it has a cure, an end.

✳

Mastersson's fingers flew across the virtual keyboard. He was in his stride, doing what he did best. He plucked the virtual construct, a subroutine, from working memory he had isolated three weeks before and began coding the first morph. His trace routines were primitive, but he was starting from the inside; the system was virgin, untainted by 'impurities' like firewalls or anti-malware. The graphic showed Carl still sifting his way through the power subsystem. Mastersson had got out thirty seconds before. *Plenty of time… or not. Carl may be unfamiliar with the insides of a computer, but he knows how to use that implant.* He was scanning gigabits of data in seconds and getting closer.

In Mastersson's mind, the virtual construct took on a shape, its form changing as quickly as his fingers could move. He did not think of the code—he knew it so well—but of the end product, a superficial duplicate subroutine composed of the system's own diagnostic algorithms.

Nearly there… But Carl was finished. *Where's he going to jump?* He swallowed hard, licking the sheen of sweat forming on his top lip before it could pool, drip, and slow him down. The icon above the power subsystem winked out. In that long second, his fingers moved like lead, each press taking an eternity, and still he was not done. *Shite. Taking too long.*

Carl's icon was still absent. Mastersson did not have time to question his good fortune. He typed frantically, knowing at any moment he could be discovered.

The icon reappeared and stopped over 'Life Support'. Mastersson let out a long, slow breath. *So close! And logical: it's a critical system.* But Carl was flying through that block of code too. Masterson completed a few more presses on the keyboard. *At that speed, there's no way he's doing a deep scan.* He stared at the screen again as Carl's icon disappeared. *What the…? Why would*

Carl keep breaking off his search, unless something's distracting him?

Helen? I could hug you.

He smiled. His fingers danced lightly through the final keystrokes until, with a flourish, it was done. *And now my virtual presence looks, superficially, just like any other diagnostic routine. A bit of time to code a few more false coats and I can move around at will. A few hours and the system's mine. I hope Helen will be alright until then.*

✻

'Mastersson, is that you? How did you get on this frequency—are we compromised?' Moira's suit glove hovered over the keypad. She tried to swallow the heart beating in her throat.

'Lovely to hear from you too, Moira. You should lighten up; things are finally going our way.'

'I'm in the middle of something. It's delicate and now isn't the time for fooling around.'

'You sound like Helen.'

Moira clenched her teeth. The remark stung.

'No need to panic, I've hidden my footprint in the station's computer and I can move between a few key systems. I've just accessed comms, obviously.'

'There's no way Carl can trace you?'

'There are several, but with enough time I'll get more countermeasures in place. Carl's quick, but no tekhead. Besides, Helen's doing an unbelievable job keeping his nose out of our business.'

'I know—something about reducing immune reactions and side-effects, complete gibberish. They lost me three hours ago.'

'A feeling I remember well.'

'Mastersson, save it.'

'I love it when you're strict. Can I help with what you're doing? If not, what do you need?'

'I'll be done out here in about fifteen minutes. I need a way inside.'

'I'm not in the external sensor array yet, so I can't triangulate your signal. I've got no idea which door to open. Opening them all is a bit too obvious.'

'Can you pull up a schematic of the station, and orientate it relative to the sun?'

'As good as done.'

'I am on the underside of the upper layer, sun-side.'

'Ri…ght. Hang on…'

'Is there an airlock?

'The sub-systems are human; the structure's Oresrian. They may be linked by sections of code which thread through the comms grid and external systems. So far, I can't access the root instructions. I could open an airlock or attempt a data-block, but they're really bad ideas, unless you want droves of aliens swarming around you.'

'I get it; you're doing a wonderful job saving my arse, but quit the information overload and tell me where to go.'

'We can discuss saving your arse later. There's an incinerator exhaust… and the inventory's showing there's enough waste to justify a burn. How good's your suit?'

Did he just—! 'Where is it?'

'On the lateral edge of the pod furthest to the left, if you're facing the sun. It's sort of a tube—'

'Mastersson.'

'Yeah, you could probably have worked that out for yourself.'

'The wind's picking up, but I should be there in about twenty minutes.'

'Okay. There'll be a warm reception waiting for you.'

'Mastersson.'

'Yes, Moira?' His mock-innocent tone made her smile.

'Stay safe. Later.'

She severed the connection, her smile not fading. Her finger tapped through the remaining sequence on the keypad. Everything that counted lit up green.

✻

Moira straightened up, sweat from the crawl up the exhaust tube quickly drying in the air circulated by her suit. The flash chamber was smaller than she expected, a space three times larger than Jane's cockpit. The walls, floor, and ceiling were thickly coated with a black, powdery residue. She did not want to speculate whether it was organic in origin. 'Mastersson, I'm inside. Talk to me.'

'Are you alright?'

Moira did not know whether to be irritated or flattered by his concern. 'Having your voice inside my head is like an itch I can't scratch.'

'Grumpy. You're fine. Did you spot the chute across the room? I think it might be the way in. Looks steep though, need a bunk up?'

'When I'm safely buckled up in a pilot's chair and about to go, I won't be worrying too much about leaving you behind.'

'At least you *thought* about taking me along. That's an improvement.'

'Enough with the… Just quit it, okay? Conversation: short.'

'Duly admonished, or is admonished too long a word to use?'

What's with him? Flippant, or skittish? 'Focus. This goes in three stages: separate Helen from Carl, free everyone else and get them out, and clean up the mess. Now I need intel.'

'Intel—love that word. There's around one hundred guards, stationed at a few strategically critical points and randomly patrolling the corridors. Active numbers are light—they keep a three shift pattern: one on, two off. Off-shift they stay in the rec-area or adjacent barracks, between you and the prisoner holding area—fifteen of us at the moment. Plus, there's a hangar bay adjacent to the barracks, opposite the holding area.'

Great, detail I can use. She stopped, fists clenching. 'Mastersson, what about Keagan?'

'Keagan's… he's alive.' Even with poor reception, his voice sounded tight.

'You have cell surveillance? Tell me what you see.'

'Hang on… no, there's nothing. I've accessed the cell camera, but the room's empty—he's been living little better than me.'

'Never mind the fucking décor. Where's my brother?'

'His new location isn't recorded. All I've got is an information stream coming from the medical database—there's one for each of the pilots—but it doesn't give his location.'

'How's he doing? Can you at least tell me that much?'

'He looks rough. His bio-signs are off: base heart rate is up, one twenty bpm; he's got a temperature of thirty-eight point five. I'm no doctor—I don't understand the rest.'

'Any clue what he's doing? Training? Exercise?' She already knew the answer.

'The sensors are recording rhythmical muscle activity throughout his body and dermal fluid loss…'

She swallowed. 'Shivering and sweating. Those figures are dangerously high. You've got to find him.'

His reply was hoarse. 'You know I would if I could. There are thousands of cameras throughout the station, it could take days, and I'm not fully in control of the surveillance system. Plus, if I don't stay several steps ahead, Carl wins by default. I'm sorry.'

Damn it! I need you at my back, Keagan, not drugged-out and foetal on some floor, again.

'Moira?'

'Spit it out, Mastersson.'

'I switched to some sort of trend monitoring. His vitals have been getting worse for the past six days.'

'He's been through more withdrawals than I can remember.' *But like this?* 'Can you at least play with the environmental controls in any areas he's likely to be? The hospital wing, the holding area, or anywhere it looks like Linnaeus might take someone for punishment? It will buy him more time.'

'Second-guessing takes too long, and if I guess wrong it won't help. I can play with the central environmental controls for the human section of the station, but…'

'Thanks. Just try. Drop the temperature by three degrees and decrease the humidity.'

'I'll get on it, and open the chute.'

'I'll be back in touch when I get to a corridor. Start thinking of a way to separate Helen from Carl; he doesn't have to survive the process.' She severed the connection. *Don't die on me now, Keagan, not when I'm this close.*

44

Mastersson was as good as his word. The sphincter at the base of the waste disposal chute expanded, revealing another tube. Despite her dismissal of his concerns, the sheer ascent was going to be a challenge. Moira unstrapped her pack and looped the retractable cord through the handle; the chute was too narrow for the pack and her shoulders together. Quickly flipping through the menus on her omni-block, she paired her smartgloves and boots. She pressed the gloves against the smooth sides, letting the inbuilt sensors scan the properties of the material and the coating of mucus-like secretion that covered them. *The burn marks on the room's walls are obvious. Why not burn out the shaft as well?* Her omni-block started to bleep and she snatched her hands back. *What the—?*

She checked the screen: 'Hazardous materials detected: organic acid, origin unknown.' *Origin unknown? These gloves aren't so smart. Trust Thargoids to go over the top with cleaning fluids.* Dubiously she eyed the slick tube walls that curved around and out of sight.

'Mastersson, I've hit a problem with the garbage chute. How long is it?'

'I'm in the middle of an epic piece of coding that's going to get us out of here, and you call me up to talk toilet tubes? I know: "Answer the question." Just over fifty metres.'

'That's too far. I need you to flash the tube.'

'You what?!'

'My suit's not designed for sustained exposure to corrosive biohazards. The thermocouples should be able to handle the heat. First, seal the upper tube door and override the safeties for the door to this chamber.'

'This is crazy. You've got no idea how hot it runs.'

'And there's no way to find out. Keagan's dying, and getting to the nearest airlock will take how long?'

'… An hour, maybe.'

'At least two. The wind's picking up outside. Do it.'

'…'

'Do it.'

'Keagan's not the only person that needs you.'

'It's going to take you too long to lock Carl out. There are other pilots on the base, and Keagan needs me now.'

'Okay, but cook and I'm not scattering your ashes, I'm selling you for fertilizer.'

Moira moved to a corner. Crouching, she made herself as small as possible, wrapped her body around the backpack, and stuck her gloves and boots to the wall and floor. 'Ready.'

Brilliant light burst past filters and closed eyelids as a rushing wall of noise tore through sonic dampeners.

Null.

An awareness of self—blind and deaf to everything except echoes of the blast.

The acrid stench was persistent, imperative—forcing her to notice. She coughed, lighting her lungs and skin with lines of fire. An insistent buzzing pulsed between her ears, from a source she struggled to locate. Her head swam as she tried to move. Everything was black. Panic gripped her. *How can I help them if I can't see?* She thought of a face, his smile.

'Mastersson…'

A break in the buzzing. It resumed again, louder and more incessant, the pulses of sound running together in an almost continuous stream. She tried to roll over, and flopped against her restraints like a hooked fish. *Carl's taken me. I'm…* her mind finally stopped spinning. *The boots and gloves.* She tried to move her hands and feet. Pain coursed through her, every part of her skin scalded raw. Several minutes passed before she could think straight. *Fucking Eejit! Didn't get sucked outside, but the suit's burnt out and I'm stuck to a wall. Omni-block.* Locking her teeth, she forced her gloved hand against the grip holding her in place. The useless effort left her sweating and breathing hard.

Think! Mastersson will have re-pressurised the chamber.

She straightened as much as she could, her muscles weak and useless, before throwing her head forward. A kaleidoscope of patterns blossomed behind her eyes and the station seemed to spin around her. She felt, rather than heard, the click of her knuckle connecting with the suit's emergency exit switch. Nano-fibres responded, the suit decomposing into wisps of nothing. She remained still, bracing herself against the nausea.

At last, it eased. She tipped her head back and a thousand fingers tickled her shoulders and back. Surprised, she forced her lids open a crack and light cascaded across her vision—welcome confirmation she was still alive. She was inside a perfect black recreation of her now-dissolved suit—the carbonised remains of the chute slime coated everything. She moved her hands and the mould cracked, flakes falling away.

The irregular buzz in her ears continued. There was an agony of scraping as she staggered, her exposed skin rasping against itself. She kicked up fine black powder that billowed around her, making her cough. *Shite. Better move before the acid comes back.*

Her backpack was crisped, the material cracking as she tugged at the fastenings. She took hold of the first handgun and hit the ammo readout. It was dead. The second and third were dead too. *Oh, come on... I survived!* Her finger pumped the button on the fourth and the ammo-display lit. The rifle and the fifth handgun were also live. *Now we're talking. Thank shite the grenades are chem-reactive, not heat sensitive. Now, out of this hole and up to Keagan.*

She mouthed words her buzzing ears could not hear. 'I hope you're there, Mastersson. The blast's left me deaf. Release the door at the top of the chute, and I need you to clear a path between the barracks and the holding area.'

There was already a thin coating of acid lining the chute walls. She stripped off her leggings, found the deepest deposit of powdery carbon she could see, and rolled in it. She bit back a scream as the powder scoured her tender skin. But acid burns would take a lot longer to heal. Forcing herself through the pain, she worked a thick layer of powder into every crevice of her hands and feet. She looked around; the grenades were still in their satchel, the backpack had taken the brunt of the blast. Although the retractable cable was still intact, the mechanism was shot. *All this tech and success depends on my ability to tie a knot.* She smothered the leggings in the black dust and quickly wrapped the weapons in them before securing the package to the line, and the line around her waist, letting it trail out behind her.

Unless I'm quick, I won't be walking or holding anything for weeks. She set her years of experience and the lithe strength of a gymnast against the incline and smooth surface. The powder mixed with the gelatinous goo to form a sticky paste that held her as she alternately braced her splayed hands and feet against the sides of the narrow tube. When she paused, she slid—powering through a rapid series of vertical frog hops was the only way to gain the top.

Panting, she found the upper hatch open and the storeroom beyond piled with refuse, but clear of people. *Good, he's listening.* Moira slid across the threshold and scraped off tingling residue from her feet, knees, hands, and elbows on the angled door-surround. Every movement hurt, but rubbing some of the virgin powder from her underclothes onto appendages and joints at least eased the rawness. She scanned the room, noting the cover and best places for ambush amidst the heaped containers, storage crates, and the powered-down droid in the corner. Movement to the right caught her eye. She grabbed for the pistol at her side, before realising it was not there. An empty doorway stood before her. *Mastersson's doing. Let's not get scared of shadows.* Despite her self-admonishment, the door's iconic octagonal shape was another sickening reminder of who built this place.

Frantic, and making more noise than she should, she hauled the weapon cache hand-over-hand up the shaft. Her movements did not slow until she freed the weapons and was holding one of the pistols. She set it to low power and cut away the leggings where the acid had attacked. There was enough material left to tie into a serviceable carrier for the rest of the cache. Sliding the rifle across her shoulders and gripping the pistol, she exited into the corridor. It, too, was empty. Despite their subtlety, the patterns on every surface made her want to vomit. Too little was hidden by the human, the familiar. The rest screamed *alien!* Moira felt no curiosity or wonder, only fear turning to hate.

Alert, she moved at speed, eyes compensating for her deafness—a trick she learnt after near-misses with artillery shells and concussion grenades. She paused at each junction. Sometimes a door would open or a light panel flash indicating the direction she should go. There were no guards. *Why patrol the station's dumping ground?* Always, fear for Keagan drove her on. The occasional buzzing in her ear was comforting.

'I still can't hear you, Masterssson,' she whispered, 'Just keep the signals coming.' She took a left, then a right and still there was no sign of life. *I wish I could ask you how far it is.* The corridor ended in a door, but several ceiling panels flashed as a side door unfolded and slid open. She dived inside. *Patrol?*

'I thought you were keeping my way clear,' she hissed at Masterssson.

She crouched in a corner as the door closed behind her. The lights went out. *Clever, at least I'll see them when*—the door unfolded, silhouetting a head against the brilliance of the corridor behind. Moira's finger twitched against the trigger, but she held back the impulse to squeeze, instead dropping the power setting to save the energy cell. The fins of the door retracted and it slid into the floor. The first figure moved fully into the light and a second figure stood next to it. They hesitated, waiting for their eyes to adjust to the dimness. Moira squeezed off two shots. The pulsed beams hit both guards square in the face. Two dull 'whumps', like the sound of over-ripe fruit being dropped, and they crumpled. The lights came on and an agitated buzzing filled Moira's ears. *Now he chooses to have a crisis of conscience.* 'This is a military operation: no time for negotiated surrenders or tying prisoners.'

She stood, squinting until the after-images faded, before quickly checking the corridor. She hauled the bodies into the room. Their armour slid easily over the smooth floor, but the larger man bucked and kicked, his body not yet realising the brain was dead.

She checked the slimmer body: a woman, also dead. *Not my size.* Both wore their facemasks down, each now filled with a paté of cooked eyeballs and brain tissue. *Why the breathing apparatus? Their guns were holstered—probably looking into the 'technical malfunctions'.*

'Lock the door behind me.'

The corridor was still clear, but she moved more cautiously. She passed more doors, all closed. The fifth had a severed hand outside. *Trying to get out? Mastersson's been playing with the ventilation system. I hope he got plenty or this is going to be a blood bath. Maybe he's got what it takes after all.*

She had gone a few more paces, darting glances in every direction, when she caught a flicker of movement behind her as the buzz sounded again in her ear. She spun, crouched and levelled her pistol, unleashing a tightly clustered array of beams at the opening doorway. Plumes of smoke erupted as the beams burned into body armour, but the intensity setting was too low. The guard spun slowly like a tank, levelled the Colossus, and fired. There was movement in the opening beside her and she dived. The detonation sent her sliding across the floor. *Great: concussive shells.* A door closed behind her. She took a moment to catch her breath. The door opened again, then closed.

'Mastersson, what are you playing at?'

More buzzing in her ear. Did it sound worried? As the door opened a third time, she rolled sideways. The concussive shell caught in the fins before they were fully open. The pressure wave did little more than ruffle her hair. A picture of Helen's blond locks came into her mind.

She kept her voice to a whisper. 'Mastersson, whatever you do, get Helen away from Carl.'

More buzzing, louder, but still unintelligible.

The guard was green—the mistimed shot, choosing a weapon they could barely lift. She cranked the pistol's power knob and waited. The tip of the Colossus' barrel came lumbering around the corner. Moira picked her spot. This time the beam sliced through armour, flesh, and bone. The body fell, a cauterised hole through the chest. She caught the faint clatter of armour and the Colossus falling to the floor. *That's the last concussion grenade I want to see.* The door opened again and stayed that way.

'Back in control are we? Carl giving you a little trouble?'

Mumbling this time, with a cross overtones.

I've got to be close to the barracks, if not in them. She darted through the door and saw the one opposite was already open. 'If I go through that, will it cut me in half?'

The mumbling sounded terse, offended.

'Good.'

The room beyond was a gym. Eight bodies, lightly clothed, lay sprawled across bits of equipment. Moira checked the neck of the nearest. There was a steady pulse. 'Low dose of carbon dioxide? Very noble, but they'll be awake in minutes. And you're losing control of the system.' She reduced the setting on the pistol and went to work.

The indignant shouts in her head continued as she moved round the room. She thought she heard 'don't' several times. Seconds later, she exited the room from the other door leaving eight corpses behind. The whistling in her ears was beginning to ease. Mastersson's words were edged with a sibilant hiss but were still too indistinct to make out. Passing through the changing room, she took a facemask from a cubicle. Pausing, she eyed the clothing inside. Being near-naked did not bother her, but the delay did. On the other hand, the black powder was rubbing off and she needed something to protect her raw skin. She grabbed the one-piece and gritted her teeth as she slipped it on. 'Which way?'

The lights brightened further down a wide, central corridor.

I hope that's you. She passed two sets of double doors; an ownerless foot guarded one of them.

'Mastersson, are these the barracks? Grunt once for yes, twice for no.'

'Right, thanks.' *Fucking great. Two rooms of unconscious soldiers, all about to wake up.* Asking Mastersson to flood the space with a gas with enough kick to finish the job was useless. She stripped the makeshift pack from her shoulders and found the grenades. Two twists armed the proximity detectors. She dropped one in the corridor, between the opposing pairs of doors. The other she left thirty metres on, covering her back. She turned a corner as the first grenade went off. *Shite, he's losing it already.* A wave of hot air billowed round the corner, carrying with it the sharp tang of explosive and pungent stench of burnt hair. Seeing a door opening ahead, she started to run. She was closing on it when she heard the second explosion. *There's something wrong—no lights flashing.* She slowed, walking warily towards the doorway. She passed her foot over the threshold, before yanking it back an instant later. Nothing happened.

'Mastersson, you still there?' Two urgent, sharp bursts of sound—*a warning?* She grabbed a grenade, twisted the top, and sent it skittering down the corridor. It slid past a boot that had just come around the corner. She hunkered down, shielding her face as the blast tore into the owner of the boot and any friends behind him. She looked up to see the door ahead closing, cutting off her escape. *A grenade won't blast through that. Damn!*

Anyone around the corner would be more cautious now, but she was running out of grenades. *Knowing my luck, these grunts have a portable blast shield.* There was no cover, nothing to hide behind if they rushed her.

'Mastersson…' Her call for a little help faded into a breathless gasp. The growing tightness in her lungs she had been ignoring was not due to exertion. She could not breathe. *Carl's taken back control of the ventilation and the doors. I am so fucked.*

Her head began to spin as words were blurted in her ear, sounding tense and edgy. She thought she heard her name, but could not be sure.

She grabbed the facemask she had taken in the locker-room and slipped it over her head. *I'm not down yet.* The artificial-smelling air was food to Moira's starving lungs. She touched the diagnostic tag on the side of the mask. Text scrolled across the small screen:

'Oxygen Reserves: 33%. Estimated Time to Depletion: 4 hrs.'

'Depletion'—there's a euphemism for dead I've not heard before. She looked down the corridor at the still-smoking boot. *I doubt they'll have the patience to wait.* Death seemed a question of when and how. She settled, sitting with the rifle resting ready across her knees. Long stakeouts took perseverance, dedication: things she had tried to teach Keagan. He would wallow in the hopelessness, curse the unfairness of it all. She felt only shame, to come through all this only to fail. *I'm the butt of a huge cosmic joke. The punch line sucks, but I'm not my brother.* She did what she did best—what she always did—and let the coldness, the rage, take over.

'Mastersson, I've got until someone down here gets bored, so bloody well get your arse in gear.'

45

His fingers were numb, leaden. *I can't let…*

'Mastersson, you still there?' Moira's voice was sharp, urgent.

'Don't move!' He rasped, his voice hoarse from constant shouting. He watched the icons change, helpless as the video feed showed the door closing behind Moira. The blocks Mastersson coded had worked, for a while, but with his implant Carl was too fast—it was impossible to close every hole. But he dare not stop typing, despite the way the muscles in his hands screamed and threatened to cramp.

Mastersson made the jump to the ventilation subroutines before Carl. He jinked sideways into the emission control subsystem as Carl assaulted the smokescreen of code around the core control routines. *Too little time.* He forced his fingers to type faster, pulling up an encryption cipher he had been saving to lock any remaining ships in the docking bay when they escaped. He embedded the cipher around the neuroxic gas release code and watched it take hold, insinuating itself until it was indistinguishable from the original. *Sorry I can't do more, but at least Carl can't poison you.*

He watched, powerless, as Carl punched through the ephemeral layer of masking data he had rushed to wrap around the door control system. Without his implant, going head-to-head with Carl would only end one way. Mastersson's fingers moved automatically as Carl appeared to stop and inspect one of the few remaining safe nodes. If Carl tagged him, the system would freeze him out.

Thought I'd be there, didn't you.

Carl's search pattern had been different for some time. No longer looking for an unknown glitch, he had come after Mastersson's virtual self, chasing him around the system. But hide-

and-seek only occupied Carl for a while. Frustrated, he threw himself at Mastersson's physical body, encased in the cell.

Fingers throbbing, Mastersson watched, somewhere between expectant and tense. *Now we'll see.*

The data-lines brightened blue, instructions flying from Carl at the cell's access controls. They disappeared. Mastersson massaged his hands. Another linear track lit—its path deviating to the prison block environmental controls. That too disappeared. He allowed himself a regretful half-smile.

The first data-lines reignited an angry red; flashing, they beat against the yellow surrounding the access control icon. Both data pathways flooded crimson, the lights alternately flicking back and forth as the assault targeted entry and life support. All red vanished from the display—Carl's override directives ended.

Can't catch me, so you try and kill me.

Mastersson knew Carl would. Weeks of brainstorming and he had seen no other option; most of his time had been spent on the codex virus—now infecting the subsystems that made his cell vulnerable. Fighting on two fronts was impossible—pushing deeper into the station's systems rendered his own defences passive and all too easy for Carl to breach. With the virus in place, *any* new instructions targeting his location would be mutated, rendering them useless. Virtually, he had dug himself in so he could push outwards. Physically, no one could get in; he could not get out. *I may as well be buried.*

Carl's icon was moving again, racing through subroutine after subroutine—*back to looking. And now he's found that...* The status indicators above Environmental Control changed: the pumps, pushing oxygen into Moira's corridor, stopped, then reversed. Mastersson held his head in his hands. *Just what I would have done. I need my implant!*

'Mastersson...'

His heart broke as he heard her gasping plea. 'Moira, hang on. I'll think of something.' He watched as she pulled the facemask over her head. *At least you're alive, for now.*

Masterssson rubbed his aching fingers, both to ease the cramp and his own feeling of impotence. *Now I have some time. There has to be something I've missed, another way... What's he doing?*

On the display, it looked like Carl had gone insane. He raced from one block of code to the next, tearing through the entire system at such a rate there was no way he could comprehend what he was seeing, implant or not.

Frustrated, are we? Masterssson stretched out his fingers and palms, waiting, suddenly alert and filled with growing hope. *I'll be there when you make a mistake.* Carl's search became erratic as he jumped, seemingly at random, through the station's software. *Better and better.* Masterssson started typing, a plan beginning to form. He grinned when Carl threw more data-streams at the protections around his cell. Even military grade code-breaking software could not get through, not when his virus warped everything thrown at it. The flood ceased, a single blue rivulet connected to 'Personnel'. *Send in your guards. You can't touch me, not here. The way these bulkheads are built, I reckon I've got two, maybe three, days before they cut through. And in the meantime...*

But Masterssson's heart froze. On the second video feed, Carl stared into the camera, mouth moving as he pointed a handgun at Helen. *There's nothing I can do, nothing faster than Carl pulling the trigger.* He had hoped it would not come to this. He had hoped Moira could reach Keagan and free Helen. *Hope springs eternal? This well just ran dry.* He stared at the screen. Carl's face was contorted with rage as he waved the gun like some mudfoot teenager with 'roid-rage. *'Surrender is not an option.' How glibly people recite that phrase in the holo-vids—I can't undo the virus-lock on the cell. I'm the only one left... there must be a better alternative to sitting on my hands.*

Helen, I would swap places with you in a heartbeat. Carl better value you more than he hates me. Masterssson terminated the video feed. He was certain Carl would hurt Helen, trying to force his hand. Watching would achieve nothing. He could not prevent it, and surrender meant, at best, a lifetime's slavery for all of them.

He went back to typing. Their only chance of getting out was hours from being finished. His hands were already locking into claws. *Why is it only in hindsight most heroic plans seem so stupid?*

Moira gasped, trying to force enough stale air from her lungs to sound out his name. Dots, blobs, and pools of colour unformed and reformed constantly in her vision. Every fibre of her being was focused on sitting up straight, looking alert. She was down to her last grenade. If Carl or the guards saw her weak, it was over. Rage kept her going. She wanted to feel free—sprinting across an open field bathed in the warm light of a familiar sun at the last—when they took her down. *Now I can't even stand.*

She had trusted him—the first and only time she had trusted anyone with her life, except Keagan. She had waited for him to come through, was still waiting… *Stupid. All my life I've known trust gets you nothing. I thought… maybe he was different. To go like this: no better than the weak and pathetic girl that watched her parents die. They weren't strong enough, and neither am I.*

✻

In his peripheral vision, Masterssson noticed Moira's head dipping yet again.

'Moira! I'm so close. Don't give in.' *No time to talk…*

Her head fell to her chest, then it inched, just a little higher—a final act of defiance. Moira went limp. Her rifle clattered to the floor.

'No!'

Holographic guards streamed around the bend in the corridor as Masterssson completed the last line of code. *Maybe Helen can use this. Maybe.* He lifted a spasming finger and hit the virtual keyboard. It was dead. A second later, the lights went out.

'What? No!' His bare fists hammered the terminal, the pain lancing up his arms his only connection to the outside world as despair overwhelmed him. Defeated, exhausted, he broke down, tears falling freely through empty air, pooling on the terminal-slab.

On its face, he read the words: 'FULL SYSTEM REBOOT INITIATED. OBEY ALL STANDARD SAFETY PROTOCOLS UNTIL NORMAL FUNCTIONING RESUMES.'

✳

In the day-to-day, it was unnerving, seeing how little Carl had changed. When caught up in his work, the scientist could be passionate, civilised, and even pleasant company. It was like years ago: conversation flowing like water and ideas as fast as thought. He was totally in the moment, captivated by the intricacy of his creation and the thrill of shared discovery.

Helen, worrying about Masterson and Moira, could not become as engrossed as he was.

He noticed. 'I do not see anything wrong with my last proposal.'

'It's fine. I was… just wondering if it had any unforeseen ramifications—whether it would be detrimental to the overall stability of the molecule.'

'We discussed that an hour ago, when we were working through the third alternative conformation. You are obviously tired. Time has not been good to you: you used to stay focused through the night, not just for a few hours. If you cannot keep up, then stop. We shall recommence tomorrow morning. I suggest you get some rest.'

'No, I want to keep going—it feels like we're getting somewhere.'

'Not when we cover the same ground twice.'

'It won't happen again. Let's crack this. If—' She realised her mistake; Carl did not like being directed.

He stepped away from her, eyes narrow with suspicion. 'You seem a little too keen to be working with me all of a sudden. What happened to your grave moral misgivings? Do you take me for a fool? Being caught up in the moment I understand—this project will be the greatest thing you ever work on—but slavish dedication, even to protect your beloved Gustav? I think not.'

I should have left, gone to my chambers to 'sleep', then maybe—

'I think it's time I tracked down my little system "glitch". When it has been eliminated, I will decide what to do with you. For now, sit there. Still. Silent.'

✳

'Gah! I will find you, Mastersson.' Spittle flew from Carl's mouth as he shouted, 'This system belongs to me, *you* belong to me. You have a few cheap tricks, nothing more.' He turned a baleful look on Helen. 'Did you know he was doing this? Time wasted, because of you. The station compromised, because of you. Yes, I think an opportunity to redeem yourself; as you two are so close, this should appeal to Gustav's reasonable side.' Carl pulled the gun from inside his clothing. The muzzle did not waver as he pointed it at her. 'Beg Mastersson for your life. Tell him to drop the protections around his cell and surrender to my guards.'

Fingers gripping the decorative hem of her dress sleeve, she tried to suppress the shaking. Do nothing and he would shoot her— she was certain of it—but everything depended on Gustav. *I won't force him to surrender.* A memory surfaced, replaying Moira's voice: *'If you don't know what to do, do something unexpected. At least it will buy you time.'*

Carl was waving the gun now, playing to his hidden audience.

She stood, arms placating. 'Carl, we've known each other for years. Surely it hasn't come to this?' She managed to keep most of the tremor from her voice. The gun lowered slightly. Desperately, she tried to think of something else to say. She took another step forward. The gun rose, twitched, and fired—a beam of brilliant white light slicing through clothing, skin, and the thigh muscle underneath. She screamed, dropping to her knees as her nose filled with the smell of charred meat. Tears streamed and she could not stem the flow. 'Carl, please.'

But Carl had already turned away. 'Mastersson, you can stop this.'

Through the haze of nausea and pain, Moira's words: *'Use what you have.'* Helen began to crawl, every centimetre sending new bands of fire running along her burnt leg.

He glanced back at her. 'What are you—?'

She grabbed his wrist, pushing the gun away while her nails dug into the softness of his inner elbow. He grabbed her hair. She ignored the pain and bit into his forearm, her teeth tearing into muscles that could pull a trigger. Agony flared as hair threatened to tear free of its roots. She bit down harder and saw the gun fall. *Anticipate.* Carl leant over and around her, grasping at the weapon with his other hand. She released his elbow, flexed her own, and rammed it point first into his groin. Warm vomit cascaded over her back as he collapsed, retching. She rolled free and scrabbled across the floor, her injured leg trailing, until she reached the gun. Spinning around, she levelled it at Carl.

He was looking at her, the gleam of insane triumph in his eyes. The lights went out.

'What did you do?' In the blackness, holding the gun gave her no sense of control.

'I reset the system: a full reboot. When it has finished, your beloved Gustav's cell will be wide open, and when my guards finish with Ms Dolan, they will take him. What they do to him is entirely up to you. My last order was to kill him, slowly. Hand the gun to me and I will give them... something gentler to do. Shoot me and they will never receive the order to stand down.'

Helen slid herself backwards across the floor, trying to gain distance and time to think. *Is he lying?* She whispered, 'Moira, tell Gustav to get clear—the guards can access his cell... Moira? Moira?'

46

Moira heard a vaguely familiar voice inside her head, calling her name over and over. But there were other voices too—closer—ones she did not recognise.

'She's coming round.'

'This bitch took out Freddy, Ravid, and Miguel. I say we finish her, let her have a little "accident".'

Bright white light flicked across her vision before coming to rest on her face. She screwed her eyes tight.

'You're new. The boss scheduled a drill a year ago. Everyone thought the surveillance was down. It wasn't. The screw-ups disappeared the next day. My bet is they didn't make it back to homespace.'

'Crap.'

'No, it isn't. We do this the way he wants it done. She stays alive, unharmed.'

Three voices. Close. I'm... lying down... still too...

'What for?'

'You gonna ask him? Thought not.'

'She found him, didn't she? She got in. He'll want to know how.'

Moira's fingers cupped the sphere in her hand. *What's that for?*

The bright light moved from her face, playing a circle over the three figures crouching over her. 'Who's got the restraints?'

'I thought you had them.'

'Can't you keep track of anything?'

She rolled her thumb over the top of the sphere, then flicked it between the legs of the nearest guard. Out of the torchlight, it quickly disappeared. She started to roll, over and over, as fast as she could.

'Hey!'

Three… two… one. She lay still, flattening herself against the floor.

Like a massive hand, the wind of the concussive blast took them; arcing paths marked by their lights, they flew at the nearest wall. As they slid down it, Moira's hair settled around her face. Through the strands, she saw their bodies lying in a crumpled heap, pooled in the light that still shone from the now-still helmet beams. She crawled towards them, eyes closed, trying to gain some night vision before anyone else came to see what the noise was. Feeling around, she found a pistol, then another. She fired at the black silhouette beneath each helmet beam. Other lights began darting over the walls at the far end of the corridor. *Time to move.*

✣

Helen slithered further away, trying to think past the searing in her leg.

'Slide the gun here. It's the only way you can help him.'

Now her eyes had adjusted, she could just make out Carl's outline in the dim emergency lighting provided by the ceiling panels. He was trying to push himself up on a nearby chair. There was a grim satisfaction in watching him collapse again. *If he's rebooted the system, he has no way to contact security. Would he have ordered Gustav's death? Not when he could do it himself—it's personal between them.*

Helen had to look at the butt of the pistol to find the power dial. She could picture Moira: *'C'mon, novice! We did this already.'*

'What are you doing?'

For a moment, she was transfixed, unmoving except for her shaking hands. 'Giving humanity a future.'

She fired.

✻

Moira leant against the corridor wall, breathing hard. The patrols had been dogging her non-stop, criss-crossing junctions attempting to cut her off. She checked the charge on the pistols; one was nearly depleted and the other down to half. Every time they exchanged fire, the guards traded a few shots and backed off. *What I'd do if I were trying to take someone alive—wear them down. At least with all the doors unlocked there's fewer dead ends.*

She caught the giveaway splashes of torch beams at one end of the corridor, and then the other. *Shite. Getting tired and making mistakes.* She crossed to the door opposite. It closed behind her. There was only one entrance; she looked around for somewhere to hide. *But why bother?* A grin spread across her face. *You'd think it was my birthday.* Weapons lay neatly arrayed in lines, floor to ceiling, along every wall. Rifles, projectile and laser; pistols of all sorts... *Ah.* Private military were the same galaxy-wide: driven by machismo fuelled overcompensation for the fact they were not in a 'proper' army. Normal station security did not need these killing machines, but they kept turning up. *Which one can I carry?*

She grabbed a choice item and some spare ammunition belts.

'Moira? Moira?' The voice was barely audible, quavering so much is was difficult to make out her name.

'Helen. Good, you're alive. Keep it brief, I'm going to have company any second.'

'You didn't contact me.'

Shite. I have to do the emotional bit before I get any sense out of her?

'There was no good news to tell you, and if you'd let anything show in your face, Carl could have spotted it. How is he?'

'Dead, I think.'

'You *think*?'

'I know, I know. Your training… But it's different when you shoot someone for real.'

'If Carl recovers and regains control of the station's systems… Are you close enough to finish the job?'

'I… I can't move quickly, but I'm on my way to the barracks. Isn't that where you are?'

Eejit, she's going to blunder straight into a patrol. 'I need you to stop thinking like a civilian. Find somewhere secure to hole up.'

'Er, okay.'

Every fibre of Moira's being screamed at her to run for the holding area. *Mastersson and Keagan*—She cut the thought dead before it ensnared her. *I need the map in Helen's implant. I don't have a choice.* 'Keep this channel live. I can use the signal to triangulate your position.' *Hopefully before they realise how we're communicating and do the same.*

'Okay, there's a small storage area en route from the barracks to the labs. I'll be in there. Could you… could you pick up a medkit on your way? I've been shot.'

'There's a medstation on the wall… done. You can make it?'

'I… I think so.'

'Good. Try and sound a little more definite—the corridors aren't a good place to be. Remember what we went through, oh, and torn clothing makes a bandage.'

'I *know*. I did that already. What about you, are you all right?'

Moira hefted her weapon. 'I'll be fine, after I rid myself of a bad case of goons.'

47

It took Mastersson several minutes to realise that the doors to his cell and the holding area would be open. *At least until the reboot ends, but what now?* With no grid connected to his implant and his console shut down, it felt as though every limb had been removed. *Is my implant everything I am? There goes Gustav Mastersson, the tech-less wonder. Moira taken, Helen at the mercy of Carl, and there's nothing I can do. What would they do? Helen: probably reason with Carl, establish an empathy. Moira? Fight, kick, and bite until she couldn't.* He remembered Helen and all the years they had spent together. He'd had so little comprehension of people, or even himself, until she had connected him to both for the first time. But even then he had relied on his tech and his own anonymity. He knew more about everyone else than they knew about him. He could 'ease' things—arrange favours. He was a useful technician. It was a role others wanted him to play and he was comfortable performing. *Everyone except Helen. I've always been Moira's pet techy, so now what do I have to offer?*

He stared at the wall. *Waiting for what? A shiny display to spring to life and make everything alright? When the system reboots, it will be Carl's.* At that moment, he wanted someone to talk to. He was not sure who he would prefer. *Helen always loved me. Moira would kick me up the 'arse' and tell me to stop being a 'soft shite'.* He had always orbited Helen's unconditional warmth like a planet around its sun—she was constant. *But if Moira would expect more from me than this, she must be able to see—something.*

He stood, catching himself on the console edge as his head swam with tiredness. He weaved his way to the centre of the transparent wall and waited as the centre panel slid upwards. *Let's see how quickly I can make some new friends.*

*

The holding area's central corridor was empty, echoing Mastersson's own hollowness—*they have Moira. It won't be long before they're back.* He ran to the first door, stopping before a surround embellished with coiling ethnic artwork. *Someone's been behaving well enough to gain a few privileges.* As he approached, the mechanism opened automatically. *If they're one of Carl's bootlickers, I'd better be careful.*

Inside, a wall of intense perfume assailed his nose, the heady scent insinuating itself into his sinuses while searching for his brain. Curtains cordoned off the far corner; swirls of patterned material spiralled in on themselves; just glancing at them made him dizzy. He smiled. There was something amusing about the way the colours played, romping with each other across the cloth. *I wonder what's on the other side? ...Hmmm, that's deep.* He grabbed at the hanging, which stretched as he pulled it. *Not that way. This is fun. Pull...this way... Aw, she's asleep.* Flailing his way through the drapes revealed a naked red-haired woman in her twenties lying on a bunk padded with thick cushions. *Oops. Pretty though.*

'Erm. Sorry. Didn't mean to disturb you or anything, but we…' *She looks so peaceful, lying there.* His eyelids felt heavy. The urge to join her and cuddle up was almost overwhelming. The room accelerated. On its second orbit, he caught sight of the burner on a shelf by the bed, clear crystals fizzing inside a silvered bowl over a little flame. *Wha—oh.* He pushed the woman hard on the shoulder. 'Hey, we have to move. Your cell door's open and the guards could be back any minute.'

Although her small mouth opened and closed, no sound came out.

'What's that? "Go away"?'

She did not stir.

The room was spinning faster now and he felt his knees fold pleasantly beneath him. The open doorway swam lazily ahead, but as he crawled towards it the rug under his hands stretched, elongating as the wall drew away. Panicked, he scurried to the shining portal and dragged himself over the threshold, before collapsing onto the smooth, cold floor. The air felt thinner and his breathing eased, bringing freshness to his thoughts. *She's too far gone, unless I can get some help to carry her.*

The second door was also shut but opened as easily as the first. More curtains hung like a fine mist across the entrance. *Not again.*

But the silence was broken by panting and some all-too-familiar animalistic grunting. He froze, awkwardly running a hand through his hair. *Now?!*

Mastersson nearly left them to it, but his conscience won out. 'Sorry to interrupt, but I thought you should know the door to your cell is open. The way's clear if you want to get out. This'll be your last chance.' He spoke over the squeal of surprise and the florid flow of curses that came with it. He did not wait to see if anyone followed, but retreated to the corridor and hurried to the next cell.

Angry now, he strode inside. From the shadows, an arm snaked around his neck. He swung his elbow back as Moira had shown him, but instead of doubling over, his assailant swayed sideways. The grip around his neck tightened. Mastersson's introduction came out as, 'Ghaak!', but his raised hand seemed to be enough to satisfy his attacker, who let go. Mastersson slid to the floor.

'Why is my door open? What is happening?' The voice was heavily accented, a polyglot of Asian and assorted planetary inflections he could not place.

'Station system rebooting.' Mastersson coughed. 'Guards in another section, but will return soon. I came to see if anyone else wants to leave. So far, they all seem very comfortable. Why haven't you tried the door?'

'Have you seen my family, a woman, two children—this high, and this?'

In the dimness he could just make out the man indicating heights at his waist and chest. The man stood like a coiled spring. Mastersson felt as if his life depended on the answer.

'No, but I haven't been to all the cells.' With the light panels down, it was difficult to make out the man's features, but the contours of his face seemed familiar. 'Is your name Isao Kishino?'

'How do you know? Who are you? Who sent you?' The man's posture changed—the ready stance of an experienced martial artist.

Too exhausted to make anything up, he gabbled the truth, hoping Kishino would accept it. 'I'm Gustav Mastersson, friend of Moira Dolan—an investigator sent to find you and your family. She has family here too, a brother.' Mastersson hoped the man relaxed slightly, but could not be sure.

'What you say makes no sense. Why is she on my case?'

'Because her boss, Ferris, is—was—an idiot.'

'Not an answer. Where is she?'

'Occupying the guards that should be outside. I hope she's still alive.'

Kishino stared, mute.

'She met your father,' Mastersson ventured.

'And he let her come for me. Good. This Moira Dolan, she is a fighter—better than you?—has a plan? She'll get my family out?'

'I know she had a plan, but I was watching on a holo-stream when security took her down. We're on our own.'

Kishino paused, considering him.

I can't look like much.

'Up, Gustav-san.'

He took the proffered hand and was pulled to his feet. It was like being gripped by tree roots. He rubbed his fingers. 'What next?'

'Your plan, but I do it better, faster. We move.' Kishino bolted out of the door, stopping briefly outside. 'You go that way… but you can't fight.' It was not a question.

'No.'

'Then keep up.'

'Wait—the people in those cells—aren't we going to help them?'

'Pah! Hikikomori. They stay in their rooms—too obsessed with their pleasures. If they want out, they catch up.'

'Why'd you stay in your cell?'

'Afraid for family. Linnaeus has something to trap each of us: addictions, blackmail, ruin financially, many threats so we do as he says. It is time for fear to end.' And he was off.

Moira would love this guy.

Mastersson charged around a corner, sliding to keep his balance as he tried to keep pace with Kishino who seemed to have glue on his feet. In the gloom of the bend ahead, a man-mountain shape loomed. The rifle in his hands looked like a toy. Two bodies lay at his feet. *Oh shite.* Mastersson watched in amazement as Kishino accelerated. *He'll be cut down.* The little man stopped dead as the figure thudded towards them. Mastersson tried not to stare; 's-he' was the biggest woman he had ever seen.

'Kishino-san, good to see you. You coming out to play? Who's your friend?'

'Good to see you, Tahira. He's okay. Is there news of my family?'

'They're fine; they're with Aaron and Honon. You need a shooter?' She flung him the rifle lying across a very-dead guard's chest.

Kishino caught it and flicked the safety.

'What about him?' The doubt was clear in Tahira's voice.

Both looked at him.

'You fight, or watch?' There was no emphasis in Kishino's question. Tahira looked like she already knew the answer.

'I can use a pistol.' *Although it's been a while.*

Tahira grunted and pointed at the other body, leaving him to pick up the weapon.

And they were moving again, Mastersson struggling to keep up as Tahira's back lumbered around the bend ahead.

✳

Mastersson had to look away as the Kishino family broke down in tears, hugging each other with a fierce warmth that left him feeling hollow inside. Even Tahira joined in, clasping forearms with a short, thin man and a stocky woman as wide as she was tall. Envy underscored his delight at seeing an open show of human feeling in a place so far from home.

The reunion lasted but a few brief seconds. Kishino rattled off several phrases Mastersson could not understand and was astounded by the family's transformation. Everyone stood straight; tears were wiped, a nose quickly blown. Tahira handed another rifle to the woman and a pistol to each child—gleanings from the small harvest of bodies they had left in their wake. *Even the small one's probably a better shot than I am. These are Moira's kind of people, what am I trying to prove?*

'What next?'

Kishino turned to Mastersson, looking at him like he was a little strange in the head. 'We go to the barracks. It's where your friend is, yes?'

Mastersson nodded. *I hope so.* 'She won't leave here without her brother, Keagan. Do you know where Carl put him?'

Kishino glanced at his family, his face becoming grave. 'She really will not go without him? He is… not good. This will not be pleasant.'

'Not a chance. They've survived so much together their bond goes beyond family. They only have each other.' The last words were loaded with bitterness and self-loathing.

Kishino's sigh was resigned. 'I know this bond. You carry, I fight.' He turned to his wife and addressed her curtly, although there was softness in his eyes. 'Yorimi—'

She nodded. 'Hai.'

He watched as Yorimi and the children moved off with the others. In the group, Mastersson had begun to feel safe. 'Where are they going?'

'Some have scores to settle, others to clear the way to the docking bay.' Kishino gestured. 'You follow.'

Their progress was good. The corridors were empty and Kishino seemed to be aware of Mastersson's limitations as he kept to an even, loping pace. They were back in the holding area in less than ten minutes. Kishino led Mastersson into a room he had not seen before.

'This is big, fancy too. What is it?' He could just make out pieces of art from several human cultures hanging from the sloped roof, obscuring most of the walls. To one side was an immense tank filled with some spectacular, if outlandish, 'fish', glowing with a pale, serene bioluminescence as they glided through the liquid.

'Pilots' lounge. Keagan is in there.' Kishino waved a hand towards the central space. He unslung the rifle from his shoulder, sweeping it in a graceful arc as his eyes darted around the room's multiple entry points. The veneer of safety was gone. Feeling exposed and vulnerable, Mastersson walked over to a large duraglass tube. It barely reflected any light in the dimness. Something angular lay crumpled in the bottom. It took him a moment to make sense of what he saw: an ashen pile of bones connected to form a body. Skin hung from it in limp, fleshy folds. 'Is he still alive?'

'I last saw two days ago, then barely.'

Mastersson walked around the display case, running his fingers over the smooth surface, feeling for a way in. 'Why did Carl do this to him?'

'A warning, to remind us to work harder.'

'I knew he was sick, but how come he's so thin? He looks starved, like he hasn't eaten in months.'

'Carl's drug; I saw others try to come off. Half the pilots are users. When I arrived, I was "the one to beat". Now, they mostly win. Keagan says to Carl, he tired of being ordered around, wants to be free. Carl says he not happy with Keagan's performance, so now his body eats itself from inside, trying to use what is not there.'

Mastersson found a barely perceptible roughness on the transparent surface. Stroking it made a section of the tube slide upwards. He bent to reach the body, but recoiled as the stench hit him.

'He's soiled.'

'Never mind, he lives?'

Suppressing an urge to vomit, Mastersson slid his bare hands through the slime underneath the body. Keagan was unnaturally light and Mastersson carried him easily over to a table and laid him out. Mastersson felt ineffectually around the upper neck. His voice was tight. 'I can't find a pulse.'

Kishino shook his head, walked over and pressed two fingers between jaw and larynx. 'There. It is weak. Without help, he does not have long.'

Mastersson jerked his head around as a high-pitched whining echoed from one of the corridors nearby. There was a scream, and then silence. He turned to Kishino for clarification, only to see the man crouching behind the table gesticulating wildly.

'Get down. No, go and stand over there. Now.'

'What? Why?'

'Just do it. I fight, you carry, remember?'

Mastersson went over to the fish tank. *What kind of noise sets a vet like Kishino on edge? Some kind of weapon?* By the time he hunkered down, the whining cry had died. His eyes jumped from entrance to entrance, each a black cavernous hole. He caught movement and spun, suddenly fascinated as he watched a hatch open inside the tank and several tiny iridescent fish swim out. There was a dull reverberation from inside and a blur of colour. The tiny fish were gone, replaced by a monster as thick as his chest. With its toothy grin, the big fish seemed to pass judgement on his life expectancy as it glided past. *Kishino's using me as bait.* He grasped the pistol more firmly. The unfamiliarity of the grip in his hand was not comforting. Panicking, he searched for the smaller man but could only make out the outline of Keagan's body lying on the table. A voice came from one of the openings, but it was distorted as the sound played around in the strange acoustics of the space. *Kishino?* Was it higher pitched? A woman's? He could not tell. The whine followed, louder now, setting Mastersson's back teeth on edge. *Kishino, I hope you know what you're doing.*

48

Moira wiped the guard's entrails from her cheek. *I hate using this thing at close range.* She was only dimly aware of Helen dry retching from somewhere behind. *How many more?* Cold-hardened rage consumed her, bringing her senses to preternatural focus—the space beyond the open entrance gave a breathy quality to the Shredder's song. She powered it down—a temporary eerie silence—before easing it to the floor. It was not suited to scouting.

She rolled the spheri-cam around the corner, controlling its pan with her omni-block. Infrared was next-to-useless; the walls, floor and ceiling lit up with vibrant fractal mosaics in reds, purples, blues and yellows. The patterns blurred her vision and removed her edge. She boosted visible light sensitivity and stopped the camera when she saw the image of the body. It looked nothing like her brother, so thin and sprawled across the table as if for some arcane ritual. And yet, she knew it was him. There was a figure too, crouching and backlit in front of a glowing tank, armed with a pistol. Inside her something broke; her thoughts stopped. She switched off the video feed. She was moving back to the Shredder before she was even aware of making the decision.

'Moira?' Helen's hissed question washed over her as white noise that pulsed with the heartbeat filling her ears. She focused on the weapon until it became her world. Images flashed: a rare time of joy camping with their patrol by a sea; Keagan smiling and splashing her with water. She tried giving herself to the memory, wanting it to be her reality, wanting not to be alone. *Another place, a long time ago.* She batted Helen's hand aside when it came to rest on her shoulder. Whatever emotions lay behind the woman's gesture were inadequate, remote and disconnected from the present. She slipped the straps around her shoulders, the weight of the Shredder familiar—a reassuring simplicity.

Helen stood in front of her. Had she seen Keagan's image on the screen? It did not matter. Moira shouldered her aside, sending her sprawling. She fired up the weapon, feeling its rhythm in her hands and listening to its song. Her cold rage fused with the melody, interweaving, strengthening. She let the feeling carry her on, further and further, to an outpouring against everything that was wrong in the universe. Helen faced her again. Moira struck her before she could say anything; the woman folded.

And Moira ran for the entrance, screaming as she turned the corner: 'PÓG… MO… THÓIN!'

It was something Keagan used to say.

✳

'Masterss—' Loud and closer. He spun, pistol coming up and loosing a wild shot into empty space. The flash imprinted a monochrome nightmare on his retinas. Shapes with too many legs and bulbous—before he could process what he saw, he felt the cold metal of a gun barrel pressing against his temple, pushing his head around.

The voice was slick with sibilant triumph. 'Hello, *Gustav*. So nice to see you again.'

Masterssons's world dropped through his stomach. 'You bastard! You killed her.'

Carl shoved the gun hard, pushing Masterson back. 'Drop it.' He pointed his gun at the pistol clutched in Masterson's hand.

Masterson's grip tightened as fury tore through him, but something about Carl caught his attention. He stood strangely, lopsided. It took a second to work out Carl's left arm was gone—a blackened plane of flesh and fused clothing fibres where his shoulder used to be. His mind swirled with a confusion of sudden possibilities. He released the pistol, and it clattered to the floor. It was savage, the primal joy he felt seeing Carl mutilated. 'I see you've lost a little weight since we last met.'

Carl raised the gun, but his head swung around in response to a chittering sound, just audible over the distant whine. The keening

358

was a constant background, but Carl seemed unaware of what it meant. He remained intent on the stream of clacking. Mastersson stared into the gloom, his eyes unable to resolve the curvilinear shapes into meaningful details.

'Incredible, aren't they?' Carl's words were softer now, almost tender. He made an extended series of glot-stops, clicks and whistles. Mastersson turned to stare, incredulous. His brain seemed to have flatlined. 'The Oresrians?'

'Oh, yes. She wants to know who you both are. I told her about you. Who's your friend? I can't see from here.'

This is insane. Stalling for time was the only thing he could think to do. 'It's Kishino. Why don't you tell them about his wife, Yorimi, and their two children?'

'Human individuality, the family unit: such quaint concepts. She is more than capable of understanding them. Like me, She recognises their irrelevance. However, She does have an insatiable appetite for knowledge, for experience. She wants to know whether you have bonded. She wants me to show you how he dies.'

Mastersson raised a forearm to cover his eyes as light panels flooded the room with incandescent brilliance. Shock gave way to despair. *He has full control of the station again. He can lock everything down whenever he chooses—everyone is going to die.*

Multi-jointed silhouettes started to resolve against the glare, along with the softer outline of Kishino's hair flowing across a floor painted with his blood. The thing had an armour-plated leg pressing down on Kishino's chest. The rifle lay splintered and useless beside him. Paralysed, Mastersson watched its mouthparts blur as they performed a series of gymnastics. More sounds came from it, like someone snapping twigs as they walked through dry leaves.

'She wants to know: would you take his place? Would you die so that he could rejoin his family?'

The keening noise of the weapon broke into Mastersson's thoughts. *Is it louder? And who's carrying it?*

‘A pause for thought. Hardly a heroic demonstration of one of humanity’s so-called strengths. Is there going to be no statement on behalf of your species? An impassioned declaration of your worth? A reasoned case, proving your superior morality and values? Do you have anything to cause Her to re-evaluate Her assessment?’

I’m sure it’s louder.

‘Very well…’ Carl opened his mouth, ready to utter—.

‘PÓG… MO… THÓIN!’

It was the faintest hope that surged and flowered when he heard Moira’s banshee cry, even as his survival instinct propelled him to the ground. *She sounds pissed.* The whine escalated to a scream as the air filled with a stream of projectiles. Above, the tank shattered, tons of water exploding outwards and accelerating him, helpless, across the floor. Everything was a tumult of images and sounds: a flickering blotch of red haze; the rushing of the water; the reverberating whine of the gun; and inhuman cries like giant fingernails over glass.

*

She surged through the entrance, the Shredder already orientated towards the figure in front of the fish tank. Bright light nearly blinded her, but she could still make out the silhouette. She squeezed the trigger, releasing a hail of explosive shells that cut the body in two, even as it tried to move clumsily out of the way. She heard rather than saw the cracks forming in the tank wall, brittle chinking sounds that built to a crescendo of splintering and a roar as the tide was released.

Through slitted eyes, she scanned the rest of the room and saw animated shapes rendered real from inside every nightmare since her childhood. They surged towards her on blurred pumping limbs, closing the distance with inhuman speed. A remote inner voice screamed at her to haul the bulk of the heavy gun around, to squeeze the trigger until there was nothing left but pulp, but she was eight, a child again and too terrified to listen.

She stood rigid, except for the tremors running the length of her body. Three of them charged. Moira barely saw them. In her mind’s eye, she watched, again, as her father fired shot after useless shot at the thing before he was skewered, thrown aside and broken. She saw her mother dissected, rendered nothing more than a specimen under the claws and mandibles that disembowelled her. Then the water hit. They slowed as the liquid surged around their legs. As one, they reached out and gripped one another, locking upper limbs, forming a three-pointed star. It held, but the water kept coming. They started to slide, moving sidelong to Moira, their screeches those of hunters denied their prey. She saw her mother's body drop to the floor as the alien held her flaccid heart.

The water surging around her thighs pushed her back against the nearest wall. Braced, she watched the aliens, the three of them, holding each other. *Like my parents used to hold me.*

The creatures had almost stopped moving, the swell of water beginning to subside. She remembered the impotence, her vow. *But I'm not helpless, not now.* She found the song again, no longer cold, but searing her with its heady elation. She pulled the trigger and watched as sections of carapace came loose, separated limbs falling free. She watched as the hail of shells tore into their bodies, rupturing the softness inside in a barrage of micro-explosions. Still she kept firing, watching the blue-green globs spray and drop into the water, fizzing and atomising to pearlescent vapour. Until there was nothing left.

Just bits of meat.

Just like my family.

Her knees gave and she slid down the wall, the Shredder discarded as it bleeped its empty warning. The pungent smell of ammonia reached her nostrils despite the station's aircon attempting to whisk it away. It stung her eyes, caught in her throat, and yet she savoured it as the rarest and sweetest of scents.

49

Helen came to and sneezed, sending droplets of water in all directions. She lifted her head and found her hair sticking to her shoulders and aching neck, the tepid liquid lapping against her body. *The lights, they're back on? Moira!* Concern mixed with anger and frustration. *What's she done now?*

Rising unsteadily on her numb leg, she took a few faltering steps through the entrance before stopping to lean on the wall. A figure was sitting—Moira from her hair colour—wrapped around a bundle of something a distance away. Her shoulders rose and fell in silent, rhythmical jerks. *Keagan? Gustav?* Desperate, she scanned the room. Over by the far wall an Oriental-looking man bent over a prone figure stretched across a bench. It was wet and dishevelled, but she recognised him straightaway. Heart racing, she splashed, slid and dodged around overturned furniture and shards of crystal as thick as her leg.

He was lying still, a nasty gash across his scalp leaking blood. The small Oriental man turned to her. Physically he was middle aged, but his eyes seemed much older. Only then did she notice his one bare arm, and the rifle-strap binding holding a pad of material over his stomach. He stood straight, calm, as if this was something he saw every day.

He seemed aware of her fear as he nodded. 'Kon'nichiwa.'

'Hello. You're Kishino? Is…?'

'Hai, he's fine; heart stronger than the rest of him. He's waking up.'

The tightness in her dissolved.

'You another friend of Moira? That is a good thing. She has lost him.'

Helen turned. *Keagan.* She felt pulled in two. Moira's devastation would be utter, but Gustav was hurt and they had been apart for so long. *Will she even accept my comfort? The last time I tried, she knocked me cold.*

'It's her brother. She'll need some time alone with him.'

The man gave a small shrug, his expression equanimous. 'Isao Kishino.' He took his good sleeve and began to dab the blood from Gustav's face. 'You?'

'Helen Mastersson.'

'Ahh… You want to do this?' He held up the bloody material.

Helen swallowed, her eyes blinking back tears; some escaped and she flushed slightly. 'Yes please.' As she moved beside Gustav, she caught Kishino looking at her.

'So, you not bounty hunter, mercenary, soldier.'

'Er…no…' She folded her sleeve and started on Gustav's injury.

'Oh.' He sounded disappointed; then he brightened. 'Ah, doctor then?'

'No…' She jerked her hand back as Gustav rolled his head away from her touch, the lines of his face creasing.

'Pah! More babysitting.'

She heard him stalk off, but did not turn around. 'Gustav, it's Helen. Time to wake up.' Although the cut was still bleeding, it was clean and shallow. More concerning was the swelling. She washed the excess blood from her sleeve in the water at her feet and dabbed the area around the lump. Behind her, she could hear a litany from Kishino, though the words were indistinct.

Gustav raised a hand, pawing the air in an ineffectual effort to remove the drips on his face.

'Gustav, wake up. We can't stay here.' Only by an effort of will did she keep the worry from her voice.

Kishino prowled the entrances as he orbited the two couples, staying away from where the water had washed the remains of Carl and the aliens. On every pass, he looked at Helen—each time she shook her head and returned to rousing Gustav. He was coming round so very slowly. *I don't know what else to do for him.* She also knew she was putting off something important.

Helen summoned her courage and crossed to Moira. Keagan was all lines and angles in her arms, wasted to nothing. She shuddered. *How many more lives will the Pivot take?* She touched Moira gently on the arm. There was no aggression in her response; there was no response at all. *Grief's consuming her like the drug did her brother.* Helen gave Moira the slightest squeeze. A wordless cry burst free of her small frame, a keening that lasted until her breath ran out, then started again. Helen kept her hand on Moira's arm, but dared do no more.

Helen looked back across the room. Gustav seemed at peace, asleep. Kishino came across, a rifle slung over his shoulder. He held a pistol and wore a second wedged in his boot.

'What's wrong?'

His expression was severe and he could not stop pacing. 'It has been too long, we cannot stay.'

'I know, but they're not ready.'

'I wait no more. I have been too long away from my family, too long away from home. We get them moving or we leave them. More guards, more Thargoids.'

'I won't abandon them here.'

'You choose. They move now, or I go.'

'I've tried everything. They just need a little longer.'

'Your way gentle, but not working. I get this one'—he indicated Gustav—'moving. You do your gentling with her, but quickly.'

'But—'

'NOW!' He walked away from her, his back an implacable wall.

Again, Helen was afraid of the little man, even though she understood his agitation. She touched Moira's shoulder but could still think of nothing to say. From behind came the sounds of someone thrashing; she turned and stared in shock. 'What are you *doing*?' Kishino had Gustav's head braced in his lap, his hands over his nose and mouth. 'You're killing him!'

'No. He wake up to fight for air, to fight for life. It's the body's way.'

Her instincts cried out: push the man away and free Gustav. Kishino's glare stopped her. *Kishino is the only one who knows the way out, and how to fight.* It seemed to take an eternity. Gustav's thrashing became wilder and Kishino changed position, pinioning Gustav's shoulders with his legs, arm muscles standing out like tow cables.

'MMMMMMmmmMmmMMMMmmm.'

'Gustav, you're back.' She tried to run, but could only stagger, as Kishino freed himself from Gustav's flailing.

'What are you doing?' Gustav glowered at Kishino.

'Saving your life. You two, fix her—very quickly.' Kishino pointed across the room to where Moira still rocked to and fro. Her keening had faded to quiet, gut-wrenching sobs.

'What happened? She came in firing, then the water…'

Kisino gabbled an impatient reply. 'She shot big tank, water hit you, you hit head. Her brother—he was too weak—did not make it.'

Gustav, who had been in the process of standing, collapsed back down. 'I can't imagine what that's doing to her. Helen, can you help get me over there?'

He's so concerned for her, but then they've been through a lot together. 'Of course. Isao, can you help?'

He said, 'Hai,' even as he gave Helen a reproving look. He pushed the pistol into his belt and pulled one of Gustav's arms around his shoulders. She took the other.

They took four awkward steps before Gustav spoke out. 'This is silly; I'm just dizzy not standing on two broken legs. Can we try holding hands?'

Kishino pointedly gripped Gustav's forearm. *Men are so*—but she cut the thought off, the levity felt wrong. *I'm just happy he's alive, that I have him back.*

Gustav took a few faltering steps, each steadier than the last.

Kishino was the first to let go. 'Quickly. We have two pistols and a rifle—only I can use them. We need her.'

Holding Gustav's hand, Helen felt light inside. But Moira needed him more. 'I've tried, but I haven't been able to reach her—she ignores me or pushes me away.'

'Is that where you got the bruise?' Gustav touched her cheek.

'Ow. My whole head aches; I hadn't noticed how badly until you so kindly pointed it out. She hit me on the back of my neck. That's probably from where I hit the floor.'

'Oh.'

'Scared of her?'

He paused, seriously considering the question. 'Scared for her. I've never seen this, not in all the years I've known her. I'm not sure where to start.'

'I think it has to be you. You've known her longer; you have a deeper bond with her than I do. We got as far as tolerance, not intimacy.'

'Tolerance, already? Impressive.'

'Gustav…'

'Right, but can I have a little space? It feels odd with you listening in—like I'm being evaluated.'

Helen moved away, stopping at a discreet distance to sit on the edge of an overturned bench. Gustav's arms were around Moira's shoulders; she did not shrug them off. A pang of jealousy pinched her, making her feel small inside.

50

Awkwardness and indecision paralysed Mastersson in equal measure. He was acutely aware of Moira's mercurial temper, and that was on a good day. Now she was a husk wrapped around a centre of pain. He carefully placed an arm around her shoulders. She did not push him away. The rocking began to slow. *There are no words for this.* His heart in his throat, he threaded his fingers through her hair, drawing her into his chest. The sobbing got louder. He nearly pulled away as the fingers of her hand circled his forearm and gripped, nearly cutting off the circulation. *At least she's reaching out to the living.* He held her awhile, but she remained curled around the body of her brother. *There's no other way.*

'Moira, can I help you carry him? The Ores—the Thargoids are coming. You don't want them to take him, do you?'

Her breath stopped, for one, two, three long seconds before she looked up at him, eyes desolate beyond words, red from spilling rivers of tears. She shook her head, jaw clenched like a vice, then unfolded like a limp marionette lifted on strings of stubborn hate. Mastersson stood back as she gripped her brother by his shoulders. She looked at him. Wordlessly, he took Keagan's feet.

Her voice was colourless, raw: 'We can't fit four into Jane.'

'I'm sorry?'

'That's Kishino.'

'Yes, his family is alive and well.'

'Good.'

'It's not for nothing—'

'Don't. Not now.'

He nodded.

'Kishino!' Her shout filled the space.

'Hai. Good. Moira Dolan is back, yes?'

'Go to your family and take Helen with you. Get out quickly, understand? I need to get back to my ship.'

'Hai. Helen-san, come with me.' He inclined his head. 'Thank you Moira-san. My father chose well.'

Helen broke in, 'Would someone please tell me what's going on?' She sounded hurt.

Moira looked like she was going to reply so Mastersson waded in. 'We have to get Keagan back to Jane…'

'And she's only equipped for two.'

'Exactly. Moira knows where Jane is, and Kishino's the only one who knows the way to the docking bay.'

'I know.' Helen was looking at him strangely. 'Your heart's with her, isn't it?'

'I… I could go with Kishino… but I thought…'

'No, Gustav, you didn't, and that tells me more than I wanted to know.' She sounded wistful, tired. 'Goodbye, Gustav—it's good to see you safe. Moira—thank you for everything. Take care of each other.'

She turned and limped towards Kishino. 'Let's find your family. Which way?'

Too late, it hit him, and there was too little time. 'Helen, sorry I—I didn't mean… I'll be in touch—when we get back.'

'Maybe, but perhaps leave it for a while.'

He stepped forward, and then stopped. His tongue felt swollen, sticky in his dry mouth. 'Goodbye. Thank you for everything, for being there.'

Moira threw Kishino a couple of small tubes, which he caught and slipped inside his clothing.

He watched Kishino follow Helen to one of the exits. She did not look back, which hurt. *I'm who knows how many light-years from civilisation. I'm tired, and my life's in danger—and apparently I've just made a life choice because I didn't think to say goodbye.* He tried to make her response irrational, as if she was reading too much into his omission, but Helen had always been better at reading his heart. *I guess it's time I found some things out for myself.*

Moira cut in, numbness in every syllable. 'So, you broke up. Can we go now?'

He looked at her, so empty and fragile. 'Let's get Keagan out of here.'

She nodded.

✣

Moira let her legs lead the way. Movement, action: these she knew; these she could deal with.

I won't let them take him, not my whole family.

Each bend, turn, and junction passed in a disconnected blur. She negotiated them on autopilot. Carried between them, Keagan was sickeningly light and they made rapid progress. She was aware of Masterson, but there was nothing to say. She pushed them faster.

They were both sweating when Moira stopped at a three-way intersection. Masterson leant on the wall, gasping for breath. 'How… far…?'

Never mind that, which way? She heard the chittering then—an arrhythmic clacking of a hundred percussion sticks. The sound flowed from the left-hand corridor. Amplified and distorted, it was impossible to judge the distance.

The thrill she felt was not fear, but savage exaltation: *I've already done enough to get noticed.*

Masterson was looking at her, his eyes wide.

'They're hunting us. We had better hope they're not herding us—if they are, they know where Jane is and we're not getting out. You good to go?'

'No… but let's get moving.'

He really isn't cut out for this, but that doesn't stop him trying.

She took hold of Keagan's shoulders again. Through her gloves, she could not tell whether he was cold yet.

✼

Kishino set a steady pace, but jogging behind him was impossible—Helen's leg ached, growing weaker with each step until she reeled, falling against the corridor wall. He stopped, turning to look at her.

'Your leg?'

'I can't…'

He ran back. 'Your friend is looking out for you.' Taking two dispensers from an inside pocket, he pressed one to the wound and the other to her neck. Both hissed as they discharged. He stood, offering her a hand.

She braced on his shoulder, dizzy for a moment. Her heart raced before settling, maintaining a solid beat. She leant on her leg. When there was no pain, she tried her full weight on it.

'It is better, yes?'

'I'll keep up.'

Helen had made sure she exercised each day since she had arrived on the station. Even as Kishino lengthened his stride, she managed to stay just behind him. He was a sure guide, moving through every intersection without stopping. The route he took matched the internal map on her implant exactly, until he branched off into an area Carl had never allowed her to go. Her leg was heavier now and she was beginning to slow. *I hope we're close.*

For the first time he paused, raising his free hand in a fist over one shoulder.

Moira taught me that one… stop.

'You stay,' he whispered, pointing at the spot where she stood, and disappeared around the bend. The temptation was too great.

She pressed herself against the wall and edged forward. Kishino had his arms in the air. His rifle and pistols lay at his feet. She stared at the wall of body armour and helmets, before ducking back out of sight. *I wish I'd asked Kishino for one of those guns.*

❋

The chittering was louder, flowing around them until it was difficult to tell whether it came from in front or behind. Moira heard Keagan's feet drop and the rest of him tumbled after, spilling out across the floor and sending her sprawling. 'What are you—?'

Mastersson was on all fours. He shook his head. '… Sorry.' The soft-spoken word was barely audible over the inhuman echoes. He lifted a hand that shook like a butterfly on a windy day and wafted it around, gesturing down the corridor.

'Get up, Mastersson; this isn't the time for some of your arcane chivalry. No one is getting left behind.'

But he shook his head again. 'Can't.'

'It's just a little further…' She tried to fight the panic, the claustrophobia walling in the maelstrom of anger. *I have to get Keagan out… I came all this way…* Seeing Mastersson down, weak—alone if she left him—bled her fury, leaked the hate that was keeping her going.

'It's okay, go.' The flatness in his voice felt like a slap across the face.

She did not want him to believe her capable of leaving him, but that sting passed. However, guilt persisted. She looked at Keagan— her brother, her only family. Had she ever known life without him? He had always been there, or at least out there—reachable if not reached. *You gave me a chance at some sort of life. You got me past the deaths of our parents, pulled me through after. I've even helped a few people—kept scum from the space lanes using what you taught me. But you never left it behind. Living with the memories ate you like a cancer. You stopped fighting and hid. I've been there every time you needed me. I wanted to carry you, the way you did me. Trying nearly broke me, cost me my career. I'm here because of you—pulling your arse from another fire of your own making.*

371

'Moira, are you all right? You need to go. I can't keep up. They can't be far behind. Finish this.'

She looked at Masterssson, propping himself up on one elbow. There was a deep sorrow there, but the strength to accept—*and move on. He wants to live, but he wants me to live even more.*

Her brother lay between them, looking peaceful she supposed— not a natural expression for him. *Maybe you finally got what you wanted.* She pushed the body, his dead body, aside. *Goodbye, Keagan. I'll always remember what you did, but now I think my debt's been paid.*

She stood, something other than the darkness of guilt and hate giving her strength. 'Give me your hand.'

'What about Keagan?'

'He's found his peace.'

'You're sure?'

'Move your arse, or I swear I'll kick it.'

Warmth flooded his face and she turned away. 'Save your breath for getting back to Jane. C'mon.' She heard him get to his feet behind her, and then stagger. 'When we get out of this, you're going to start exercising.'

'Are you going to be around to make me?'

'If I am, I'll make sure you regret it.' She slipped his arm around her shoulders, taking his weight. Inside, she was suffused with a comforting glow—like nothing she could remember.

51

Helen tried to keep her breathing steady and even so she could hear what was being said.

'… no need to fight. Your boss, Carl, I see him die.'

That Kishino's negotiating shouldn't be surprising; I've spent too much time around Moira.

'Did you check his pulse?' The woman's voice was deep, with rounded tones.

At least she sounds intelligent.

'Didn't need to—cut in half by a Shredder.'

'Oh, he's gone. Shredders are mean.' Another woman's voice, gravelly with an edge.

'Yeah? Linnaeus is meaner. Unless I see his cold, rigid corpse on a slab I ain't gonna believe it.'

Male. Stupid.

Kishino's voice remained calm. 'He is no longer the threat. Up here, there are Thargoids. You have seen them?'

'We've seen them; they took Jenkins, Greph, and Pesto.'

At least the intelligent one speaks for them.

'Small group, about three?'

'Yeah, how did you know?'

'I think they toy with us—hunting parties—many, they could wipe us out.'

'Not without a fight.'

'That is the point. They watched while we fought ship-to-ship. Now they come in small groups to see how we fight now, like this.'

'Or because they enjoy killing us.'

'Reason less important. Soon they decide it is time to finish the job. I can fight, and I have a doctor with me—'

What?! Helen caught her shout of protest.

'—I think now we on the same side, yes?' Kishino spoke with a surety Helen did not feel.

'Don't trust him.'

'Shut it, Cassidy.'

'Who made you boss, Malik?'

'I did, because I have a brain and I can shoot straight. I've seen this guy around, he's a pilot, idiot, *a really good pilot*—or were *you* planning on flying us out of here, past a horde of Thargoid drone ships?'

'Good, then we are agreed. Doctor Mastersson, you can come out now.'

I hope I can pull this off. I don't know how much physiology I can remember. At least Moira taught me a bit of field medicine. She straightened her hair and stepped around the bend, trying to look professional.

'Aw, she's cute. My middle leg is really sore, doctor, wanna take a look?'

'Ignore Cassidy, Doctor Mastersson. Good to have to have you along.'

Kishino did not wait for permission to pick up his weapons. He handed a pistol to Helen and whispered, 'The safety is off, so careful. This is not civilisation—watch the one called Cassidy; I've seen men with that hungry look. If he touches you, shoot him. He won't give you a second chance.'

She took the pistol, holding it like a live scorpion.

‘Try to look comfortable with it. He may leave you alone, but I doubt it.’

Malik hefted her rifle. ‘The pilot and doctor go in the middle. The rest of you, try not to be bug food.’

*

They moved quickly, only pausing at junctions when the seven guards and Kishino fanned out to cover each exit before the group tightened again and moved on. Helen tried to keep the bile in her throat as they came across the first pile of dismembered bodies. There were scorch marks over the walls.

Cassidy came up behind her, putting his hand on her rear. ‘The “Doc” dun’t like the sight of a liddle blood?’

‘Don’t.’ She knocked his armoured glove away with the pistol butt.

He laughed it off.

‘Do we have a problem, Cassidy?’ Malik shouldered past the smaller man.

There was a mean glint in Cassidy’s eye. ‘No, *ma’am*.’

Helen saw Kishino raise his eyebrows. He tapped his rifle with a finger.

I don’t know if I can shoot two people in a day, even if one of them is Cassidy.

More corridors and several minutes passed uneventfully, but Helen felt herself growing ever more tense. *Won’t the Oresrian ships just pick us off? What if Moira doesn’t make it? What if she does make it? She’s not exactly subtle.*

‘Just another couple of corridors—shit.’ The bodies had been surgically taken apart, armour discarded in a pile, and the bones laid out in parodies of sleeping humans. Helen spun around and threw up.

Cassidy was right behind her. ‘What the fuck! Watch what you’re doing, bitch!’

Malik hissed, 'Keep it down or they'll know we're here.'

At the back, someone mumbled, 'Like it's going to make a difference.'

But Cassidy had not finished. 'Look what you did! I'm gonna—'

Kishino's rifle muzzle appeared under Cassidy's chin. 'You be quiet, or you not speak again.'

The tension in the group was palpable now. Weapons were clutched tighter, eyes darting around as they moved along, huddling together for protection.

A multi-legged nightmare, taller than a man, came hurtling around the bend ahead, legs undulating in a hypnotic rhythm.

'Up front!' Malik's voice boomed and the guards turned as one organism, scouring the alien with multiple beams of flaring energy. Bits of—*skin?*—flaked off where the focused light hit and burnt, but it kept coming.

'Hold your rifles steady. Focus your fire on the head.'

As if the Oresrian heard them, it jumped aside causing most of the second volley to go wide. Helen screamed.

Malik still had her rifle to her shoulder. The beam it emitted was brighter than the others and she kept it targeted on a single spot as the Oresrian recommenced its charge. It travelled two more metres before its face caved in and exploded, sending blue-green liquid arcing into the air that boiled off as a white vapour before hitting the floor. The body kept coming, apparently unaware it was supposed to be dead. It struck the group like an out of control vehicle. Kishino grabbed Helen, pulling her against the wall as it slid past. It took Malik and five others to the ground.

Cassidy was grinning, his rifle pointed at Kishino's head. 'No one threatens me, little man.' The chittering from the corridor behind them was getting louder. Some of the guards were stirring, although seemingly unaware of the danger.

Kishino wore a look of extreme sadness. 'Cassidy—'

'Oh, I dun't think so.'

Helen knew Kishino was thinking about his family. Her hand moved of its own volition; the pistol beam caught Cassidy in the hip. He flinched, his rifle discharging into the wall.

Kishino grabbed Helen by the arm. 'Run!'

She followed slowly, too shocked to protest at the way his fingers dug into her arm.

'Never look behind.' Moira's remembered instructions came back to her, but too late.

Cassidy's rifle was trained on them. Even favouring one leg, his aim was steady. Prone, three of the other guards opened fire on the Oresrians as they came into view, but their shots were hurried and the beams went wide. Helen stumbled, nearly falling. As the nearest standing target, Cassidy was the first to go down—mandibles shearing through his armour like gauze.

Kishino tightened his grip on her arm. 'Come!' He pulled her around the corner as a sizzling bolt of energy scorched her hair.

'They have weapons!'

'Hai! Move!'

52

They emerged into a huge hangar bay, Helen hobbling and holding Kishino's arm. Half the docks were empty. Helen watched as a stubby, fat ship, twice Jane's size, manoeuvred towards the exit. Like the craft, the opening hangar bay doors were obviously manufactured by humans, their harsh utilitarian lines contrasting with the organic smoothness of the chamber walls—*mankind's perversion of the biotic.* The crafted Oresrian shapes seemingly spoke of serenity and beauty, but she had seen what the creatures were capable of: they were an anathema to human life. *Humanity isn't an apex predator.*

'Yorimi!' Kishino's cry was jubilant.

'Isao!' A woman came sprinting towards them from one of the nearest ships, a flattened-out trigonal pyramid of pentagons with a beetle's face. The couple threw their arms around each other, a desperate embrace following their long separation. Helen looked at the landing pads—some empty—and gave a wan smile. *I want to go home.* She tried the transceiver. 'Moira, where are you?'

Before she could hear an answer, the couple came striding over, talking as they came.

Kishino scanned the docking bay, frowning. 'Did you have trouble? What about Tahira and the others?'

'We did not see the aliens, or any guards. Tahira and her friends got away in three of the ships. I said we would wait for you.'

'That is good. Now we move.' Kishino's hand was on the grip of his pistol, eyes flicking back the way they had come.

'Please, come.' Yorimi gently gripped Helen's elbow, steering her towards the ship. Kishino trailed watchfully behind.

As the outer portal closed behind them and she entered the spacious cockpit, she found herself squeezed into a corner by the Kishinos. As the family exchanged hugs, the joyous shouts of 'Otōsan!' from the two children cracked the hard shell of shock surrounding her thoughts, reminding her of normal lives lived light-years away.

Kishino prised himself loose. He indicated each family member in turn. 'Helen-san: my wife, Yorimi-kanai; my son, Ichirou-bō; and my daughter, Kiyoko-chan.'

'Pleased to meet you.'

'I like her hair, Otōsan. She's pretty.'

'Yes, Kiyoko-chan, she is.' Isao was smiling, laughter lines creasing his face. He looked complete. 'Helen-san will be coming with us.'

Yorimi smiled. 'It will be nice to have another josei to talk to on the trip. You are most welcome.'

Kiyoko–chan was staring at her with big eyes.

Ichirou-bō stood, small arms folded, assessing her shrewdly. He indicated the ship. 'This is Otōsan's. When I grow up, I'm going to have one even bigger.'

'I bet you will.' Helen managed a smile. *That's what this is really about: ensuring a child can dream.*

As he sat at the pilot's console, Kishino spoke, his tone firm but patient. 'You will work for it though, properly, not how I did. What do we always say?'

'"With my own hands", Otōsan.'

'Good boy.'

Yorimi was already strapped in. At her nod, the children took their seats, moving with the discipline of miniature soldiers. 'Please, Helen-san, sit. You've been in combat before?'

'No.'

'If Yorimi and I are incapacitated, or hull about to fail, hit that big red button.'

'Thanks. I'm already overly familiar with the workings of an escape pod.' *Moira would love this. Your everyday battle-ready family-friendly transport.*

As Helen slid into her seat, she saw the others were already strapped in. They sat quietly, still and expectant. *Carl picked Isao as one of the best pilots he could find. I wish I wasn't here for the demonstration.*

She whispered into the transceiver. 'Moira... If you can hear this, I'm aboard Kishino's ship with his family. It's sort of flat, with a beetly nose. I hope you and Gustav are okay, and whatever you're planning isn't too dangerous.'

Beyond the viewscreen, the hangar doors opened and Helen's stomach tightened as the ship shot forwards. *They're going to chew us up and spit us out.* With centimetres to spare, they were through.

Helen screamed as the screen filled with the metal carcass of a vessel, its sparking innards floating in the cloud vapour. Her head was thrown sideways as Isao's shoulders flexed and the metal bulk slid past, accompanied by the screeching of wounded shields.

'SHHHH!' Both children were glaring at her, each holding a finger to their lips.

'Sorry.'

All she could see in the viewscreen was cloud, until she caught sight of another craft spiralling through the planet's atmosphere, two smaller, angular craft pursuing, sending flash after incandescent flash into its rear shields. They disappeared as the ship reoriented, pulling her forward into the harness. She knew that Kishino wanted to concentrate, so she hissed at Yorimi, 'Why are we flying down? I thought we were leaving?'

Yorimi frowned. 'Cloud cover is thicker below. Isao knows what he is doing.'

Abashed, Helen resolved to stay silent. The craft plummeted and Helen managed to bite back another scream. They twisted around the outside of the station, passing between fungus-shaped sections and what looked like the roots of a giant tree. She winced as they slipped through another gap barely wider than the ship.

Isao jerked right, throwing her hard against the harness as the ship twisted. Facing them was a fan-shaped array of bulbous balloon-like structures interspersed with half octagonal disks. She was thrown the other way as the ship lunged between them. She saw movement to the left. Another craft—*Jane!*

'Moira, it's Helen. You got out!'

'Yes. Stay off comms. I need to talk to Kishino—it's important.'

✻

'Get clear. I've rigged the station with charges, big charges. Take point. I'll cover your six.' Moira pulled Jane in behind Kishino's ship as he began to level out, accelerating away.

'Isao guess Moira-san would do something like this. How far until we are clear?'

'Several klicks, at least.'

'I thought Moira-san said they were big charges?'

'Do you back-chat your father like this? They *are* big charges, but that station is huge. I'd need an anti-mat bomb to shatter that thing. All I can do is knock some bits off—what matters is they're the *right* bits. Check your rear view.'

Jane's holo-display already showed the scene behind. Moira zoomed in on the large sections clustered like fruit segments. Where they anchored to the base, flames blossomed. Exhaled plumes of gas caused the clouds around the station to churn and boil as several tanks pirouetted away, falling in different directions. Other, smaller, chunks fell, sparking and smoking as they went.

'Destroy the stabilising thrusters and buoyancy tanks. Simple, effective, but—'

'That station's going down. Even Thargoid engineering can't cope with the pressures at the centre of a gas giant. Not long, and I'll have squashed us a few thousand bugs.'

'Moira-san, they will evacuate before the station sinks.'

Moira smiled as a second wall of flame seared the clouds.

'Was that—?'

'The Thargoid docking bay doors. And a line of proximity mines. No more bugs get in, or out.' Grinning, she turned to Mastersson in the co-pilot's seat beside her. He gave her a weak thumbs up.

'And the human docking bay?' Kishino's tone was sharp.

Shrewd. But you don't survive to be an Elite pilot if you don't use your brain. 'Did everyone get out?'

'Half the ships were still docked when we left; corridors filling with Oresrians.'

'Then I don't have a choice.'

Helen shouted, the words cracking as she overloaded the transducer. 'Moira, you can't! There could be fifty, sixty—more—people still on board.'

'And there's a few hundred Thargoids blocking the only exit.'

If enough people said, 'No,' to arses like Carl, people like me wouldn't have to do things like this. She touched her omni-block. Behind and below, the clouds lit up, silhouetting the station. It was listing as it went down; a few of the buoyancy tanks hanging grimly on. The vibration rippled through the fabric of the station, severing more connections. Two more tanks ruptured as they came free. They floated up and away, before losing gas and altitude, disappearing from sight.

Helen's voice was shrill. 'I don't believe—I thought you weren't a murderer! They could have used escape pods.'

'Calm down! There aren't any. It's a Thargoid-built lab and prison. Linnaeus may have had one, but it would be hidden and booby-trapped. You know him; would he install escape pods for test subjects and underlings?'

'But those people…'

'Those people made their choice. You all got out. Any prisoners in the detention area were close enough to make it. Those who could get out already did, right, Kishino?'

His voice was heavy. 'Hai, but this is not a good thing you do today.'

'No, but it's necessary.'

Moira angled Jane away before wheeling around and priming her forward armament array. She aimed and fired. Beams of blazing light followed the missile salvo. The seams joining the tanks to the station melted and shattered. Twisted and brutalised, they gave up their hold and floated lazily into the upper atmosphere.

'Survival of the fittest.' Helen's whispered words sounded in her head.

'What was that?'

'Something Carl said once. I have a horrible feeling you just proved him right.'

'No time for philosophy; we have incoming.' Moira glanced over at Mastersson as Jane peeled away, re-routing her power to rear shields, guns, and the engines. He looked green. 'Helen, anything we can do to stop Mastersson decorating the cockpit?'

'He never did fly well. Giving him something to suck usually helps.'

'Thanks. Mastersson, you've got thumbs—use them. I won't be the one clearing up in here when this is all over, understand?'

He managed a feeble nod. The briefest thought tickled the edge of her conscience: *Maybe I could fly a little more gently.* She slapped it aside as she spun Jane to avoid the first beams. In the rearview, the sights locked onto the small angular Thargoid craft. She unleashed a barrage, grinning wolfishly as it hit home. The smaller craft's shields flickered, died.

'Enough silly talk. You need help? I can turn around.' Kishino's voice was taut, resolved.

Honour before family? One thing would never change: *family comes first.*

'Get your people away from here, Kishino.' Another trailing craft lit up in a dazzling display. 'I've got this. Besides, I fly better alone.' Six more drones appeared on the scope. *Jane, I hope you're tougher than you look.* Another five, this time from the left. A cluster—*twenty?*—behind those.

Kishino's ship neared the edge of scanner range. *At least you're all away.*

But he was turning around.

Fucking eejit! 'Keep going! I'm coming to you. We'll punch through together.' She pushed the throttle full-forward, holding nothing back. *And a little after-burner.*

'NnNnnnnnnngghh.'

She heard Mastersson beside her, even over the singing from impacts on Jane's rear shield. *Poor guy.* On the scanner, Kishino pivoted and two of the advancing lights winked out.

Oh, shite. Beyond the first wave, a wall of drone-ships lay ahead, clustered so close on the display it was hard to make out individual vessels. She waited, agonising seconds passing while she watched Kishino's ship dancing through the cloud of attackers.

We'll be there before the second wave. But against so many?

It had always been a question of timing, of how the Thargoids responded. She had hoped that they could stay hidden in the clouds, the puny humans perceived as little threat and the aliens would swarm the docking bays trying to free... She had hoped to face a fragmented force, that other ships would become targets. But the Thargoid response was instantaneous, total. *That must be every single drone-ship from their security perimeter—all coming for little me.*

And she flew to meet them.

'Helen, Kishino, Mastersson'—she looked across at her companion, now an alarming shade of puce—'I'm sorry. I hoped we'd all get clear.' Jane was drawing level with Kishino's ship now. She could see his port shield flickering, struggling to recharge before the next wave. *Maybe I can buy them some time, or something.*

'Jane, more power to front shields.'

'Acknowledged.'

She slid Jane in, ahead of Kishino.

'Moira-san—'

'You've got the civilians onboard; your family. Mastersson knew what he was getting into when he came with me, right?' She looked over.

Mastersson had his face in a sick-bag. 'Hhhuuunnn… hhuunnn…'

'I'll take that as a "yes". Your front shield's low. Put everything into your rear shield and engines. Jane's in better shape, she can get you through.' *Maybe.*

'You are a good person, Moira-san. Okay.' Kishino eased his speed, letting her pull ahead.

Likely, we'll all be cut apart, but… She began a spiral as the first beams filled the space before them, flashing through the clouds like rays of sunlight. *At least we're partially obscured.* It was small comfort, an unrealistic hope. *But why are the drones closing so fast? Slower, and they can pick us off at their leisure.* Beams played across Jane's shields, the level indicator's concentric circles contracting towards gone. *A few seconds…* She jinked wildly, knowing Kishino would follow her moves. The front shield winked out. *They're right on top of us.* Jane screamed as the beams cut into her hull, raking her nose and flanks… *but so few hits? What the fuck?*

The Thargoid host streaked past the two human craft, disappearing rapidly astern.

'Kishino, did you see that?'

'Hai. We should be dead. Only those in front of us fired. They do not chase. I am happy, but do not understand.'

'Neither do I. Something's wrong.' Moira swung Jane around and stopped, watching the scanner display as myriad bright points converged on the station. The dots were disappearing, the station outline on the scanner growing bigger, fatter. It took her a moment to work out what was happening.

'We're alive—' Helen's words overflowed with relief. '—but what are they doing?' before trailing off into awkward silence.

It was like iron filings to a magnet: the lights flying together, joining at the station, seeming to fuse into a single entity. Moira stared at the altimeter. *It's not going to work.* Struck dumb and paralysed, she watched her hopes unravelling on the screen before her.

'Moira-san. The station, it's rising.'

Just die! Give up and die you fuck!

Helen's voice broke in, fear and awe colouring her words. 'They're working together; they're trying to lift the entire structure. They're trying to save the ones left behind.'

So sentimental… Alien or not, Elite or not, multiple pilots can't coordinate with that level of precision. You were supposed to be distracted. You were supposed to waste time hunting down other useless humans that couldn't fly and trying to dock your ships. Minutes were all we needed—minutes—and you'd be crushed at the bottom of the planet's gravity well under a billion tons of atmosphere.

The ships plucked at the station, hundreds of fingers lifting a tree with feather-light touches. And she could not stop it. She could destroy a few, maybe a couple of dozen before she was noticed and swatted aside. It would not be enough.

'Moira-san. We should go.' Kishino's voice was commanding, urgent.

But she could not move. *All for nothing.* She watched the scanner, the station's continuing resurrection.

She was dimly aware of Masterson's stomach doing his talking for him in the background. Helen was speaking, soft and persuasive. Something about getting home. Letting go. Living a life.

Living a lie.

Some dots clustered below the station, breaking away from the main body. *And now she's coming for us.* Moira stared. 'Jane, increase scanner magnification, focus on the base of the station.'

On screen: an object, not a ship, increased its range as it fell. A bright cluster of dots separated from it—drone ships swarming upwards to hug the main body of the station once more. Moira could not pull her eyes away from the descent. *Debris!* Another cluster of bright dots separated, flowing up the main structure, pressing in tighter. A second piece of station dropped—larger this time—freefalling into the clouds.

'It's breaking up.' She had not realised she had spoken aloud. Her ears were filled with the hysterical entreaties of Helen and the barked orders of Kishino. Even Mastersson was attempting to croak something at her from inside his bag. She could not stop watching. The station continued to rise, but slower now, as if the multi-jointed hand cupping it was being gentler, more careful. She held her breath, and waited. And waited.

The scanner showed a flurry of activity on the lower left side. As if a quarter of the structure atomised, the clustered ships flew clear and released the section. The dark, dead part fell, leaf-like, into the gloom below. The newly-free dots buzzed the remains, but there was no clear surface left—every square metre was already in the drone-ship embrace. The dots orbited faster and faster, frantic. A few collided and winked out.

Now you'll learn what it's like to die slowly.

'You knew. How could you know?' Kishino's disbelief was clear.

'It was a hunch.'

The station split. The right side was rising again, carried by the drones. The left peeled clear, spinning as it descended. *You're not that clever. Even with a thousand fingers, you won't be able to catch the last grain of sand.*

The station broke again and again. Ecstatic, Moira pictured the bulkheads snapping, sundered corridors and chambers spilling their contents to freefall into the void. She checked the readout. They were dropping. Frenzied, the drone-ships flew in helpless circles, following the fragmenting station as it fell—slipping away, piece by piece. *Enjoy your last few minutes, bitch.*

'I… I don't understand.'

Battle-bemused, as always. 'Mastersson could explain, Helen, but he's still puking up his guts. The station wasn't designed to be supported externally. Now nothing can stop the fall. And we need to move.' *She knows, and she'll want to take us down with her.* Moira pulled hard over, punching the engines and rear shield to full, but never taking her eyes from the scanner.

'Here they come.' Kishino did not sound surprised. The drone-cloud formed in seconds, flowing out and reaching for them. *But our ships are quick and we have a lead.*

Kishino was already with them; Jane's scanners showed he had also re-configured his ship.

'But—'

'Not now, Helen!' Moira and Kishino's voices sounded in unison. Moira felt a pang of guilt. *But doesn't the woman know some times are not meant for talking?* She watched the drones accelerating, knowing they were faster; seconds passed, the range-meter counting down the decreasing distance between them.

The first laser bursts flew wide, the distance too extreme for accurate targeting, but soon they were pounding an irregular rhythm on the shields. *C'mon Jane, hold together.* More of the drones were in range now. Jane's shields were flagging, unable to keep pace with the incoming energy beams. *At least they're spreading their fire.* Kishino's rear shield was dangerously low. She looked over at Mastersson. He had seen the screen too.

'Feeling better, now we've been flying straight for a while?'

'Yeah, a bit.'

'You know what I want to do?'

'Do it.'

She hit the retros, pushing them straight to full. Mastersson threw up again, or tried. His dry retch sounded more like a bark.

'Moira-san, don't.' The Thargoid drones were only a klick away. They weren't firing. *Like with Ma—playing with us, or savouring our end. At least it buys Kishino the time he needs.* 'Get out of here, there's nothing you can do.'

'Moira!'

'Helen, stop screaming. Let me concentrate long enough to take a few with me.'

The drones were all around them. Moira powered up the forward guns and brought Jane around in an arc. *At least we are going together.* The first drone was cut in half, taking a full barrage. She swung for a second, and a third, energy beams… *ripping into dead drones—dead-in-space drones!* She let out a whoop of exultant vengeance—and went to work. Volley after lethal volley punched through the inert ships, but there were always more. And she kept shouting, relishing every explosion. She knew the others wanted to talk, but at that moment she did not care.

'Weapon system overheated.'

'Jane, not now! For the first time in months, I'm having fun.'

There was a muffled, 'I'm not,' from the sick bag.

Relenting, Moira eased back on the throttle. The drone cloud was spreading out now—filling the space between them and the planet. *Now a grave.* She turned her attention to the voices coming over the comm:

'Otōsan, shoot that one!' Giggles followed.

A whispered muttering in her ear. 'This is barbaric.' Then louder. 'Will someone please tell me what's going on?!'

'She's your passenger, Kishino. You tell her.'

'Moira-san used what any experienced pilot already knows. Facing a Thargoid ship and drones, don't attack the drones—destroy main ship and the drones become useless. They just float.'

'Get that one! Yayee!'

Helen seemed to be struggling. 'So when the station fell far enough into the planet's atmosphere, and was destroyed…'

'Exactly!' Kishino, too, was carried away in the moment and loosed another salvo to the accompaniment of gleeful shouts from his children. 'The drones went dead. They're not waking again.'

Moira saw another one disappear from the scanner.

'But how did you know it would work for an entire station, that all the drones were being controlled—'

Moira grinned. 'Sometimes you just have to use your intuition and experience to see what's not there.'

Mastersson coughed, rasped, and coughed again. 'Moving…' More coughing.

'What?'

'Moving, that one…'

Moira turned to the scanner. A single ship, powered up, was heading into deep space. *Wha—it can't be. They're all drones…* She double checked; the rest of the ships still floated on their merry way, an expanding cloud of inanimate coffins.

She kicked up Jane's engines.

Kishino had seen it too. 'There's a ship. It scans as human.'

'Survivors? Can we pick them up?'

I do try so hard to like her. And breathe… 'No, Helen. Survivors would be heading back to human space. That one's going the other way. The systems where that one's headed are uncharted, possibly Thargoid.'

'But who's on board? What if they know about Carl's experiment? If there's an Oresrian left alive, they could be carrying our pilot's tactical knowledge—'

'I know, to a Thargoid base or planet.' It seemed impossible, but the ship was there, accelerating away.

'I will follow it.' Kishino spoke with finality. 'If Helen-san is correct, too much is at stake. It must be stopped.'

Moira was already swinging Jane's nose towards the fleeing craft. 'You game, Mastersson? You wanted to know if I'm sticking close. Are you? I could chuck you out of an airlock. You should survive long enough for Kishino to pick you up.'

'Uh, we'll be flying mostly in straight lines, right?'

'Depends on that ship, but it's going to be a long trip. You'll have time to get your space-legs. Maybe you'll get to see some sights, meet new and interesting... things.'

'You can go off some people, but I'm in.'

'You getting this, Kishino? You can't take your wife and kids into the void.'

'Hai. Thank you, Moira-san. It... is good to stay.'

'Shite—sorry kids—Kishino, I just remembered, your father, Masayoshi, he gave me an heirloom to pass on—a small lacquered box with horses on it. How do I get it to you, out the airlock?'

'I know it. Did my father say anything when he gave it to you?'

'He said, "To remember why".'

'Then the box is not meant for me—I already know why, Moira-san. Keep it—it will give you something to think about on your journey.'

'Thanks...' She reached up and felt the box inside the pocket of her flight suit. Awkwardness left her struggling for words.

'Sorry to interrupt, and presents are lovely, but I should be going with you. I'm the only one with any xenobiology experience. I—'

'Helen, my trigger finger has all the xenobiology experience we need. There's no time to double back. Besides, there's no hairstylist for hundreds of light-years.'

'But—'

'We're not going there to talk. However much I've come to respect and even like you, I could do without a blonde conscience wittering in my ear.'

There was a burst of angry muttering, but not loud enough to decipher.

Jane accelerated, and Moira found she was not sad to be leaving. *What's there to go back to? Mastersson's here.* The thought crept in, unbidden. *Maybe going back would be easier.* But for the first time in her life, she felt free to make her own choice. *No one's memory to live up to, and I've had enough vengeance to keep me going until tomorrow.*

'You are brave, Moira-san. Fly well. Mastersson-san, take care of her.'

'I will. Goodbye, Kishino.'

Moira felt irritated and oddly comforted. *How would Helen say it? 'Men!'*

Helen was the next to speak. 'Goodbye. Take care of each other. *Both* of you, look me up when you get back.'

Would I be that strong, or content, watching the man I still had feelings for fly off with someone else? Moira tried to get her head around the concept that she could even be a 'someone else'. *Plenty of time to deal with that.*

'Thank you, Helen. Goodbye.' Mastersson gabbled his parting words before his head went back into the bag.

And now it's my turn. Moira tried to put the clamour of feelings into words. *I have friends.* It was too much, too soon. *If in doubt, revert to type.*

'Kishino, Helen: Póg Mo Thóin!'

They would understand, when they worked out what it meant.

EPILOGUE

Deep Space, on the Way Home

Helen sat, clipped into her harness while Kiyoko read to her from a slate. Ichirou floated over her head, giggling as he attempted to tie her hair to one of his toys. She had been on board ship with the Kishinos for two weeks and, just yesterday, she had been called 'Obasan' for the first time. Yorimi told her it meant aunty. Helen liked it.

Kiyoko had already mastered most of Helen's favourite hairstyles. All Ichirou could talk about were his two heroes. They had scheduled another game of 'Matter-sama and Moira-sama Save the Universe' for later. She got to be the 'Tar-goid'. After hearing Moira, he was never going to use the proper term. She was not sure she wanted to, given the way Carl had eulogised it.

Ichirou loved playing out the events—essential for him to process the experience, she knew. Otōsan rescued his family and brought them home, but Moira-sama and Matter-sama were exploring deep space, flying ships and fighting aliens, and chasing someone—or something—with knowledge that could destroy humanity.

The five-year-old had no way of knowing where they were or what they would find. But in his imagination, the tales would grow with each retelling.

OTHER *ELITE: DANGEROUS* BOOKS

From Fantastic Books Publishing:

Elite: And Here The Wheel, by John Harper.

Elite: Lave Revolution, by Allen Stroud.

Elite: Mostly Harmless, by Kate Russell.

Elite: Reclamation, by Drew Wagar.

Elite: Tales From The Frontier, a short story anthology by various authors.

From Gollancz:

Elite: Docking is Difficult, by Gideon Defoe.

Elite: Nemorensis, by Simon Spurrier.

Elite: Wanted, by Gavin Deas.

All released before publication—other *Elite* titles may now be available.

ACKNOWLEDGEMENTS

A project of this size is made up of smaller parts, many of which were achieved only with the help of others. I'd like to express my thanks to:

My editor, Allen Stroud: your dedication to pace and intolerance of fluff were invaluable;

My proofreader, Zoe Markham: you gave this work the polish it needed;

Frontier's frontman, Michael Brookes: your levels of patience, dedication, and hard work were inhuman;

My alpha, beta, and gamma readers, Matthew Lee Adams and Rich Weatherly: your dauntlessness in the face of the earliest draft was inspiring;

My creative art consultants, Colin F. Barnes, Alex Bowden, and Liam 'Mobius' Rafferty: you are Visual Ninjas and Imaging Sensei;

My family: your honesty pushes me towards becoming a better writer; your support gives me the courage to reach.

∞

And thanks also go to:

David Braben (and Ian Bell): for years of enjoyment;

Frontier Developments: for doing the extra work necessary to open your creation to others;

Martin Gisle and Drew Wagar: for the genesis and pioneering of the Kickstarter-to-fund-a-Kickstarter idea.

COMMUNITY CREDITS

The Kickstarter Backers' Hall of Fame

'A successful commander must possess courage, quick reflexes, a keen mind, and the savvy to know when to empty his pockets for an investment.'

This novel had its genesis in a Kickstarter fundraiser, necessary to buy the rights to set a story in Frontier Developments' *Elite* game universe. 508 souls from the *Elite: Dangerous* online community gave their hard-earned and raised the needed credits. Their ranks were legion; their faith, uncompromising; their generosity, astounding.

Backers, I am indebted to each and every one of you. After reading *Out of the Darkness*, my hope is that you consider the eighteen months I spent working on it adequate recompense.

With heartfelt thanks,

T. James.

THE ADMIRALS

'Sacrifice is a strategy.'

Michael Brookes

Brad Roberts

Commander Evergrey Jameson

THE VICE ADMIRAL

'A good tactician always looks behind, stands their ground, and thinks ahead.'

Christian Ullrich

THE COMMANDERS

(Not ordered by competence)

'Everything above and beyond the call of duty—the mark of a great commander.'

Mark 'Zesago' Burger

Cmdr Kevin Jameson

Oliver Smith

Paul Garcia

Justin W. Turner

Michael Lefevre

Howard Chalkley

Anne Tweed

deusx_ophc

Michael Berglund

Alan Stiles

Kimmo Friman

Sander Bloem

Roland J. Veen

Gerrit Lugwig

Trygve Jensen

Simon Morton

Stephen Burnside

Jeff Bristow

Stephen T. Taylor

Nicholas 'Buz' Penney

James R. Lealan

Robert Blanker

Stephen Arthur Blower

Steve Barrett

Robert Vale

Gunnar 'Gunny' Kentzler

David 'JP' Bodger

Kristian 'Mad Mullah Hastur' Bjørkelo

Max Eloranta

Gabriel Garret Green

Martin Laver

BattleFalcon

Iain C. Docherty

David Braidwood Allan

Ian Crawford

Darren Vallance

Sarah Jane Avory

Jedra

F. Alströmer

Mikko Issakainen

Janne Lehtikangas

Neil T. Pritchard

Bloocheez

A. Stevens

Dave Vint

Steven Parry

Although we commemorate the bravery of the above, those others who rallied in such numbers and committed credits, time, and resources to this cause will never be forgotten.

Your collective legacy is graven in these pages.

ABOUT THE AUTHOR
AND
OUT OF THE
DARKNESS

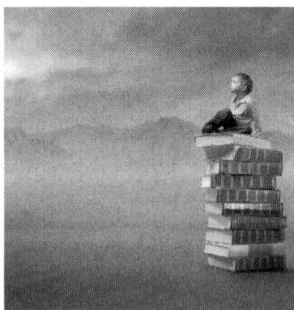

Mature in years, young at heart, and sideways in outlook T. James aims to bring his inquisitiveness and varied life experiences into his writing to create something just a little different.

The breadth and scope of speculative fiction has always had a special attraction for him as a reader and, as a fan of the *Elite* games since 1984, the opportunity to set a story in the first galaxy he flew a spacecraft in was too good to miss. Having spent several months working with Frontier, contributing to the backstory and lore of the *Elite* universe, his imagination finally took flight—one which ended with this book, his first novel-length work. Now that it's finished, he may actually get some time to play *Elite: Dangerous*!

And the future? Anything could happen. Keep an eye on the websites below:

Elite-Based Work:

outofthedarkness.info

Personal Blog:

thewordonthe.net

More about T. James:

tjames.info

Publishing Website:

writerandauthor.com

Printed in Great Britain
by Amazon.co.uk, Ltd.,
Marston Gate.